PERFECTLY IMPERFECT SERIES
SPECIAL (DISCRETE COVER) EDITION

Darkest
sins

NEVA ALTAJ

License Notes

Copyright © 2024 Neva Altaj
www.neva-altaj.com

All rights reserved. No portion of this book may be reproduced in any form without permission from the publisher, except as permitted by US copyright law.

This is a work of fiction. Names, characters, places, and incidents either are the product of the author's imagination or are used fictitiously. Any resemblance to actual persons, living or dead, events, or locales is entirely coincidental.

Editing by Andie Edwards of Beyond The Proof
(www.beyondtheproof.ca)
Proofreading by Yvette Rebello (yreditor.com)
Manuscript critique by Anka Lesko (www.amlediting.com)
Stylistic editing by Anna Corbeaux
(www.corbeauxeditorialservices.com)
Cover design by Deranged Doctor
(www.derangeddoctordesign.com)

The quote used in Chapter 16 is borrowed from the online essay *"The Ruminant Digestive System."* Extension at the University of Minnesota. Accessed December 15, 2023, by Authors: James Linn, Donald Otterby, W. Terry Howard, Randy Shaver, Michael Hutjens, and Lee Kilmer

Perfectly Imperfect Reading Order & Tropes

1. *Painted Scars* (Nina & Roman)
Tropes: disabled hero, fake marriage, age gap, opposites attract, possessive/jealous hero

2. *Broken Whispers* (Bianca & Mikhail)
Tropes: scarred/disabled hero, mute heroine, arranged marriage, age gap, Beauty and the Beast, OTT possessive/jealous hero

3. *Hidden Truths* (Angelina & Sergei)
Tropes: age gap, broken hero, only she can calm him down, who did this to you

4. *Ruined Secrets* (Isabella & Luca)
Tropes: arranged marriage, age gap, OTT possessive/jealous hero, amnesia

5. *Stolen Touches* (Milene & Salvatore)
Tropes: arranged marriage, disabled hero, age gap, emotionless hero, OTT possessive/jealous hero

6. **Fractured Souls** (Asya & Pavel)
Tropes: he helps her heal, age gap, who did this to you, possessive/jealous hero, he thinks he's not good enough for her

7. **Burned Dreams** (Ravenna & Alessandro)
Tropes: bodyguard, forbidden love, revenge, enemies to lovers, age gap, who did this to you, possessive/jealous hero

8. **Silent Lies** (Sienna & Drago)
Tropes: deaf hero, arranged marriage, age gap, grumpy-sunshine, opposites attract, super OTT possessive/jealous hero

9. **Darkest Sins** (Nera & Kai)
Tropes: grumpy-sunshine, opposites attract, age gap, stalker hero, only she can calm him down, he hates everyone but her, touch her and die

10. **Sweet Prison** (Zahara & Massimo)
Tropes: age gap, forbidden romance, only she can calm him down, opposites attract, he hates everyone but her, touch her and die, OTT possessive/jealous hero

Trigger Warning

Please be aware that this book contains content that some readers may find disturbing, such as gore, violence, attempted SA (not by MCs), abuse, self-inflicted injuries, animal cruelty (not by MCs, this chapter will be denoted in the book in case you need to skip), and graphic descriptions of torture.

This is a work of fiction. Do not try any of the medical procedures described at home. If you need help, please see professional services.

Author's Note

My dearest reader,

I'd like to ask a favor of you. When leaving the review, please keep it **spoiler-free**! Allow other readers to find out what Kai's darkest sin is on their own. As you can imagine, it's the key element that drives the story, revealing it in advance may influence the enjoyment of other book lovers like you.

Thank you so much.

I hope you love Kai and Nera's journey as much as I do.

With love,
Neva

DARKEST
PERFECTLY IMPERFECT SERIES
sins

prologue

Nera

Present day
The Leone Villa, Boston
(Kai 34 years old, Nera 24 years old)

HE'S HERE.
My eyes are not yet adjusted to the surrounding darkness, so I can't discern anything except the general shapes of the furniture in my living room. Nothing moves. No sounds, other than my breathing.

Nothing.

But I know he's here.

It's a sixth sense that seeped into my bones years ago, since the first moment I met him. His presence creates an imperceptible shift in the air, stirring the very atoms around me. I don't have to see him or hear him move to know he's there. My body and mind can feel him. Always could.

I close my eyes and slowly start turning, hearing nothing but my heartbeat. It's faster than normal, but steady. I've nearly completed the turn when my heart flutters. There. When I open my eyes, darkness is still the only thing that greets me, but it doesn't matter. I know he's directly in front of me.

My heart always knows.

"Long time no see, tiger cub." The deep, raspy voice washes over me.

Hearing it is like being swaddled by a thick fluffy blanket. I'm safe and secure, in a place where no one can do me harm. For a few rapid beats, I let it just sink in, absorbing the vibrations of his tone. The sound is different from the last time I saw him, his voice is more raw somehow, but it's him. How many sleepless nights have I spent curled up in my bed, trying to relive the specific timbre of it? Probably hundreds.

The reading lamp on the side table comes to life, its dim glow partially illuminating the huge male frame leaning back in the recliner. For the most part, his face remains in shadows; only two silver eyes seem to glow in the surrounding murk.

It's a punch to the chest, seeing him again after all this time.

"I thought you were dead," I choke out.

He inclines his head to the side, and more of the light falls onto his face, allowing me a glimpse of his tightly pressed lips, and more . . . A scar on his left cheek—an uneven line of raised flesh, beginning at the corner of his mouth and curving up toward his ear. Another mars his skin above the left brow, and two more are visible across his chin, somewhat obscured by the dark stubble covering his jaw. None of those marked his face the last time I saw him.

The urge to run to him overwhelms me, but I snuff it out. My feet stay rooted to the floor, my eyes locked on the man who was once everything to me. Too many nights I've lain in bed imagining what it would feel like to see him again. I knew it would hurt. But I didn't expect that it would hurt *this much*.

Time is a tricky thing. Hours. Days. Years. The human brain has a limited capacity for storing information, and, as time passes, slowly and without notion, it forgets things. Sounds. Smells. Words. Situations. Memories peel off and are swept away by the winds of time, like dried leaves fluttering on the breeze just before the onset of winter. And when the spring arrives, the only thing left is a vague awareness of their past existence.

Time.

They say that time heals all wounds.

It's all lies and a crock of bullshit.

Time didn't take away my memories of him, even though I wished for that on numerous occasions. I still remember every single thing about this man.

"Did you miss me?" he asks in that husky voice, the tone reminding me of a brewing storm, the instant before the first crack of thunder.

Miss him? No, that word doesn't describe the anguish and despair of the past four years. The desperate hope I felt while scouring every dark corner, praying for a glimpse of him. And then, the inevitable disappointment and agony upon discovering he wasn't there. Because I've always felt his eyes on me, even when I couldn't see him, the sudden certainty that he was truly gone was crushing. Horror gripped me when I finally accepted that he must have died and I'd never see him again.

"It's hard to miss a man whose name I don't even know." A nearly physical pain squeezes my chest. All this time, he let me believe he was dead.

A corner of his lips tilts up, making the new scar on his face more prominent.

"I missed you, too, cub," he whispers, raising a big black gun, fitted with a suppressor. "Do not move."

My breathing stops.

The muffled gunshot wheezes through the air.

Part 1

past

Chapter one

5 years ago
(Nera 19 years old, Kai 29 years old)

"My dear Nera, you look stunning tonight." The woman in a dark-red silk gown leans in to give me a quick peck on my cheek. Her heavy perfume invades my nostrils, and I struggle to stifle a cough. "Simply glowing."

"Thanks." I manage a smile, one that's just as fake as the woman's sentiments.

I got my period yesterday and spent the entire night tossing and turning, unable to sleep because the cramps were killing me. There are dark circles under my eyes that the foundation couldn't cover, and I'm pretty sure my face is still swollen. We both know I look like a wreck, but no one would ever dare say anything of the kind to Nuncio Veronese's daughter.

"And I love the blouse you're wearing," she continues. "Who's the designer? It must be a super expensive label."

"My sister made it," I mumble and throw a glance over my shoulder, searching for my friend Dania, hoping she would save me.

"Oh. It's adorable." She smiles. "I was just saying to Oreste how the two of you would make a perfect couple. I'll tell him to give you a call next week, Nera, my dear. He just bought a new car, the latest Tesla model, and I'm sure you'd enjoy a ride."

I shudder. Oreste is a well-known manwhore who uses way too much hair gel and practically bathes in cologne, even worse than his mother.

"I'm busy next week. Maybe some other time."

"Perfect. I'm sure that Don Veronese would approve of the two of you seeing each other." She grins and leans in to whisper into my ear. "Your father is very fond of my son, and I'm sure he is considering making Oreste a capo."

And there it is. The real reason she's trying to set me up with her spawn. Not because she likes me, or because she believes we actually would make a good match, but because her son would have an easier climb up the hierarchy ladder with the don's daughter as his girlfriend. It doesn't even surprise me anymore.

"I'm sure he is. Oh, there's Dania. I need to go say hi." I grab a glass of iced lemonade from the nearby table and dash toward my friend on the other side of the garden. She's frantically trying to beckon a waiter and is completely oblivious to my slow suffocation by social politeness. I keep my focus on my best friend as I squeeze my way between the party guests, hoping I won't get snagged by unwanted eye contact with another person.

"Nera, sweetheart!" Someone from a group to my left brushes my arm as I pass them. "Your hair looks amazing."

"Thanks." The ponytail at the top of my head is hardly impressive, but it was the most effort I could manage after I washed my hair this morning.

"Oh, Nera, I didn't know you were here." A guy who looks vaguely familiar materializes right in front of me, bringing me to a sudden stop. I think he's one of the underboss's nephews. "It's rather boring here. How about we sneak out and go grab a drink somewhere?"

"Um, no. Thanks." I step around him, only to come face-to-face with Jaya, Dania's cousin.

"We missed you on Saturday." She offers me a huge, fake smile. "Melinda was disappointed when you didn't turn up."

Yeah, I'm sure her sister was devastated I didn't come to her baby shower. Not because she wanted me there to share in her happiness, but because now she can't say that the don's daughter attended her party.

"I've only met your sister once, Jaya," I say. "You invited me to her birthday, but when I arrived, she just took the present and didn't even bother introducing herself to me."

"She didn't know who you were! If she did, I'm sure she would have treated you differently."

"My point exactly. Please pass along my best wishes."

I leave Jaya staring at my back and rush toward Dania. She's trying to convince the poor waiter to bring her an alcoholic drink, by the looks of things.

"I need to get out of here," I whisper as I tug on her arm. "Now."

"Sure." She snatches a glass of white wine off the waiter's tray and lets me drag her across the lawn toward the stone fountain at the back of the garden.

"This should work." I gesture to the iron bench next to the water feature and take a seat. The shadow of a big oak tree hides us in this spot, despite the nearby lampposts.

Dania throws a look over her shoulder toward the crowd enjoying the night outside the colonial-style mansion on the other side of the property. "Do you think someone will notice us gone?"

"Some big shot will be giving a speech soon. Everyone will be too busy listening to his rambling and clapping like mindless fools."

I take a sip of my lemonade. "Dad said they were able to persuade this guy to push a Bill through the State Legislature that'll help the Family."

"Something about casinos?"

"Could be. I'm not up to speed on all the business ventures since I left home."

"I still can't believe the don let you move out." She takes a seat next to me.

"Me neither." I shrug. "When I told him I bought a place with the money Mom left me, he threw a fit. I got a long lecture on how outrageous it is for Nuncio Veronese's daughter to live alone, in some 'small shitty shed' of an apartment. 'What would people say?'"

"So, you managed to sway him?"

"I tried. He threatened to drag me back home if I dared to leave, then threw me out of his office. But the following week, he told me he'd thought about it and decided to let me have my space."

"I wish my dad was more like yours." Dania takes a big sip from the glass and coughs. "I'm turning twenty next month. My dad has already started playing matchmaker. This time next year, I'm going to be married."

I cringe. "Sorry."

"What about you?"

"No matchmaking is going on at the moment, thank God. I told Dad I'm sick of doing nothing every day and want to go to college, or at least take some online courses, before I let him trap me in an arranged marriage. When he disagreed, I told him I'd strip naked and go dancing through the City Hall Plaza, ruining my reputation and, possibly, all future marriage prospects—for good."

"I think you'll still be a catch, even after flashing your naked butt." Dania laughs.

"Maybe. But can you imagine the scandal that would create? My rear end would be the main subject of Cosa Nostra's gossip for years."

"I still don't understand why on earth you want to go to college. You guys are so loaded, you'll never need to work a day in your life. And I'm pretty sure that when you get married, your husband won't allow you to have a job anyway."

"I know. Still, I got my acceptance to the online vet tech program. I'm starting classes this fall."

Dania chokes on her wine, spit flying everywhere, and bursts out laughing. "The don's daughter, giving shots to chickens and delivering piglets?!"

"Well, I guess I might have to go through all that at some point." I laugh, too.

"So, that's the real reason why you started helping at that vet clinic! I thought you were just bored."

"Let's just say that I needed a change of scenery. And it's fun. They brought in a stray dog last week and I got to watch the vet stitch up a wound on the little rascal's stomach."

"Nera! That's gross."

"Not really. I quite like it. Pretending to have a normal life and all that." I sigh. "Oreste's mother cornered me earlier. She wants to set me up with him. I think I'm going to call it a night and go home."

"What about your security detail?"

I tilt my head toward the sky, gazing at the stars. Dad insists I take along security guys whenever I'm out anywhere late, but I'm not in the mood. It's hard to act like you're living a normal life when you have bodyguards following you. "Not tonight."

"The don will be mad if he finds out."

"Most certainly." I snort. "Well, I'm off, then. I need to be up at seven. We have a cesarean on a cat scheduled for tomorrow morning."

"I envy you, you know. Playing animal doctor while I need to start the search for a perfect wedding dress."

"Don't be. I'll be searching for one soon enough, too. Dad allowed me just a few years of grace, but then I'll be bound for the marriage market, as well." Every time I'm over for the Sunday lunches Dad still insists I must attend, I dread that he'll tell me he's changed his mind. Since I turned nineteen, he's been not-so-subtly hinting that I'm ripe to be married. "I just pray he keeps his word and lets me be until Massimo gets released."

"Yeah," Dania says. "You're too valuable an asset to not be used."

"Yup. An asset."

"Do you have any idea who you might end up with?"

A shiver passes down my spine. "No. I just hope it won't be anyone from the Camorra Clan. I overheard Dad talking to the underboss, and there seem to be negotiations taking place with them recently."

"God, Nera. I hope your dad won't choose to side with Camorra and marry you off to Alvino. There's been some talk that he beat up the girl he was seeing pretty badly. She ended up in a hospital."

There have always been rumors about Alvino being a bully. I guess that doesn't hurt him as the leader of the Camorra Clan. "Good thing my father hates Alvino, and Camorra. I don't think he'd ever sign a truce with them, but even if that happens, he would never make me marry that bastard."

"Are you sure?"

"Of course I'm sure." I give Dania a quick peck on the cheek, then rise from the bench and grab my purse. "I'll see you on Friday. Have fun."

As I walk across the lawn, heading to the parking lot, I take another look at the party guests drinking and laughing in the backyard of my childhood home. When I was little, I loved hiding behind the stairway banister with my younger sister, Zara, watching the elegantly dressed men and women as they milled about the big hall below. My father always enjoyed hosting parties, and when the don sent out an invite, no one dared to turn down the invitation. The preparations often took days, and Mom made sure that everything, from the silverware to the music, was arranged to her high standards. She was never a fan of parties, but she always shined as the great hostess. Keeping the high-ranking Family members happy was important. Keeping them close, was crucial.

I remember staring in awe at those beautiful people, wishing I was older so I could be allowed among them. I imagined the dress I would wear to my first party—white, with a big ruffled skirt. And little heels, maybe gold or silver. I was so eager to be a part of their world.

Until that night fourteen years ago.

It was New Year's Eve, and the whole house was decorated in beautiful gold ribbons with little red details at the fringes that I helped Mom pick out. Well, she was actually our stepmother, but neither Zara nor I ever called her that. Our mother died giving birth to Zara, and Laura had been the only Mom we ever knew.

That night, the tables were covered in white satin cloths with big gold bows pinned to the corners. Magnificent flower arrangements served as centerpieces atop each spread. Our parents were standing by the big Christmas tree—Dad in a streamlined black suit and Mom in a beautiful silk dress that matched the blue of her eyes. The New Year's party was always a big deal, and in addition to the Family members, many politicians and other government officials were in attendance. I didn't know who was who, but I remember pointing at a man with a long white beard, who was laughing at a joke our dad had made, and telling Zara that he was a judge, and not the sultan I saw in the *Aladdin* movie. Dad told me so when he checked up on us earlier that night. But Zara said the man looked more like Santa.

Massimo, our stepbrother, was in the entry hall, just below the stairway where Zara and I were hiding on the top landing, deep in a serious discussion with two men. He was twenty then, but he always seemed older. Maybe because he was constantly grim-faced and serious. Massimo never paid much attention to me and Zara, we were probably too young for him to bother with, but he and our older brother, Elmo, were inseparable.

Over the years, I've often wondered how the two of them got along so well back then. Massimo's broody, antisocial personality was the complete opposite of Elmo's cheerful, outspoken one. Although they were close in age, Massimo acted like he was at least a decade older than the fun-loving and carefree Elmo.

So, while my stepbrother engaged in business, Elmo was leaning on the marble column near the front entrance, flirting with a pretty red-haired woman. Not that I knew what "flirting" was when I was five, but remembering that night as I got older, more and more details became clear in my mind.

Elmo had just turned eighteen not long before that party, and I recall thinking how grown-up he seemed in his black tuxedo. He was teasing a woman almost twice his age, making her break out into a funny-sounding laugh that kept making Zara and I giggle. He probably should have been mingling with the capos, as the don's son was expected to, but no. Massimo was always the one who did what was expected.

The smell of cigar smoke, alcohol, and fancy food reached all the way to the upper floor where Zara and I were spying on the activities below. My sister squealed each time she noticed a new pretty dress, and I had to remind her every few moments to be quiet so we wouldn't be discovered.

I wish I hadn't.

I wish someone had spotted us and sent us back to our rooms.

It was almost midnight, and everyone was laughing. A man in a white suit played a tune on the piano which was brought in specifically for the occasion. Waiters were weaving among the guests, carrying trays of delicate tall glasses raised high above their heads. The champagne for the toast. A truly extravagant, festive event.

I barely noticed the commotion by the front door when two men started arguing. I couldn't hear what they were saying over the clamor of the party, but it seemed important because the raised voices suddenly transformed into shouts. When the men started pushing each other, their faces flushed and angry, Elmo abandoned the red-haired lady and rushed toward them. Always the peacemaker, my brother undoubtedly intended to break them up.

He didn't see the weapon one of the men pulled out. But Massimo obviously did, because he was running toward the entrance, yelling at Elmo to get back.

An ear-splitting boom exploded inside the gold-and-red-decorated room as the gun went off. Elmo stumbled backward, holding a hand to his chest. The voices and music suddenly died, as if someone flicked an off switch. The silence lasted less than a second before Massimo's animalistic roar filled the void. My heart was beating like a drum as I squeezed the wooden posts of the banister, watching Massimo catch Elmo as my brother fell. Instantly, other screams reverberated through the room as people started running into the entry hall. And in this chaos, my stepbrother reached behind his back and pulled out his own gun.

Another boom rang out as Massimo fired at the man who shot Elmo.

I heard the echo of those gunshots for hours. Not even the piercing siren of the ambulance that rushed to our house or the rumble of the coroner's engine that later carried Elmo away could drown out that sound. And it still thundered in my head, over the deafening slam of the police car's door splitting the stillness of the night, as the cops took Massimo away.

That's when the idealistic notion of my family's perfect world popped like a big soap bubble.

"Do you want me to get your car, Miss Veronese?" the voice of the valet pulls me out of the painful memory, dispersing the imagery of gold ribbons and blood.

"Yes, please." I nod and wrap my arms around my middle. "Thank you."

He throws over his shoulder, "Beautiful night, yeah?"

I look up at the sky covered in countless twinkling stars, surrounding the big full moon above the line of trees in the distance.

"Yes," I whisper. "It truly is."

Kai

Gravel crunches under the soles of my shoes as I walk across the empty parking lot, heading toward the still unfinished six-story residential building. The street lamps around the block are off, but the bright light of the full moon presents an unwelcome complication, requiring me to keep to the shadows.

Just as I'm approaching the service doors which are standing open, a muted clank reaches me from the inside. Keeping my stride casual, I take out my gun and step into the stairwell.

"Can I help you?" asks a man in overalls from the top of the stairs. A bucket with cleaning supplies is next to him. A janitor.

The whole block is still under construction and the tenants haven't moved in yet, so there shouldn't be any custodial staff around at this hour. Obviously, the intel I got was wrong. I lift my weapon, aiming at the janitor's head.

"Please," the man chokes out. "I have a family. Two kids and—" I squeeze the trigger before he can finish the sentence.

There is a loud thump as the man hits the floor, his body falling down the stairs and landing at my feet. Blood is oozing from the big hole in the center of his forehead while his unseeing eyes seem to be staring at me. Some cultures believe that the souls of the dead stay in this world and follow the person who ended their life for all eternity. Haunting them. He's welcome to join the army already at my back.

"I'm in," I say into my Bluetooth mic and step over the body. "Estimated time to complete the mission—fourteen minutes."

"Copy. Commencing radio silence." With that confirmation, the audio feed gets muted.

My target should be in one of the apartments on the third floor, conducting a secret meeting with two Middle Eastern oligarchs. Whether it's about oil or guns, or something else, it's not important. The only aspect that interests me is the preferred method for eliminating the mark, if there is one. Military-issued contracts rarely have that detail specified. Typically, the only requirement is that nothing at the crime scene can be traced back to them. Private contracts, however, often come with a set of specific requests, which are at times too fucking bizarre to even think about. Luckily, this is a plain old "hit and split, no witnesses" kill order. No stupid-ass requests to worry about. I like these types of contracts much better.

I reach the landing on the third floor and head down the hallway toward two men standing by the last door on the right.

"Hey!" the first one barks, reaching inside his jacket for a weapon.

I lift my gun and fire two shots in quick succession. The bodyguards drop where they stood, flaunting identical bullet holes between their eyes.

The apartment door flies open. Even with the silencer, the sound of a gunshot can't be completely suppressed and will draw attention. I shoot the guy standing at the threshold, then switch my aim to the next man coming through the doorway. Just as my bullet finds its mark, a burning ache explodes in my right leg. The fucker managed to hit me. I grit my teeth, push through the pain, and step inside. Keeping my back to the wall, and holding my gun at the ready, I move down the narrow hallway toward the door at the other end.

A spray of bullets pierces the wooden surface before me, peppering my upper body with several hits. I stagger back, allowing myself only a second to gasp for air, then kick the door open. In the middle of the room, a goon is in the process of changing his gun's magazine. Without hesitation, I shoot him twice in the chest. He stumbles backward, his gun clanging to the concrete flooring. Another shot to his forehead, and his dead body topples to the ground, as well. One of my former colleagues had a saying: "Never presume someone is dead until he's sporting a hole in his head." It's a solid mantra.

I brace my free hand on my hip and look around. The spacious studio is empty, the once-pristine white walls are now sprayed with red and feature newfound perforations. No sign of my target or his partners anywhere. The smell of fresh paint hangs heavy in the air, but I still detect a faint, acrid bite of gunpowder as I walk toward the bathroom and kick the door open.

Three suits are crouched by the toilet—fancy threads for dying by the john—their faces pale and eyes frantic. I shoot the closest in the head, then take care of the other two in the same style. Checking to make sure the dead men were actually my target and his associates, I tap the comms button on my earbud.

"You fucking idiots said there'd only be two bodyguards."

"The client . . ." a shaky voice comes through the line, " . . .the client assured us that no more than two security personnel will be with the target."

"And what about the damn surveillance intel?"

"Um... Captain Kruger said there wasn't time for it." The man's voice is reaching a hysterical pitch. "I'm so sorry. This was a rush job, Mr. Mazur."

Figures. "Tell that motherfucker that if he wants me dead, he should try killing me himself."

"Yes, I'll let him know." The guy clears his throat. "Can you tell me the mission's status, Mr. Mazur?"

"Fucking accomplished!" I take the earbud out and stuff it into my pocket.

The nature of my relationship with Lennox Kruger, the head of the Z.E.R.O. unit, has always been ambiguous. He likes to say that he saved me when he removed me from the psychiatric facility for juveniles deemed too dangerous for society. In truth, he wanted a pet he could condition to kill people without remorse. Well, he got what he wanted, and then more. I'm pretty sure he would have disposed of me by now if I wasn't the only operative left from the original Z.E.R.O. unit. With Belov and Az gone, I'm the last one of his psycho minions.

Once upon a time, our dysfunctional band of brothers was pulled together for one sole purpose: to kill targets fast, and do it without leaving a trace of who did the deed. After Az disappeared and, later, Belov ditched too, Kruger decided to leave the military behind and become an independent contractor. He assembled new teams to take on both government and private jobs. Extortions. Protecting anyone—even high-level criminals—with pockets deep enough to pay the fee he demanded for unscrupulous methods and no questions asked. Even taking down warlords or the governments of small countries if the price tag was right. And of course, assassinations.

Those missions were primarily assigned to me. I got 50 percent of the contract value for every completed job—quite an incentive to keep working for the man who terrorized me throughout most of my adolescence. But the thing is, even without the padded bank account, I probably would have just kept doing it. Killing is the only thing I know how to do.

Droplets of blood mar the shiny white ceramic sink and the right side of the mirror over it. As I look at my reflection, a big red stain clings to the spot aligned with my eyes in the glass. How fitting. I put my gun on the counter and start unbuttoning my suit jacket.

"Fuck," I groan as I unstrap the Kevlar I'm wearing over my shirt.

Several of the bullets hit me in the chest, making it hard to draw a breath. I let the bulletproof vest fall to the floor and lift my shirt to inspect the wound near my hip. The anti-ballistic fibers didn't catch that one. I grit my teeth and feel the skin around the wound with my fingers. The bullet doesn't seem to be that deep. The combined obstacle of the door and my protective gear definitely slowed it down.

I don't bother picking up the vest or my jacket as I leave the apartment. My DNA is already all over this place with me bleeding, but it can't be traced to my identity through any law enforcement databases. Hopefully, Kruger's cleanup crew can take care of this shit. If not, so be it. Another unknown sample to keep company with all of the other unsolved cases.

The first hit grazed my thigh, causing a minor nuisance. The one to my side, however, might be a problem. I didn't plan on getting shot tonight, so I left my car several blocks away. Covering that distance with a bullet lodged just above my hipbone is going to be a bitch.

No one is around as I limp across the parking lot—only me, the stars, and the full moon casting its light over the deserted surroundings.

I stop my advance for a moment and observe the sky. When I was a kid, I'd often sneak out when everyone in my foster home fell asleep and climb onto the roof to watch the sky. It wasn't the dark expanse or its apparent endlessness that captivated my attention, but rather, the twinkling dots of those distant stars. They seemed so small, yet, their glow penetrated the darkness as if they were beacons, lighting the path for anyone lost in the dark. I would reach out and imagine capturing one in my fist, as if I could hold that saving light. But opening my hand revealed it to be empty. The light lingered in the sky—gleaming, tempting me to try again, but always remaining out of reach.

The last time I tried catching a star, I was eight years old. My foster father found me on the roof and dragged me down by my hair. He took me to the basement where he beat the shit out of me. I couldn't even stand afterward. He called me an imbecile and left me lying in a puddle of my own blood while he went upstairs to get the razor. I was too far gone to fight him when he grabbed me by the hair again and shaved it all off.

Two days later, when I was finally able to walk, I found the same razor, went into his room, and cut his throat. After that night, I never again tried to catch a star. I guess that cemented my belief that the heavenly shine was not meant for me.

I turn my face toward the shining globe in the dark sky and close my eyes, imagining how good it would be to never open them again.

The traffic light changes to red, so I turn up the music a bit and glance out the open window. Dad doesn't like me going through this part of town, he thinks it's dangerous, but it's a much quicker route. I come this way quite often because the vet clinic is just on the next block, and there's no one around at this time of night anyway.

I'm humming along to the tune from the radio, drumming my fingers on the steering wheel, when a movement in the alley across the street catches my eye. It looks like a man, walking slowly while supporting himself with his hand against the wall. He stops for a moment, then takes two more steps before his legs give out, folding under him.

Shit. Should I go over and see if he needs help? Nope, someone else will come along, give him a hand if he needs it. I look toward the traffic light. Still red. My eyes swing back to the man in the alley. He's sitting on the ground now, leaning on the side of the building, and his head is tilted up. Probably just a drunk who's lost his way or is so inebriated he can't even walk straight. *He'll be okay,* I tell myself, but I can't pull my eyes away from him.

He seems to be looking at the sky, just as I had done earlier. It wasn't the first time I'd stared into the night and wondered what life had in store for me. Is he doing the same? Is he like me, also asking, "What's waiting for me out there?"

Maybe this guy doesn't have a phone. He would have called someone for help already if he did, right? *Crap.* I step on the gas as soon as the light turns green and crank the steering wheel, making a U-turn, then nudge my car to the desolate sidewalk, stopping at the gap between the two buildings.

Leaving my vehicle and heading into a dark alley to check on some random dude is stupid, but I can't just ignore him. I reach under my seat to pull out the gun I've hidden there. Sticking it into the waistband of my pants at my back, I exit the car.

The street light outside the alley entrance bathes the surroundings in a yellowish glow. I keep my right hand on the handle of my gun, ready to withdraw it at a moment's notice. Reckless I might be, but stupid I am not. Two years ago, I caught one of my father's men banging a maid while he should have been on guard duty, so I blackmailed him to teach me and my sister how to shoot. Zara didn't want to at first, but she ended up being a natural. I might not be the best shot, but I do pretty well at short distances.

I approach the man and come to a stop by his legs. He's wearing black pants and a black dress shirt, the top two buttons undone. His left pant leg looks wet, and there are smears of blood on the pavement beneath him. My eyes glide to his enormously wide chest, rising and falling slowly with each labored breath, then continue up to his face. The air leaves my lungs.

He must be the hottest guy I've ever seen. Definitely older than me, and not like one of the immature peacocks I left behind at Dad's party. The lines of his face are sharp as if etched in stone. High cheekbones. A strong jaw with neat short stubble, and a slightly crooked nose. His closed eyes are framed by thick black eyebrows, and several strands of jet-black hair have fallen over his face, the ends reaching nearly to his waist. I've never known any man with such long hair.

"Do you need help?" I ask when I come to my senses.

The man doesn't respond. I throw a look over my shoulder. Still no one around. Great. Keeping a grip on my gun, I crouch and lean closer to him.

"Hey." I poke his chest with my finger.

I don't even see him move. One moment he's slumped against the wall like he's passed out, and the next, he has a gun pressed to my temple, his eyes boring into mine. My body goes utterly still. Cold sweat breaks across my skin, and a frisson of fear runs down my spine. There's no time to draw my own weapon, so I just stare into the most unusual eyes I've ever seen. Such a light shade of gray they almost look silver.

"Who the fuck are you?" he asks in a deep raspy voice.

"An idiot, apparently."

He furrows his brows and scans my flowery blouse and white pants. His eyes move up until they stop at the top of my head where my dark-blonde hair is gathered into a high ponytail and tied with a red silk scarf. The touch of cold metal at my temple disappears.

"Get the fuck out of here, cub," he rasps and leans his head back on the wall again, closing his eyes. "Stupid girl."

I slide my gun from behind my back and press the barrel to his chest, just over his heart. "Stupid, but armed."

Those magnificent eyes snap open. He holds my gaze as he wraps his fingers around the barrel and shifts the gun, butting it up against the bridge of his nose.

"Do me a favor. Don't miss." His voice is flat, lackadaisical, as if his life means nothing.

I stare at the lunatic before me, unable to break eye contact. Some people may say that they don't care if they live or die, for whatever reason, but when faced with an actual survival situation, they'll do whatever it takes to save themselves. Self-preservation is a basic instinct, regardless of circumstances.

"Come on, tiger cub. I don't have all night." With those words, he lets go of my gun and closes his eyes again.

The wise thing to do would be to get back into my car and leave the hottie with a death wish to die of blood loss, but I can't do it. And we've already established that I'm an idiot. I lower the gun and return it to the back of my pants. Then, I tug on the scarf holding my hair.

The guy's trouser leg is ripped midway up his thigh, revealing a long gash that's oozing blood. I wrap my scarf around his trunk-like leg, just over the wound, and tie it off with a tight knot.

"My car is over there. I'll take you to a hospital." I stand up and extend my hand toward him.

The silver eyes meet mine once again, then lower to my extended hand, regarding it as if it's going to bite him. Slowly, he raises his arm and wraps his fingers around mine. Pushing off the ground with his other hand, he starts to rise. Up, and up. When he's finally vertical, I have to tilt my head to the heavens to be able to hold his gaze.

"No hospital," he says, releasing my hand. "I'm parked several blocks away, just drop me off."

"Sure," I croak. "Um . . . Do you need help?"

His lips quirk at the corners as he surveys the entire five feet and four inches of my body and shakes his head. I might be an average height for a woman, but he has more than a foot on me.

"Isn't this a school night?" he asks as he heads toward my car, supporting himself on the wall of the building to his right.

"Not since my senior prom over a year ago," I retort, hurrying to open the passenger door for him.

I watch as the mountain of a wounded man shuffles across the sidewalk and grabs the edge of the car's door. His face is pale, and the scarf I tied around his thigh is completely saturated with blood.

"There's no way you can drive yourself anywhere in that condition." I head around the vehicle while he practically drops onto the seat. "Knife fight?" I ask, starting the engine.

"Bullet." He throws his gun onto the dash. "My car is about a mile down the street."

I try my best to keep my eyes focused on the road, but they keep sliding to the stranger at my side. Who starts unbuttoning his shirt!

"What are you doing?"

He ignores my question and takes off his button-down, groaning in the process.

"Dear God!" I yelp, staring at the bloody mess on the side of his upper body.

"Eyes on the road, cub."

"I'm driving you to a hospital."

"No, you're not," he says as he presses the bundled garment to the bloody wound above his hip. "I have a doctor waiting for me at... home. I just need to get there."

"I'll take you home, then."

"No."

I squeeze the steering wheel and steal a look at him. Wherever that home of his is, he'll bleed out before reaching it. Not my problem. I've already reached the boundary of "extremely stupid" by allowing an armed stranger with gunshot wounds into my car. Doing anything more is aiming for "astronomically idiotic" level. I curse under my breath and take the next right.

"I'm taking you to the vet clinic where I work. I'll try to stop the bleeding, and then you can be on your merry way."

"Can you get on that?" I nod toward the metal table in the center of the room.

When I turn around, I find my wounded stranger leaning on the doorframe with his shoulder, holding a gun in his hand while scanning the space with his eyes.

"It's just us," I say. "The clinic won't open until eight tomorrow morning."

He assesses the room one more time, and then he pushes off the jamb and limps toward the surgical table. He's almost reached it when he suddenly stops and grabs onto the cupboard to his left.

I dash to him and seize his arm, swinging it over my shoulder. "Come on, a few more steps."

The heat from his body seeps into me as we slog across the room. My left palm is pressed to his bare back, just above the gun he's tucked into the waistband, while I grip his forearm with my right. I have several male friends with whom I'm moderately close, and random hugs are a regular occurrence. *This* may not be an actual hug, but with my body basically tucked into the stranger's, I'm hyperaware of every single point of contact between our bodies. The weight of his arm on my shoulders. A slight brush of my hip against his thigh. The corded muscles of his forearm under my fingertips. His warm breath as it tingles the top of my head. It's as if he's surrounding me with his presence, and everything else seems to fade away. I've certainly never felt *that* with any of my friends.

We somehow manage to get to the table. I help him up, then I pull the cart with the surgical instruments and supplies closer.

"Okay." Trying to gather my courage, I take a deep breath as I rummage through the first drawer. "We'll do your side first. There should be a pack of pressure bandages somewhere around here." My fingers finally curl around a familiar tubular shape, and I set the roll on top. Straightening out, my eyes snag on a box of nitrile gloves on a nearby counter. My hands shake while I tug two out and pull them on.

Crazy. Everything about this is crazy. This idea didn't sound so complicated when I came up with it in the car, but now, I'm slowly sliding into panic. *Stupid. Stupid. Stupid.*

"You need to remove the bullet first, cub."

My head snaps in his direction, and I gape at him in horror. *What?* There's no way I'm digging into his flesh to take out a bullet. I just thought I'd bandage him up to help stop the bleeding.

A small smile lifts the corners of his lips. He seems to find the situation amusing. My pulse skyrockets while I peer at the two silver orbs that have captured my gaze. I can't help but wonder what secrets are hidden in their depths. Something about those pale irises makes me feel as if I'm staring death right in the eye, but the wild thumping of my heart is not because of fear.

I'm well aware that it's the middle of the night, and I'm all alone with a stranger—a man who's more than twice my size, and who, even wounded, can easily snap my neck. But no, my frantic heartbeat has nothing to do with fear.

More strands of hair have slipped out of his braid, the dark tendrils framing his handsome face. In full light now, I can see it's not as perfect as it seemed. There is a scar on his forehead and another on his left cheekbone, but they don't distract from his looks.

"The bullet is close to the surface." He reaches for the forceps on the cart and places them in my hand. "You'll manage just fine."

I squeeze the instrument and look down at the hole in his side. "We only have animal anesthetic here."

"I don't like drugs. We'll go without," he says and lies down on the table.

"No anesthetic. Sure." I swallow. Dear God, he's nuts.

Trying my best not to freak out completely, I start cleaning the skin around the bullet wound. The only thing I see is blood, but somehow, I will my hand not to shake as I bring the forceps closer to the injury.

"It's half an inch or so in," he says. "You should be able to feel it right away."

Don't faint. Don't faint. Bile rises up my throat as I place the tip of the forceps inside the wound. I've watched animals being treated numerous times, including some pretty nasty lacerations, but I have never witnessed anyone taking out a bullet. The urge to shut my eyes, to block out the images of blood and torn flesh, is overwhelming. I grit my teeth to overcome it.

Strong fingers wrap around my wrist, moving my hand slightly to the left. The force behind his hold is nonexistent, as if he's afraid of hurting me.

"There." I hear him, but I don't dare to look away from the wound. "Can you feel it?"

I nod.

"Good. Now, take it out."

I hold my breath and squeeze the small object with the forceps. The stranger's body tenses but he doesn't let out a sound. Cold sweat breaks across my forehead as I slowly pull the bullet out. Instantly, blood starts seeping from the hole in the flesh. I toss the forceps and the bullet onto the cart and grab a huck towel, pressing it over the wound.

"Now what?" I choke out.

"Clean the blood first. Next, apply a dressing—maybe add a few—and cover it with a bandage. Then, use the tape to secure everything."

I follow his instructions and, when I have the bandage on his hip secured, I grab the edge of the table and try to bring my erratic breathing under control. There's blood all over my hands and arms, halfway to my elbows.

"Now, the leg," he grunts as he pulls himself into a sitting position. "Do you have elastic bandages?"

Nodding, I take off the bloody gloves and reach inside the drawer to pull out two packs. My fingers are shaking, and I barely register my own movements as I place the packages in his outstretched hand. The skin on his palm is rough, and a thick raised scar splits it diagonally.

"Cub."

My gaze jumps from his hand to his eyes. They are watching me intently. There's a light touch on my right wrist as his fingers circle it, just as they had done a few minutes ago. He raises my hand and presses his lips to the tips of my fingers. And I suddenly forget how to breathe.

"You did good." His husky voice washes over me, almost like a caress, while he releases my hand.

Stunned, I just stand there as he tears off the casing around the roll and starts wrapping the bandage around his thigh. He doesn't even flinch. My panic starts to subside, so I'm finally able to process the sight of him in all his beautiful male glory.

I let my eyes wander over his huge naked chest, every muscle of which is so perfectly outlined that he'd make a phenomenal subject for studying anatomy. What? Yeah, "studying," that's exactly what I'm thinking as I watch the way his biceps flex while he works on wrapping his leg. Those things might be thicker than both my thighs together. Heat spreads across my cheeks as I ogle him without an ounce of shame.

Similar to his face, there are small imperfections on his upper body. A five-inch line of raised flesh on his left forearm. An old knife wound, probably. There are also several small scars on his stomach and chest, but I'm not sure what could have caused them. The round mark on his shoulder near the right collarbone, however, is most definitely from a bullet.

When he's done, he slides off the table, and again, I need to tilt my head up to be able to meet his stare.

"Next time you stumble upon a man with a gunshot wound, you either run or you kill him." He leans in until his face is mere inches from mine, and one of the loose dark strands of hair brushes my cheek. "You got that, tiger cub?"

"Yes," I whisper.

He picks up his ruined shirt, then reaches for my silk scarf discarded on the table and stuffs it into the pocket of his pants. The next moment, he's limping across the room, heading toward the exit.

"No 'thank you for saving my life'?" I mumble.

My mysterious stranger stops, but he doesn't turn to look at me. "You're alive, aren't you?"

"Yes. So?"

"That's the biggest 'thank you' anyone ever got from me, cub."

The bell above the door chimes as the door closes in his wake.

I look down at my hand. The tingling feeling where his lips touched the tips of my fingers is still there. Was it a kiss? I remain standing in the middle of the operating room, staring at my hand for nearly five minutes. When I finally shake the fog off my mind, I run to the door, afraid I'll find the long-haired guy face down in the parking lot.

There is no one around when I step outside. I turn, my eyes searching for the tall figure but finding nothing. A crumbled newspaper, tossed by a breeze, rolls down the deserted street. The trash can down the block rattles as a stray cat jumps on its lid and then leaps onto the balcony above. But, there is no sign of *him*. It's as if he just... disappeared.

I pull out the phone from my back pocket and open the news app. Several articles with bold headlines flash across the screen as I swipe through the contents. All of them are about the shooting that happened earlier tonight, barely five blocks from here. I click on the most recent one, skimming the text. Nine victims, according to police. A prominent real estate mogul and members of his security team. A reporter interviewed the nearby residents, but no one saw or heard a thing. The only potential lead came from a woman working the night shift in the nearby pawn shop. She saw a man heading toward the unfinished complex where the shooting took place. Unfortunately, she didn't see his face, only his back and long hair, twisted into a braid.

Chapter Two

Nera

"How's that work of yours going? Anything interesting happened?" The words are spoken between bites, and it's my dad's usual easygoing tone, but Nuncio Veronese, the don of Boston Cosa Nostra, never says or does anything without a reason.

A piece of broccoli almost gets lodged in my throat, because for a split second, I think he might have somehow found out about my long-haired stranger from last week.

"Um . . . It's great, Dad." I swallow. "Nope. Just the same old, you know. Oh, but a boy did bring in a tarantula the other day."

"Dear God." He sighs then turns to my sister who's sitting on the other side of the table, "Zara, please pass me the bread."

My sister moves the glass bowl closer to him and continues eating in silence. She is always so quiet that, sometimes, I forget she's even in the room. When we were kids, Zara was so joyful, constantly laughing and babbling about something. Mom used to say that if Zara didn't have a mouth, she'd grow one out of sheer will. That changed after the night Elmo was killed. Since then, she hasn't been that smiling little girl who loved mischief.

"I know I agreed to go along with this crazy idea of yours, Nera, but don't you want to reconsider?" my father continues. "If you want to study something, why not economics? Or finance? Something that would be of actual benefit and you could use in the future?"

"Nope."

"You do understand that it's only temporary, right? When you get married, your husband won't let you spend your time inseminating horses or whatever. It's absolutely unbecoming for someone of your pedigree."

"There are hardly any horses in need of insemination in Boston, Dad." I sigh. It's the same conversation every Sunday when I visit. "We mostly treat pets."

"Thank God." He reaches for his wine and takes a big sip. "I should have married you off the moment you turned eighteen, but Massimo said I should wait."

I raise an eyebrow. I didn't know that my father discussed my future with my stepbrother. Massimo is serving an eighteen-year voluntary manslaughter sentence for killing the guy who shot Elmo, and Dad visits him once a week. Every Thursday morning, Dad travels to the correctional institution outside of Boston and stays for hours. I've always wondered what they talk about. My father is the only person my stepbrother allows to visit him in prison. Neither I nor Zara have seen Massimo since he got locked up. As far as I know, he hasn't even let Salvo, his childhood friend who is now one of my dad's capos, come see him.

"How is he doing?" I ask.

"Quite fine, actually. You know Massimo, nothing rattles him much."

"He's been locked up in the maximum-security prison for more than a decade and he's 'fine'?"

"Yes," he says. "He's been asking about the two of you."

A sharp intake of breath comes from across the table. I glance up to find Zara staring at her plate, her fork hovering halfway to its destination. It lasts for only a moment before she resumes stuffing food into her mouth.

"But he still won't let us visit?" I look back at my father.

"He has his reasons." Dad shrugs and changes the subject. "Tiziano's son is being baptized this fall, and there'll be a big Family lunch afterward. I need both of you to attend and look your best. Get yourselves custom-made dresses, something no other woman there will have. My daughters need to stand above every capo's wife or girlfriend. I don't want to be embarrassed in front of the Family, you hear me?"

"Which day is it? I'll have to check my schedule at the clinic."

"I don't care about your hobby schedule, Nera. You're going to be there," he snaps, then points his fork at Zara. "You, too. In an outfit that's appropriate for the venue and the weather. I'll get back to you with a date."

Keeping her eyes downcast, Zara sets her utensils on her plate and slowly rises. She doesn't say a word as she steps away and leaves the dining room.

"That was mean!" I hiss as soon as my sister is out of earshot.

"She's not a kid anymore. Your sister is almost eighteen, and she needs to start paying attention to how she presents herself. She can't go around covered from head to toe in a hundred-degree heat, for God's sake. People will talk."

"Then let them fucking talk!" I throw the napkin onto my plate, then rush after Zara.

Her room is on the second floor, right next to my old one. They are adjoined with a connecting door, and since I'm not spending time here anymore, I let Zara use my childhood bedroom as her sewing studio.

I find Zara sitting on the edge of her bed, gripping the bedspread in her fingers. Fashion magazines, sketches, and various pieces of fabric are scattered all around. I lean my shoulder on the doorframe and take in the mess.

"My room isn't enough, huh?" I smile, trying to keep the mood light. "Come on. Show me what you're working on."

Zara just shrugs, her shoulders seem to slump even more after. I step into her domain, trying my best not to trip or dislodge any of the sewing patterns she has spread out on the floor.

"This looks amazing." I bend and pick up a sketch showing a sleeveless gown with a halter bodice that ties around the neck. "I could use a dress for that lunch with Tiziano if you have the time."

My sister's lips instantly widen into a smile. She springs from the bed and rushes around the room, collecting the tape measure and a notepad off the recliner.

"Are you sure about the design?" she asks as she crouches to grab a pencil from under the bed. "I can make changes if you want."

"No changes. It's going to be perfect. Like every piece of clothing you've made for me."

I run my hand over the puffy sleeve of her white blouse. She told me the style is known as "lantern," where the material balloons out toward the wrists and the cuffs are held together with pearl buttons. The shirt's collar is high and tight, forming a big bow around her neck. She's so talented.

Shortly after our brother was killed, Zara developed vitiligo. It started on her fingers and wrists, but then the white spots appeared on her chest, legs, and arms. Around the time Mom died, it progressed to include areas around her eyes. No matter the temperature outside, Zara always wears high-necklines and long sleeves because she doesn't like it when people stare. Last year, she tried covering the discolored parts of her face with a foundation, but her skin didn't handle it well. Still, she kept switching the brands, trying different ones, until she developed such a rash that I had to sit her down and put a mirror in her hand. She is absolutely gorgeous, and I tried to make her see that. There isn't a single thing that isn't beautiful about my sister. I wanted her to realize that about herself, to recognize that she is pretty and perfect, just as she is. She didn't believe me, but at least she stopped using the foundation.

"How about lavender silk?" Zara asks as she wraps the tape measure around my hips.

"Yeah, lavender sounds great." I raise my arms so she can measure my bust. "So . . . I met someone at the vet office last week."

Zara arches an eyebrow.

"Tall. Like, really tall. Amazing body. Long black hair. He's probably the hottest man I've ever met."

"Did he bring a pet for a checkup?"

"Um, not exactly." I laugh. "He ended up being the patient."

I give her the details of my run-in with the stranger, starting with how I found him in an alley, but I skip the gun part.

I still think about him. His rough, broken voice. The way he lay on that table, utterly still, as I dug the bullet out of his flesh. A couple of years back, one of my father's guards was shot just outside our gates. While the thug who was stupid enough to do it was swiftly dealt with by our security guys, the wounded man was brought into the house. Our family doctor arrived to treat him, and even though I heard the man was given an anesthetic, he still wailed loud enough for me to hear it in my room. The whole neighborhood probably heard him.

But the thing that left the biggest impression on me was my stranger's eyes. So beautiful. And so empty. There was nothing in those two silver orbs. No fear of dying. No concern. Nothing. Looking into them felt like I was looking at a soul made of stone.

When I'm finished recounting our run-in, Zara just stares at me for a couple of moments, then grabs my shoulders and shouts into my face.

"Are you out of your fucking mind?!"

I blink at her. Zara never curses. And I don't remember the last time I heard her raise her voice.

"Alone," she continues, shaking my shoulders. "In the middle of the night. Treating gunshot wounds on a stranger?"

"Listen. I know it was stupid, okay? But when I saw him in that alley, just staring at the dark sky, it reminded me of me, somehow. I couldn't just leave him there to bleed out."

"You could have called 911."

"I know. But I didn't." I sigh. "It doesn't matter now. I won't see him ever again anyway."

"Thank God!" Zara shakes her head and moves to the dresser.

She kneels on the floor and starts rummaging through a stack of colorful fabrics piled up on the right side. There is another stack on the left, but it contains all the neutral colors—beige, white, brown, and black. No vibrant shades, no patterns whatsoever. These are the fabrics she uses to make clothes for herself.

"Do you have enough of that lavender to make something for you, too?" I ask. "We could go in matching outfits, like we used to when we were kids."

Zara looks down at the big folded bundle of fabric on her lap and lovingly strokes the pinkish-purple silk with the tips of her fingers. She would look lovely in that color, especially in one of the designs I saw strewn on the floor—a magnificent evening gown with an off-the-shoulder V-neckline and a high slit along the leg.

"No," she whispers and approaches me, holding the fabric in her arms.

She drapes the pretty material around my waist to see how it would flow, then checks her sketch, and, while I watch my talented sister, my heart breaks for her for the thousandth time. I wish she would see herself as I do—beautiful, inside and out—and wear one of the astonishing dresses she loves creating so much instead of just making them for me and our friends.

"How are things here, at home?"

"Same," she says while scribing the numbers on her notepad. "Batista Leone came over the other day, and he and Dad spent almost three hours in Dad's office."

That's nothing new. As Dad's underboss, Leone spends quite a bit of time at our house. He was also the previous don's underboss. I heard that he expected to take over the Boston Family when the old don died. However, during the meeting where the capos and the biggest business investors gathered to discuss succession, my father was voted in as the next don. It was at that same meeting that the marriage between my father and the previous don's widow, Laura, was arranged. Elmo was sixteen, I was three, and Zara was barely a year old when our new mother arrived at our home. Massimo, Laura and the late don's son, was eighteen when he became our stepbrother.

"Do you think Dad let Batista remain as his underboss because he felt bad that the don's position was basically stolen from him?" I ask.

"Maybe. Dad was never cut out to be a don, and he knows it."

"What?"

"Um . . . I mean, he enjoys being the center of attention and having people reach out to him for advice, but his temperament isn't one that befits a don."

"What do you mean? He's been handling things for the Family and maintaining perfect order for over fifteen years."

"Yeah, it certainly seems that way," she mumbles. "Do you want the zipper on the side, or back?"

I narrow my eyes at my sister, wondering what she meant with her cryptic comments. I could probe a bit more, but it wouldn't do any good. When Zara decides a subject is closed, it's the end of the discussion.

"On the back works for me," I say.

Zara adds another note next to her sketch, then takes the lavender fabric from my hands and starts folding it. "I need you to promise me something, Nera."

"What?"

"Should you ever run into that man you saved again, you'll walk away."

"He was just a random hot guy." I shrug, pretending to be disinterested. "I helped him. He left. I don't see how we would ever meet again."

"That man knows where you work."

"He's probably already forgotten about me, Zara. Don't worry."

I deflect with a laugh, but the truth is, I'm secretly hoping to meet my long-haired stranger again.

Kai

A man in yellow shorts and a white T-shirt moves within the circle of my scope as I track him with my rifle. This entire park space is part of Mr. Jogger-Extraordinaire's property and is heavily guarded. Someone on the inside provided Kruger with the guy's daily schedule, but they didn't have the code for the alarm on the gate. I had to scale the wall and sneak in during the guards' shift change at midnight, and then I spent the night lying behind a shrub, waiting for my target.

The running man stops for a moment, stretches, then resumes his lap. I'll never understand an urge to jog at five in the morning as a form of recreation.

During my basic training with the Z.E.R.O. unit, extensive physical fitness activities were held daily, missing them was out of the question. Running and other forms of cardio. Conditioning drills and weight lifting. Rope climbing. Sparring with other recruits in close-quarter combat, either bare-handed or with various blades. Four hours each day of honing our bodies, building agility and endurance, all so we could form the muscle memory we'd need to handle the strain of the field. The rest of our days were spent on military tactics and weapons training, including the fundamentals of a variety of handguns and rifles, throwing weapons, and also explosive devices and light artillery. That second part was meant to shape us into perfect killing machines. So, I understand the need to exercise the body when there is a specific aim behind it. I do not understand the urge to run for fun.

The jogger stays in my scope, but instead of focusing on my target, my mind drifts to that night last week. The girl. For what is probably the hundredth time in the past twenty-four hours. Actually, if I'm honest with myself, since the moment I left the vet clinic, I've been constantly thinking about her. She offered to help me without any expectation of getting something in return. It puzzles me. I've been conditioned not to expect anything from anyone, so I can't comprehend her actions.

I also can't seem to get the image of her—all serious and sure of herself, with her tiny Sig P365 pressed to my chest—out of my mind. Young. Petite. But brave and determined. And too damn reckless. Just like a tiger cub.

Her red scarf is still in my pocket. I told myself I took it with me because I didn't want to leave my DNA at her workplace, but that's all a load of shit, of course. There was so much of my blood in that clinic when I left, that the amount soaked into her hair accessory was pitiful in comparison, and wouldn't have registered. I wanted to have something of hers—a memento—so I stole it. Until then, I've never stolen a single thing in my whole life.

I should check up on her.

The need to make sure she's safe rises within me like a tidal wave. It's an unexplainable, ridiculous pull messing with my head, and no matter how hard I try, I can't shake it. It's been haunting me every minute of every day for the past week, and I don't know how to deal with it. I don't care about people. In fact, most of the time, I barely care about myself, so this concern for someone else's well-being is completely foreign to me.

I'm going to look in on her today.

The moment I make that decision, it gets easier to draw a breath.

Yes. I'm heading back to Boston once I'm done here.

But the thing is, I never planned on leaving Mr. Run-For-Fun's property alive.

In my line of work, the smallest mistake or a slight oversight could mean certain death. I figured it was high time for me to make one. I'd never give Kruger, the motherfucker who made me into what I am, the satisfaction of thinking he had won this unspoken war between us by taking my own life. Never. But everyone makes mistakes in the field.

The jogger veers to the left, taking a trail toward the small pond, two bodyguards following a few feet behind. There are cameras on the lampposts along the running path, but they are not directed at the area around the body of water. If I take my shot when they return to the path, the surveillance people will see it, and the whole compound will go into lockdown.

That's my plan. Just one tiny mistake—firing after my target has moved out of the camera's blind spot—and I'm dead. If there is hell in the afterlife, I'm sure that's where I'm going to end up. I don't give a shit. I'm already in hell, and I haven't even left the earth, yet.

Shoot now, while they are out of the camera's range? Or wait until they are back in view, make the kill, and sign my own death warrant? Cub or my demise?

If I let myself be taken out, I wouldn't be able to make sure the girl is okay. I *need* to make sure she's safe, and that need is stronger than the wish to finally end my existence.

I slide my finger to the trigger, ready to squeeze. The jogger keeps his pace around the pond. His security detail is trailing him, lined up like ducks in a row. With my scope aimed at one of the bodyguards, I fire. The man stumbles, falling facedown on the grass. The other bodyguard has already drawn his gun and positioned himself in front of Mr. Soon-To-Be-Dead-Anyway, covering him with his body. The way they are standing, if I shoot at the bodyguard's neck, the bullet will probably pass through and end up in my target's face. Two birds, one stone. Too bad this contract arrived with a special requirement—the jogger's face must be left untouched.

I lower my scope and send the bullet flying. It strikes the bodyguard's upper torso, just above his collarbone. The man's legs buckle under him. I aim at his head next, the shot hitting him between his eyebrows. Mr. Yellow-Pants has turned around and is trying to escape. I bet he's pissed himself by now, but it'll be hard to tell with his fashion choice. I shoot both of his legs.

My position is all the way on the other side of the pond, so it takes me almost five minutes to reach the jogger. He's wailing as he rolls back and forth on the grass. I take out my phone, turn on the video camera, then crouch next to him.

"Hold this." I grab his hand and place the phone into his palm. "There. In front of your face."

"Please!" the man whimpers and shakes his head. The phone slips from his grasp.

"I don't have all day." I place the phone in his hand again. "Hold it in front of your face."

He continues whimpering but keeps the phone raised in front of him.

"Just like that. Nice." I pull out my knife and press the blade to his throat. "Now, I need you to look at the camera and say: 'I'm sorry for banging your wife, Mr. Delaney.'"

"I'm . . . I'm sorry . . ." he stutters, then starts crying. "Who are you? Why are you doing this?"

"That's not in the script." I stop the recording, then hit the start button again. "Once more. Loud and clear, please."

"I'm sorry for banging your wife, Mr. Delaney!" he screams.

"Perfect." I nod and slice his throat open.

I send the video to Kruger, then turn around and head back to get my rifle. Fucking private contracts and their special requests.

There's just one thing I hate more than people. Traffic jams.

I picked an indirect route to Boston to avoid the packed roads, so why in hell is there a line of vehicles in front of me blocking the on-ramp to the overpass? It has nothing to do with the rush hour, because the cars aren't moving, and some of the drivers have exited their rides. A crowd has gathered in the middle of the road. I leave my car and head over there to check out what's going on.

"Please, don't do it," a female's voice reaches me. "We can work it out, Jeremiah."

The group is standing in silence, staring at the man on the other side of the bridge railing who's looking at the road below as if he's intending to jump. The woman I heard earlier is a few steps behind him, gibbering something about a divorce. I fucking hate drama.

Pushing through the lookie-loos formed into a half circle around the couple, I approach the guy and take out my gun.

"Get back over to this side." I press the barrel to his temple. "Or I'm going to blow your brains out."

The future ex-wife and a few other people scream, their cries blending with the thumping of several dozen feet. It would be easier to just push the guy off, but that would mean cops, maybe even road closures or whatnot, and I'm in a hurry.

"Now, Jeremiah," I say.

The would-be jumper gapes at me, his body shaking. He's going to slip.

"I-I can't," he stutters. "I'm scared."

Of course he's scared. He doesn't want to die. If he truly wanted to kill himself, he would have jumped by now. And he wouldn't have brought his wife along to bear witness. Fucking manipulator. I put my gun away, then grab the idiot by the scruff of his jacket and haul him over the railing. He lands on his ass next to my feet.

"Get in your car and out of my sight," I snap.

The wife rushes toward the guy as he scrambles to his feet, and they both run to a green pickup truck abandoned in the middle of the road. A few moments later, the truck peels out at high speed, followed by the rest of the cars that were blocking my way. Good. I throw a glance at my watch and head back to my car.

I make it to the intersection near the vet clinic just in the nick of time, catching my tiger cub leaving the building. She throws her purse onto the back seat of her Volkswagen and then gets behind the wheel. Staying at a distance, keeping at least one car between us, I follow her toward the east side of the city. As we approach one of the traffic lights, my curiosity gets the better of me and I switch lanes, pulling up right next to her vehicle. The tinted window on the passenger side won't allow her to peek into my car, but I can see her clearly.

Think more clearly, too.

My brain was a bit scrambled due to the blood loss when we met, but I did notice that she was pretty. Moron. She's more than "pretty." Delicate facial features, with a small nose and big almond-shaped eyes. Rounded, soft cheeks. I could look at her for hours. Honey-blonde locks gathered at the top of her head, with a few stray strands falling around her face. I remember the smell of her hair, so near to me while she leaned closer to extract the bullet. Flowers. She smelled like flowers.

A rock song is blaring from her car speakers, and she's tapping her dainty fingers on the steering wheel, following the rhythm and singing along. It doesn't come out right because she misses almost every note.

See? The girl is fine, I tell myself. *Now, turn around, and get the hell out of here.*

I can't.

I thought that seeing her one more time, making sure with my own eyes that she's all right, would be enough.

But, it's not.

Why? Because she was "nice" to me?

The last time anyone did something nice for me was nearly fifteen years ago. It was when that old bastard, Felix, snuck into my room at the Z.E.R.O. base and pointed his gun at my head, saying he would shoot me if I wouldn't let him treat the knife cuts Kruger gave me earlier in the day. I probably would have killed him on the spot, but I was still groggy from whatever cocktail was pumped into me before Captain Kruger got busy with his little torture session. My dear boss had very distinctive ways of punishing his recruits.

And now, this girl.

I told her I never thanked anyone in my life. It's not only because I never actually had something to be thankful for, but because "thanks" is just a word. One syllable without a true meaning. Like *love*. Or *care*. Empty words people use but don't mean. Like *forgiveness*.

But I want to give her something. More than a kiss on her hand. I've actually never kissed anyone or anything before. I don't have much to offer, so that night, I gave her what I had. A kiss for the hand that treated my wound with such care.

But, I can also give her safety.

The traffic light changes to green, and I follow her to a nice residential neighborhood where she parks in front of a three-story building. I wait for her to get inside, then take two spins around the block to make sure the neighborhood is as safe as it seems. Once that's done, I pull up in front of a closed store and grab my laptop out of the bag I left on the passenger seat.

The shortcut to access the confidential database is at the upper left corner of the screen. I breeze through the four-factor authentication to log on and enter the street name into a search query. The list of all known offenders and their addresses fills the page. I narrow the search down to a ten-block radius around my cub's building and scrutinize the results. It takes me almost an hour to scan over the three bios that come up. The first one is a woman who was sentenced twice for financial fraud, so I rule her out as a potential threat. The other two, however, are men with histories of assault and battery, and one of them was convicted of attempted rape. I check both of their addresses through the nav app, then take my gun and get out of the car.

The whole idea of second chances is one big illusion. People very rarely change, if ever.

And I will not allow a potential threat to live anywhere near my tiger cub.

Chapter Three

Kai

26 years ago from the present day
Psychiatric residential treatment facility
(Kai 8 years old)

"I'm afraid not much can be done with the boy, Captain Kruger," says the woman in a white coat as she stands in the doorway. "He can't write and he can barely read. He can only marginally be considered socialized. When a nurse tried to bathe him, he scratched her face and bit her arm. We had to sedate him just so we could wash the blood off him."

The man in a military uniform steps into my room. "How old is he?"

"We're not certain, but we think he's around eight, at least according to the child protective services' records. He was found half-starved and completely neglected inside an abandoned apartment two years ago. When the doctors examined him, they figured he couldn't be more than six at the time."

"Parents?"

"Unknown. But they found syringes scattered everywhere and

assumed that whoever was taking care of him was a junkie. Probably overdosed someplace else. The boy was speaking a mix of Polish and English when he was found. He spent the last two years being moved from one foster home to another because of his behavioral issues."

"Mm-hmm." The man takes another step toward me.

I study his body from head to toe, looking for anything he could use as a weapon against me. There's nothing, but that doesn't mean he won't try to attack me. I keep standing in the corner, my back plastered to the wall, and watch him for the slightest threatening movement.

"Did you try placing him together with the other kids?"

"Yes, sir. It didn't work out well. The other kids are scared of him."

The man in a uniform takes another step, and now he's in the middle of the room.

"I thought he's the youngest here."

"He is. But he seems to be the most violent. His records indicate an incident where he bit off a boy's ear and stabbed another with a fork while living in a foster home."

"The boy doesn't look violent to me. Has he expressed any kind of regret over killing his foster parent?"

"No."

"Interesting. Is it known what triggered him to kill the man?" Two more steps, and he stops right before me.

"The medical report showed numerous fractures and other clear indications of repeated abuse. The incident, however, occurred because the caregiver shaved the boy's hair. Um . . . Sir, I don't think you should be that close to him."

The man's eyes meet mine for a moment, then move up to focus on the top of my head. "Yes. He did do a lousy job."

He extends his arm, like he's going to touch my head. I kick his hand away and swing at him, trying to hit him in the balls. The man moves back, avoiding my fist, but his lips curl into an ugly smile. I charge at him with all I have.

The bastard doesn't even try hitting me back. He dodges most of my jabs, but I still manage to land my elbow into his side—once, and graze his chin with my fist. When I try jumping on his back to get to his neck, he jerks backward and swipes at me. The heel of his palm connects with my forehead. The hit is so hard that I end up sprawled on the floor, my ears ringing.

"Nice." The man adjusts his army jacket and glances over his shoulder at the woman in a white coat. "The military is starting an education program for troubled youth, and this boy would be a good candidate. I'm taking him. The documents will be delivered to you within an hour."

"Oh. I'm glad he's getting a second chance after all."

"Indeed." The man meets my gaze, and this time, there is a wide satisfied smile on his face. "I'll make sure his potential is fully utilized."

Chapter four

Nera

"You look stylish tonight. Benito seems to be smitten with you," Dania says, motioning toward the other side of the karaoke bar.

I throw a look over my shoulder, finding the son of one of my father's capos nursing a drink. He winks at me as soon as our eyes connect.

"I'm not interested," I say, turning away.

"He just texted, asking for your number." Dania nudges me with her leg. "He's cute."

"I hope you didn't give it to him."

"Why?"

"I want nothing to do with a guy who only wants to ask me out because of who my father is." I sigh. This is one of the reasons I usually avoid places owned by Cosa Nostra members. It happens all the time.

"Not all guys are like Lotario," Zara whispers next to my ear.

"All the Cosa Nostra guys *are*," I whisper back.

Status and position are the most important things in Cosa Nostra, and as the eldest daughter of the don, you could say that

I'm the most sought-after prize. I learned that the hard way last year.

Lotario, the guy who runs one of the casinos, approached me at one of the parties hosted by my father and asked me out. I couldn't have been more thrilled and it felt like I was floating on a cloud. He was twenty-five. Impossibly gorgeous. And had impeccable manners. Lotario knew just what to say and how to say it to make a girl feel special. We went on a date to a fancy restaurant, where he had a private booth hidden away from the other restaurant guests' view, reserved for us. A big bouquet of dahlias was waiting for me when we got to our table. "So we won't be disturbed," he said, when in actuality, he simply didn't want anyone spotting us together.

We started seeing each other regularly, in secret of course. Lotario was afraid my father might not approve because of our age difference. He wanted to wait before telling him. I agreed. I would have agreed to anything—I was so naive, or maybe just stupid. Definitely blinded by all the attention he was showering on me. Expensive jewelry. Beautiful flower arrangements every time we saw each other. I was sad I had to throw them away as soon as I could because of my pollen allergy. I mentioned it to Lotario, but he insisted that I should be surrounded by pretty things. And then, there were extravagant dinners and his sweet compliments that had me enthralled, especially since I knew I wasn't really a beauty. My looks are rather ordinary. At best, I guess I might have a bit of a "girl next door" look about me. But this charming and handsome man was smitten with me, and it felt so good. *I* felt beautiful and special.

When he asked me to come over to his place one night, I said yes. Of course I did. I thought I was in love with him. And that he was with me. I gave that asshole my virginity. It was quick and it hurt, but I didn't mind. Then, he left the room, saying he needed to get something downstairs.

I don't know why I followed him. Maybe, deep inside, I knew the truth. I found him on the porch, speaking with someone on the phone. He was bragging about how he finally banged Nuncio Veronese's daughter, and how he plans on doing it every night until he gets me pregnant. I still remember his cackle as he said he'd be made a capo once he married me. By the time I collected my things and snuck out through the back door, I was crying so hard that I barely managed to order a taxi.

"Do you want to go home?" Zara asks, pulling me from my unpleasant thoughts.

I brush the painful memory aside and put on a smile. "After three hours of trying to talk you into coming out? No way."

"Well, I didn't think that I'd enjoy karaoke, but it's kind of fun." She shrugs.

"Of course it is," Dania smirks and smacks my thigh. "And since Nera suggested it, she should go first, show us how it's done."

"Nope." I laugh and shake my head. "You know how much my singing sucks."

"Oh, come on. It's not that bad. Off you go."

"Fine." I drain my glass of lemonade. "Don't you dare laugh."

Setting my empty glass on the table, I hurry toward the small raised platform on the other side of the bar where a guy with a microphone is waving me over.

As soon as I reach the stage, he hands me the mic, and the first soulful notes of "Un-Break My Heart" start.

"Oh, God." I cringe. I like music, but I couldn't hit the right note or carry a tune if my life depended on it. Sometimes, I sing in the shower or inside my car, but never in a room full of people.

Watching the words fade in on the small wall-mounted screen,

I start the first verse. As expected, everyone around bursts into raucous laughter. I continue the song while my eyes wander to our table. Dania is nearly falling off her seat, giggling like crazy. Beside her, Zara squeezes the bridge of her nose, her hand blocking her face and her shoulders shaking uncontrollably. It is so unexpected that I lose track of the lyrics for a moment. I only managed to convince her to come with us tonight by threatening to find the first dangerous-looking guy I could and persuade him to let me practice first aid on him.

A quick glance at the screen helps me catch up on the words, and I resume butchering the song, howling even louder than before. I'm aware that I'm making a fool of myself, but as long as it puts a smile on my sister's face, I don't give a fuck.

Mercifully, the song ends, but I stay on the stage and look at the karaoke host.

"One more, please," I say. "'My Heart Will Go On.'"

A collective shriek fills the room as people laugh and beg the guy to take the microphone away from me. I guess they've had enough of my "talent." Well, they'll have to endure one more song. I don't get to see my sister having fun too often, so I'll make sure to prolong this as much as possible.

My second rendition is even worse than the first. One of the girls sitting close to the stage has her hands over her ears, gaping at me in horror, but the rest of the crowd is cheering me on. All I care about is Zara, though, and I notice she has her palm pressed to her forehead as she shakes her head in disbelief. Still, a wide grin is gracing her lips.

I'm in the middle of the chorus, laughing my ass off, trying to hit the high notes and failing miserably, when a slight shiver runs down my back. It feels like someone has just put the tip of their finger at the base of my neck and slowly slid it along my spine. An atavistic instinct alerting me that I'm being watched. But it doesn't make any sense. More than fifty people are watching my idiotic performance, and I haven't sensed anything until this very moment. I let my eyes glide over the room, finding nothing amiss, so, ignoring the weird feeling, I focus back on the second verse.

The sensation doesn't dissipate, though, even after I'm done with the song. In fact, it becomes even stronger. As I'm heading back toward our table, it stays with me, like an invisible net of gossamer threads that I somehow got myself tangled in.

Someone else gets on the stage and starts singing. They aren't any better than I was, and the audience is cheering and laughing again. No one is paying me any attention anymore, but I can feel it, that . . . *something*. Dangerous. Dark. Lurking somewhere in the shadows. Watching me.

"Nera? You okay?" Zara reaches out and grasps my hand.

"What?" I shake my head and laugh. "Yeah. Sure. So, how was I?"

"Magnificently terrible."

"Hey, do you remember when we were in school, and the teacher wanted us to sing a Christmas song for all the parents?" Dania asks.

"You mean when she got so emotional she teared up at the end of the performance?" I say.

"Um, I don't think that was the reason, Nera. I'm pretty sure it was your singing."

"Oh, don't be so mean! I was eight!" I pinch her arm. "And I wasn't that awful."

"If you say so."

Dania goes up on stage next, picking an eighties rock song. She's dressed in a pretty pink top with spaghetti straps and jeans, as suitable for a casual evening in a karaoke bar as could be. I, on the other hand, am decked out in a designer-label pencil dress and wearing high heels that are hurting my feet. Zara is similarly attired, only her outfit has long sleeves and is ankle-length. There are certain unwritten rules when your father is the leader of the Cosa Nostra Family. One of these is that you can't be seen in casual clothes in public. Upholding a certain image is imperative, after all.

I've never truly understood the impact my father had on every element of my life until I moved out. Sometimes, I wish I had never left home. I know that one day soon I'll have to go back to that existence, and it might have been easier if I didn't get to know the other side of life. The alternate reality. The normal side—where you don't need to pretend to be someone else in order to be accepted.

But for now, I'm determined not to think of what will come. About a random man who'll never know the real me, but who will marry me only because the don decrees it. One who's going to buy me diamond necklaces and take me to expensive restaurants, but won't actually care about how I feel. Someone who'll likely bring me huge bouquets of flowers, despite me telling him numerous times that they make my sinuses irritated and inflamed.

"Louder! We can't hear you!" I shout as Dania starts the song's refrain, then lean closer to Zara. "Maybe, next time, you could sing one, too?"

"Maybe..."

I drop a light peck on my sister's cheek, then wrap my arm around her shoulders and turn my attention back to our friend on the stage. It's strange how two people born of the same flesh and blood, can wish for absolutely different things. My quiet sister, always wanting to be invisible. And me, wishing for someone to finally see me for who I truly am, not as whose daughter I am.

I keep my focus on the stage, while the tingling sensation keeps feathering my spine, and, for some reason, it doesn't feel unpleasant anymore.

Kai

Shrieks of laughter and cheer rise all around me as I lurk in the shadows, concealed by a wooden column near the entrance to the kitchen area. Waiters move past while they go in and out, some of them glaring at me for blocking their way. Typically, I'd do something about those looks, but I can't be bothered right now to pay attention to anything other than my tiger cub sitting at a corner table across the room.

As I watch, she leans in and kisses the cheek of the girl sitting on her left. This girl's hair is darker, but she and my cub look quite a bit alike. Cousins? Or maybe sisters? I tilt my head, and my gaze follows my cub's hand as it comes to rest on the other girl's back. I'm trying to figure out this gesture. Human interactions, especially between people with familial connections, have always fascinated me. Probably because I've never understood them that well. This move, for example. Is it an unconscious action or a deliberate one? Is she offering comfort, reassurance? And if so, what's necessitating the need? The other girl seems fine to me.

And the whole setting here, with random people taking that damn mic, wailing into it just so the rest of them can laugh? What a fucked-up way to pass the time. My cub seems to be enjoying it, though.

I heard the amusement in her voice while she sang her song. Though, I'm not sure it could actually be called singing. Whatever was coming out of her mouth sounded more like a banshee's cry. It was awful, and slightly painful to listen to, but the corners of my lips tilted up regardless. She's gutsy. It takes someone with a lot of confidence to purposefully make a joke of yourself in front of a room full of people.

My eyes slide down her body, taking in every single detail. The way her hair is twisted into some complicated knot at her neck. The classy dress, one that makes her look somehow different from the girl wearing pants and a blouse that I followed home two weeks ago. The heels—the sky-high heels that match the color of her dress.

I watch her for over an hour, soaking up every single movement she makes. The way she laughs, with her eyes creasing in the corners. How she tends to fidget with her glass, rotating it in her hand. She goes up on the stage one more time. I don't know the song, but I'm fairly certain it's not supposed to sound like *that*. She's so bad at singing, that it's just damn cute. When she messes up the chorus for the second time, I find myself laughing with the rest of the crowd. It feels strange, probably because I can't remember the last time I laughed. When she heads to the bathroom, I follow her at a distance, and then again when she returns to her table.

Eventually, the three girls have a brief discussion before taking their purses off their chairs and heading toward the exit. As they walk by one of the back tables, a man occupying it follows them with his gaze. Late fifties, much older than the rest of the patrons in this place. He continues to ogle my cub as he lowers his hand below the table to his crotch, rubbing and squeezing the bulge between his legs. Once the girls reach the door, he gets up and trails in their wake. I step away from the column and head after the perv.

The guy steps through the door, then pauses on the sidewalk, looking left and right. I halt behind him and press the tip of my knife between the ribs at his back.

"Not a word," I say next to his ear. "Walk."

He must hear in my tone of voice that I'm not fucking around because he does as I command. I usher him down the street, in the opposite direction from where the girls are headed, then slip us into the entrance recess of a residential building.

"I have money," he chokes out. "You can take it. Please, just..."

"Turn around."

"Of course. Here, I'll give you my wallet," the man mumbles as he faces me. "There isn't..."

Grabbing his throat, I shove him against the brick wall and throw a quick look down the street, catching my cub and the girls getting into a black sedan. When they're safely away, I return my focus to the scumbag before me, getting right into his face, searching his distraught eyes. Just as animals in the wild can sniff out other members of their species from miles away, human predators recognize their kind. And I can see it as clear as day—this man was going to hurt my girl.

The asshole's pupils dilate as he returns my stare, and panic seeps into his features. Without a word, he starts clawing my arm. He must have got a whiff of my intentions.

With one quick move, I bury my knife in his neck.

Chapter
five

Kai

A CRISP LATE SUMMER BREEZE BLOWS INTO MY FACE AS I step out and approach the rooftop guardrail. The rusty old metal is cold under my palms, so I lean my forearms on it and gaze at the building across the street. The penthouse boasts floor-to-ceiling windows, allowing me a glimpse into a spacious living room full of modern white furniture.

I reach into my pocket and pull out the soft red fabric, rubbing it between my thumb and fingers as I watch my tiger cub inside her apartment. She's sitting cross-legged on a big pillow tossed on the floor near the balcony, focused on the book in her lap. Her hair is unbound, cascading down her back.

For some reason, keeping an eye on my little savior has an unusually calming effect on me. She did save my life on the night we met, but not in the way she probably thinks. It wasn't the makeshift bandage, which I keep in my pocket wherever I go. And it wasn't her inexperienced extraction of the bullet from my side. But, had I not met her, the next mission likely would have been my last.

There is a limit to how much shit someone can take before calling it quits and checking out of this world. That night, just moments before the girl found me, I realized that I had my fill. As I sat on the ground in that alley and watched the dark sky above, I decided to make my next job the final act of my life.

So, I closed my eyes and imagined the bliss of just... not existing. Only to have my reverie and visions of finally being free interrupted by a silly girl.

And here I am now. Still alive and breathing. Previously, I didn't much care if I completed my assignments and came out alive or in a body bag. But I do now. How could I watch over my girl if I'm dead? The night she tied her scarf around my thigh and then offered me her hand, my life became hers.

I've spent quite a few nights on this rooftop over the past three months, observing her. The first time I ended up here was when I followed her home after wasting the creep outside the karaoke bar. Once I saw my cub enter her building, I made my typical rounds of the neighborhood, then broke onto this roof and just watched her. It has now become part of my routine. Check everything out around her building to make sure nothing is suspicious. Climb to this roof across the narrow street from her place. Spend hours watching *her*.

Just watching, because learning anything more about her may mean I'll never escape her gravitational pull. Thus, I don't know much about my girl, other than what I've noticed during my viewing stints.

Most evenings, she reads or uses her laptop. I think she might be studying something. Since she still works at the vet clinic, I figure it's something related. She likes music. One night, she spent two hours cleaning up her place, and while she vacuumed, dusted, and washed her windows, she danced to songs I couldn't hear. So, I imagined what she would sound like—off-tune and out of sync—and felt my lips pull into a smile. Then, the other night, I watched as she tended to plants growing indoors. She keeps the pots lined up by her window, where they are prominently displayed like cherished decorations. I thought girls liked flowers, but her "garden" is all just a bunch of green leaves. That night, she spent twenty minutes misting the overgrown weeds.

She has a few girlfriends, who sometimes hang out at her place. Her sister or cousin, whoever the young girl from the karaoke bar is, pulled up in a taxi once. She went up carrying two big paper bags. I assumed she must have brought takeout, but the contents ended up being clothes. My cub spent quite a while trying on the things from those bags.

One dress in particular—long and purple, with an open back—had me leaning over the railing as I ate her up with my eyes. She twirled around her living room in it, then took it off right there in open view. I had a hard time swallowing as she unintentionally gifted me with a glimpse of her mouthwatering body. I stood, unmoving, while my cock hardened into granite, straining the fabric of my pants. Never before had I been this turned on just by looking at a woman. It made me feel like a fucking freak, but I couldn't look away.

The ping in my pocket alerts me to an incoming email. I wrap the silk scarf around my left palm so it doesn't slip off, then fish out my phone and scan the attached files. The first is a photo of a woman—senior, thick glasses, speckled short gray hair. Several lines of text are underneath—name and, I assume, her short bio. The entire life of a person, condensed into less than half a page. If I did want to read it, it would probably take me an hour to decipher the meager amount of text. But the grandma's life doesn't interest me in the least. I don't care to know who my targets are. I don't give a fuck if they have a family. Or the reasons why they landed on Kruger's hit list. I get the job done, no questions asked.

The second file is a copy of a flight itinerary to Berlin, and the next contains the street address and the exact location coordinates, as well as the code for the alarm. It appears that Captain is in a good mood today, considering that's more than what he usually gives me. Or maybe he's simply minimizing the risk of losing his only remaining "top-tier" asset.

Even after all these years, I still have a hard time deciphering his actions or the motivation behind them. All too often, he would send me into the field with minimal intel. During one such particular time, I barely managed to make it out alive. When I confronted him about it, he said that part of his objective was to hone my reactions when faced with unexpected situations during the missions. But then, barely a month later, I was ambushed on an op and was brought back to base severely wounded, Kruger fucking lost it. He killed the entire surgical team after they patched me up because they weren't quick enough for his liking. If I didn't know him any better, I might have believed he was worried for me.

The last attachment is a screenshot of a contract, highlighting the particulars of the kill order and the one-point-five-million-dollar fee. Looks like the granny is a major leaguer, but I already knew that. She would have to be.

I slide the phone back into my pocket and resume watching my tiger cub as she continues to read her thick textbook. The silk of her hair scarf feels so soft in my hand. It must have been an expensive item, but she didn't hesitate to use it to stop my bleeding. I've tried several times to wash out the blood, but the stains remain. The pretty thing is ruined. Maybe I'll buy her a new scarf and leave it in her room. This one is mine now.

With one last look at my girl, who is now getting ready for bed, I tuck the ruined scarf back into my pocket and lean away from the railing. It's a four-hour drive back to New York, and I still need to gear up before heading to the airport. There's shit to be done. And people to be disposed of.

Nera

One week later

Carefully, I poke the slimy, little brown thing on my plate with the fork.

"I think mine might be still alive." I nudge Zara with my elbow. "What is this again?"

"No idea," she whispers through her forced smile.

"You don't like the escargots, Nera, dear?" Tiziano's wife, a shocked look on her face, asks from across the table. "We had them imported from France, specifically for this occasion. The head chef here is famous for preparing this dish. Come on, give it a try. They practically melt on your tongue."

As if to confirm her declaration, she places the nasty-looking thing in her mouth, making a strange squashy sound as she chews.

"I'm not that hungry, actually. The potato and leek soup was more than enough for me," I deflect. "But I'm sure Salvo will take another serving."

The capo, who's been pretending to be engrossed in his food while secretly watching my sister during the entire meal, snaps up his head. I offer Salvo an apologetic grin and sigh with relief when Tiziano's wife switches her attention to him.

"Want to go get burgers after we're done here?" I nudge Zara again, with my leg this time.

"Yes, please." She pushes her own escargot into the napkin lying next to her plate and quickly folds it.

"I can't believe that Massimo's parole was denied once again," Armando, the capo sitting a few settings to the left, says between bites. "Are they really going to make him serve his full sentence?"

"Appears so," my father replies from the head of the table. "I've been pulling stings left and right, even got a senator who owes us a favor involved, but he said nothing can be done. Someone is intent on keeping Massimo locked up for the duration. The Parole Board cannot be bought, it seems."

"He should have been wiser and waited for the Family to handle the retaliation at a later time," Batista Leone, the underboss, throws in. "Killing a man in front of several witnesses, members of the law? Boston's chief of police was at that party. I'm amazed Massimo didn't get a murder conviction and a life sentence."

He takes a big swig of his red wine, and a few drops end up on his tie, right next to the salad dressing stains. Signaling the waiter to bring another bottle, he leans toward Armando, saying in a hushed voice, "That boy has always been too impulsive. Hopefully, the time in prison has cooled him off."

I stare at Leone, open-mouthed. The underboss often pecks at my stepbrother. More than once I've heard him commenting how Dad never should have allowed Massimo to live with us. Batista figures that Massimo should have been sent away to a boarding school when my dad married Laura. I've never liked the man. His greasy hair and body odor make me gag, but it's his ass-kisser attitude that sickens me the most. Living at my father's house, I've noticed that Leone has often come by uninvited. At least once a week he'd show up at our door. Even when my father had friends over for a social occasion, the underboss somehow had always ended up being included. He would glue himself to my father, praising the don's achievements for hours, never missing a chance to point himself out as an important element in whatever endeavor was discussed.

The conversation around the table switches to investment plans, with Brio, another capo, proposing we expand into the hospitality industry. He goes on and on about how hotels could increase profits.

"I'll consider it," my father says. "There were some unexpected expenses at the new casino. Business expansion may need to wait until next year."

"Why?" The man sitting next to Tiziano turns toward my father. He's one of the biggest investors in the Family's enterprises. "The cash flows show a significant increase in revenues. Why wait?"

"Just a precaution, Adriano. We need a better analysis of the hotel market before investing heavily into a large project like that." My father waves his hand casually, but I notice a glance he exchanges with Batista Leone. He quickly rises, saying, "I'm afraid I have to leave you all now. Duty calls. Girls?"

I conceal a sigh of relief for being spared from pretending to eat more weird dishes, and after saying my goodbyes, hurry after the don.

"Zara and I will grab a taxi. We need to pick up some rolls of fabric for her," I say while our dad is getting into the back seat of his car.

"Hopefully, it'll be something other than black or brown." He scrutinizes Zara's maroon outfit, a set of wide-leg pants and a matching blazer.

"Ignore him," I say, squeezing Zara's hand as we watch the limo pull out onto the street.

As we head in the opposite direction, a light prickling at the back of my neck urges me to turn and take a look around, but I don't notice anything amiss. It happens quite often—now and then, I get this weird feeling as if someone is watching me, but when I look for a potential cause, there's no one there.

"Strange," I mumble, then link my arm with Zara's. "I think there's a good burger joint down the street."

We spend the rest of the afternoon eating junk food and treats, hanging out at the fabric store, and trying on clothes at a small couture dress shop, but all the while, I can't shake that feeling of eyes following me.

Chapter *six*

Kai

Fall in New England. The scenery might be nice, but the unseasonably cold wind makes the pedestrians hold their coats tightly to their chests as they hurry along the sidewalks. I wait for the traffic light to change, then cross to the other side of the street, heading toward the vet clinic. It's almost seven in the evening, so they'll be closing soon. I should have been back at the base by now, delivering my mission report to Kruger, but I chose to make a slight detour to Boston and check up on my cub again. A *short*, eight-hour round trip out of the way.

It's been four months since she found me in that dark alley, and I still can't get her out of my head. The need to know she's safe consumes me. It's more than an obsession—it's a primal urge. One that must be obeyed or I'm going to lose my shit. Something that started as quick checkups every couple of weeks, has now turned into hours-long sessions of just watching her. Keeping my eyes on her, because nothing can touch her on my watch. Nothing can harm her when I'm near.

Lately, I've had to be more mindful to keep out of sight. She nearly caught me looking at her about three weeks ago. I was too fucking stunned watching her from across the street as she tried on dresses at a little store with her friend. The vision of her—so beautiful—had me nearly drooling like a teenager. I almost lost my head and forgot to move into the shadows when she swept her gaze through the massive storefront window. I've had to be more careful ever since and have been timing my "visits" so they happen in the evenings, when she's done at the vet clinic. And that way, I can follow her home to make sure she arrives safely.

I stop on the sidewalk across from the clinic. The glass double doors give me a clear view of a middle-aged woman moving around the reception area, collecting her belongings. My cub is further back, restocking the shelves with packages of pet food.

The woman throws something over her shoulder, and they both fall into a fit of laughter. I wish I was closer so I could hear it. Hear the happiness in my cub's voice as it washes over me. Her smile is bright, and her movements are graceful, so I tell myself to simply be content with seeing her be free. Free to live in the light. Free to experience the warmth of that life.

The other woman approaches my girl and nudges her with an elbow, saying something in the process. I snap to attention immediately, ready to head over and wring the shrew's neck for hurting my tiger cub, but my girl just giggles. Why is she allowing it? Why is she not fighting back, defending herself? Even if it was just a little shove, she should be returning the hit, or others will start mistreating her. She definitely shouldn't be hugging the woman as she's doing now.

My eyes narrow into slits while I try to analyze this strange behavior, but come up with nothing. Did I misunderstand the woman's intent? Give me a target, and I'll have it eliminated in under twenty seconds. But this—ordinary people—I don't get.

I've lived in foster homes with a lot of different kids. A lot of boys who, at the time, were older and bigger than me. For as long as

I can remember, I tried to avoid being around other kids, adults—anyone really—because they enjoyed taking out their frustrations on the scrawny kid that I was. Inevitably, those situations didn't end well for the other party. They hurt me. And I would hurt them back. Tenfold. I might have been smaller and younger, but I had a lot of prior experience in defending myself.

That proficiency was gained hard and fast. Call it an intrinsic condition. Because, no matter what people believe, the fact is, life is a fucking jungle, and there's only one rule in it. Kill, or be killed. Figuratively, or literally, it doesn't matter much. That's how this world of ours works. I've adapted to live it in. Survive in it. I know the dangers and the threats.

What I don't get is "normal" for the folks who haven't seen the ugly underbelly of our so-called enlightened society. So, as the older woman leaves, and my girl stays behind, I dismiss their interaction as beyond my grasp. I refocus on my purpose here, on heeding that inherent instinct.

I watch my cub as she wipes the counter, using a white cloth while rolling her hips. Left then right, a shimmy follows her hand movements. It looks like she's dancing. And even though I can't hear the tune, I'm fairly certain she's offbeat. Once she's done with her task, she does a rather clumsy ballet twirl, then throws the rag across the room, directly into a basket in the corner.

She's fine. She's always fine.

I should turn around and head back to New York, but I can't make my legs move. What would she do if I walked in there now? I have no fucking reason to be here, and less than that to speak with her again. And what would we even talk about? I have no idea how to make small talk. I suck at any kind of conversation.

Keeping my eyes on my cub, I unbutton my left shirt sleeve and roll it up to my elbow, then grab the knife I keep sheathed at my ankle. My blades are always razor-sharp, so it only takes the slightest pressure to puncture the skin on my forearm. Purposefully, knowing exactly what it takes not to sever the muscle tissue, I slowly drag the tip of a knife from my elbow toward my wrist. Blood runs down to my hand once I'm finished with the grisly deed, big red drops fall onto the sidewalk and land at my feet. The cut is shallow, but long enough to require several stitches. Enough of a reason for me to seek her out again. Returning the knife to its leather holder, I head across the street.

A cheery chime sounds above the door as I step inside. The upbeat notes of a popular song I've heard on the radio stream from the phone that lies on a small shelf by the coat rack. My girl is standing in front of a wall cabinet, rearranging a few supplies, and humming to herself.

"Forgot your car keys again, Leticia?" she chirps while still focused on what she's doing.

I take another step forward, dripping the blood onto the floor. "Not exactly."

Cub's hand goes still halfway to the shelf. Slowly, she turns around, her eyes flaring wide.

"You! What are you doing he—Oh my God!"

"I need . . . help," I mumble as she stares at my arm. It's not the lie that makes the words sound strange coming out of my mouth. I've simply never, in my twenty-nine years, asked anyone for help.

She blinks a few times, finally coming out of her momentary stupor, then rushes into the nearest exam room and starts pulling out the drawers.

"You're aware this is a vet clinic, not an ER?" she asks as she grabs a squeezy bottle of sterile water. "Come here."

I take a seat on a rolling backless stool that's been left next to a metal table attached to the wall. Meanwhile, my girl continues to rush around, searching for something. Her face doesn't give anything away, and she appears calm and collected, but I notice that she has opened the same drawer more than three times.

"I think this needs a few stitches," I say as I lay my arm on the stainless-steel surface.

She swivels to face me, her eyes as huge as saucers, while she clutches packs of gauze to her chest.

"What? No, it won't." Her gaze drops to my forearm. "Shit. I'll call Leticia and see if she can get back."

"You won't be calling anyone, tiger cub."

"Ah, yeah, I will. Last time I practiced giving stitches, poor Todd didn't fare too well."

Instantly, tension grips me, and a barely suppressed rage boils in my stomach. Who the fuck is Todd? A male friend? A boyfriend?

"And where is Todd now?"

"Back home, hidden in a suitcase under my bed." She comes to stand in front of me and looks down at my arm. "This is a really bad idea."

She killed the guy and stuffed him in a suitcase? It's a pain in the ass to fit a body in a suitcase—I know that from experience. You need to break the limbs first, at every joint. Depending on the size of the bag, the neck might need to be broken, too. I narrow my eyes and watch her as she methodically cleans the blood from the cut. And what about the smell? Dead bodies start to stink after twenty-four hours.

"How long has... Todd been under your bed?" I ask as she puts a numbing spray around the cut.

"Um, ten, maybe twelve years. You're distracting me."

Twelve years? She must have started young. Younger than I was when I made my first kill at just eight years old.

"I don't think it was wise to keep him there all this time. You should have got rid of him right away, cub."

"I'm sentimental. Besides, I couldn't separate Todd from his buddies. I like to pull them all out from time to time." She takes a deep breath and reaches for the needle and thread. "Okay, here we go."

"Them? How many do you have under your bed?"

"Besides Todd? Maybe five or six more." The needle pierces my skin. "Can you please be quiet now so I can concentrate? I can't do this and talk about my plushies at the same time."

"What are plushies?"

"Stuffed toys. Please stop talking."

Toys? I go over the whole exchange in my head again. Yes, it makes more sense now.

I eye her as she works on my cut. Her face is as pale as a wall, and her lower lip is bloodred from repeated biting. She's wearing jeans and a plain navy T-shirt, but even in this casual outfit, she looks sophisticated somehow. Her hands are small and delicate, and her long nails are painted red. They don't resemble hands that are accustomed to sewing up wounds or working with animals. I raise my eyes back to her face, it appears even paler than a few minutes ago. Her almond-shaped amber eyes, ringed by long dark eyelashes, are wide, focused on her task. The wavy dark-blonde strands that remind me of liquid honey frame her angelic face, and my fingers itch to reach out and touch them. Not that it will ever happen.

There's a saying about "hands dipped in blood up to the elbows" that describes men like me. However, in my case, I earned that depiction long before I was considered an adult in the eyes of the law. Now? Now, I'm so submerged in blood and death that the stink of it is permanently lodged in my nostrils. I won't dare set my dirty hands on something so pure and innocent as her, even if it's just to feel her hair. For me, she's like a treasured painting in a museum, open to view, but marked with a brass sign warning "Do Not Touch."

I look back at her lips and notice she is muttering something under her breath.

"Don't faint. Don't faint. Fuck, I forgot to put on the gloves." Her voice is barely audible, but I can still detect a slightly hysterical tone. "Don't faint. Just don't fucking faint."

"Haven't you done this before?"

"No. I've just watched Leticia do it a few times." She ties the thread and looks up, meeting my stare. "To dogs and cats. Not people. Why did you come here instead of going to a hospital?"

"This was closer."

The girl shakes her head and resumes her work. "What happened?"

"A homeless guy attacked me."

I get another look, paired with a raised eyebrow this time. She doesn't believe me. It's the truth, though. Besides my apartment in New York, I have a few other places scattered around the US where I crash between jobs. But none of them feel like "home." No place ever has. I guess that makes me "homeless" in a way.

Cub moves on to the next stitch, carefully holding the skin together with her fingers. Her muscles clench, making the tendons on her arms stand out the moment she pierces my skin. Is it the sickening sight of the wound?

"I'm so sorry," she whispers. "I suck at this. It must hurt like hell."

My body goes still. Pain and I have been close friends most of my life. I've learned to block it out. Her caring about how I'd feel because of the pinch of a needle is so strange.

It takes only twenty-two sutures to close the cut. They're uneven and messy, but I don't mind. The whole ordeal lasted barely ten minutes. I should have made a longer cut.

Cub puts away the needle and exhales. "I need a drink."

"Are you old enough to drink?"

She meets my gaze and leans slightly forward. "I don't remember you asking my age when you insisted I sew you up, buddy."

"I'm pretty sure there isn't an age limit on that."

"Smart-ass." Her lips widen into a small smile. "I think we've got some printouts with wound care instructions. They'd be about animals, but make sure you read them anyway. I'd offer you an E-collar as well, but I don't think we have one in your size."

"What's an E-collar?"

"Something the vet clinic patients get." Her smile grows, and watching it light up her face feels like I'm looking at one of those shining stars again.

I seize her right hand and slowly raise it to my mouth. She sucks in a breath but doesn't pull away. My lips touch the tips of her fingers, tasting blood. She looks so innocent and pure. What the fuck am I doing? The plan was just to check up on her and head back the moment I knew everything was all right. It didn't include slicing my forearm open just so I could talk to her again. Or contemplating doing it again tomorrow. And the day after that.

She's just a nice girl, probably from a good family, with zero awareness of what happens in the shadow of sordid society. I have no business seeking her out, absorbing her warmth and light, just to steal a few moments before heading back to my bleak existence.

"I should go now," I say, but I can't let go of her hand.

Nera

My stranger's breath brushes the tips of my fingers where they are still grazing his lower lip. With him sitting, our faces are at the same height and barely a few inches apart. Once again, I'm captured by his eyes. I can't escape the magnetic pull of that unwavering stare, compelled to drown in the pale-gray depths. I'm not sure why I'm so fascinated by them. Maybe it's because everything else about him is black—his clothes, his hair, even the air around him seems darker somehow. His eyes are the only light in his gloomy sphere.

"Do you always wear black?" I whisper.

He tilts his head to the side, perhaps surprised by my question. "Most of the time."

"Why?"

"Blood stains are harder to see on the dark fabric."

I drop my gaze to my blood-covered hand still held in his. "You do seem to get hurt a lot."

"Lately, definitely more often than usual."

"Maybe, next time, you should go to a hospital."

"Why?" He releases my fingers. "You wouldn't want to help me again?"

I meet his stare, and the breath gets stuck in my chest. There's something in his eyes, something different. They no longer look like empty shells. A sliver of hurt seems to have pierced their stony depths.

"Of course I would," I say.

"Then why?"

"Because I almost fainted. And because your cut looks even worse after my 'help.'"

He looks down at his left arm. The uneven line of raw, puckered flesh that I clumsily stitched together is an ugly, screaming-red sight. "Looks fine to me."

I shake my head. "It's sepsis waiting to happen."

"Antibiotics will take care of that, cub."

My heart leaps, as it does every time he calls me by that

nickname. No one has ever called me anything but Nera before. "Why do you call me tiger cub?"

"Because it fits you." He reaches out and brushes the tip of his finger along the back of my hand. "Will you help me again, if I come?"

I bite my lower lip, leaning slightly forward. It might be crazy and stupid, but I would like to see him again. Soon. "Yes."

"Why? You don't know me. Why did you help me before?"

"I couldn't let you bleed out. Do nothing. It's not who I am."

"Some people may deserve to bleed to death."

"Do you?" I ask.

The touch on my hand disappears, and for a few moments, he simply watches me. I glance down at his lips, where a few red stains mar the corner of his mouth. Probably from when he kissed my fingers.

"Yes," he rasps.

"No one deserves to die in such a way."

"You're very naive if you believe that."

"Maybe." I take a clean piece of gauze from the cart and reach out to wipe the blood off his lips. His gaze stays focused on my hand so intently, as if he's expecting a punch from a flying fist. I pause just an inch away from his mouth. "Um . . . You have blood on your face. I'm just going to . . ."

I slowly press the gauze to his lower lip, then move it to the corner of his mouth, letting the material soak in the red. His eyes hold mine, like two magnets, not allowing me to look away.

"I told my sister that I took a stranger to my place of work and extracted a bullet from his hip," I whisper. "She called me crazy because you could have been a serial killer or something."

"Serial killers kill their victims to satisfy their inner urge to inflict pain. I don't have such compulsions. But your sister was right about the first part."

"She also told me to turn and run if I ever see you again."

"Wise advice. She must have been the one wearing a long brown dress at the place where you went to sing."

I blink. Karaoke night, three months ago. He was there? Self-preservation kicks in, and I take a step back.

"I guess I shouldn't have said that." He cocks his head to the side. "Don't be afraid of me."

"You just told me you've been stalking me. Isn't that a good reason to be scared?"

"I wouldn't call it stalking. Your safety is important to me, so I drop by from time to time."

"From time to time?"

"Once or twice a month. Just to make sure you're okay." He shrugs.

"Why?"

"You helped me. I'm reciprocating."

"That's a disturbing way of thanking someone."

"I know. But it's the only way I know how." He rises—slowly, and with measured movements, as if he doesn't want to spook me. "It was the wrong thing to do, and I understand it now. I'm sorry for scaring you. You won't be seeing me again."

What? No! I don't want him gone. I clasp my hands in front of me and take a step closer to this mysterious man.

"You can come again," I blurt out. "If you need to have a bullet dug out or to be stitched up again, you know where to find me." I pause, then add, "If you don't mind looking like Frankenstein's monster afterward, that is."

He lifts his hand as if he's going to touch me, but then slowly pulls it back. "Real monsters rarely look like one."

I watch his broad back as he heads to the front door, his steps sounding hollow in the room. With every foot of distance, the tingling in the tips of my fingers from his kiss turns into a quake.

"You won't even ask my name?" I shout at his retreating form.

He halts at the entryway threshold and places his hand on the frame. "If you give me your name, then I'll need to give something back. That's how conversations work."

"And what's wrong with that?"

"There's nothing wrong with it. I just don't have much to give."

I start to say that it can't be true, but he's already opening the door.

"You can give me *your* name," I call after him.

There is a strange stillness in his body as he stands there—a big marble statue in the doorway, while cars zoom by on the street beyond.

"I could give you a name." His voice is low, I can barely hear the words at this distance. "But it wouldn't be mine, tiger cub."

I stand in the middle of the clinic, staring at the door that shuts with a click after him, wondering what he'd meant by that. And hoping I'll get to see him again. Hopefully it won't take as long until the next time.

Chapter seven

Kai

26 years ago from the present day

Z.E.R.O. unit base

(Kai 8 years old)

BRIGHT LIGHT SHINES ON ME FROM THE FIXTURE ON THE ceiling. I squint my eyes and shake my head, trying to clear out the dizziness. The last thing I remember is two nurses at the psych ward holding me down, while a third plunged a syringe into my thigh. When the guy in the uniform stated that I was to come with him, I kicked his nuts and tried to escape. I got to the middle of the hallway before the nurses caught up to me, tackling me to the ground.

"You want to keep the boy's name?" A voice I don't recognize comes from my right. "What about his records?"

"Make him disappear, Felix." Another voice, but this one I've heard before. It's the military guy.

Keeping as quiet as I can, I turn my head to the side, taking a look around me. This seems to be some kind of clinic. There are two wheely beds and shelves with medical supplies. The walls are gray and look unfinished, and electric wires stretch along the floor. No windows.

My eyes slide to the opposite side of the room, to where the two men are standing. One is the guy in uniform. The other is older and wearing a tweed jacket. He's got thick brown glasses on his face and a laptop under his arm.

"Wouldn't it be easier to just give him a new identity?"

"No," the uniformed jerk says. "His file makes it sound like he's not mentally stable. Changing his name again might fuck him up even more."

"Again?"

"He was found abandoned, neglected, and half-wild when he was six. The social worker couldn't get the boy to state his name, so he gave him a new one. Apparently, he picked the first name based on a movie he recently watched. And, since the boy spoke partial Polish when he was discovered, his last was chosen at random from an online list of ethnic names."

The man in the tweed jacket turns and looks at me over the rim of his glasses. "So, the boy doesn't know anything about his past? Not even his real name?"

"Nope. An ideal candidate and first recruit for my Z.E.R.O. program, don't you think?"

Chapter eight

Nera

"I'm coming down in a minute, Dania," I say into the phone as I rummage through the closet, searching for my other red heel. "But just a heads up, I can't stay long. I still haven't finished my paper that's due next week."

"What's it about? Treating constipation in goats?" She giggles.

"Very funny."

"Are they really going to teach you how to deliver piglets and things like that?"

I spy the shoe in the corner and pull it out. "Probably. Where are you parked?"

"Just out front."

"Okay. I'll be there in a sec."

I put on my shoes and head to the mirror to take a quick look. The black bandeau dress Zara made for me is strapless and reaches halfway to my knees. I wore it two weeks ago to a cocktail party my father hosted, but it's the only one that doesn't need ironing. It'll do. After grabbing my purse and coat, I open the front door and stop in my tracks. Tied in a bow to the handle on the other side of the door is a length of red silk. My heartbeat speeds up as I gape at the scarf, so similar to the one I used to stop the bleeding on my long-haired stranger. The one he took with him. Did he leave this? I look right then left down the long hallway, but there is no one there. My eyes drift back to the knob, and I reach out to untie the scarf. It's not the same as the one he pocketed, but I have no doubt it was him who left the replacement.

I probably should be concerned, considering that a strange man knows where I live. And, I guess, I am a little bit. But I'm also feeling something else. Excitement.

Despite my reckless actions that have set this whole thing in motion, I'm not completely clueless. The man was shot! And, it happened on the night when all those people were killed. Was it him? A witness pointing to a long-haired man heading to that building complex isn't proof, but somehow, I *know* he was responsible. I should probably ask my dad to assign someone outside my building. Or even better, I should sell this place and find another apartment.

But then . . . I run the scarf through my fingers and gather my hair at the back of my neck, tying it with red silk.

"Are you going to Romina's bachelorette party?" Dania asks as we make our way to the table at the far side of the pub where two of our friends are waiting.

"I'm not sure," I say, trying to hide a yawn and failing miserably. I've pulled an all-nighter studying, so I'm dead tired. "Zara has a math test next week, and I promised to help her this weekend. She failed the last one."

"Oh. And . . . how is she?"

I bite my lower lip so I don't lash out at my friend. I hate it when people speak about my sister as if there's something wrong with her. "Fine."

"So, she still doesn't want to socialize? I have to admit, I was rather surprised she came with us to a karaoke night."

"If my sister doesn't want to go out, it's her choice. You have a problem with that?"

"Whoa, girl. I didn't mean . . ."

"I know." I offer her an apologetic smile. "I'm sorry. The first round is on me, okay?"

"You bet."

I hang my coat over the back of the chair, then wave over a waiter before leaning over the table to give each of my girlfriends a peck on the cheek. Romina launches into recounting her bachelorette party plans right away, and I can't help but feel a bit of envy. Romina's dad works in one of Cosa Nostra's casinos, but he's not high enough within the hierarchy to be considered a major player. She's marrying for love, not because she needs to sacrifice herself for the sake of the Family. I may still have a few years of freedom left, but the knowledge of what awaits me all too soon hangs above my head like the sword of Damocles.

We need to show our fake IDs before the waiter agrees to take our orders. If we had gone to one of the Cosa Nostra-owned bars, no one would have dared to card me, but I don't frequent those too often. If anyone from the Family spotted me at a bar without a bodyguard, they would contact the don straight away. Dad would then call to give me a lecture for being irresponsible and send two goons to follow me around for the rest of the evening.

As I reach for the mojito the waiter sets on the table, a strange feeling overtakes me. It feels like thousands of tiny little needles are pricking the exposed skin at my nape. It's the same sensation

I've been occasionally having for months, but it's never been this strong before.

I rub my palms over the back of my neck and throw a quick look around. Dania and the girls are still gabbing about Romina's party, discussing who'll wear what. The group at the table on our left is laughing as one of the guys entertains everyone with a story, his arms waving wildly all over the place. It's the same all around—people are just talking and having a great time. About a dozen men are sitting at the bar, a few look fairly wasted. Nothing seems to be out of the ordinary, but still, I can't shake the sense that something *is* different. I just can't figure out what.

"Nera?" Romina nudges me with her elbow. "Will you be coming with us?"

I try to snap out of it and take a sip of my mojito. "Where to?"

"To shop for shoes. I need something that will go with my outfit for the rehearsal dinner. We're going tomorrow afternoon."

"Can't. I need to finish my paper on the role of regulatory agencies in veterinary practice."

Romina blinks at me twice, then falls into a giggling fit. "I really don't understand why you would do that to yourself. Veterinary technology? Really?"

"Can you imagine if your worth in life was based only on what you could contribute to the Family?" I ask. "That your skills and experiences couldn't be used to make a difference for society as a whole, if that's what you wanted, but only to further the Family's prosperity? But no one asks a woman for advice in our world, even if she were to be the most brilliant expert in whatever field. And, as a woman, *I'm* simply the means to ensure a good business relationship or to strengthen a man's position in the organization. So, I chose the vet tech program because I like animals, and because the benefit of gaining that knowledge is *mine*. Not Cosa Nostra's. Only mine."

An uncomfortable silence descends around the table. I know I shouldn't have been so harsh, but I just couldn't hold my tongue anymore.

"I'm going to get some air," I say and, grabbing my purse, leave the table. As I walk away, that strange sensation follows me, yet I'm still unable to pinpoint the reason for it.

The pub has gotten crowded in the last ten minutes, so I have to squeeze among bodies as I head across the room. At the bar, a group of men is loud and contentious, and the bartender is trying to calm everyone down. Between the overall confrontational atmosphere and the heavy aroma of alcohol hanging in the air, I feel like I'm suffocating as I head down the narrow hallway to the exit.

I step out onto the street and take a deep breath. To my right, four people are hanging out, smoking. Needing to distance myself, I turn left and head down the sidewalk, away from the smell, until I reach the corner of the building. The music and raucous laughter from inside the pub reaches all the way here, to this side alley, but it's much more peaceful than at the front. Closing my eyes, I lean back onto the cold brick wall and finally inhale fresh air. I love being out with my friends, but sometimes, everything is just too much.

"You'll catch pneumonia, cub."

I tense, and my eyes fly open. My long-haired stranger is leaning on the opposite wall, his arms crossed over his chest and head tilted to the side, watching me. My heartbeat soars just from being near him once more. He's wearing an all-black outfit again—a suit that looks tailored and expensive even in low light, and an unbuttoned coat overtop. I don't see any weapons, but I have a feeling he's got more than one on him. Every single molecule of air around him seems to emit a very clear message: *Danger! Menace! Keep Back!* I ignore the warning, wanting to be closer to him, not further away.

"I needed some air," I whisper. That odd feeling is buzzing within me now, as if invisible hands are lightly stroking my skin. It was him I sensed.

"I see you found the scarf." He moves his gaze to my hair accessory.

"Well, it was tied to the handle of my front door. Hard to miss it."

He just nods. No explanation for how he knows where I live or why he left it there.

"You seem well," I add. "No bleeding wounds tonight?"

"Unfortunately, no."

I raise an eyebrow. "Unfortunately?"

"I quite enjoy our little doctor-patient adventures. Maybe next time, when I get shot or stabbed, I'll seek you out again."

Just the idea of him getting wounded again makes my chest constrict. Even though it would allow me to see him. Touch him. Maybe, he would even kiss my fingers again, like at our previous two encounters. My guess is it's his particular way of thanking me. Still, I don't want him hurt.

"Please don't."

He suddenly stiffens, his eyes flaring.

"Please don't get shot or stabbed again," I clarify. "What are you doing here?"

"This isn't a very safe neighborhood. I wanted to make sure you're all right."

"I can defend myself when the situation calls for it."

"Yes, I have a feeling you can." Pushing away from the wall, he covers the distance between us in a few long strides until he's standing at arm's reach. "Turn around."

I stare into his eyes as he towers over me like some beautiful dark specter. Nothing is even remotely normal about this situation. Casually chatting with a strange man in a deserted alley as if we are neighbors who happened to unexpectedly meet up. A *dangerous* man who has obviously been following me. Who in their right mind does that? It's beyond stupid.

And yet... Slowly, I turn around, giving him my back.

Rough, heavy fabric lands over my shoulders. The coat is still warm from his body heat, and a faint smell of his cologne invades my senses. It's not an overbearing, pungent fragrance like many of the Cosa Nostra men prefer, making it difficult to identify his particular scent. It's more of a subtle comfort than a specific aroma. Something fresh and wild, like the mountain wind.

"Thank you," I say as I turn to face him.

"No singing tonight?"

"Not that kind of place."

"Mm-hmm... I don't know much about music, but you were quite bad."

"I know." My lips curve up. The guys I know would never say something like that to me. They would shower me with faux compliments, saying how beautiful my singing is because that's what they think I want to hear.

"So why did you do it?"

"It was fun. And because it put a smile on my sister's face."

His forehead furrows. "You wanted your sister to laugh at you?"

"She wasn't laughing *at* me. She was laughing because of me."

"Isn't that the same thing?"

"Um, nope. True friends and family would never laugh at you, no matter how stupid your actions may be."

"Mm-hmm... I never thought about it like that." He retreats and leans back on the wall again, crossing his arms as before. His stance stretches the black fabric of his shirt over his muscular arms and across his broad shoulders.

Heat floods my cheeks as I recall him sitting in front of me—shirtless—that day at the vet clinic. I guess, any woman would be beguiled by a man like him. I can't say I haven't imagined him naked. But my fascination with my stranger goes beyond the physical attraction. On one hand, his turning up out of the blue only to disappear again soon after, leaves me with few cryptic answers and more questions following our short time together. He remains a complete enigma. On the other, he outright confessed to stalking me. Any sensible woman in my place would run, far and fast, screaming all the way. Me? I just want to know more about him.

"Can I ask you something?" His raspy voice breaks the silence, and, I swear, I can feel the vibrations against my skin.

"Sure," I breathe out.

"What's with the weed?"

"The what?"

"The green things you keep along your windows?"

I arch my eyebrow. "How do you know about my plants?"

"The rooftop across from your building has a good view of your place. I saw you spraying the leaves when I came to check up on you."

"They're herbs. Oregano. Mint. Parsley. Rosemary. I like their smells. Though, I'm afraid I might've killed the parsley. It's almost completely dried out." I sigh. "I'll have to buy a new one when I have some free time."

"I thought women liked flowers. Not grass."

"Herbs," I point out again. "I like flowers, too, but I tend to get into a sneezing fit whenever I get too close to most varieties."

"Mm-hmm." He nods. "So, this stuff can grow on its own, yes? Like grass?"

I snort. "I can't believe I'm discussing houseplants with the guy who's been stalking me."

"Why? I think it's been a nice, interesting chat so far."

My brows hit my hairline. "You need to go out more, buddy."

A tiny little smile transforms his lips, and a swarm of butterflies invades my stomach.

"Why are you here, instead of with your friends?"

"I didn't like the direction of our conversation and needed a break." I put my hand over my mouth to cover a yawn. "Sorry. I didn't sleep much last night."

"Why don't you go home?"

"I would. But my friend drove me here." I meet his gaze. "And I'd rather not take a taxi if I can avoid it."

He tilts his head to the side. "Are you covertly asking me for a ride?"

"Maybe." I bite my lower lip.

"What about your sister's advice?"

"I've spent several times alone with you, and I'm still alive, with my virtue intact. My guess is, you're a safer bet than a psycho taxi driver I might get."

"You're beyond reckless, cub." He gestures with his chin toward the building across the street. "I'm parked over there."

I wrap the massive coat tighter around me as I walk next to my stranger while he leads us to the black Dodge Charger. For every step he takes, I need to take two of my own to keep pace. Our arms brush ever so slightly as we walk. Just an occasional tiny graze, muted by the thick fabric of his coat. Nevertheless, to me, each contact feels like a small electrical shock through my system.

When we reach his ride, he opens the passenger door for me, then heads around the hood and gets behind the wheel. While he starts the car, I shoot a message to Dania, saying that I went home, then lean back in the leather seat.

"I guess I don't have to give you my address," I say.

The corners of my stalker's mouth tilt up by a minuscule degree. If I wasn't openly looking at him, I would have missed it. "No."

I press my lips together, hiding a grin. "And should I be concerned by the fact you know where I live?"

His gaze captures and holds mine. "No."

I've been lied to my face numerous times and failed to notice it, but there is something in this man's eyes that makes me certain he's telling the truth.

"Okay." I nod and focus on the streetscape beyond the windshield.

We drive in silence after that, but the quiet is comfortable. Typically, I hate being in the company of others I don't know well, when that awkward silence reigns. The need to fill it with empty small talk gets overwhelming, but so is the fear of sounding dumb. My stranger doesn't appear pressured to break the tranquility between us. Me, neither. It's nice to simply be with someone and be at peace.

It starts to rain, puddles quickly forming along the road and reflecting the array of white and red lights of the cars around us. The windshield wipers are swishing rapidly, trying to keep up with the downpour.

Left-right.

Left-right.

Left . . .

"Cub." The husky voice barely penetrates my haze. "We're here."

"Okay." Instead of opening my eyes, I bury my face deeper into the coarse wool. It faintly smells like the forest—a citrusy pine and earthy aroma.

A car door shuts somewhere. Another click, and the scent of fresh rain invades my senses. Hands adjust the earthy warmth around me, and then, I'm floating. Held in someone's arms. Not someone's. *His.* God, it feels so good.

Cars sound in the distance, wind blows in my face. I turn my head and snuggle my nose into my dark stranger's neck, inhaling. Calm.

Heat radiates around me. A slight bounce against his chest. I stay adrift, lulled by the hollow echo of his footfalls. Lots of them. He's carrying me up the stairs.

"Where's your key?"

"I don't know. Let me sleep."

Stillness. Silence. Then, a loud bang.

"Your door sucks."

More steps. Soft squeaks of wooden floorboards. The balm of my favorite fabric softener as my cheek touches the pillow. Hmm. I miss the aroma of the forest as it starts to fade away.

To dreamland... No.

Gruff, broken voice speaking quickly. "Right away!" It sounds like an order. Makes me want to obey.

I crack my eyes open and find my stranger standing by my bed, holding a phone to his ear.

"Sleep. Someone will be here to fix the door."

"Sure," I mumble and close my eyes.

As I'm drifting back to slumber, I feel a rough hand wrap around my wrist, and then a light feather of warm lips across the tips of my fingers. Or maybe it was just a dream.

Kai

"I'm very sorry, sir, but we don't have parsley."

I narrow my eyes at the flower shop attendant and take a step closer. The man quickly retreats, his back hitting the wall behind him. This is the fourth flower shop open twenty-four seven that

I've checked, and none of them had the damn herb. And I'm losing my patience.

"I need parsley." I lean forward until I'm growling into his face. "Now."

"I'm truly s-sorry. I-I," he stutters. "My neighbor may have some. He runs a local greenhouse and grows vegetables and herbs. They haven't yet harvested all the crops. If you come back tomorrow, I will have some for you."

"I have a double hit on the schedule tomorrow."

The man blinks at me in confusion. "A hit?"

"Kill job," I clarify. "Give me the address to this place."

The man swallows, his face turning a greenish hue, then rattles off a street name and a number. I nod and leave the flower shop.

The location he gave me is in the suburbs. It takes me almost an hour to reach a gravel lot in front of a cozy one-story building with a couple of long, glass-enclosed greenhouses on the side, and a half-acre garden out back. The sky is dark, and the glow of the streetlight doesn't reach behind the main structure, so I have to use my phone as a flashlight while I step among the messy greenery, wondering what on earth possessed me to go on a hunt for the damn parsley at three in the morning. But I know the answer—I owe it to my cub for tonight.

No one speaks to me like I'm just a normal guy. Frankly, other than business-related exchanges I have with Kruger and the support crew, people rarely talk to me at all. And I'm completely fine with that.

Or, was.

Tonight, in that alley, my girl had talked with me as if I wasn't a monstrous freak, hiding in the shadows. It was strange. The good kind of strange. For a short while, I actually felt like a person. Something I haven't felt for a long, long time. And then, she let her guard down, falling asleep in my car. With me beside her. Trusting that I wouldn't do anything to harm her while she was in her most vulnerable state was beyond reckless.

It shook me to the core.

Not once has anyone ever trusted me with anything, especially their own life. The majority of missions for Z.E.R.O. were assassinations or other nasty shit, however, there were a few times when our unit was tapped for a rescue mission. Typically, it was Az, and on rare occasions Sergei Belov, who was assigned to carry those out. Never me. The only thing I was ever good for, was ending lives. Never saving them.

At first, I figured that Kruger might have been worried I'd go berserk during the mission and get my charge unintentionally killed. But then, it dawned on me—it had never actually crossed his mind to consider me for a rescue. Lennox Kruger selected operatives' assignments based on their qualifications and skills. And I was deemed unsuitable because, apparently, accepting the notion that someone may need my protection was not an ability he thought I possessed. Maybe he was right.

And still, my girl trusted me with her safety. Even gave me her unprotected back when I asked, then fell asleep while alone with a monster. Allowed me to carry her inside. Into her home. Into her safe space.

I glance down, realizing that my flashlight is off. The fucking phone battery picked the perfect time to die. There's a bit of moonlight peeking through the clouds, its bluish luster illuminates a patch of greenery around me, but not enough to clearly distinguish between different weeds. I yank the closest green bush that looks like parsley, pulling it out from the ground. It gives after the third tug. I raise it to my eyes and turn it left and right, checking out the leaves. Then, the root, which is long and orange.

"Fucking carrot," I mutter and throw the thing over my shoulder, shifting a bit to the right. More green shit. In the gloom, the leafy tops all look like the pictures of parsley I searched out earlier online. Walking around the garden, I pull out a couple more at random, lifting the plants toward the scant light overhead. All the fucking leaves look the same. Well... almost; the roots are different. Some are long and somewhat skinny—undoubtedly ground veggies. But she said parsley is a herb. What's the goddamned difference?

I pull on one and come up with... an albino carrot? Another, and it's round like a gnarly ball instead of a normal-looking root. With my phone dead, I can't check what is what, and I can't remember what parsley actually looks like. I have maybe an hour before the carpenter is supposed to arrive at my cub's place to change the door I managed to jerry-rig shut when I left, and I intend to be there while he goes about his business. One, because there's no way I'd let a man get inside her apartment without me being there. And two, I want to make sure he works quietly as I instructed, so he doesn't wake her up.

Fuck. I bring each variety of yanked greenery to my nose, smelling the leaves. Jesus Christ. If Kruger could see me now, crouching in the middle of vegetable bushes, he would think I'd finally completely lost my shit. When asked to determine the caliber of a weapon based on the sound alone, I can answer correctly nine times out of ten. But this? I don't know shit about this. I keep sniffing at the crap, but everything just smells like wet dirt.

"Fuck it." I straighten and, fisting a bunch of plants in my grip, head back to my car.

Chapter
nine

Nera

"I SEE YOU HAVE A NEW DOOR."

I take another bite of my pizza and follow Zara's gaze to my front entrance. "The lock was broken. I had the door changed a few weeks ago."

"You couldn't have just changed the lock?"

"Um . . . It was a significant break, some of the wood around it had cracked."

The morning after my stranger brought me home, I woke up thinking I dreamed it all. A shiny new, steel-reinforced front door proved me wrong. As well as two keys that I found lying on the kitchen counter. When I glanced over the balcony, I noticed two guys in overalls loading my old door into the back of a pickup truck. The wood all around the deadbolt was splintered.

"Salvo's mother called me yesterday," Zara says as she reaches for her water. "She's going to a charity event next month and wants me to design a dress for her."

"What?!" I shriek. "That's amazing!"

My sister just shrugs. "Yeah. I told her I'm going to think about it."

"You'll think about it?" I reach across the table and grab her hand. "What's there to think about?"

"It's not the same as making dresses for you and our friends, Nera."

"You bet it's not. You're going to say yes, design a magnificent gown for her, and everyone is going to go crazy over it. Every single woman in the Family will want to have one, too."

Salvo has been friends with Massimo and Elmo since childhood. His family is one of the most long-standing members of the Boston Cosa Nostra. A few years ago, he took over the capo position from his father and has been handling the negotiations for various transactions with our partners ever since. If his mother turns up at a party wearing a dress designed by my little sister, there'll be a lineup of women in front of our house the following day.

"Yeah. Dad's going to love that," she says with a sour smile. "Nuncio Veronese's daughter working as a seamstress for women below her social standing."

"But . . ."

"No buts. I'm going to tell her I'm busy with school assignments and can't do it."

My shoulders sag. "You said your biggest dream is to have your own fashion label one day."

"A dream. That's all it is." She stands up and starts gathering the dirty plates, effectively shutting down the discussion on this subject. "How are your courses going? You skipped lunch on Sunday."

"The courses are fine. And I've been putting in more hours at the vet clinic, so I couldn't make it."

"You haven't seen that man again, have you?"

I flinch, and a piece of pizza crust gets lodged in my throat. "Man?" I cough. "What man?"

Zara's hand stills halfway to the empty pizza box. Her eyes snap to mine, and it feels like her pointed gaze is drilling holes into my skull. "Nera!"

I cringe. Zara could always see right through my bluffs. Even though she's two years younger, sometimes she's more like an older sister.

"Maybe?" I offer her a sheepish smile. "Listen, it's not what you think. He just dropped by the clinic, needing help."

"Help? What kind of help?"

"He needed a few stitches."

"He had Leticia patch him up?" She shakes her head. "She's a vet, for God's sake."

I slide a napkin into my hands and start folding it. "Um . . . It wasn't Leticia. I did it."

"You?"

"It was messy, but he didn't mind. And I also ran into him when I went out with Dania and the girls. He . . . he drove me home."

"You got into a car with a man you don't know? What's wrong with you? He could have—"

"He did nothing," I interrupt her. "I asked him to drop me off. He drove me home, and then he left. That's all."

Well, it's not exactly the whole truth. There's the door. And the "present" he left for me.

"Why are you grinning? This is serious, Nera! Who is he? Do you even know the guy's name?"

"I don't know his name. Actually, I don't know much about him." I glance at the new gray pots I arranged beside the balcony doors. "He brought me celeriac." Spotting the blank expression on Zara's face, I clarify, "Celery root. And some parsnips."

"What?"

"I think he thought it was parsley."

When I headed out to the library that day to pick up the

reference book I needed for my paper, I found a bunch of vegetables hanging from the outside knob of my new door. Some were parsnips, but most were celery root plants. I gaped at them, wondering what the hell they were doing there, until it dawned on me. They were meant to be parsley. I stood on my threshold, staring at the "offering" for several minutes, while a warm feeling swelled inside my chest.

"Men who need bullets removed from their bodies and wounds sewn up don't go around bringing girls parsley, Nera."

"This one does. There was still dirt on the roots. I'm fairly sure he stole them from somewhere." I look away from my new "herbs" and meet my sister's gaze. "Do you remember all the gifts Lotario used to bring me?"

"What does that have to do with this?"

"Flowers," I say. "He kept bringing me flowers even though I told him several times that I was allergic. Diamond earrings, which I never wore since my ears aren't pierced. That crazy-expensive snakeskin purse that I gave away because I would never use real leather."

"Lotario was a tool. You shouldn't use him as a reference."

"And what about our friends?" I ask. "Friends who I thought knew me well, always seem to be in competition to buy the most expensive gift for my birthday without bothering to find out what I actually like."

"It's not like that."

"It is. And you know it. You've experienced it yourself. Last year, Dania bought you a watch for your birthday. And she knows you never wear jewelry because your skin is so sensitive and won't tolerate many things. She picked that particular watch because she knew everyone would be talking about it for days. Not because you'd like it."

Zara looks away, but I still catch the tears in her eyes. "I do like that watch."

"I know," I whisper and take her hand in mine. "And I know you love the jewelry Dad keeps buying for you. Even though you only keep it in that velvet box on your vanity."

"He probably forgot." She brushes away a stray tear and smiles. "So . . . parsley?"

"Well . . . celery root." I snort.

Zara eyes me for a few moments, then bursts out laughing. "I didn't know you have such a peculiar taste in men, sis."

"Me neither." I grin.

"But, be careful, Nera. And for the love of all that's holy, next time, ask him his name."

Kai

The elevator doors ping open.

I step out and head left toward Kruger's office at the end of the hall. Two tech guys who handle surveillance are hanging out halfway down the corridor, shooting the breeze while slugging from their takeout coffee cups, but the moment they notice me, their discussion comes to a halt. They plaster themselves to a wall, watching me with wide eyes as I approach, their focus bouncing between my face and an unconscious man I'm carrying over my shoulder. My eyes cut to them as I pass. One of the pip-squeaks gulps—loudly—and his coffee cup slips out of his grasp, crashing onto the concrete floor with a resounding thud. As soon as I move past them, two sets of running feet patter in the opposite direction. I adjust my hold on the unconscious guy and step inside Kruger's office.

"I expected you on Friday," he says without lifting his eyes from the laptop and scribes a note on the pad lying on the side of his desk.

"Something came up." I dump the limp body by the door and take a seat on the lone visitor chair in the room.

Kruger doesn't even spare me a look, just resumes typing and periodically making notations. He's always needed to appear as if he's unperturbed by my presence, but we both know that's not the case. After he took me in, under the pretense of enrolling me into the "troubled youth program," this man spent years using the most sinister methods to shape me into his vision of a perfect killing machine. I was his first recruit. Or, "patient zero" in the insane project of his, molded since the age of eight to become a remorseless slayer. As far as experiments go, I guess you could say I surpassed the expectations.

"And what's the nature of the thing that 'came up,' Mazur?" he asks and finally meets my gaze after circling his last line on the pad of paper.

"Not your fucking problem."

The pen in his hand cracks in half.

I lean back in the chair and cross my arms over my chest. As a child, I was terrified of "my savior," but then, there came a time when our roles reversed. I can still vividly remember the look on his face when it happened.

I returned from a mission and threw a severed head on his desk. It belonged to a well-known terrorist whom the military had been trying to kill for years. Kruger stared at the bloody thing for nearly a minute before he pulled his shit together enough to glance my way. That was the moment, I think, when he realized just what he had created.

It was then that I'd first seen fear in Lennox Kruger's eyes. He was afraid of me. I was barely seventeen. But something else was also in his eyes. Pride. I'd never had anyone be proud of me before that day. It felt good. Still, in that moment, I wanted to put a gun to his temple and kill him. At the same time, though, I wanted to see that look of pride in his eyes once more. My feelings about the whole thing confused the fuck out of me.

I'm not sure why I never tried to kill the bastard. God knows I had numerous opportunities. Like now, for instance. I could easily shoot him in the head before he can get to the gun he keeps strapped under his desk. Still, I don't want to waste him. Maybe because I enjoy seeing that look of fear in his eyes way too much. Or maybe because my fucked-up psyche sees this asshole as the closest thing I've ever had to a parent. And, to make the whole situation worse, I'm fairly certain that, in his own deranged way, he thinks of me as his kid.

"I don't want your private matters messing up my business," he snaps.

"When have I ever affected your 'business'? You do remember my fucking completion rate, right?"

He grumbles something and looks away.

"I didn't hear you, Kruger. What's my fucking rate?"

"A hundred percent."

"Exactly. So mind your own shit." I nod toward the man on the floor. He seems to be stirring. "What do you want to do with him?"

"The client has changed her mind. She doesn't need him anymore. You can take him back to wherever you found him."

"The return trip wasn't included in the contract. Will she be paying for the extra work?"

"No."

"Well, if that's the case . . ." I take out my gun and shoot the hostage.

Kruger looks at the corpse littering his floor and says, "Take care of the body." Then, he gets back to his notes.

I ignore his order and head straight to the door. My cub is working a late shift today. If I floor it, I'll get to Boston just in time to follow her home. And maybe, I can watch her a little bit longer.

It's been more than a week since I checked up on her last. A small smile pulls at my lips. She liked the parsley. It's planted in a matching set of three gray pots, sitting just by the balcony door where she likes to study, not by the window where the rest of her weeds are. My parsley's living in the best spot.

"Mazur!" Captain snaps. "The body!"

"Suck my dick, Kruger," I say over my shoulder and slam the office door.

Chapter Ten

Kai

I COCK MY HEAD AND WATCH MY GIRL AS SHE CLIMBS THE STEPS of the fire escape to the roof of her building. She's carrying what looks to be a blanket under her left arm and a bottle in the same hand, while gingerly holding on to the railing with the other. Her dark-blond hair is piled into a messy bun on top of her head and is tied with red fabric. The scarf I left for her.

The condo block I've been using as my watchtower is a story higher than her walk-up, so I can clearly see her cross the flat, snow-dusted asphalt to take a seat on a makeshift bench someone has set up there. Seems like she likes hanging out on rooftops, too. We have that in common. Getting comfy, she wraps the blanket around her shoulders and then just stares straight ahead into space.

Something has happened. Something that has shaken her.

During my random visits over the past eight months, I've gotten to know her rather well. She doesn't drink coffee, but she likes lemonade. Compulsively neat, based on how spotless her apartment is. Unhealthy sleeping habits. She can go all night, working on her laptop, until she practically passes out at daybreak. Last week, she conked out on her couch with a power cord wrapped around her leg. Good thing I kept a key to the new door I had installed. I didn't have to break in when I headed up to untangle the damn thing so it wouldn't cut off her circulation.

Other than joining her girlfriends at a bar every Friday night, she doesn't seem to go out very often. I adjusted my work schedule so that I'm free those nights and can watch over her. The establishments she frequents are fairly subdued—more like neighborhood pubs—and not very likely to attract major problems, but I won't take any chances with her. I want to be sure she's safe. No. It's not just a *want*. Need. I *need* to know that she's safe.

Sometimes, I drop by and check on her during the day. So far, though, I haven't encountered anything that might be considered a potential threat during the sun-filled hours. Most of that time she's studying at home, only once in a while venturing out to a library, or working at the vet's. No boyfriend. And no pets. That's really bugging me, for some reason. She's learning a whole bunch of stuff about animals, so why isn't her place overflowing with cats and dogs, or whatever other critters are usually kept as companions?

Cub opens the bottle and takes a big swig. She seems sad. I don't like it.

I push away from the railing, intending to head over there and demand to know who has made her unhappy so I can kill the little shits, but stop after two steps. I promised myself that I'd keep my distance. I'm going to make sure she's safe, but I'll do it from afar. Lurking in the dark corners is what I am best at. I don't "do" people unless it involves disposing of them.

Gritting my teeth, I turn around and look at my girl again. She's clutching the blanket around her shoulders, looking down at her feet as she slowly swings the bottle in her hand.

The urge to find out what's troubling her is eating me up inside, battling with my resolve to stay in place. But, I'm a stubborn motherfucker, so my resolve wins.

For a full five minutes.

Nera

Subtle prickles on the skin across the back of my neck and, a few moments later, the sound of approaching steps. Slow. Deliberate in their movement.

"I see you finally decided to show up again," I say, keeping my eyes on the city skyline. "It's been two months."

The wood creaks beneath me as my stranger takes a seat on the other end of the bench. "I was never far away, cub."

"Yeah, keeping tabs on me from a distance. I felt you, you know." And each time I felt the tingling sensation that's solely associated with him, I hoped he'd show up so we could continue talking. About nothing. And yet, everything.

"How so?"

"It's a sixth sense, in a way." I lift my wine bottle. "Want some?"

"Are you typically this relaxed with men you don't know?"

"Nope. I guess you're special." I turn, meeting his gaze for the first time. He's slouched with his elbows on his knees, his head tilted to the side—watching me. The bench we're sitting on is rather long, and there is at least an arm's length between us. I wish he was closer so I could snuggle into his side. For some reason, I'm drawn to this man like a moth to a flame, but with him, it's not the shiny light that beckons. It's the darkness. The urge to glimpse what hides behind that silver stare of his.

I've missed his gloomy presence. In a strange way, he is one of the few, rare genuine things in my life right now. It says a lot about my mental state, I gather. God, I shouldn't have gone to Romina's wedding. She was so happy. And I was jealous of her happiness, knowing I'd never get a chance to experience what she had, to have what she does. It just made me feel like shit.

"Why are you sad?" His eyes are focused on mine, and once again, I'm taken aback by the absolute absence of any kind of emotion in them.

"A dog that was hit by a car was brought in today." I sigh and look back at the rooftops visible on the horizon. "Poor thing didn't make it. He died."

"Everything dies, tiger cub. Dogs. Cats. People. From the moment we're born, we're all heading in the same direction. Toward our death. It's how life works."

"Yeah . . ." I take another sip of my wine. There is less than half a bottle left, and I'm feeling slightly dizzy. "Should that make me feel better?"

"I don't know. Maybe."

I snort. "Word of advice for you. If you ever get invited to deliver a motivational speech, decline."

The wind blows, sending a few stray hairs into my face. I secure them behind my ear and wrap the blanket tighter around me.

"Are you cold?"

"No, just sleepy. Wine usually has that effect on me." Holding on to the bottle in one hand and clutching the sides of the blanket with the other, I slide my ass along the wooden bench until I'm sitting right next to him. He smells like a forest again. "I see you got yourself a new coat. Can I keep the one you left behind, then?"

"If you want." His voice sounds huskier this close.

I close my eyes and lean my head on his shoulder. "What are you doing on my roof, stalker?"

"I'm not sure."

The sound of traffic drones below us, lulling me into slumber. I turn my head so my nose is pressed into the sleeve of his coat and inhale his scent. He tenses but doesn't pull away.

"Thanks for the celeriac."

A few silent seconds stretch between us before he speaks again. "It should have been parsley."

"I figured that out. Did you steal it?"

"I don't steal." He picks up the edge of the blanket and moves it to cover my legs. "I left money at the till."

"I guess that's all right, then." I lean a bit more on him. He seems more at ease with my closeness this time. A moment passes, and then he wraps his arm around my back. The excitement courses through my veins from having his body touching mine. Yes, there's the blanket and his coat, along with the rest of our clothes as a barrier, but still, it feels so good to be snuggled against him. I tilt my head until my nose nudges his coat, just as a stray thought invades my mind. "Are you married?"

"No."

A small sigh of relief leaves my lips. "One of my friends got married last week. She had the prettiest dress I've ever seen—snow-white and made of delicate lace, with little sparkly crystals along the hem. And the groom . . . He wore a white suit. They seemed so happy. Maybe because it was a real wedding."

"Are there fake weddings, as well?"

"Most of our Family's weddings are fake because couples get married out of obligation, not for love. It sucks." I yawn and lift the bottle to my lips, but before I have the chance to take another swig, he takes it from my hand.

"I think you've had enough."

"Party pooper." I reach out, trying to snag my wine. "Can I have my bottle back, please?"

"No." A curt response above my head and, a moment later, something crashes behind us. Probably my wine. "You looked more beautiful than the bride."

"And how would you know that?"

There is no answer, just the steady sound of his breaths. I crack one eye open and find him watching me. His head is bent, our faces are barely inches away.

"You were there, weren't you?"

"Yes." He holds my gaze, unblinking. Waiting for my reaction.

"Why?"

"Too many people. Too many potential threats. I needed to know you were safe."

"I don't need a guardian angel," I whisper and lift my hand to trace the line of his chin with the backs of my fingers. His breath brushes my hand as he leans into my touch ever so slightly.

"Good. Because that's not what you got."

"And what did I get?"

He dips his head until our noses almost touch. "A demon, tiger cub."

A small smile tugs at my lips. I can still hear the rumble of the passing cars on the street below, but the traffic has lessened. It must be well into the night by now. My dark protector looks away, turning to stare at the night sky.

Tranquility descends, and my eyelids feel heavy. I should probably head back inside, to bed, if I'm to be of any use tomorrow, but I can't make myself leave. Closing my eyes, I let his scent and closeness envelop me.

"Are you sleeping?"

"Trying to," I murmur.

"Letting your guard down while you're with someone you don't know isn't wise."

"Are you planning to hurt me?"

"Never."

"Then, I'm good." I adjust my blanket and close my eyes again. "Just for the record, you make an excellent pillow, demon."

"Is that... a compliment?"

"Definitely."

He's so warm, and being snuggled into him feels like I'm leaning up against a furnace. But even outside that cocoon of body heat, he makes me feel comfortable. Protected. And not only in a physical sense. Secure to say what's on my mind. Safe to just be... myself.

Drifting into a blissful haze, I'm dimly aware of the regular world that continues to turn. The less-than-empty streets. A siren in the distance, breaking the hum of traffic. The not-quite stillness of the night.

"You don't have any pets," he says in that broken voice.

"Nope."

"Why?"

"Because, keeping an animal indoors means keeping them confined. Almost like a prison. There's nothing worse than knowing your life has been relegated to a box, and no matter how pretty that box is, it's still a cage. Maybe one day, if I have a house somewhere outside the city limits, and a big yard where they could roam free. Maybe, I'll even have horses." I chuckle sleepily, remembering my dad's comment on horse insemination. "What about you?"

"I don't really have an opinion about animals."

"You don't have an opinion?" I snort.

"No. Animals are just nuisances. Things that come across my path from time to time. They don't interest me, so I ignore them." He rests his chin on the top of my head, and a shiver of awareness runs down my spine. "But I think I'm becoming partial to felines, tiger cub."

"You don't look like a cat guy to me."

"I don't like animals in general."

"Not even dogs?" I ask, wanting to know every little thing about him.

"Especially dogs."

"Do you know that saying: 'people who don't like animals, don't like people, either'?"

"I guess the saying is true. I don't like people."

"But here you are, sitting on a roof, chatting with one. While she's dozing at your side, I might add."

"Yes. And she's freezing, as well. I'm taking you home." He slides his other arm under my knees, lifting me onto his lap, blanket and all, then rises.

I wrap my arm around his neck and meet his pale-gray gaze.

"For someone who doesn't like people, you seem rather worried about my well-being," I whisper.

"Seems that way."

As he carries me toward the roof exit, his long strides swiftly covering the distance, I slide my hand to the back of his head and run my palm down the length of his braid. He comes to a halt so suddenly that I yelp.

"Sorry." I snatch my hand away. "I shouldn't have done that."

With his eyes focused on the building access door in front of him, he stands completely unmoving for a moment, then turns his head to face me. I stop breathing, absolutely captivated by his eyes boring into mine, and the sensation of being wrapped in his arms.

"I don't like anyone touching my hair," he says.

I suck in a breath. Considering all the pinching, prodding, and squeezing I've done while patching him up, I didn't expect that he would care if I touched his hair. "I won't do it again."

His eyes lower to my lips, and linger there for a heartbeat. Then, he quickly looks away. "I don't mind when you do it, cub."

I resume stroking his hair while he carries me down the stairs and then across the hallway toward my apartment door. The alcohol haze and the drowsiness from earlier have vanished. Banished by the thrill of being held by him again, feeling his warmth beneath my touch. His eyes keep straining on the path ahead, but mine are glued to his face, trailing over each sharp line, devouring the sight of him. What would he do if I tried to kiss him? Kiss me back? Or walk away and never show up again? I have no idea how to define this . . . thing between us.

When we reach my door, he stops before it but doesn't set me down. A moment passes. He keeps staring right in front of him, at the new door he was responsible for. And I keep looking at him.

We're both lost in our visions until there's a sudden click, and the motion-activated hallway lights turn off, leaving us in complete darkness. I thought I couldn't be any more aware of him, but now, in the blackout, his presence is immense. The softness of his hair under my fingers. The rise and fall of his chest. Warm breath tingling the skin of my face. The beating of his heart just next to my ear. It's well after midnight and, other than our breathing, there's not a sound in our world.

"Why don't you like it when someone touches your hair?" I whisper.

"It's the only thing that's mine."

A shiver runs through me, caused by the timbre of his broken voice. It sounds like the darkness itself is speaking to me.

"How so?" I ask, my words barely audible.

"Everything else I have belongs to someone else, tiger cub. My past. Knowledge and skills. Even my name. I don't mean it like it's some figure of speech, either. None of those are mine."

"I don't understand."

He must tilt his head to the side, because I feel his chin brush my cheek. "I know."

"Can you explain? How can a person's name belong to someone else."

"Some things you're better left not knowing." He bends and slowly lowers my legs to the floor.

The hallway lights, triggered by the movement, flick to life, and I have to blink to adjust to the sudden brightness. My stranger takes my hand and, raising it to his lips, just barely brushes my fingers with his mouth. I'm still trying to draw a breath when he steps back and locks his gaze with mine. "Sleep well, cub."

I follow him with my eyes as he walks down the hallway, his huge frame making the space appear much narrower than it is. For a fraction of a moment, he stops at the end and glances back at me, and then, disappears around the corner.

Chapter Eleven

Kai

22 years ago from the present day

Z.E.R.O. unit base

(Kai 12 years old)

*Trigger warning – animal abuse in this chapter.

"Aim at its hind leg and shoot. Now, boy, that's an order."

I look at the big brown dog lying on the floor, tongue hanging from his mouth as he happily waves his tail at me. Since the day Captain Kruger brought that dog six months ago, I knew something wasn't right. At first, I considered that the dog might be a wild stray, and he wanted to see how I'd defend myself if the animal charged me.

Captain enjoys creating and observing situations where I'm forced to act on instinct. Spiking my drink with something that caused light sensitivity and made me dizzy before he sent me to a shooting range for practice, all so he could assess how well I could shoot under the influence of similar drugs. Cranking up the overhead brightness, and then playing loud sounds through the speakers in my room, so he could measure how long I could last without sleep and how functional I was under the depravation. Ordering the guards to attack me from time to time to determine the quickness of my reflexes in such situations.

But I didn't understand the purpose of a dog.

Now I do.

I've been taking care of that dog for months. Feeding him. Taking him out with me on the mandatory PT run every morning. He's even been sleeping at the foot of my bed. Captain saw it, and he never asked me to stop taking care of the dog. I figured it must have been a present, after all.

"What are you waiting for, boy?"

"No," I say, meeting his stare.

"You're disobeying a direct order?"

Keeping my lips tightly pressed, I release the gun I'm holding, letting it fall to the concrete floor. I'm not hurting my dog, even if it means I'll get punished.

"Mission failed, boy," Captain barks into my face. "And when you fail a mission, you can expect consequences."

I steel myself, expecting a kick to my stomach or a punch to the head. It never comes. Instead, Kruger turns around, aiming his weapon at the dog, and shoots.

Chapter Twelve

Kai

The front door opens, revealing a dark-haired man in his early thirties. "Can I help you?"

"Yes." I nod. Then punch him right in the face.

The guy falls backward and ends up sprawled in the middle of the hallway. Maybe I shouldn't have hit him that hard. I step inside, then close the door behind me and grab a handful of the guy's shirt. I drag him across the living room into the small, untidy kitchen and drop him onto one of the chairs. There is a hollow bang when his head hits the table as he slumps forward, still unconscious. I take a seat across from him and lean back to wait.

The operative who was assigned to this mission got pulled over for a traffic violation, and during the stop, the officer spotted unregistered guns in the car. The dumb schmuck was taken into custody immediately. He's out of commission for tonight, or at least until Kruger's people can bring their top-secret papers to the police station and get the guy out. Since this contract needed to be carried out today, I got tagged, because of my proximity to the location, apparently.

The man stirs and groans. He straightens slowly and blinks at me in confusion.

I take out my phone and slide it across the kitchen table, screen up. The guy looks at the image of the USB drive on the phone and quickly shakes his head.

"I don't have it. I swear." He spits out a mouthful of blood onto the kitchen floor and continues talking. "I don't know who took it, but it wasn't me. I don't even know what's on it. You have the wrong person."

I cross my arms over my chest and sigh. Information extraction is not my specialty. It requires the mark to be kept alive and coherent. Maintaining his living status long enough for him to ponder his life choices while I work him up is not a problem. The snag is, I'm not sure how coherent he'll end up being when it's time to sing. As I'm pondering my dilemma, I grab one of the tasty-looking apples from the bowl in the middle of the table. I take a bite, but it's not as sweet as it appeared.

The guy stops fidgeting in his seat and gapes at me. I think he's interpreting my relaxed pose as indifference. His eyes dart toward the door, then back to me, zeroing in on the apple. In the next moment, he's leaping from the chair and running to the door. I take another bite, then reach into my jacket and pull out my gun. The idiot is hysterically jerking on the doorknob like a maniac, trying to pull it open. Unhurriedly, I screw the silencer on the gun, aim at his hand, and shoot. A pained scream fills the room.

"Come back here," I order.

The man keeps sniveling as he trudges back to the table, clutching his hand to his chest.

"Shut up and sit." I put the gun away and point to his seat.

He manages to plug his trap and slithers onto the chair.

"Now, listen to me well, because I'm not going to repeat myself.

My orders for this shitty mission are clear—retrieve the flash drive by any means necessary, but let you live." I nod at his hand. "Shooting to maim isn't exactly my thing. Looks like I hit an artery there. If you don't get help in twenty minutes, you're done for."

"Sugar jar," he chokes out.

"What?"

"The flash drive is in the sugar jar."

I rise and get the white ceramic jar from the counter. Buried just below the surface of the fine white crystals, lies the elusive memory stick. As I'm about to grab it, a faint squeak of wood scraping on the linoleum floor sounds behind me.

"Fuck, you're stupid," I say, turning around as the guy rushes at me with a kitchen knife in his good hand.

I grab his wrist and squeeze. A muted crunch of bone follows. The knife slips from his hand. I catch it in midair and plunge the blade into the side of the idiot's head, right through his ear.

"I told you," I say into his glassy gaze and let the body fall to the floor. "Occupational habit, asshole."

I get the flash drive from the sugar jar, then look up at the wall clock hanging over the counter. Half past two in the afternoon. If I head out now, I could be in Boston by seven. My cub should be working the afternoon shift today. She typically does on Thursdays.

Twenty-seven days. Ten hours. And twenty-five minutes. That's how long it's been since I've spoken with her. I've been checking up on her regularly, but I've kept my distance.

Nera.

I never intended to discover her name, too worried that knowing it would drag me even further into this obsession, but one of her friends called out to her while I was close enough to hear.

Nera.

I wonder how it would sound if I spoke it aloud.

I want to talk with her again.

Taking a fillet knife out of the knife block, I check the sharpness of the blade with my finger, then stride up to a long mirror mounted in the hallway.

Nera

The chime above the door rings out, breaking the silence in the small vet clinic.

"We're closed," I say as I'm reaching for my jacket.

"I know."

My head snaps toward the voice. The designer all-black suit fits him perfectly, hugging his broad shoulders, the top two buttons of the black shirt underneath undone. The collar is completely covered in dried blood. Diagonally, across his cheek, is a long nasty-looking cut.

"Are you serious?" I gasp and throw my jacket back on the hanger.

My demon looks around the office, then casually strolls into one of the exam rooms and takes a seat. "How's life, cub?"

"Unbelievable," I say under my breath as I rush around, collecting disinfectant and gauze. "Just . . . unbelievable."

I can feel his eyes on me the whole time I'm rummaging through the drawers to find the rest of the things I'll be needing and set them beside him on the table. After washing my hands, I march toward him as tiny little butterflies flutter their wings in my stomach, the sensation clashing with the horror of seeing him hurt.

"I think I need stitches again."

I blink and focus my gaze on the cut along his cheek. "Steri-Strips would suffice this time. The bleeding has already stopped, so you just need something to keep the wound closed."

"Oh... That's a shame."

"Shame? Are you some kind of masochist or something?" I ask as I clean dried blood from the cut and surrounding skin.

"No."

It's really hard to focus on my task when he's so close. My leg is pressed against his thigh, and my breasts are touching his upper arm. "Um, can you tilt your head a bit?"

He lifts his chin.

"That's not what I meant. I need you to . . ." I place my palm on his other cheek, gently angling his head to the side. "Like that."

The tip of my thumb is grazing the corner of his lips, and his breath is fanning across the back of my hand. The silence in the room is so absolute, I'm pretty sure he can hear my heart beating like a damn metronome set to its highest tempo.

"This looks like a clean, sharp cut, almost surgical," I say and reach for the box with Steri-Strips.

Applying these requires both hands, unfortunately, because I really like feeling his skin.

Keeping my eyes locked on his, I move my hand away from his cheek, "accidentally" brushing his lips with my fingers. "With all the experience you're providing me, I should consider changing my major to nursing."

A barely there smirk forms on his face. "I'm happy to be of use."

"Was it another homeless man?"

"Yes, the same guy as before."

"I didn't know there were transient people hanging out around here."

"Well, you never know what's hiding in the dark corners."

"Yeah, I guess you're right." I stick the second strip over the cut.

"You seem to frequent those quite often. I've noticed you lurking in the shadows, you know."

It's been a month since our last meeting on my roof. At first, I thought he was gone, and I wouldn't be seeing him anymore. But then, every once in a while, there was that prickling sensation again, usually when I was out with my friends. So, I started paying more attention to everything around me. And, it was always just a glimpse, a movement in the shadows or the glint of watchful eyes in the dark. I never actually saw his face, but I knew he was there.

"How did you manage to slip inside my friend's birthday party?" I ask as I set another Steri-Strip in place. "It was by invitation only."

"Through a window in the coat room."

My hands go still. "Jaya's party was on the third floor of a private club."

"Building's downspouts were rather solid," he deadpans. "And their security is a fucking joke."

Once I've attached the last strip, I let my eyes drift down and then up his body. He's well over six feet tall and heavily muscled.

"Were the drainpipes made of steel?" I ask when I meet his gaze again.

"Mm-hmm." He keeps his eyes glued to mine as he reaches for my hand. Even before I feel his touch, my heart is beating out of my chest because I know what's coming. My wrist feels so small and fragile in his huge hand, and it seems he notices that also because his hold is as gentle as if he's handling a delicate glass figurine.

"Thank you." His voice is rough, and he feathers his lips over my fingertips.

"I thought you didn't thank people."

"Never had the reason to. Until recently."

"Don't you thank your friends when they help you?"

"I don't have friends, cub."

"Everyone has friends."

"I had one. Kind of. He was my colleague, but he left."

"Did you thank him when he did something nice for you?"

He lowers my hand but keeps holding on to my wrist, and his eyes become distant as if he's lost in his memories, searching for a particular one. "He almost blew me up, along with another unit member. The trigger in the bomb he'd made malfunctioned, but he managed to fix it in time. I punched him in the face and broke his nose."

"That doesn't sound like a 'thank you' to me."

"I left him breathing."

He says it so matter-of-factly, that I can't help but laugh. "He made it through okay, then."

"I believe so, yes. What about your friends? Can you rely on them when you need help?"

"Isn't that what friends are for?"

"I guess. But you haven't answered my question."

"Friends are . . . complicated in my world."

"And what world is that?"

"One that values status and social position above all else," I say. "My father is a very important man. People always try to please him. So, when someone does something nice for me, I never know if they are being genuine, or if it's only because of who my father is."

"Yes. Actively or passively, parents impact their children's lives," he responds as his thumb sweeps the inside of my wrist, just above my pulse point.

"What about yours?" I ask.

"They died well before they could have a significant impact on me."

"I'm sorry."

"Don't be. I'm not. Some people are not meant to have children."

"What did they do?"

"Not a single thing." He moves his gaze to the coat hanger just outside the exam room. "You're wearing the scarf again."

"Yes. I've become quite fond of it." I turn my hand around so that our palms touch. "You said 'unit member' earlier. Are you in the military?"

"In a way," he mumbles, his eyes cast downward, staring at our joined hands.

"What does that mean, 'in a way'?"

"It means nothing is black and white, cub. There are just shades of gray." He looks up and our gazes lock. "Except you."

It's becoming impossible to keep my breathing under control while he looks at me like this. As if I'm the only person in the world. "And what am I?"

"You, my tiger cub, are a ray of light in the absolute darkness my life has become and has been for a very long time."

I suck in a breath, shaken by his words. No one ever said something like that to me.

"If you'd asked my name, you'd know how contrary it is to that sentiment," I whisper. In Italian, Nera means "black." But he couldn't possibly know that since I never told him my name.

My demon cocks his head to the side, his eyes lowering to my lips. "Yes. But on the other hand, it also means *light*. Radiance. Or brightness."

"And how do you know that?" My voice is barely audible now.

"I heard one of your friends say your name."

I take a step closer so that I'm standing between his legs, our eyes are nearly level, and stroke the side of his chin, careful not to catch the cut on his cheek. "When?"

"A few weeks back. You were leaving a downtown boutique."

Yes, I remember that day. I was keeping Dania company while

she shopped for new boots. That pleasant shiver I've been associating with him was present the entire time, and I kept looking over my shoulder. "I didn't see you."

"I'm only seen when I want to be."

"What about those other times, when I did notice you?"

"Maybe I wanted you to see me in those instances."

"Why?"

"So you could have fun with your friends without worry. And know that nothing would happen to you because I was watching over you, cub."

"Cub? You know my name. Why won't you use it?"

"I heard it by accident. You never gave it to me. I don't like using things that were never given to me. It's stealing."

"You have unique principles for a stalker." I shift my gaze to his lips. "Can I tell you a secret?"

"Yes."

I lean forward until my mouth is ghosting over his ear and whisper, "I like the idea of you watching over me, demon."

He keeps impossibly still—hardly moving for several silent moments—our quickened breaths the only sound in the room.

"I'd like to do much more than just watch over you." Deep, raspy words crash over me like a waterfall. He takes my face between his palms, and even though his touch is light, I can feel every ridge of his skin. "But some things are never meant to happen."

He continues to cradle my face as he stands up, his massive body casting a shadow as he towers over me.

"You're leaving?" I ask.

"For the light to shine, darkness must retreat. It's what's meant to be."

His hands fall away, and I watch his broad shoulders as he heads toward the outer doors.

"That's it?" I call after him. "You come out of nowhere, ask me to patch you up, and then just leave?"

"I wanted to talk to you. Looks like I can't help but resort to stealing, after all."

I don't want him to go. I never know how much time will pass until he decides to show himself again.

"Can I steal you?" I blurt out as he reaches the threshold. "Only for one Sunday morning."

He halts. "What for?"

"I want to show you something."

With his head tilted to the side, he watches me for a few moments before answering. "Sunday after next. Eight o'clock. I'll wait for you in front of your building."

"Should I give you my number? In case something comes up and you can't make it?"

He looks at me over his shoulder, and it seems as if his eyes are piercing through mine. "Even if all hell breaks loose, I'll be there, tiger cub."

His long braid swishes in the air as he turns away and vanishes into the night.

Chapter Thirteen

Kai

People. Hordes and hordes of people meandering between stands overflowing with baked goods, canned products, seedlings, and a surprising number of fruits and vegetables for this early in the season, navigating between the arrayed crates holding more of the same, and lingering over other tables to barter with somewhat frantic-looking vendors trapped behind the endless produce lines. Old, young, with clinging children, they all push at each other as they traverse among the booths, seemingly carried by a current of human mass.

It's a fucking nightmare.

"So?" Nera asks next to me, her lips wide with a broad smile. "Where do you want to start?"

It's warm today, and she's wearing a light coat over a flannel white shirt that she's tied at her waist, and pale jeans. Her honey-colored hair is gathered in a low bun at her nape, secured there with the red scarf I gave her.

"Why are we here?" I ask, my eyes glued to her lips. A smile is something that's rarely directed at me. Most of the time, when the situation requires me to be close to a person, they are either crying or screaming.

"This is a farmers' market. I'm giving you a crash course on herbs and vegetables." She takes my hand, ushering me forward.

Someone bumps my arm with an elbow. I ignore it completely, staring at our interlocked fingers as she drags me ahead, hurrying toward the closest stand. For months, I've been struggling with the urge to touch her each time we've met. Kissing a hand that nursed my wounds was the most intimate contact I allowed myself, aside from that one weakened moment when I could not resist touching her face. It nearly broke me. But, I've known that if I let myself go any further, there wouldn't be a way to go back.

I rarely wish for things in life, because I know how seldom I get them. But when I do, the urge to keep them is a maniacal, visceral need. To never let go.

"Parsley first." Nera halts by a table with an overhead sign for a local greenhouse above it and lifts a tied-up bunch of green leaves on thin stems with her free hand. "See this? It's flat-leaved parsley. It's a herb, but its tops resemble those of the root veggies you got me. Actually, there is a parsley root variety. The smell is more vibrant, though, and it looks like a white carrot."

She starts pulling her other hand from mine. Not happening. I squeeze it, keeping my fingers tightly wrapped around hers.

"Um. I need that hand," she mumbles, looking down at our hands.

"No, you don't."

Her perfect eyebrows rise in question. "Because?"

"Because you have two," I growl.

This hand is mine. She offered it to me freely, and I'm not releasing it unless it's absolutely necessary. One day, maybe she'll allow me to touch more than just her hand, but for now, this has to be enough.

"All right." The corners of her lips tilt upward. Slowly, she brings the bunch she's holding up and brushes its leaves under my nose. "Parsley. Smell."

The elderly man in a checked shirt minding the booth gives us a quizzical look as I sniff at the leaves.

"Good." My cub replaces the parsley and picks up another bunch of green crap, but this one has the gnarly-looking ball at its base. "And this, this is celeriac. It's a root vegetable, just like the parsnips you got for me. The root is big and round, not the long and skinny one that resembles a carrot. Now, smell."

Another handful of leaves ends up in my face. I wrinkle my nose and sneeze. "That's enough, I get the idea."

"Are you two buying something?" the old-timer grumbles.

I pin him with my gaze, giving him a look usually reserved for my targets before I break their spines.

"We're just browsing, if that's okay?" Nera grins at the man, whose eyes are still glued to mine.

"Yes, yes of course. Absolutely." He takes a step back. "Take all the time you need."

My girl resumes perusing through the displayed veggies and herbs, lifting things she finds interesting, making me sniff or poke them. Fennel. Dill. Radishes. She keeps her right hand in mine the entire time. I pretend that I'm paying attention to the stuff she's showing me, but really, I'm focused solely on her.

More people pass by, squeeze in next to us, so I take a step to the side, closer to my tiger cub, creating a barrier to keep away the pests. I didn't know where she wanted to go today, so I came carrying two guns concealed in my shoulder holster, a knife strapped to my ankle like usual, and a garrote in my jacket pocket. It doesn't seem like I'm going to need any of those on this outing. Still, I watch our surroundings from the corner of my eye, making sure there are no unexpected threats anywhere near her.

It's hard to focus on her words with the warmth of her at my side. I want to move away, afraid I may get addicted to touching more than just her hand, but at the same time, I want to invade her space, press myself against her. My mind is screaming to move back. My body doesn't listen. I take another step, moving behind her and releasing her hand in the process. The moment is brief, just a split second, but it feels like hours without her touch. The instant I'm behind her, I entwine our right hands again and place my left on the table on her other side. Once I have her surrounded with my body, it's easier to breathe.

She's discussing plant fertilizers with the guy running the stand, who still looks a bit sick in the face, absolutely oblivious to the turmoil happening within me. I try remaining stoic but lose the battle soon enough and dip my head, inhaling the scent of her shampoo.

Nera

The vendor in front of me is speaking, and I nod, keeping up the appearance that I'm listening to whatever he's rambling about. From the moment I felt my demon come to stand at my back, his body enveloping mine on almost every side, my mental capacity to process anything flew the proverbial coop. A faint touch of his chin at my temple. Huge calloused fingers holding my own. His breath in my hair. His scent drowning me.

"You said you're allergic to flowers." A husky whisper right next to my ear. "And yet, you smell like one."

There are dozens of people around us, so many voices and other sounds much louder than his words, and still, he's the only one I hear.

"It's the pollen I'm allergic to. Not the smell," I choke out.

"Mm-hmm... good to know."

His thumb brushes the back of my hand in small, tender strokes, and each one makes it harder to draw a breath.

"Thank you."

"What for?" I ask.

"For bringing me here. I've never been to a farmers' market before."

"So, you like it?"

"It's awful, cub."

I laugh. "Well, you could have lied and said you like it."

His breath tingles the skin on my neck as he dips his head, bringing his mouth to the level of my ear.

"I don't want lies between us, tiger cub." His hushed, raspy voice floods my senses, making my whole body buzz with an electric charge because of his deep resonance alone. "Just secrets."

"Okay," I whisper back.

A woman nudges her way to the booth's counter on our left and starts chatting with the seller. Although she's less than a foot away, aside from the high-pitched quality of her words and the fact that she's there, nothing else in our immediate space seems real. The world dissolves, and both my body and mind attune solely to the man standing behind me, his chest plastered to my back. I close my eyes and tilt my head to the side until my cheek touches his.

"Will you tell me your secrets one day, demon?"

"One day. Maybe."

"But not today," I say under my breath but with conviction. "Just one tiny secret? Please."

He cocks his head, lightly nuzzling the skin on my cheekbone with his nose. "I don't dream. Ever. Even when I was a kid, I would go to sleep and just wake up in the morning, with only blackness and emptiness filling the gap in between. Up until recently, I believed that dreams are just a lie."

A shiver runs down my spine. "But not anymore?"

"Not anymore," he rasps. "Can you guess what I dream about, tiger cub?"

I bite the inside of my cheek and shake my head. The ringing of a nearby phone penetrates the haze I'm in. My devil takes my wrist, raising my hand.

"I dream about you, tiger cub." Whispered words, just before he places a fleeting kiss on my fingertips. "But my every dream is interrupted by an alarm clock."

He lets go of my hand, and then the warmth at my back disappears. I turn around and find him standing two steps away, his gaze glued to mine, even as he holds the phone to his ear.

"I'm on my way," he barks into his device, then puts it away without moving his eyes off me for an instant.

People pass around and between us, hurrying to check out other vendors, their colorful clothes flash in front of my eyes, obscuring the view of my demon's black-clad form every few seconds. Red. Yellow. Black. White. Black again.

"When will I see you again?" I ask.

Blue. Black.

"Soon," he replies.

Pink. Orange. Black.

"I'm going to a club with some friends on Friday night. Not the safest place in town."

White. Yellow.

The crowd dissipates for a moment, allowing me a clear view of him again.

His mouth quirks into a tiny smile. "I'll be there."

A family of four comes to a stop between us, obscuring my demon once more. I take a step to the left, looking around. Green. Red. Purple. Brown. But no black. Black is nowhere in sight.

Chapter Fourteen

Kai

19 years ago from the present day
Z.E.R.O. unit base
(Kai 16 years old)

THE PAPERS RUSTLE IN MY HANDS AS I TURN THEM OVER, scanning the messy handwriting. Yesterday, Kruger sent me to the unit's resident shrink for an evaluation. It didn't have anything to do with my well-being. He just needed to know if I could handle the pressure before he sent me into the field, and if I had enough smarts to adapt should something unexpected come up. Apparently, I passed with flying colors.

Earlier tonight, I broke into the psych office and took my file, but it doesn't do me any good since I can't read worth a damn. I shove the papers into the side pocket of my tactical pants and head into the armory. One of the guards is stationed there at all times.

I find the man slumped on his chair, snoring. I slap his face, then press the tip of my knife just under his Adam's apple.

"Read this to me." I dump the folded papers onto his lap.

The man blinks at me in confusion, then starts reading. Mostly, it's the same old shrink nonsense: profound psychic numbing as a result of traumatic childhood events, including abandonment, which led to manifestations of extreme rage associated with multiple violent episodes involving struggles for self-preservation.

"*Total absence of empathy or care for others. Inability to form connections with anyone around him. The only exception is the subject's superior officer, Lennox Kruger. However, the degree of the subject's emotional attachment is inconclusive due to his continued unwillingness to cooperate,*" the guard reads. "*Overall, evaluation findings are as expected given the subject's background and ongoing program stressors.*"

"Continue." I bark.

"*Mental and physical capacities are well above average. The subject is deemed fit for duty, able to meet the challenges of mission assignments. He is expected to fulfill required tasks without fail.*"

The man stops reading and looks up at me.

I put more force behind my blade. "Anything else?"

"Just another note," he chokes out.

"Read it."

The guard swallows before continuing. "*In conclusion, it is unlikely that the subject will ever progress to be able to form deep-rooted personal relationships of any kind. Should it happen, however, the history of observed behavioral range—from utter calm to controlled rage—cannot be ignored. The subject presents an extreme liability risk, and his unpredictability could potentially lead to objectionable situations, up to and including potential case(s) of Absent Without Leave (AWOL). Regular disciplinary actions may provide no effect. Upon suspected gross misconduct of duties, immediate termination is advised.*"

I rip the papers out of the guard's hands and head back into the dorm.

Nothing new in that shit sandwich. Evaluation, my ass.

Chapter Fifteen

Nera

"For God's sake, Nera. Why are you fidgeting this entire evening?"

I quickly turn back toward my friends and grab my drink off the table. "No reason."

"Are we waiting for someone else to join us?" Jaya prods. "Because from the moment we stepped inside the club, you've been looking around nonstop."

"Nope," I mumble into my glass while stealing another look at the entrance directly across the room from me.

He's not coming. We were supposed to have gone out last Friday, but Dania got a stomach bug and we rescheduled our club night for a week later instead. Since my demon and I never exchanged numbers, I couldn't let him know about the change of plans. I've been hopeful he'll be here tonight anyway.

"I heard my dad talking with some of his buddies who came over for a drink last night." Dania leans over the table, whispering, "Apparently, Alvino walked in on his girlfriend giving one of the Camorra soldiers a blowjob. He killed them both and dumped their naked bodies in front of a mall. Their genitals were cut out."

I shudder. "That certainly sounds like Alvino."

"One of my sister's friends was dating him when she was still in high school," Jaya says. "She broke up with him after only two weeks, and she and her family left the country shortly after. I think they were afraid Alvino would do something to her. He doesn't take rejection well, it seems."

A shiver runs through me again, but unlike last time, the sensation doesn't ebb. It remains as a faint tingling at the back of my neck. Slowly, I lower my glass to the tabletop. The conversation shifts to ex-boyfriends and then to Dania jabbering on about her latest crush—some guy she met online—and I tune it out. My eyes wander around the club, skimming over the random men all around us, searching for that familiar tall figure. Finding nothing. I look further, peering into the dark recesses, hoping to spot the glint of my demon's eyes. Still nothing. But, I know he's here.

"I'll be right back," I tell Dania and head into the crowd.

There are hundreds of people in this club, squished together, and I have to push between their bodies to keep going, keep searching. The tingling is stronger now, but in this crowd, I can't look more than a few feet in front of me. I notice a small raised platform up ahead, one of the huge speakers placed on top, and hurry toward it, elbowing everyone out of my way.

The dais is several inches high, and when I climb up, my eyes survey the mass of clubgoers. Scouring. Where is he? Two weeks might have passed, but the feeling of his hand clutching mine is still very much imprinted on my mind. His breath in my hair. The way his stubble tickled my face when I pressed my cheek to his. The need to see him again, to feel his body pressed against me, is all I've been thinking about for days. *Where is he?*

A gentle caress down my exposed back, and then warm breath across the nape of my neck. "Looking for someone, tiger cub?"

I smile and close my eyes, savoring his light touch. "Not anymore."

"I like the dress." Husky words whispered right next to my ear. Then, another stroke of his fingers from the base of my neck all the way down to my waist. "I had to resort to stealing again."

"I'm glad."

His palm glides over my hip bone to my stomach, pulling me closer, plastering my back to his front.

"I hoped you'd come visit me sooner," I whisper.

"I dropped by twice."

"I haven't seen you."

"I know." His other hand wraps around mine, threading our fingers together. "I can't allow myself to come to you too often."

"Why?"

"Because I wouldn't be able to leave."

Slowly, I turn around and meet his heart-stopping eyes. My heels and the raised platform are giving me quite a boost in height, but the top of my head still barely reaches his nose.

"Maybe I don't want you to keep leaving." I touch his lower lip.

"Light and darkness don't mix, tiger cub. They cancel each other out." He dips his head and kisses the tip of my finger. "And I would never dare to shroud your flame."

I grab a handful of his shirt, scrunching it in a tight grip as if that would hold him here. With me. I want more. More than these stolen moments. My body yearns to be close to his, the same way my mind yearns to know more about him. Why won't he tell me his name? Where does he go when he leaves? What does he do? Why does he keep pulling away? I'm afraid to ask. And afraid of the answers.

He reminds me of a stray kitten who was brought into the clinic last week, barely alive after obviously being seriously tortured. It scratched and bit anyone who came close to him, even when it was just to give the poor thing some food. One evening, while I was alone at the clinic, I left the cage door open and went about to do my nightly tasks. Nothing happened. I repeated my actions for three days, always with the same result at the end of the night. The kitten remained at the back of his enclosure. On the fourth day, the little rascal finally left his cage, jumped onto the counter, and just watched me work. The next day, he allowed me to feed him.

I have a feeling I'm in a similar situation with my stranger. There's something awful hiding in his past. In his present, as well, more than likely. I have my suspicions about what it might be. He won't hurt me if I push too much, of that I'm certain. He would just . . . disappear.

But if I leave the door open, leaving him to take that step . . .

"I wouldn't mind sharing your darkness. You just need to let me in." I lean on his chest and inhale his scent. "I've never been afraid of the dark, demon, because sooner or later, daylight always follows."

"Not always, my beautiful shining star." He drops a kiss on the top of my head. "Your friends are coming."

I stare into his depths as he steps away. "Don't go."

"I won't. Not until you're safely home."

Another step. Then, two more until he disappears into the crowd.

"Nera!" Dania grabs my arm. "We thought something happened to you! What are you doing here?"

"Who was the guy you were talking to?" Jaya throws in.

"No one," I whisper. "Just the darkness."

Kai

The phone in my pocket starts vibrating again. It's the fourth time in the past ten minutes. I ignore it and keep my eyes glued on my cub while she stands with her friends around a tall table on the other side of the club. The goddamned caller is being persistent, so cursing the dickhead under my breath, I pull out the phone and bring it up to my ear.

"Your target is still alive," Captain Kruger bellows through the line. "Explain."

"The contract stated that there's a six-day window."

"The recommended optimum time for eliminating the mark was today, while he was occupied at the spa."

A guy in front of me moves, stepping to the left and obstructing my view of the group. I grab a handful of hair at the back of his head and shove him to his previous spot. Roaring, he swivels around to come at me with a raised fist.

"Your advice has been rejected, Kruger," I say and backhand the advancing bonehead. He ends up sprawled on the floor. "The target will be neutralized tomorrow evening. Make sure my payment is ready."

Short silence reigns over the line, but I can still hear him breathing. I know he's pissed. He's been pissed for nearly ten years, ever since I demanded 50 percent of the fee for every kill, and insisted on picking and choosing what contract I want to take on. After that little tête-à-tête, he's been fuming like a toxic sludge, trying to bring me to heel, but he can't afford to openly oppose me or my methods. The man whom Kruger needs to be taken out has a small security army that follows him around wherever he goes. If I refuse the job, Kruger would need to dispatch one of his regular teams. And their mission success rate is a mere 63 percent.

"Where are you? Your GPS location has been turned off," he grumbles.

"There's no possibility of me ending up dead at the moment. If that changes, I'll make sure to turn it back on so you can locate my body should my mission fail."

Kruger continues yammering about God knows what, but I cut the call and creep along the wall, coming closer to Nera and her friends. I pick a spot in the corner and lean my shoulder on the wall so I can watch my girl.

The long purple dress she's wearing hugs her curves like a second skin. It's the dress her sister brought over a few months ago, and I nearly swallowed my tongue seeing her in it. And then, out of it. The dress has no back to it, just ties around her slender neck, leaving her gorgeous flesh exposed. I couldn't help myself earlier—I had to feel her smooth skin. Couldn't resist running my hand along her spine, inhaling that intoxicating scent of her. Letting go of her again was torture. My only reprieve is continuing to watch her while she's having fun.

One of the girls at Nera's table says something, and the rest of the group falls into fits of laughter. My tiger cub is laughing too, creases appear at the corners of her eyes, and I find myself leaning forward as if I'm being pulled toward her by an invisible string. I want to feel some of that warm light she seems to be emitting. To soak it up and brighten my miserable soul. She reaches for her drink, smiling broadly, but suddenly looks up, her gaze narrowing right on the spot where I'm standing. I quickly take a step back. Retreating into the shadows where I belong, where I can simply watch her.

It was a mistake, to allow myself to get closer to her. Looking at Nera now as she laughs with her friends, makes everything so much clearer. I should stay away from her. For her sake.

The music changes to a slow tune, and the overhead lights dim. A few guys approach the table of Nera's friends, speaking with the girls, and making them giggle. One of the newcomers—a guy in his early twenties, wearing a white shirt and khaki trousers—offers his hand to Nera. She shakes her head, but the woman to her right seems to be encouraging her to go, whispering into my girl's ear. The guy's hand wraps around Nera's delicate fingers, and then he pulls her toward the dance floor.

Rage ignites inside my chest as I watch him slide his arm around her back, drawing her closer.

Mine! The voice in the back of my head roars, urging me to end the motherfucker who's dared to touch her.

I'm halfway to them, on the dance floor, before I even realize I've moved. Seeing them this close-up, I come to a sudden halt. I can't dismiss how they seem to fit together. Both young. Blond. The guy's clothes appear to be of good quality, pricey. He might be a student, like her, on a path to becoming something great in life. A lawyer. Or maybe a doctor.

Not a man who kills people for money because it's the only thing he knows how to do.

Like me.

My eyes remain glued to them as I take a step back.

I don't fit. Not me.

Not a low-life scumbag who can barely read at grade school level.

Another step, then a few more, until I'm back at my spot in the corner, watching my tiger cub in the arms of another man. The fire inside me is still burning, right there in my chest, scorching everything in its way. And I let it. I let it incinerate the silly hope that took root there, that grew each time I came to see my cub, feeding me lies that I might have a chance at something good in my life. I guess I forgot that hope is a luxury doomed souls like me are not entitled to.

The music carries on, and I keep watching, imagining myself in the blond guy's place.

Nera

"How about another dance?" the guy asks me after the song ends. He seems nice and is rather handsome. I probably would have been attracted to him. Before. Now? I can't even remember what name he used when he introduced himself. "Thank you, but I think I'll head back to my friends now."

"Why? Is there someone else?"

Yes. No. I sigh. I wish I knew the answer to that question. "Maybe."

"Well, he's not here, is he?" He shifts his hand to the small of my back, sliding lower.

"Remove your hand from my ass, please."

"And if I don't?"

"If you don't, I'll punch you right in the face. I'm sure your friends will find that entertaining."

"Fine." He releases me while an evil smirk pulls at his lips. "Haughty bitch."

I turn on my heel and head back to the table where the girls are giggling hysterically.

"What? Only one dance?" Dania asks.

"Yup. And it was one too many," I say as I grab my purse. "I'm going to the restroom."

I slip through the crowd behind our table, taking the long way around, searching for my demon. He's been watching me from the darkness this whole time, but hasn't shown his face again. Dancing with that idiot was my last-ditch effort, a desperate attempt to draw my dark protector out. I imagined him rushing toward me and the handsy prick on the dance floor, ripping the guy away, and taking his place. It's hard to picture my stalker as a dancer, but I have a feeling he would be good.

When I round the corner of a short hallway, only one girl is waiting in the line for the single-stall unisex restroom. The facilities at the front of the club are way busier but also have more stalls, so people tend to go to those instead.

The door opens and the previous occupant leaves while the girl in front of me stumbles inside. I move up and reach into my purse for my phone to check the time just as hands grab me from behind. My phone slips from my grasp, clattering onto the floor, while the assailant pushes me face-first into the wall. A scream builds in my throat, but a big palm covers my mouth before I can get it out.

"Not so haughty now, are you?" my dance partner's voice croaks behind me.

I thrash from side to side, trying to free myself from his hold, but he's using his weight to pin my chest to the wall, and I don't have the leverage to push him off.

"I'm going to show you how a good girl should treat a man." His hand wedges between our bodies, and he unzips his pants. Bile rises up my throat as I feel his hard dick pressing against my ass. He grabs a handful of my skirt, tugging the hem of my dress upward, then paws at my panties. Reaching behind me, I grab his balls and twist with all my strength.

A predatory howl breaks behind my back, but it lasts less than a second. The hand over my mouth jerks away, and, suddenly, the pressure on my spine disappears. The muted beats of the club's music are now joined by a strange new gurgling sound. My heart rate skyrockets as I turn around. A broad male back fills my field of vision, with a long thick braid swinging slightly between shoulder blades. I move my eyes up, and up, until my gaze stops on the red face of the assailant. My demon has his huge hand wrapped around the guy's neck, holding him suspended against the opposite wall.

I take a step to the side, staring fixedly at my attacker. He's clawing at the fingers squeezing his throat, trying to make words come out, but the only sound leaving his lips is muffled wheezing. His feet are dangling almost a foot off the ground.

Without looking away from the bastard, my demon asks, "Did he hurt you, cub?"

For a moment, I'm taken aback by the tone of his voice. It's steady, as usual, but infused with so much brute force that he sounds like Death incarnate.

"No," I choke out. "But he tried."

"Go back to your friends."

I can't make my legs move.

"Do as I say," he growls and turns toward me. "Now."

All the air leaves my lungs. I can't believe I once thought his eyes seemed empty. Looking at them now, it feels like I'm staring into the magma chambers of two volcanoes—pure rage, just waiting to erupt.

"Why?" I ask.

"Because I don't want you to watch what happens next."

I throw a look at my attacker again. He was going to rape me. I might have been able to fight him off and get away before he succeeded, but I'm not completely sure. And if another girl was in my place, she might have frozen up, and then the bastard would have done the deed.

There aren't many beliefs that I share with Cosa Nostra, but there's one I wholeheartedly approve of. No man is allowed to force himself on a woman. So, if my demon wants to kick the fucker's butt, I don't have a problem watching him do it.

"I'm staying," I say.

My dark protector turns to face my assailant. The corded tendons of my demon's bare forearm pop, arm muscles bulging and straining against his rolled-up sleeves as he tightens his hold. Blondie's eyes roll back, his limbs twitching a few times before falling slack.

My demon releases his hold, letting the would-be rapist's body hit the ground. He killed the man in less than five seconds, using just one of his hands.

For me. He killed him for me.

"Why?" I ask.

A light touch of a finger at my chin, tilting my head up.

"I'll annihilate anyone who dares to touch a hair on your head." His deep voice is infused with so much menace. "No one. Nothing will ever do you harm. I thought you understood that."

No. Not really. But I do now.

And the feelings that swell with that realization completely snuff out the horror of witnessing the man die.

A life for a life? Is that fair? Is that our truth?

Every time I've thought about my future, I've always seen myself as some sort of side character. A person who gets tossed this way or that, all dependent on which direction the wind was blowing. Nothing but the means to keep the narrative flowing along. Always an object, one that just waits to be used however someone sees fit. Never the subject of the story. Even my own. But is it possible that I'm worth more than the "superiority" of my birth based on coincidence and circumstance, more than a speedway to gain rank, more than merely an asset? That someone... *him*... would end a man's life just because the perpetrator threatened to harm me?

"Cub." My demon cups my cheek in his palm. "I need to get rid of the body."

I nod. That girl is still inside the restroom, but she could come out at any moment. When she does, she'll see the dead guy. Awareness hits, and I grab the handle in a mad grip, keeping the door closed.

"There's a back room down the hallway, I think." I motion with my free hand to indicate the unlit passage to the side. "If you move him there, no one will find him for hours."

He narrows his eyes at me in what I'm pretty sure is confusion. I might not know his name, but I think I'm starting to read him rather well. In the time we've spent together, I've shared things with him I've never shared with anyone else. His subtle reactions are familiar to me now.

His gaze moves along my arm, stopping on my firm grip on the knob. "Someone's in there?"

"Yes. I'll make sure she doesn't come out until you're gone."

Pale-gray eyes meet mine again. He takes a step forward, coming up so close that I need to tilt my head all the way back to maintain our locked stare.

"You surprise me, cub."

"Well, I'm glad we have our roles reversed for once."

The edges of his lips curve upward. I've always found him handsome, but that tiny smile transforms him into drop-dead gorgeous.

"Head back to your friends and enjoy the rest of your evening."

"So, I won't see you again tonight?"

"No."

I try to stifle the onslaught of disappointment as I watch him grab the dead guy by the back of the shirt and drag him down the hallway. Is this all I'll ever get from him? Short, sudden visits before he disappears again?

"What if someone else bothers me tonight, and you're not there?" I call after him. It's a pitiful attempt to make him stay, but I'm working with the only thing I have.

"I said you won't see me. Not that I won't be there," he says just before turning the corner. "No one will touch you on my watch, tiger cub."

Chapter Sixteen

Nera

THE STEADY TAPPING OF RAINDROPS HITTING THE window mixes with the low tones of a song streaming from my phone. I continue stirring the ravioli and throw a look out at the balcony where I have my pots of herbs all lined up. My original plants are maintaining a steady growth rate, providing me with a plentiful supply of freshness for my cooking. But I'm amazed at how well the celery root and parsnips are doing. Not only did they survive the winter inside my apartment in the small planter box I transplanted them into, but they seem to really like it because they've almost doubled in size since my demon brought them.

It's been almost a year since we met, and we're still playing this strange game of hide and seek. Sometimes, I would stand out on the balcony, and when I'd look down, he'd be across the street, leaning on the hood of his car. We'd watch each other for a few moments, and then he'd get behind the wheel and drive away. Or I would notice him lurking on the roof across the street, looking down into my windows. We would have our usual staring contest, and then he'd disappear again, leaving me with a thousand questions.

For a long time, those questions left me frustrated, but along the way, I accepted this crazy situation we're in.

Every time he surprised me with a visit, I learned something new about him. Like last week, when I found him at my door, his shirt sleeve saturated with blood. Another knife wound, on his biceps this time. A straight clean cut right above his elbow, running almost all the way up to his shoulder. I sewed him up at my dining table. Thirty-six stitches. Then, I offered him a piece of cake that Zara had made the day before, certain he'd say no. He said yes. And I found another puzzle piece to fit into the mystery of him. My demon has a sweet tooth. The man ate his dessert before I even put the rest of the cake back into the fridge.

Every time he lets me see him, each time he comes by, I fall for him a little more. And every time he leaves, my heart aches. Little by little, without a conscious thought or even an effort on his part, I've fallen in love with a man who is still very much an enigma to me. The walls he keeps between us are more than impenetrable rock. They are a fucking mountain bastion. He won't let me in. The little things he lets slip here and there, help paint a picture of his life before we met, and some things I've figured out on my own. But that's all I have.

Secrets. There are so many secrets between us, they have become our norm.

We've never even brought up what happened at the club a month ago. There was no "thank you" on my part, no explanations on his, either. Just us, and that unspoken understanding.

In the dark.

I remove the pot from the burner, drain the ravioli and set it aside to cool off, and then walk up to the balcony doors to glance at the top of the building across from mine. It's been raining nonstop since this morning, so my demon likely hasn't come, but I still slide my eyes across the expanse of the roof. There's nobody there.

I'm turning around when I catch movement below, on the street. A figure in a black coat, leaning on the wall by the building's entrance, his arms crossed over his broad front. Rain is pouring down on him, soaking his hair and his outer layers as he stands there like some dark wraith. Our gazes clash, and like always, I feel the impact as a punch to the chest. It's ever the same when I see him. My heart swells, and I forget to breathe—as if seeing him keeps all the air from my lungs.

Breaking our locked stares, I turn around and head across the room. I only pause at the door to put on my rain boots, then leave the apartment. My building is old, and there is no elevator, but it only takes me a minute to reach the ground floor.

As soon as I step outside and onto the sidewalk, his eyes are on me, following me as I cross the street and come up before him. The unrelenting rain pelts my face as I tilt my head to meet his unwavering gaze.

"It's cold," he says. "Go back inside."

"What about you?"

"I'm used to harsh conditions. Spending a bit of time in the rain has never been a problem for me."

"You could have skipped your check-in today. You're soaked."

"I'll be away for the next few days. It had to be today."

Fat raindrops cascade down his face, falling into a puddle at his feet. He has always had this menacing aura around him, but as I look at him now, he doesn't seem so dangerous. Just . . . lonely.

I take his hand in mine and squeeze a little. "Come on. Let's have dinner together."

He lets me lead him to my building and up four flights of stairs to my place. When we get inside the apartment, he stops at the threshold and looks around as if seeing the space for the first time.

"Are you okay?" I ask.

He bends his head and locks his eyes with mine. "You've invited me into your home."

There's a strange quality to his voice, a hidden meaning to his words, but I'm not sure what it could be.

"Yeah. Why? I mean, you've been here before. Several times. Or did you forget that I gave you stitches at my dining table last week?"

"No. But I came to you then. This is different."

"How so?"

"It just is." He looks down at the floor. "I'll make a mess of your carpet."

"Don't worry about it. Um . . . I'll get you a towel."

"A towel?"

"For your hair. It's drenched."

I let go of his hand and rush to the linen closet. A hand towel won't do any good in his case, so I grab one of the yellow bath towels. When I enter the kitchen, I find my demon standing in front of the fridge, checking out the colorful magnets I have hanging there.

"My sister gifted me those," I say. "She went on a vacation to Europe with her friend from school and her family and bought me one from each city they journeyed to. I've always wanted to visit overseas."

"Why didn't you go with her?"

I bite my lower lip. Within Cosa Nostra, there is one very important unwritten rule—never reveal your weakness. People change. Loyalties switch. Friend one day, enemy the next. Whenever someone asked why I hadn't joined Zara, I always said I was too busy to go and couldn't fit it into my schedule.

"I'm afraid of flying," I whisper.

He cocks his head to the side, observing me. "There's nothing wrong with being afraid of something."

"That's a noble sentiment, and, maybe for you, it's true."

He looks away, his gaze traveling back to the fridge magnets. "I'm afraid of kids."

"Kids? Why?"

"If someone is a threat, I make sure I take them before they could ever get to me. And my preemptive strike is tenfold anything they could have done. But I could never harm a child." He takes the towel I'm holding out for him without elaborating anything further.

I hoped he was going to unbind his hair, but he just rubs the towel over the braid, drying up most of the moisture.

"I made ravioli with cheese. Is that okay?" My hands are shaking a little as I move to the cupboard to take out the plates. I wasn't this nervous stitching him up last week, but I am now. Something has changed between us. I'm not certain what, but I can feel it. Maybe he's right. This time feels different from a mere week ago.

"I don't have a preference for food. It's just sustenance. But I did like the cake."

"Is chocolate your favorite?"

"I'm not sure. Could be." He falls silent for a moment. "I've never tried cake before."

My hand stills on the stack of dinnerware. "You've never had cake?"

"No. I don't think I have."

He says it so casually, as if it's just an ordinary declaration. I can't wrap my mind around it. How is it possible?

"What about on your birthday?"

"Birthday celebrations aren't something that's done where I come from. I'm not sure of the exact date, but I believe I was born sometime in winter."

I set the plates on the table while dread pools in my stomach. How terrible it must be, to not know something as basic as your own date of birth? My arms ache to wrap around him and pull him to me, to offer the warmth and love he's obviously never experienced.

"I think you should pick one," I say.

"One what?"

"Date." I move the bowl of ravioli to the center of the table and then take a seat across from him.

"I'm pretty sure birthdays don't work like that, cub. But if I can choose, I'd pick June second."

I suck in a breath. My heart swells while my demon keeps me pinned with his eyes from the other side of the table.

The day we met.

"Why?" I choke out.

He switches his gaze to the plate in front of him. And just like that, his walls are back up.

He slayed a man for trying to hurt me, but he still won't let me glimpse into his life. Even after nearly a year, he barely touches me. Kissing my fingers. Holding my hand. On a few rare occasions, he's touched my face. That's all I've gotten. It's not enough.

Not anymore.

I need to feel his skin on mine. I want to know the taste of his lips. The weight of his body as it presses against me. I want everything, but I'm afraid that if I bang too hard on the barrier he has set between us, I might lose him. For good.

Kai

I follow Nera with my eyes as she scurries around the kitchen, putting away the leftovers and loading dirty dishes for a wash. She probably thinks that inviting me over was nothing special, completely oblivious to the consequences of her actions. An invitation into her home. Another part of her to which she granted access. There's no going back now. She can't revoke it. It's mine.

"What would you like in exchange?" I ask.

"In exchange for what?"

"For the food."

She turns around, hurt written all over her face. "I don't want you to pay me back. It was a . . . gift."

I take a step toward her and place my hands on the counter, caging her in. There isn't a feeling similar to this—being this close to her, with our bodies almost touching.

"There are no free gifts, cub," I rasp. "Not for me. Name your price."

Nera's breathing picks up. Her eyes drift down, stopping on my mouth. "I want a kiss."

I freeze. For a moment, I think I've misheard her. I've been dreaming about her lips on mine for months. It was a fantasy, an unattainable wish, but now she's offering to make it a reality.

There's a slight trembling in my fingers as I lift my hands and gently cradle her face with my palms. I stroke the skin under her eyes with my thumbs, then run them along the line of her eyebrows, and nose. Stealing. Stealing touches that weren't offered to me. I brush her cheeks with my knuckles, feeling the delicate texture of her flawless skin. So soft. Softer than anything I've ever touched. And now, I'm tainting it with the killer's hands. I want to kiss her so damn much. And more. I want her to be mine, body and soul. My tiger cub. My twinkling star. Am I really selfish enough to drag her into my darkness? I can't. Could never do it. Never.

But I'm taking the kiss that she offered. For someone like me, it's more than I deserve.

A small yelp leaves her lips when I grab under her thighs and lift her onto the counter. Seizing her chin, I tilt her head and capture her eyes, wide and gleaming, with my own.

"Another piece of you, mine now," I growl. "You can't have it back."

I slam my mouth to hers. Hard. Taking. Claiming every inch of her lips and mouth all at once. *Mine!* Her breath, mixed with the air from my lungs. I inhale it, drawing it into myself. *Mine!* Her small teeth bite my lower lip. I nip her back. The warmth of her palms seeps through the fabric of my still-damp shirt as she squeezes my upper arms. It feels as if she's singeing my skin. Another bite, more ferocious this time. I reciprocate. Wanting more. So, so much more. I want all of her. Not want—need. Like air. Like the blood flowing through my veins. Each beat of my heart, it's hers. For nearly a year, every cell of my being has been hers.

It might be just our lips that are touching, but she has etched herself onto my soul. I kiss her again. Stealing her breath away. It feels as if I've been drowning, and it's the only thing that gives me life. Again. More. Never enough.

The phone in my pocket starts vibrating. My lips go still on hers. For a fleeting moment, she made me forget what I am. She keeps kissing me, but the phone keeps ringing. Almost as if my sins are calling, wanting to be known.

"Demon?" she whispers into my lips. "Everything okay?"

I want to lay myself at her mercy, beg her to take me despite the wreck of a human being that I am. Maybe she would, but it wouldn't be right. Because I need *all of her*, but in order to get it, I'd have to offer *all of me* in exchange. Every sin. Every dark deed. A fair trade.

I close my eyes and inhale her scent. Innocent. Untainted. She would never accept me if she knew the truth.

"I have to go, tiger cub."

Her eyes search mine, confused but trusting. "Where?"

"I can't tell you."

"Why?"

I caress her silky skin with the pads of my fingers, stealing yet again, then step away. "Because, there are no lies between us. Only secrets."

I can feel her eyes on my back as I walk toward the front door. And all the while, my phone keeps ringing. My sins are eager to connect. The past. The future. And most of all, the present.

Rain beats on the windshield, distorting my view of the second window from the left on the third floor. My flight to Budapest leaves at nine, which means I have a few more hours.

I pull out my phone and go over the mission parameters once more, trying to figure out a way that would allow me to shorten the time I need to spend in Hungary. There isn't any.

The initial plan was for me to fly there, execute the target, and head right back. Three days max. But when I returned Kruger's call after I left Nera, he said the surveillance team in Budapest had been taken out. Before they had the chance to submit their report. This means I'll need at least a week, probably two, to follow my target and establish his daily schedule and patterns before I can get to the kill.

Fourteen days. Two weeks without seeing my girl. I don't know how I'll ever survive being apart from her for so long. Short periods now, mere days, I can hardly manage. But more than that? Weeks? I might go insane. At times, I feel like I'm already dead, but then I come to see her, and it's as if life flows back into my soul. I live for my stolen moments with her—it's the only thing that keeps me going.

The dashboard clock shows two a.m. I've spent four hours sitting here, trying to make myself leave. Couldn't do it. I need to steal another look at her before I go. Another glimpse that I hope will preserve my sanity. So like a thief in the night, I step out of my car and hurry across the street.

The faint light steaming through the window bathes Nera's sleeping form. She's curled into herself, resting at the edge of the bed. Her hair is gathered at the top of her head, tangled strands sticking out of the messy bun in all directions.

Her bedroom isn't big, perhaps only half the size of the living room, but it's similarly decorated in tones of white and pale brown. A few red accent pieces here and there—a vase on the vanity, a knitted bed cover neatly folded atop a recliner set in the corner of the room, and several scattered beige throw pillows embroidered with poppy flowers—make the room uniquely hers. And there, hanging on the mirror above the vanity, is the red silk scarf.

My steps are muted by the thick white carpet as I head across the room and crouch by the bed, staring at the lips I tasted just hours earlier. I'm certain I haven't made a sound, but Nera still stirs, as if she somehow felt my presence. Her eyes flutter open, and, for a few moments, she just watches me. There is no alarm or even a hint of surprise in her gaze, as if finding me next to her bed in the middle of the night is absolutely normal.

"I thought you left. What happened?"

"Nothing." I take the edge of the blanket and tug it up, covering her exposed shoulder.

"You promised there won't be any lies between us, demon. Only secrets."

It amazes me sometimes, how well she knows me, while not actually knowing a single thing about me at all. "The trip I'm taking. It'll be longer than I expected."

She bites her lower lip. I wait for her to ask me *why*, but she just keeps gazing at me and nods.

"How long will you be gone?"

"Ten days. Maybe a bit more."

Another nod. "Are you leaving right away?"

"In a few hours."

She reaches out and strokes my cheek. "Then, stay here tonight."

"Cub..."

"Please."

I shut my eyes for a moment, arguing with myself that I should leave. I lose. Again.

"All right."

Nera's palm tenderly glides along my chin, to the back of my head, pulling my braid from behind my shoulder to let it fall over my pec. Other than Nera's gentle hand, the last time someone handled my hair was more than two decades ago, and that son of a bitch did not survive the aftermath of the encounter. But her touch is different. I crave it. Welcome the feel of her delicate fingers as they move along the tangled tendrils until they reach the elastic band holding everything together.

"May I?" she asks.

"Yes."

A small, sleepy smile pulls at her lips as she removes the hair tie and starts undoing my braid. Her movements are slow and careful as she does it, threading her fingers through the strands. Despite being fully clothed, I somehow feel as if she's stripping away every layer, leaving me bare before her eyes.

"Are you going to spend the rest of the night squatting beside my bed, demon?"

"That's the plan."

She rakes her fingers through my hair once more, then scooches back in bed, until she's lying next to the wall. An invitation to lie down with her. She won't ask me to climb in bed the same way she wouldn't inquire where I'm going. I've established the rules of this game we've been playing, and even after all these months, she's still adhering to them. But the problem is, it's not a game anymore. Not for me. It hasn't been for a long time.

Every morning I wake up with her face on my mind, and each night I go to sleep with her name on my lips. It's wrong. Everything about this is wrong. She's so young, and not just in terms of her years. I'm barely thirty, but I feel ancient in comparison. My three decades on this earth are filled with violence and death.

My eyes dart to the thick textbook lying on her nightstand. It would take me days to read one chapter in that thing. She's too smart, too gentle and caring to tie herself to someone like me. Earlier this week, I watched as she helped her vet friend save the life of a little bird with a broken wing. They spent two fucking hours fumbling with the stupid thing. Me, on the other hand, I take lives without a second thought. Without a speck of remorse.

I have no idea why she allows this weird relationship of ours to continue. She has family. Friends. Every time I come to see her, I expect her to ask me to go away and not return. She will, eventually. It would be a grave mistake to let her get closer even an inch. She'll realize that there's nothing left in me that's worth a damn. Maybe there never was. Just an empty shell of a man who treads through life leaving behind corpses, misery, and terror everywhere he's been. If I had an ounce of decency, I would have let myself be killed. Years ago. The world would have been better off without me in it.

"It's okay." Nera's soft whisper fills the silence. "You can stay where you are, if you prefer."

My eyes wander away from the textbook to meet my cub's unrelenting gaze. A mistake. Because the moment I do, a strange force pulls me forward, luring me closer. I'm tempted by her warmth, seduced by her sunshine. I need to take it with me when I leave.

Straightening up, I take off my coat and throw it onto the recliner set a few steps away. My suit jacket is next. Nera turns on the bedside lamp and watches me as I start undoing the straps of my shoulder holster that has my two guns tucked in it. She doesn't even blink. Disarmed, I take a seat on the edge of her bed, my eyes retracing their path to that thick book on the nightstand.

"I couldn't sleep after you left, so I studied a bit." She sits up in bed and leans against the headboard. "No better way to make a person fall asleep."

"Is it interesting?"

"Some parts, yes. But that one is rather boring." Her hand is in my hair again, stroking it. "See for yourself if you want."

"I can't." I grit my teeth. "I can't read, cub."

Her hand halts for a moment, but then she resumes combing her fingers through my hair again.

"Dyslexia?" she asks.

"No. I only finished first grade."

"How is that possible? Isn't that against the law?"

"As far as anyone was concerned, I got homeschooled until I was sixteen. But where I come from, reading and writing wasn't high on the list of priorities."

"So"—a stroke on the side of my chin—"how bad is it?"

"I can handle short sentences, and words I already know," I say, not looking at her. "To get through half a page, I need a couple of hours."

"Okay." She takes my chin between her fingers, turning my head to face her. "Would you like to know what I was reading about after you left?"

"Yes."

"Come sit beside me. And pass me the book."

I climb on the bed and place the heavy textbook in her hands. Nera leans her head on my shoulder and opens the text, setting it on my lap.

"Tonight, we're learning about the digestive tract of an adult cow," she states and points the tip of her finger under the heading at the top of the page. "I'll go slow. If you need me to repeat any words, just tell me."

"Okay."

"Stomach compartments." Her finger slides across the page as she reads:

"*The rumen is the largest stomach compartment and consists of several sacs. It can hold twenty-five gallons or more of material depending on the size of the cow. Because of its size, the rumen acts as a storage or holding vat for feed. Aside from storage..."*

I wrap my arm around her back and listen to the sounds of her voice blending with the raindrops beating on the window. Every now and then, she yawns, but she continues reading, her finger moving under the words until the sun rises above the horizon and she finally falls asleep on my chest. I lift the book off my lap and keep holding my girl pressed to my body for a bit longer. Then, I carefully lay her down and rise from the bed.

Before I leave, I shut off the light and lean over my sleeping cub, taking her hand in mine.

"Thank you," I say and kiss her fingers.

Chapter seventeen

Kai

Two weeks later

"Good evening. How can I—Oh, it's you again, sir."

I glare at the florist with a steely stare, then switch my focus to a guy standing in front of the shelf laden with rose bouquets.

"Out," I order.

"Excuse me?" He gives me an exasperated look.

I reach into my jacket and pull out my gun, pressing the barrel to the idiot's forehead. "Now."

The guy drops the flowers he's holding and hightails it out of the store. I reholster my gun while approaching the shop door, then flip the sign to *closed*. When I turn around, the florist is gaping at me with bulging eyes.

"I need flowers that don't have any pollen. My girl is allergic."

"Um . . ." He pulls at his collar. "Perhaps, some roses?"

"They don't have pollen?"

"Well, they do, but um . . . they are considered hypoallergenic because the pollen particles are far too big, so they won't become airborne and cause issues for allergy sufferers."

I throw a look at the shelf containing various colored roses. A few years ago, I had a hit that came with a special request. The client wanted the victim's severed tongue placed on a bed of rose petals and delivered to him in a gift-wrapped box.

"No roses. What else?"

"Maybe a cactus?"

I lift an eyebrow.

"No cactus. Right. Okay, then . . ." The florist turns around looking over the displayed arrangements, then rushes toward another shelf in the corner. Sweat glistens on his forehead, and droplets start to slide down the side of his face. "Tulips are a great choice."

He brings over a vase filled with red-colored flowers and lifts it in front of me. I pull out one steam and start inspecting the inside of the bloom.

"What's the little black dart-like things?"

"Um, well, those are stamens, but there is very little pollen on them. You see, every plant reprod—"

"Spare me the biology lesson, grandpa." I grab the scissors hanging on the wall beside the wrapping paper, then turn the flower upside down and carefully cut off the dangly things with the black powder on them. "Does this make it pollen-free?"

The guy stares at the flower I'm holding. "I-I guess so."

"Perfect." I toss him the scissors. He almost stabs himself in the stomach trying to catch them. "I need you to cut off the little fuckers from each one. You have five minutes."

"But, sir. There are at least seventy tulips. I—"

I take a step toward him.

"Sure. Five minutes."

As the florist gets to work on depollinating the tulips at a nearby workbench, I take a seat behind his counter and start going through the drawers, looking for a red pen. I find one in a box full of paper clips, then grab one of the fancy cards from the display rack.

By the time the florist finishes with his task, I've ruined more than a dozen cards, and the floor around my feet is covered with crumpled glossy paper. I glare at my latest attempt, narrowing my eyes at the two words I wrote. My handwriting looks terrible, but it's the best I can do.

"Until next time, gramps." I throw a few Benjamins on the countertop and grab the bouquet out of the florist's hands. Stuffing my note into my pocket, I leave the shop.

Nera

No milk. Great.

I slam the fridge door shut and carry my bowl of muesli to the living room. The TV is playing the news on mute as I slump onto the cushions and start shoveling my dry breakfast cereal into my mouth.

At Dad's house, breakfast was always a lavish affair, just as lunch and dinner were. Eggs, sausages, pastry, cheese, fruits, and whatnot. It was always served in the large dining room at eight thirty, sharp. The possibility of skipping it was nonexistent. Dad always insisted that he wanted the whole family to eat at least one meal together. I always found it depressing. With Mom and Elmo gone, and Massimo locked up, those dreadful breakfasts always reminded me of just how broken our family actually is. However, eating anywhere besides the dining room was unthinkable, and it was only after I moved out that I realized how liberating it was to have your food whenever and wherever you wanted.

The anchor is reporting an international news story while images of several people are shown over his left shoulder on the screen. I grab the remote and turn up the volume. Something about an assassination of an oil tycoon in Budapest. The man and his entire security team were gunned down, execution style, at his private estate just outside the capital. At present time, the local authorities have no leads on the parties responsible for the massacre, or information on a potential motive for the killing.

As ghastly as the news story is, I can't help but think that if it was a professional hit, the police wouldn't find a thing.

Using hitmen-for-hire is typical within the Mafia world. They are ridiculously expensive, but if you want someone gone without any trace that could lead back to you, it's the only guaranteed way. It's not a secret that Camorra tends to use these assassins quite often, especially when someone stands in the Clan's way. I know of at least five situations where high-ranking members of other crime organizations in the US ended up dead, and their deaths were left unsolved for years.

I guess we're kind of lucky. Since my dad took over the Boston Family, he's been trying to maintain good relationships with other Cosa Nostra factions as well as with our competitors. He does his thing and never steps on anyone's toes. I know that some of the capos don't support this strategy, but our business investors do. Skirmishes and internal wars eat into the profits too much.

I turn off the TV and take my empty bowl into the kitchen. As I'm heading toward the sink, I catch a flash of red out of the corner of my eye. Stopping, I turn toward my "study nook" that I've set up by the balcony door. Wedged between two oversized floor pillows, just next to my laptop, is a big blue pot, similar to the one

I use when making pasta. Inside is a bunch of red tulips. Butterflies invade the pit of my stomach as I approach and crouch in front of the flowers. Next to the pot, on the floor, is a beautiful silver card. Its glossy, satin-like elegance is in complete contrast with a barely readable note scribed in red ink.

No pollen

I cover my mouth with my hand and stare at the tulips. Now, I can see the pot *is* actually mine. I used it to prepare ravioli when my demon was here two weeks ago.

"He's back," I mumble into my palm.

My phone starts ringing somewhere in the bedroom, but I don't move from my spot. It's likely Zara with a reminder that I'm expected at Dad's for lunch later today. As if I could forget. He called me yesterday, demanding my presence, and my unquestioning obedience in this case.

Carefully, I take one of the flowers from the pot. When it comes to tulips, I get into sneezing fits more often than not. They are always a gamble for me. This time, though, I don't care if it happens. I bury my nose into the bell-shaped blossom, inhaling once. Then one more time.

No sneezing.

I pick up the pot and take it to the dining table, setting it in the middle. It looks completely out of place on the spotless glass surface, but I don't even think about exchanging it for a more appropriate vase. Returning my long-forgotten empty cereal bowl to the kitchen before heading into my bedroom to get ready for my day, I spot a new magnet on the fridge. It has been placed low, all the way under the set Zara had brought for me. The image shows a bridge and an old-looking building in the background. The caption under the bridge reads *Hungary*.

I stare at my father, at a loss for words.

"You promised." I can't believe this. "You promised you'd let me finish my courses! Is that so much? Just a few more years to live my life as if it's actually my own, before I need to surrender it to serve Cosa Nostra and be married off?"

Nuncio Veronese reaches for his whiskey glass and takes a seat on a big recliner in the middle of his study. "Things change, Nera. The situation was different then."

I bite my tongue in an effort not to scream. "So, how long do I have left?"

He looks down at his tumbler, rotating it, the ice cubes cracking and clinking within the glass. Each fractured sound makes me feel as if I'm facing the countdown clock on death row, waiting for my sentence to be carried out. Waiting for the inevitable. Without hope.

I know that my father loves me. He would take a bullet for me without a second thought. He'd jump after me into rushing waters, even though he doesn't know how to swim.

My father loves me.

But he loves the Family more.

"You can finish this year of schooling," he says and takes a big gulp of his drink. "We can announce the betrothal in August, and aim for a fall wedding."

"Dad . . ."

"You are the only person I can count on. Massimo is in prison. Elmo is gone. Zara is . . . well, you know. There's only you. And I . . . I've made some bad choices, Nera." He's looking down at his glass as he says it. "Some really bad choices. And if the Family finds out, everything I've worked for would crumble into dust."

I stare at him. My father would never work against the Family's prosperity. Cosa Nostra is his life. "What bad choices?"

"I allowed Camorra to invest in our casino business."

A shocked gasp leaves my lips. The Cosa Nostra business can only be owned by the members of the Family. Allowing someone from the outside, especially another criminal organization, is blasphemy.

"We had losses," he continues. "I have been forging the revenue reports for the last few months. Some of the loans had to be paid back. We needed the money—fast, and I said yes. Batista and I planned on repaying Camorra before the annual Family meeting in December."

"The underboss knew? Why the fuck didn't he caution you against this?"

"It was his idea, actually. We had no other choice, and it should have been temporary. But Alvino changed his mind. He said he wouldn't accept the payoff unless we offered something in exchange. He wants you."

The room starts spinning. I'm not marrying a guy who landed his girlfriend in an ER, and who also cuts off people's genitals. And what about my demon? Just the thought of not seeing him ever again sends me into a full-blown panic.

The horror must be written all over my face because my father stands up and grabs my shoulders.

"He won't hurt you," he says. "I had a serious conversation with him, and I made certain he's aware of what will happen if he dares to lay a hand on my little girl."

"Please, Dad . . . I can't . . ."

"The Family needs you, Nera. I need you."

I stare at my father's face while the scenes pass through my mind like a movie on fast-forward. Me, in a wedding dress, walking down the aisle toward the man I don't know. Me, sitting with him at the head table, eating in complete silence because we have nothing to talk about. Me, in a room full of elegantly dressed people, with a big fake smile on my face and in jewelry that equals half my bodyweight. Accepting their empty compliments while trying to hide the tears and despair at being turned into a trophy. Me, lying naked in bed, letting my husband fuck me because it's his right.

Is that all I can expect now from my life?

A year ago, if my father had given me this news, I would have cried but would have felt resigned to my fate. Marrying for the sake of the Family is not only expected, it is common. Being tied to a man who won't give a fuck about me seemed normal. Not anymore. Not when I know what it feels like to have someone who actually cares about who I am, as a person. Who looks at me as if he really sees me. Not as the don's daughter. Not as a strategic move. Just . . . me.

"I'm sorry, Dad," I whisper. "I . . . can't."

"You can't?" He leans toward me, glaring with eyes that seem so cold. His face is set in a grimace, a strange mixture of fury and desperation. I don't recall seeing my father angry more than a handful of times before.

I make myself keep steady and meet his furious gaze. "I won't."

"I am your don. You're going to do what I order you to do, no questions asked." His voice has a dangerous edge, somewhere between a warning and a threat.

"You are my father, first and foremost." My voice is trembling. "Shouldn't your child's happiness come before work? Dad?"

"It's not work. It's legacy, Nera."

"Yes. A sparkling legacy of false glow, fake friends, and the tears of your daughters who would give anything to be regarded as something other than pawns in games of power." I reach out and take his hand. "You should always be a safe harbor for me and Zara. We need a father. Not a don."

His brows draw together, and a haunted look enters his eyes. "I tried my best, Nera. I made sure you had everything you ever wished for. Whenever you or your sister liked something, I bought it for you."

"You gave Zara a golden necklace for her eighteenth birthday."

"The one with the diamonds that she saw at the mall. She stood in front of the display and looked at it for more than ten minutes. I didn't even care about the price."

"She can't wear it, Dad." I squeeze his hand. "Zara gets a rash from wearing most jewelry. The necklace has been sitting in a box on her vanity, like a pretty sparkling reminder that her father somehow forgot that little detail about her life."

The color completely drains from my father's face, and he rears back as if I hit him.

"I did forget," he chokes out. "How could I have forgotten something like that?"

"Because you've spent years being surrounded by people who always tapped you on the back and congratulated you, no matter what you did. So you just stopped thinking about how your actions impact others."

My father looks away, his gaze distant as he stares somewhere beyond the window.

"When you lose someone you love, it kills something inside you, you know?" He sighs. "I lost your mother. Elmo. And then, Laura. It was . . . too much."

"I know. We lost them, too."

He looks down at me, and I can almost see the man who loved giving me and my sister piggyback rides through the house.

"I don't want to lose you, too." He lifts his hand and strokes my cheek. "I'll tell Alvino that my daughter is no longer an option open for discussion."

"Will he make problems for you?"

"Don't you worry. I'll handle my own mess." He bends and places a kiss on my head. "I'll be seeing you at my party next weekend?"

"Of course, Dad."

"Good. Now, go to the dining room. Zara is probably waiting for us."

"Thank you."

I'm halfway across the room when I hear his voice behind me. "I'm so glad you'll never have to be in my place."

"Me too."

***

"Are you still seeing that stalker of yours, Nera?"

I sprawl on Zara's bed and rest my head on my crossed arms. My sister and I have never kept things from each other, but when it comes to my demon, I don't like volunteering information. Maybe because I don't think she'd understand. Or maybe I'm just selfish.

"So?" she prods.

"We had dinner at my place two weeks ago."

"Mm-hmm. That's quite a development," she mumbles around the pins held between her lips, then sends me a pointed look. "Considering you still don't know the man's name."

I shrug. He's my demon. I'm his cub. I don't need his name.

"What did you make?"

"Ravioli with cheese." I bite my lip. "It wasn't actually planned, or I would have cooked something more appealing. I prepared dinner for myself, but when I looked out the window, I noticed him across the street."

Zara lowers the pattern piece she's pinning to the fabric. "You and your stalker guy have the weirdest relationship I've ever heard of. How long has it been going on, this bizarre thing you two have? Six months?"

"A year."

"Christ." She shakes her head. "And how often do you two see each other now?"

"It depends. In more recent months, he's been dropping by the vet clinic and following me home twice a week. But, we've also hung out on the roof and talked. Or just sat there in silence and watched the sky. A lot of times, I've spotted him lurking across the street or around the corner, but as soon as I do, he vanishes." I grin. "I think he intentionally let me see him those times. The truth is, I'm fairly certain that more often than not, I don't even know he's there."

"That's . . . twisted."

"I know. It's also the most healthy relationship I've had with anyone since I can remember. Excluding you, of course."

"You know nothing about him. How can that be a healthy relationship?"

I turn onto my stomach and prop my hands under my chin. "Have you ever met anyone with whom you could talk about the things that you can't discuss with other people? Even though you don't know much about that person?"

Zara's body suddenly goes very still. "Maybe."

I spring up in bed. "What? Who?"

"Don't want to talk about it."

"You know you can tell me anything, Zara."

"Not in this instance." She goes back to her sewing. "So, how did that dinner go?"

I narrow my eyes at her. She's obviously avoiding the subject. Maybe she has feelings for someone she shouldn't. A man who's not from the Family, or maybe someone much older than her? Considering I was just thinking that there are some things I'm not willing to share, I decide to let her have her secret. For now.

"It was nice," I say. "But after we were done, he asked what I wanted in return."

Zara's eyebrows arch in question.

"He has this weird notion that nothing is free. So, I asked for a kiss."

"Was it good?"

"It was like I've been living in a vacuum, and then, when his lips were finally on mine, I breathed fresh air for the first time in my life." I close my eyes and sigh. "He had to go on a trip—couldn't tell me where—but he returned this morning. Or maybe last night."

"How do you know?"

"He left me flowers."

Zara snorts. "Men. You should have told him that you and the flowers don't get along."

"I did. He cut off the stamens, Zara."

My sister's head snaps up from her sewing, and the surprise is clear in her eyes.

"He brought me back a magnet," I whisper. "From... Budapest."

Chapter eighteen

Nera

"Is something going on?" Dania asks as we step out of the movie theater and head toward the car and driver my dad insisted I use. My own car is in the shop to fix a failed fuel pump, and I won't have it back for two more days. And Dad has been somewhat paranoid since last Sunday when I refused to marry Alvino, so he demanded I have one of his men drive me around instead of using taxis or rideshares.

"Nope. Just the don being his protective self." I shrug.

The driver opens the back door for us when we approach, and as I look up to thank him, I notice it's not the same man who drove me here.

"Where's Pio?" I ask.

"A family emergency," he replies. "Your father sent me to take over, Miss Veronese. I'm Gerodi."

"I hope it's nothing serious?"

"Absolutely not." He smiles and shuts the door after me.

Since Dania's home is close by, we drop her off first. Halfway to my place, though, the driver misses a turn.

"Gerodi, you should have taken the right."

"Oh, apologies, Miss Veronese." He meets my gaze in the rearview mirror. "No worries, I'll find a place to do a U-turn."

I lean back but keep my eyes pinned to the mirror. Every few moments, Gerodi glances at it, then looks away. My purse is right next to me on the seat, and I move my hand toward it as inconspicuously as possible.

"So, have you been working for my father long?" I ask.

"A couple of months." Another smile.

We reach an intersection where he could easily turn around, but he keeps driving straight. My hand slips halfway inside my purse, and I can feel the phone under the tips of my fingers.

"It's hard. Starting a new job," I say casually. "Have you made any friends? Did you ask Teobaldo to show you the ropes? He's been working for us for more than a decade."

"Yes, he was very eager to give me the basics."

"That's great." My pulse skyrockets. There is no Teobaldo working for my dad.

Another intersection, another missed turn. It looks like we're heading out of the city. I grip the phone and slowly pull it from my purse, just enough so I can see the screen. I have Zara on speed dial, and I only need to click the button. Both my hands and legs have started to shake.

"I really wouldn't do that if I were you, Miss Veronese."

My head snaps up. Holding my gaze in the mirror, the driver pulls a gun from his holster and places it on his lap.

"What do you mean?" I try to play dumb, even though I know I'm busted.

"Alvino's orders were quite explicit, Miss. No harm is to come to you unless you try something," he says. "Please don't make me hurt you."

My stomach drops, and, for a moment, I can't seem to draw a

breath. There's only one reason for the head of Camorra to order someone to grab me. Dad must have already told him that the marriage won't happen.

I let go of the phone and fold my hands in my lap. As long as I'm in the moving car, my options are limited. The doors automatically locked soon after we started moving, and I'm certain the asshole behind the wheel activated the override so I won't be able to open the door from the inside. Besides, I can't jump out of the vehicle at fifty miles per hour.

"Where are you taking me?" If I have an idea of where we're going, I might think of a way to escape.

"You'll see." His lips widen in a highly disturbing grin as he gets onto the interstate.

We drive in silence for more than two hours. During this time, I consider all potential reasons for Alvino to resort to doing this. I don't think he would dare kill me, but there are a lot of other nasty things he could do. And based on what I know about him, nastiness is his favorite pastime.

The driver takes the off-ramp onto a narrow, deserted road. There's hardly any other traffic here, not surprising considering that the dashboard clock shows it's one in the morning. We continue for a couple of miles and then make a turn before coming to a stop in front of a building, though I don't know more than that since there are no lights around it.

With gun in hand, the driver opens the door for me. I grab my purse as I exit the car, but he snatches it away.

"You won't be needing this for the time being," he says, throwing it onto the passenger seat.

A line of SUVs is parked in the otherwise empty lot, and hope sparks within me upon seeing them. Perhaps there's someone here who could help me.

The driver gives me a shove from behind, pushing me toward the huge wooden door. It's only then that I realize what this building is. A church.

"Come on, Miss Veronese. Your groom is waiting."

Kai

Years of the most intense and rigorous physical and mental training. A decade and a half of active duty. Over one hundred high-risk and psychologically challenging missions, executed with absolute calmness and detachment. Since I made my first kill, my hands have never once trembled. There has never been a situation that made me feel unhinged or even slightly agitated.

"THE FUCKER HAS MY TIGER CUB!" I roar as I hit the steering wheel with all my might.

I've been following the dark navy sedan for over two hours. From the moment they didn't make that turn leading to Nera's after dropping off her friend, I knew something wasn't right. When the vehicle started heading out of the city, it became clear that my girl had been kidnapped. I don't give a fuck by whom or why. Their death sentence has been signed.

The shit-for-brains driving the sedan takes the next exit off the highway and then proceeds down a county road. I follow, keeping my distance so as not to raise suspicion. When they make another turn and pull into a middle-of-nowhere church parking lot, I keep going. Once I'm far enough, I drive off the road and into a thicket. Branches scratch at the hood and the sides of my vehicle as I urge it deeper, out of sight. I don't even shut the door when I launch out and run to the trunk to load up.

It takes me four minutes to reach the edge of the parking lot attached to the church. A line of black cars is parked on the side, and behind the wheel of the last one, a man is smoking. The navy sedan that brought my cub here is parked in front of the church entrance, but it appears empty now. Two men with automatic rifles are guarding the front doors, and another is making the rounds outside the building.

Inside the church, the lights are definitely on, but the stained glass windows make it impossible to get a read on of what's happening within. I look up, assessing the upper level. There should be second-story access that leads to the choir loft.

Using the darkness as cover, I sneak up behind the last SUV in the line. The man inside is in the process of lighting another cigarette, and he blows smoke out through the open window. I pounce and bury my knife into the side of his neck, just below his ear. His body jerks, and a gurgling sound leaves his throat. Pressing my free hand over his mouth to muffle the noise, I rotate the blade. A rather quick death, unfortunately.

The guard doing the rounds is next. I take him out from behind, wrapping my arms around his neck and dropping him on his ass. His neck snaps like a twig in the process. After confirming he's dead, I creep along the outside of the church and throw a quick look around the corner. The two guards are still positioned at the front doors, just over ten feet away. This close, I could take them both out with my handgun, but it may draw whatever numbers are hidden inside the building. Since I don't yet know what I'm dealing with, a silent kill is my best option.

I take two of my throwing knives, one for each hand, and step out of my cover. The guards spin toward me while I send both blades flying. One lodges in the first target's eye, the other in the second's forehead. I doubt they have any awareness of what's happening to them when I cross the distance between us and, in one fluid movement, swipe my Bowie knife across both their throats.

Leaving their bodies slumped before the doors, I double back to grab my rifle from under the bush where I left it, then head to the rear of the church.

Nera

Fear claws at me, crawling over my skin as I stare at the man sitting before me. His arms are spread on the back of the front-row pew, while his eyes roam up and down my body as if assessing his new possession. I've never met the head of the Camorra Clan before, but I've seen a few images of him on social media. He's lankier than in the photos, and his hollow cheeks and the grayish tint of his skin are even more pronounced in person.

"I knew your daddy wasn't the sharpest tool in the shed, but I never expected him to be so stupid as to back out of our deal." He smiles, revealing two rows of nicotine-stained teeth. One of his eyes seems to be misaligned, turned inward, which makes his grimace more grotesque. "I expected you to be prettier."

He rises and grabs my chin, his fingers bruising my skin as he tilts my head to the left and then right. His breath stinks of onions and cigarettes, making me want to puke. I swallow the bile and keep very still, enduring his inspection.

Along with Alvino and the driver who escorted me here, there are over two dozen men inside the church. Camorra soldiers, all armed, sitting in rows of pews on the right side of the aisle. And the priest in his ceremonial robes, standing at the altar. There is no way I'll be able to escape.

"Pity. I may need to fuck you with my eyes closed," Alvino sneers. "Let's get this over with."

He grabs my upper arm, dragging me toward the dais. My left heel gets caught on something, and I stumble, twisting my ankle. Pain shots up my leg, and I can't help but cry out.

"Shut the fuck up." Alvino slaps my face.

I barely manage to stifle another cry as I'm dragged in front of the priest. Keeping my weight off my left leg, I stare in horror at his elaborately decorated chasuble while nausea threatens to suffocate me. From the moment I stepped out of the car and realized we were at a church, I knew what was coming, but it still felt as if it was happening to someone else. With a municipal ceremony, Dad might have had some pull to get it annulled. It's nearly impossible to do so with a church wedding.

The priest starts speaking, and I squeeze my eyes shut. I won't cry. I won't let the bastard standing next to me gloat at my misery. My mind leaps to my beautiful demon instead. I'll likely never see him again. Camorra is not like Cosa Nostra. They keep to their traditions. After the nuptials, it's expected that the wife stays at home. If I'm ever allowed to leave Alvino's house, it will always be under a heavy guard.

I draw in a shaky breath and make myself open my eyes, scanning my surroundings, hoping to find a means of escape, all the while knowing it's futile. There are too many armed men, and my injured ankle can barely support my weight. There's no way I'll be able to run.

The priest continues to speak. Alvino turns toward me, that awful evil smile plastered on his face. He opens his mouth to say "I do" just as a single, sharp bang rings out. Alvino's head jerks back. His legs fold beneath him, and he starts falling backward, pulling me along. I find myself sprawled over him on the floor—my face just inches from his wretched one, gaping at the big hole at the center of his forehead—when gunfire explodes.

Maybe it's the adrenaline, or simply a pure self-preservation instinct, but I don't look up, not even to see what's happening around me. Staying as low as possible, I crawl toward the nearest wall. Once I reach relative safety behind a thick stone pillar, I chance a quick glance toward the middle of the church. The priest is dead, splayed on the floor a few steps from Alvino. Several other bodies are scattered nearby. I can only partially glimpse them through the gaps among the pews. But those who are facing my way, have identical red holes in their heads.

The Camorra members who are still alive have taken cover between the wooden seats. Their shouts fill the vast space as they point and shoot at random. I don't see who they are shooting at. Considering the number of dead bodies, I figure Dad must have somehow found out what happened and sent our men to rescue me. But I don't see anyone except Camorra soldiers.

The shooting dies down, and, for a moment, there are no sounds at all. Two Camorra goons who were hiding behind the first pew rise, holding their guns out.

Bang. Bang.

That sharp sound again. It's a different pop than a regular gun makes. With the echoey acoustics, it's hard to pinpoint where the shots are coming from. Both men drop dead. Another round of rapid firing erupts as Camorra soldiers shoot in all directions, then silence descends once more.

The faint tingling feeling creeps up my neck. I look toward the altar and notice a movement in the shadows behind it. A figure in black steps into the light, and my breath gets caught in my lungs. He lifts his guns, one in each hand, shooting at the remaining Camorra men while walking to me. Walking. As if on a stroll through a park on a sunny afternoon, birds chirping in the distance. As if there aren't God-knows-how-many goons still out there trying to shoot him. He just rains bullets on them without pause. My angel of death. My salvation.

"Cub?" he says as he reaches me.

"I'm okay," I choke out.

He nods and steps behind the column that's served as my shelter. A barrage of bullets hits the wall on our side the moment he stops shooting.

"When I tell you, you're going to run." Two empty magazines clatter to the floor. "There's a door at the back, behind the altar. The car you arrived in is parked just outside, keys are in the ignition." He slots a new magazine into each gun. "I'll cover you from here."

"I can't," I say, as I slowly rise. "I twisted my ankle. I could probably walk, but I can't run."

His eyes snap to mine. I can see the storm brewing in their depths as he goes over our options. There's at least eighty feet between here and the dais. Too many of Alvino's guys are still alive. He'll run out of ammunition before I manage to drag myself there.

"Okay." He turns to send a few bullets toward the Camorra men, then places his guns in the holster. Smoothly, he grabs under my thighs and lifts me against his chest. "Hold tight. We'll have to be fast."

I gape at him. If he's carrying me, he won't be able to return fire. And his back will be exposed to the shooters. *Fuck no!* Feeling his heat beneath my touch, I slide my hand between our bodies and pull a gun from his holster.

"Heads up, demon. I'm a lousy shot unless my target is up close." I cross my ankles at the small of his back, locking myself in. Then, I wrap my left arm around his neck and extend the right over his shoulder, gun at the ready.

My demon smiles. "Give them hell, tiger cub."

He runs.

The scent of gunfire and forest fills my nostrils as I squeeze the trigger again and again. My entire arm shakes from the recoil and the weight of the too large weapon in my hand. There's no time to aim, so I just shoot in the general direction of the pews. A bit of stone shrapnel or maybe something else hits my exposed leg. Tears well in my eyes. But I tighten my hold around my demon's neck and keep firing, despite barely being able to feel my grip.

Fresh air rushes into my lungs, sweet summer smells replace the stench of blood and gunpowder. We're out. That fact barely registers before I find myself deposited behind the wheel of a car.

"Floor it," my demon barks as he snatches the gun out of my hand and shuts the door. "Go directly home."

"I'm not leaving you," I scream through an open window.

"I need to do a cleanup here, and I can't do it if I'm worried about you."

He turns and shoots toward the back of the church. An instant later, a bullet hits the hood of the sedan. Alvino's men have obviously followed us, but I can't see the exit we came out of because my dark protector is standing in the way, blocking my view.

More bullets rain.

My demon suddenly jerks back, crashing into the car beside me. He tosses the weapon he took from me and pulls another from his holster, making a guttural noise in the process. His low grunt is cut off by the exploding rear window as a bullet shatters the glass and lodges in the padded seat.

"Nera, go! I can't focus!" he yells, slamming his palm on the car roof.

I step on the gas.

Chapter nineteen

Nera

Half past nine.

Over forty-eight hours.

The hands of my oversized wall clock seem to be moving super fast, but at the same time, much slower than they should. Sometimes, a minute feels like an hour. But the next passes in a heartbeat. Where the fuck is he?!

When I made it home after escaping that disaster with Alvino, I collapsed on the couch and, with my eyes fixed on the front door, waited for my demon. And waited. Panic gripped me in its claws, squeezing. It became harder to breathe. I didn't move my eyes from the door for hours.

Morning came. The panic transformed into madness. I grabbed my phone and searched the news sites for any speck of information. Nothing. I limped outside and walked around the block in my day-old dirty clothes, hoping to spot him lurking in some dark corner nearby. He wasn't there. And not on my roof. Nor on the roof across the street. Nowhere.

Returning to the apartment, I resumed my vigil on the couch. I didn't go to work, just stared at my front door. That's where Zara found me when she came over to check on me that evening because I wasn't answering her calls. I almost lost it when that front door opened, but I realized it was my sister and not him.

"Where are you, demon?" I whisper into the empty living room.

A year, and we never managed to exchange numbers. If I had the energy, I would have laughed. How am I supposed to know if he's okay? If he's... alive?

Slowly, I stand up from the couch and trudge to the kitchen to get a glass of water. I took a quick shower earlier and must have crashed for a couple of hours. After jolting awake from a restless slumber, I just threw on a T-shirt I usually sleep in. I'm not going anywhere until he comes back anyway.

My phone starts ringing on the counter. It's my dad. I'm not really in the right frame of mind to speak with him now, but I do need to answer the call. I can't tell him about what happened at the church two nights ago. If I do, I'll have to tell him everything about my demon, too. And my father might order him killed. No man outside of the Family is allowed to get this close to the don's daughter.

"Yes?" I croak into the phone.

"Nera, you sound awful. Zara said you're sick."

"Yeah." I throw back my water and lean my forehead on the cupboard door. "I don't think I'm going to make it to your birthday party tomorrow."

"We may need to postpone it anyway. An epic clusterfuck befell Camorra, and I'm still not sure how it'll affect us. Alvino is dead."

My head snaps up. "What happened?"

"No one knows. He was found dead in some church outside the city limits yesterday morning. Along with about half of his crew. As I heard it, the scene looked like a bloodbath. Bodies all around, over thirty dead."

"And... and it was only Alvino's men?" I close my eyes,

squeezing the phone hard enough to make my hand ache. "The dead bodies?"

"As far as I know, yes. Why do you ask?"

A sigh of relief escapes me. "No reason. It just seems strange."

"Well, there's speculation that it was an internal conflict. I don't particularly care one way or another, I'm glad that bastard is off my back. I'll know more after the meeting with Efisio this afternoon. He's taking over."

"That's good." I have no idea who Efisio is, and I don't give a fuck. "I have to go, Dad. I have a headache."

I throw the phone back on the counter and shuffle to my spot on the couch to continue my watch. My eyes are tired, and my lids seem to be closing on their own. I drag one of the study cushions off the floor and prop it on my lap and under my chin, slouching forward, so I have a direct view of the apartment door.

Where are you, demon?

A light stroke along the line of my cheekbone. Fingers moving hair off my face. A scent that reminds me of a mountain wind.

My eyes snap open.

"How's your ankle, cub?"

I choke back a whimper. My demon is standing by the couch, looking down at me. His face is pale, and there are dark circles under his eyes.

"Does it still hurt?" He gestures with his chin toward my leg.

"You were gone for two days, and you ask about my leg?" I whisper with a shaky voice. "I spent hours staring at my door, waiting for you to appear. A piece of me died each time I heard retreating footsteps in the hall. They didn't stop, didn't draw near. It wasn't you. Two days. It wasn't you."

"I had to take care of some things first, before coming here."

I spring off the couch and brush away my tears with the back of my hand. When did I start crying? "I thought something happened to you! I thought you were dead! And you had to 'take care' of something?"

"Yes."

"I was so damn scared! You don't get to do that!" I poke my finger at his chest. "Never. You hear me?"

He bends and slides his arm around my waist, lifting me against him. "I'm sorry."

"Jesus, demon." I wrap my arms and legs around him and slam my mouth to his.

Life. His lips on mine feel like life itself. Every stroke of his tongue. Every nibble. I revel in every single thing he's giving me. A whole year, and this is only the second kiss we've shared. The second kiss he's allowed me. Not anymore. I bite his lower lip and squeeze my legs tighter around his waist, grinding my core on his pelvis. He's hard, his cock pressing on my pussy.

"Cub." He grazes my lips with his one more time, then lowers me down. "I think I should go."

My feet touch the ground, and I want to cry again. Leaving. Again. It's nothing new. But every time he departs, he takes a part of me with him. Not tonight. I grab the lapels of his suit jacket and meet his gaze.

"No. You're not claiming another part of me tonight, demon. Tonight, we're going to trade."

I can feel his breaths on my cheek, deep but rapid. "A trade?"

"Yes. A part of me, for a part of you."

He stiffens. "Please, Nera. I don't have much restraint left."

A tiny smile pulls at my lips. He's used my name just once before. "You're staying."

"You don't know anything about me." He lowers his head, his eyes downcast—avoiding meeting mine.

I start pulling his jacket off. It's black, just like the shirt he wears underneath. Always black. I'm pushing the jacket down his arms when he hisses, as if he's in pain.

Instantly, I stop. "What's wrong?"

"Nothing."

I strip off his jacket and start unbuttoning his shirt, while he remains unmoving, just standing there staring at the floor. Only after I remove his shirt do I notice a length of bandage wrapped around his left bicep.

"That's what I had to handle. Why I couldn't come right away," he mumbles. "It's not that bad. Low caliber bullet, but I had to find someone to pull it out and fix me up."

I press my palm over my mouth. When I was in the car, he stumbled, just before he bellowed for me to drive home. He got shot while covering me with his body. And I left—left him behind not even knowing he was hurt.

I reach out to stroke his arm with my free hand. "I'm so, so sorry."

"I'm not. The alternative wasn't an option. I won't let anything bad happen to you as long as I live."

"But you also won't let me get any closer to you than a kiss?"

"If I do, there's no pathway back for us." His voice sounds hollow. "I'm not a good man, cub. If you knew even a fraction of the things I've done . . . What I'm *still* doing. You wouldn't want anything to do with me."

I cup his face, lifting his head to force him to meet my eyes. "You mean, the fact that you're a hitman?"

I didn't think a person could go as still as he does when those words leave my mouth. The only part of him that moves are his eyes, searching my face for answers. I can't even be sure he's drawn a breath.

"I know," I whisper. "I'm not as naive as you think."

I suspected as much since the first night I met him. Especially once I saw that headline. There were other clues, as well. Military background. Mentions of a unit. His reluctance to talk about his life, where he goes, what he does. The magnet from Hungary he left on my fridge—the same day I saw that Budapest news story. And of course, the way he single-handedly defeated over thirty men at the church. Efficient. Deadly. Killer.

"It doesn't change how I feel," I say as I caress his cheeks with my thumbs.

His eyes flare, and in the next instant, I find myself crushed against the wall, with his hand gripping my chin.

"And what is it that you feel?" Leaning closer, he presses his forehead to mine. "Tell me."

"Excitement, while I wait for your arrival. Happiness, when you finally decide to show up. And sadness, every time you leave. I feel joy when I stumble upon the little gifts you leave for me, when I find them around my place." I reach out behind his back and pull away the hair tie holding his braid as I continue. "Warmth and serenity when we sit next to each other on my roof, doing nothing but staring into the night. Contentment and acceptance because you see me as I am." My fingers tunnel through his hair, slowly gliding among the long strands. "You. I feel you. With every fiber of my being, demon."

A long exhale leaves his lips, as if he held his breath during my admission. His arm comes around my waist again, lifting me, carrying me across the room.

"I'll owe you a bowl," he growls as he deposits me on the kitchen island and swipes his arm along the surface on my left. My bowl of lemons crashes to the floor, glass shattering everywhere.

I take his face in my hands, pulling him toward me until our noses touch. "You owe me much more than a bowl, demon."

His nostrils flare, and then he's demolishing my lips again. A small gasp leaves me when he grabs a fistful of my hair, tugging on it, and wetness instantly pools between my legs. His other hand slowly trails along my neck and chest, pushing me down until I'm sprawled on the kitchen island. I wrap my legs around his waist, his hard cock pressing into my core as he leans forward. His long hair falls to the sides of my head like a silky black veil, shrouding everything from my view but his face.

"Do you know what demons do to their victims?" The rough timbre of his voice penetrates the silence, making me shudder.

I smile and squeeze my legs around him even tighter. "What?"

"They consume them, tiger cub."

In one smooth motion, he tears my T-shirt from neckline to hem. His hands slide over my throat again, then move along my arms until his fingers encircle my wrists like manacles. He pulls my hands away from his face, bringing them down to the edge of the countertop.

"Hold on," he says.

I bite my lower lip and grab the blunt edging, pressing my fingertips against the quartz on either side of my ass.

"Good." He dips his head to whisper in my ear. "I've been dreaming about this moment for so long."

A kiss lands on the side of my neck. Then another on my collarbone. One more, a bit lower, just above my left breast. These are not light butterfly kisses, but rather hard and possessive, like he's branding every inch of my skin with his mouth.

So long. I have waited so long for this. Dreamed about his hands and lips on my body, imagined how it would feel. This surpasses everything my desperate mind conjured up. My skin seems charged, pins and needles prickling everywhere he touches. Just like when he watches me, but a billion times more intense. Warmth swells inside my chest, filling the cracks in my soul. I hadn't even known they were there until this moment. I didn't know there were parts of me that were missing, but now, they are suddenly there. I feel complete. Only in my demon's arms do I feel that way.

My core clenches and my legs shake as he drags his lips down the valley of my chest and stomach. When he reaches my soaked panties and inhales, I almost come from the sensation alone.

"I'll have your scent on my mind each time I think about you, cub." One more deep breath, and then he tears my panties off.

Rough palms slide along my thighs and grab behind my knees before pulling my legs over his shoulders.

"My Nera. You are so damn beautiful," he purrs, slipping his hands under my behind.

Air leaves my lungs in short bursts, my body shaking hard as if I have a fever. His warm tongue laves my folds, slow and torturous. The tip of that masterful muscle slides inside me. Delves deeper, French-kissing my core. Tremors shoot down my spine as I arch my back, whimpering. Wanting. I'm not sure what does me in more—his tongue on my pussy or hearing him say my name. The quivers heighten with every hard, relentless stroke. My entire being feels like it's coming apart—my body, my mind, my heart—every cell is ready to explode in one perfect union.

One languid but deliberate stroke up my slit, and then he presses his lips over my clit and sucks it into his mouth. White lights flash before my eyes, and a devious cry, something between a moan and a scream, leaves my lips as I teeter on the brink of climax.

But then, so suddenly, the pressure of his lips is gone. My eyes fly open, and I find my demon watching me from between my thighs, a small satisfied smirk pulling at his lips.

"I wonder, should I finish you with my mouth"—he slowly lowers my ass down onto the counter—"or with my cock?"

That ship sailed long ago. Since the moment I met him in that dark alley, I've been drawn to him. He's burrowed under my skin, literally making me feel him. His presence. His dominion over me. I *am* already "finished," irrevocably ruined for any other man.

Fast, short breaths escape me as I watch him. Stormy eyes lock on mine as he reaches for the button on his pants, while his other hand lands between my legs. Deft fingers stroke my already sensitive pussy, each sensual caress wreaks havoc on my nervous system.

"Please," I moan, arching my back, mad with need. If I have to endure much more of this torture, I might just go crazy.

He unzips his pants while teasing my clit with the pad of his thumb. "Please, what?"

My gaze wanders down his chiseled chest, across the three lines of perfectly defined abs, and rests on his huge cock. My core muscles clench at the mere thought of having him inside me. "Please, fuck me."

"Fuck you? No, I don't like that term." He grabs me behind my knees, pulling me closer. "I'm going to take you, Nera."

"What's the difference?" I pant while the tip of his cock teases my entrance.

"What I take, I keep forever," he says with a wicked smile. Then, he buries himself all the way to the hilt.

My shriek of pleasure fills the room, but it quickly transforms into moans as he pounds me relentlessly. His breaths are sharp and fast, coming out in a steady rhythm. Every muscle on his body seems taut as his cock enters me, plunging deeper with each thrust while his eyes bore into mine. They are not empty now, and I can see the tempest roaring to life in his turbulent state. Hear the cry of rampant desire as clear as if he voiced it. *"Mine,"* his eyes say.

When I allowed myself to hope, to imagine how it would be between us, it was always like this. Hard. Unrestrained. Wild. Raw. Like him. I've always known there's a fiend behind his usual detached and dark demeanor. And I love seeing it come out into the light.

My inner walls spasm around his length while an ardent fever singes my body, seeking a way to burst free. I let go of the counter edge I've been gripping, grabbing at his forearms instead. My nails dig into his skin as I stare at him. He hasn't looked away from my face since the instant he plunged inside of me.

His piercing gaze holds mine captive while his right hand moves up my thigh, my stomach, stopping on my chest. My guardian demon—my possessor—presses his palm over my heart.

"Now, come for me, tiger cub," he growls, thrusting until he bottoms out.

I scream. Stars flash before my eyes as I let myself fall into beautiful oblivion, annihilated and consumed by my dark demon in the light.

Chapter Twenty

Nera

The early morning breeze wafting through the open window caresses my naked flesh. I reach out and move the black strands that have fallen over his face. We've been lying in my bed for nearly an hour, just watching each other.

"What happens now?" I whisper.

I've been meaning to ask this ever since we collapsed exhausted onto the sheets after making love for the second time since the sun came up over the horizon, too afraid to hear the answer. But I can't keep it back anymore.

"I don't know, cub." His hand lifts to my face, the tip of his finger tracing the line of my left brow, then down my nose and to my lips with cautious, gentle movements. "What do you want to happen?"

My heartbeat picks up as I gather the courage to speak. "I want you to stay. And I don't mean only today."

"I don't know how."

"Go home. Pack. And come back here." I smile. "It's not that hard."

"That's not what I meant." His hand cups my cheek, and his thumb strokes the skin under my eye. "I don't know how to live a life like yours. The things you know about me—those are just a murky surface on the black pond of my existence. I'm too fucked-up to live among normal people, cub."

"Then, we'll unfuck you."

A sad smile tugs at his lips. "I'm not one of your animals, Nera. Some things cannot be stitched back together."

"We can try."

"Is that the life you want for yourself?" He clenches his jaw. "Wouldn't you rather have a nice, educated man like you deserve?"

"Is that what you think?" I lean forward, getting in his face. "So if I say yes, you'd just leave me again?"

"I'm never going to leave you," he says. "Even if I wanted to, I know I never could. I'll be watching over you till the day I die, cub. And as long as I live, no one will dare touch a hair on your beautiful head."

"Will you be watching over me even when I walk down the aisle and pledge myself to a *nice* and *educated* man?" I bite out and shove his chest.

His face is completely blank, showing zero emotion, but the thumb stroking under my eye goes still.

"Will you hide in some corner while I give myself to him the way I gave myself to you?" I continue. "Are you going to watch when he *takes* me on the kitchen island while I scream in pleasure?"

The rigor overtakes his whole body, only his heart seems to be functioning. I can feel its thunderous beat under my palm. Something dangerous flashes in his eyes as they peer into mine, but he still doesn't utter a word.

I lean forward until my lips almost touch his. "Will you let me belong to someone else, demon?"

Kai

Will you be watching over me even when I walk down the aisle and pledge myself to a nice and educated man?

A continuous high-pitched tone rings inside my ears, mixing with Nera's voice. It began as a faint buzzing when I forced myself to tell her that she should be with someone else, but now, the frequency has shot up, bouncing inside my skull like a vengeful drill.

Will you hide in some corner while I give myself to him the way I gave myself to you?

Images fill my mind, scenes of her kissing a faceless man while he has her pinned against the wall. Then, the vision shifts and rearranges to Nera sprawled on the kitchen island, her face flustered and bathed in sweat. Not a bittersweet memory but a haunting, because it's not me pounding into her. That shrilling sound in my head skyrockets, and white dots appear before my eyes.

. . . let me belong to someone else, demon?

"Over my dead body," I growl.

Grabbing her around the waist, I roll us until I'm lying on top of her. "I don't care how much better than me the motherfucker is, or if he's more worthy of you. I will fucking gut any man who comes within fifteen feet of what is mine."

"Good." Her mouth ascends, pressing to my lips. "Because there is no one better than you. Not for me."

I take her face between my palms, raining kisses on her lips, nose, eyes . . . everywhere I've imagined kissing her but haven't dared. Monsters like me are not allowed to dream, and I never have. Not until I met her. For the first time in my life, I see the possibility of having something of my own. Her. My tiger cub.

"I'm going to buy us a house," I mumble as I trail my lips down her neck. "And a few dozen acres of land around it so you can have your animals. No other people nearby. I hate neighbors and I don't want any."

"That sounds expensive." She giggles as I kiss her earlobe.

"I have money."

"Maybe you shouldn't spend it all on a house."

"Unless you want me to buy the whole damn state, I'm good."

I return to her neck. The spot under her ear is my favorite, I think. Another fit of giggling. "How good?"

"Five hundred. Maybe six. I haven't checked my account balance in the last year or so."

"There are certainly some nice houses for five hundred grand around here, but I'm afraid you're going to have to downsize on the property."

"Million, cub. Not thousand." I nip her collarbone. "Offing people pays well. Offing people who are hard to kill pays even better."

Nera seems to freeze beneath me. Fuck, I shouldn't have said that. I lift my head and meet her warm amber eyes.

"Do you enjoy doing it?" she whispers.

"Do you enjoy doing laundry?"

Her hand comes to my face, stroking my chin. "They are people. I'm sure some have deserved it, but not all. You must feel something when you end a person's life. They have families. Friends. People who love them, who will be devastated by having them gone."

And here we are. The moment I've been dreading. I could say that it bothers me, or that I think about the people I kill, but it wouldn't be the truth. Friendship. Family. Those are just words for me that bear no meaning, like a foreign language I can hear but cannot comprehend.

"I don't know, cub," I say, then decide to risk it all and be honest.

Even if it means she might not want to have anything to do with me afterward. "And I don't care."

She watches me in silence for a few moments, but, unlike I expected, there's no disgust in her eyes. Just sadness.

"Who did this to you?" she asks, her voice barely audible.

"Made me into an unfeeling killing machine? Just life, Nera. There's no one to blame."

"You might be a killing machine, demon"—a sad smile forms on her lips as she reaches inside her nightstand drawer—"but you are not unfeeling. In fact, I think you feel too much and too strongly, and because of that, you found a way to suppress your emotions."

"I'm afraid you're wrong, cub." Narrowing my eyes, I wonder why she has pulled out the small manicure scissors.

"Am I?" she asks. And then, she plunges the sharp tip of the scissors into the middle of her left palm.

"Jesus fuck!" I leap off the bed, staring at her hand as blood seeps from the wound. Grabbing the closest thing I can get my hands on, I remove the white pillowcase and, as carefully as I can, take her injured hand in mine. "Why did you do that? Fuck! Let go of the damn scissors."

The entire tip is buried askew into her flesh, and, as soon as she pulls it out, the blood begins to gush from the puncture even faster. I press the bundled fabric to her palm and grasp behind her neck, pinning her with my gaze.

"What the fuck, cub?!" I didn't mean to yell at her, but I'm fucking losing it over here. Seeing her hurt has shaken me to the core. I'm flabbergasted; my damn brain doesn't want to accept the possibility of that ever happening.

"You said you don't care about other people getting hurt."

"You are not other people!" I lift the bloodied fabric to take a peek at her palm. There is still some bleeding, but it seems the cut isn't as deep as I feared. "Does it hurt?"

"A little." She cocks her head to the side. "Does it hurt you?"

"As if you plunged a fucking knife in my chest."

"And yet, you said you don't feel anything." She presses her lips to mine.

"No more demonstrations like this one," I say into her mouth. "You hear me?"

"Loud and clear. Now, can you please answer that? It's been ringing for five minutes."

The ringing of my phone somewhere in the apartment finally registers. I get up, then slide my arms under Nera's body and carry her out of the room.

"Are both of us needed to answer your phone?" she asks as she threads her fingers through my hair. I still find it strange, to have someone touching it. But I like it.

"Both of us are needed to deal with the consequences of your insane experiment." I set her on the kitchen counter and open the drawer on the left-hand side. "You moved the first aid kit."

"It's in the cupboard under the sink. I added more supplies to it and needed more room for the box. I wanted to be better prepared since you tend to get into confrontations with people in my neighborhood and come here bearing the most bizarre wounds."

I place the plastic box next to her, then walk around the island to get the damn phone from my suit jacket. The blasted thing is still ringing, and the screen shows Kruger's name.

"What?" I ask and lodge the phone between my shoulder and my ear to keep my hands free.

"I've been calling you for twenty minutes."

"I've noticed. What's the urgency?"

"There's been a change of plan. Where are you?"

"Not your fucking problem. I'll call you in half an hour."

I throw the phone onto the counter and inspect my work. "Is that too tight?"

"It's fine. You seem to have more skill than I do." She drags the tips of her fingers down my bare chest. "I must insist you treat me wearing this exact outfit next time, as well."

"There better not be a next time." I trail my hands along her thighs and up her delicate ribcage, still finding it hard to believe that I finally have her.

"You have to leave?"

"Yes." I take a deep breath. It goes against every instinct I have, but this time, I'll tell her everything. "It's work. I have to head to Mexico."

"You're wounded."

"That doesn't change anything. I still need to go."

"When will you be back?"

"I'm not sure. It shouldn't take longer than a week."

"Please take care." She cups my cheek with her palm. "And, come back to me."

I don't remember if anyone has ever asked me to take care, even when I was a kid. I don't recall much of my early childhood, but I doubt I would have forgotten that. The worry and concern clearly visible in Nera's eyes gut me. Is this how it feels to have someone to call my own? Someone who actually cares if I live or die, beyond the fact that my death would mean the loss of an asset? For the first time in my life, I feel like an actual person and not just a scrap shaped to resemble one.

"Nothing on this earth would stop me from coming back to you, my tiger cub." I slam my mouth to hers. "I promise."

I press the phone to my ear and exit Nera's building. "I'm listening."

"You said you'll call back in half an hour!" Kruger barks. "It's been almost two."

I smirk. "I had more important things to do. What do you want?"

"We're moving the Mexican job to a later date. Another contract just came up, and it must be executed tonight."

"Specifics?"

"Long-range weapon is required. I'm sending you the details. No deviations on this one, Kai."

"Noted. Oh, and one more thing. You need to assign the Mexican job to someone else."

"Why?"

"Because tonight's hit will be my last. I quit."

I cut the line and slide behind the wheel, then open the email from Kruger with the job specifics. Usually, the files include both the headshots from the target's ID documents and the photos Kruger's surveillance team have gathered. Considering this job came up on short notice, there are no surveillance images or the target's daily routines noted within the email. The only information provided is the time window of two hours when the hit is to be made and a short bio with the identification photos.

I skip the target's particulars like name and occupation, which do not interest me whatsoever, and pause on the included headshots. A man in his midfifties—swiped back, light-brown hair, peppered with gray at the temples. He's wearing a suit and tie in each picture and has a serious air about him. Probably a business mogul who managed to step on the wrong toes. Seems more than likely considering the contract amount of three million, with a bonus of half a million if the execution is done with one bullet to the forehead.

I move to the details specifying the location, noting that the target will be giving a speech at an invitation-only event that will be held on private property. Likelihood of infiltration—nonexistent. The closest spot the assassination can be accomplished from is a building fifteen hundred yards north of the property.

No wonder Kruger decided to delay the Mexico mission so he could get me onto this one. Although he has two teams of mostly ex-military personnel at his disposal, they are generally only used in situations requiring blunt force. Eliminating a target with a single bullet from nearly a mile away requires tremendous skill and precision. And nothing beats the experience of someone who has been executing targets with long-range weapons since he was sixteen.

I plug the coordinates from the file into the map app on my phone. The location pings at thirty miles north of Boston. The last time I had a job in this area, I met Nera. The display clock reads nine a.m. That means I have twelve hours to get back to New York, arm up, and reach the mission location.

Taking one last look at Nera's window, I pull onto the street and floor the gas pedal. Even on a Sunday morning, the traffic is heavy, but it doesn't bother me as it typically does. Spending time with my cub has a strange calming effect on me, and sometimes it lasts for days. Things that usually irritate me or make me go ballistic, don't seem to affect me that strongly, as if the world isn't such an awful place anymore. I don't feel like it's just me against the fucking universe. And instead of a dumpster fire, I think that life can actually be something good. But as time passes and the tranquilizing effect her presence has over me dissipates, the reality of my world reverts to its original state—enemy territory. And I don't want to live in that wasteland anymore.

Not once in my life have I thought about changing my vocation. All I know how to do is kill. It's the only thing I've ever been good at. The only future I had. But now, another path has formed in front of me. A path that I never dreamed would be open to me because souls like mine don't get second chances.

Not that I believe myself to be redeemable. No, there's no absolution for my sins. And my general stance about people hasn't changed—I still don't give a fuck if they live or die. But Nera does. And I would do anything if I could become more worthy of her. A good man I will never be, but I could be better. For her.

I'll find a night school or a tutor, something that would allow me to finally learn how to read properly. I'll even rein in my temper and not kill the teacher if they call me a dummy for not being able to read more than basic words. And I'll find some stupid regular job, even though I don't need the money. Normal people have jobs. I don't really have any particular skills other than eliminating targets, so it would have to be something simple. Working with people is out of the question. I'd probably end up strangling my superiors and colleagues before the end of my first day. Maybe a warehouse worker? No, there'll be people around there as well. The only type of people I can work with are the dead kind. Maybe I should work at a funeral home.

Kruger won't take my retirement well and will try to stop me. I'll have to deal with that whole issue once and for all. After twenty years, I've had enough of his shit. It's time to break up this dysfunctional family of ours. Family... fuck. Simply thinking of him as such speaks to just how deeply fucked-up I am. Regardless, if he insists on standing in my way, I'm going to kill him despite all that. I'll kill every person in this world if they dare to come between me and my cub.

After I'm done with this last job, I'll finally reply to Felix Allen. I have no idea how that crackpot geezer got ahold of my phone number, which isn't listed anywhere, but he's been messaging me every couple of months, asking if I want him to help me get Kruger off my ass for good. I've ignored each text so far, but he keeps sending them. I don't need him to save my ass, I can handle that on my own, but I'll ask him to get me a new identity. The name still wouldn't be mine, but the one I've been using nearly my whole life isn't, either. Maybe I could ask Nera to pick one for me. I don't care what it is as long as she likes it. Yes, I'll do that.

One last job.

And then, maybe I'd be able to start a new life. With my cub.

Chapter Twenty-one

Nera

Private property, 30 miles north of Boston

"This reminds me of the parties Mom liked to host." I pass Zara her drink and nod toward the crowd in front of us.

String lights hang from the iron supports that have been set up around the lawn, casting the area in a warm yellow glow from hundreds of swaying, globe-shaped bulbs. An array of intimate tables with white satin tablecloths and big bows tied around each pedestal and similarly adorned chairs are spread all across the grass. White flower arrangements and tiny lantern-shaped replicas of overhead lights make up beautiful centerpieces on every table. Elegantly dressed men and women mill around, enjoying overpriced champagne from thin crystal flutes as a mix of heavy fragrances competes with the fresh evening air.

The entire Family is in attendance at the don's birthday celebration, of course. When Dad called this morning to say that "the party is still a go," I told him I'd be coming as well since I was "feeling much better."

"One of the reasons I don't like these parties is because they remind me of her," Zara whispers.

"Me too." I look down into my glass, watching the ice cubes floating on the surface. "Happy to be done with school?"

"Yup." She just shrugs and takes a sip of her juice.

"Your dress is lovely." I gesture to her tight, floor-length dark-gray gown. It's very pretty with its long sleeves made of lace and high neckline, but a bit too prim and proper for her age. "You look beautiful."

She forces a smile and quickly looks away.

"Zara." I take her hand, compelling her to look at me. "I know you don't believe me, but you are the most beautiful woman at this party."

"Sure." She tries to pull her hand away, but I hold on tightly.

"You are. And I'll keep telling you that until you get it through that thick head of yours. Got it?"

Zara just sighs and nods.

Even when she was a baby, Zara was a pretty child, but now, with her long chestnut hair and pixie face, she's stunning. I tried to explain to her that people look at her because she's beautiful, but she won't hear it.

"Did Dad make you come here tonight?" I ask. I know she hates all Family events and will skip them anytime she can, unless our father doesn't give her a choice.

"Yes. It is his birthday celebration, after all." Spoken so softly that it's barely audible.

"I'll talk to him. He shouldn't force you to come to Family gatherings if you don't want to. I mean, I can understand him wanting you here this evening, even though his actual birthday is next week, but still," I say, even though I know he's not likely to listen to me, since "parading" daughters who will soon be of marrying age is a regular thing in Cosa Nostra.

"So, your stalker is back. I hope he was sorry for making you worry so much. Is everything okay with him?" Zara asks before taking a sip of her drink.

"Yes." I lean closer to her to whisper into her ear. "We slept together last night."

She chokes on her juice.

"I know what you're going to say—I don't know him. But you're wrong." I lift my glass toward the people gathered in front of the stage set up on the other side of the lawn. "Look at them. The crème de la crème of the Family. I've known most of them since we were kids. Many have been coming to our home, having meals at the same table with us. I know what they do, which schools they've gone to, the names of their children and pets, and I know with whom they cheat on their spouses. All that information, all the years I've known them, and I'm not certain if any of them actually like me. Or who might bury a knife in my back if the situation suits their favor. So, what good does knowing all that stuff do me?"

"You don't even know the guy's name, Nera."

"I don't. And I don't need to." I turn to face her. "You heard about Alvino and his men being wiped out?"

"Yes."

"I was there. Alvino had one of his goons grab me and take me to some middle-of-nowhere church."

My sister's face pales.

"My demon came for me. Carried me out in his arms while they were raining bullets on us. That's why I was distraught Friday night. He saved me, but I had no idea if he made it out himself. He took a bullet for me, Zara." I meet her gaze. "I'm in love with him. And after this party, I'm telling Dad that I won't let him marry me off. Ever."

Zara grabs my hand, squeezing it, fear and shock written all over her face. I squeeze hers back and smile.

"I know. You'll understand it one day. You'll find a man who makes your heart beat twice as fast. Who'll make you feel like the world isn't revolving unless he's next to you. It's scary and beautiful at the same time." I press a light kiss on her cheek. "You should head home. I'll talk to Dad and ask him not to drag you to any more of these. And then, I'll tell him I'm choosing someone else over the Family."

I watch my sister as she rushes inside the house, probably to look for a bodyguard to take her home, then turn around and head toward Dania who's standing among a group of our friends near the stage. String lights similar to those dangling over the tables but with smaller bulbs are decorating the tree just behind the platform, making the whole setting resemble a wedding celebration. I guess it is, in a way, considering the announcement my father is going to make. He's made a deal with Efisio, the new leader of the Camorra. And he's going to announce it tonight.

But, I am concerned about how the rest of the Family is going to take the news of us partnering with Camorra, and I tried to convince Dad to keep it on the down-low for now, and, instead, try to pay them off before the annual meeting, but he wouldn't listen.

My father, wearing a broad smile on his face and carrying a flute of champagne in his hand, climbs the steps to the stage. Everyone around starts to clap. Nuncio Veronese has always had a natural charisma that allowed him to persuade people to do things that otherwise would require threats. If anyone can manage to pull this off without everything dissolving into a civil war, it would be my father.

Eagerly awaiting his address, the don's inner circle gathers around the stage. All the capos, that is, except for Batista Leone. He remains standing off to the side, by a table with the drinks. It's rather out of character for him. He usually tries to be as close to my father as possible. The underboss appears to be in a good mood but keeps fidgeting with his glass and throwing looks over the assembled guests.

Someone within the crowd yells out a sleazy joke, and my father laughs, throwing one back. Yes, he still knows how to smile, but his smiles seem to be reserved only for the Family now. He starts his speech by recollecting a funny story from his youth, and people soak it up with wide eyes. I watch him entertain the mob while I play with one end of the red scarf I've tied around my ponytail.

After my demon left this morning, I felt that familiar dejection that comes with each of his departures. But this time, my heart didn't ache so much because I knew he'd be coming back to me, once he's finished doing whatever he needs to do. He promised to return to me, and when he does, we can start anew.

I lift my drink, hiding my smile behind the rim of my glass. Maybe I'll even offer him my hand next time he comes through my door, introduce myself properly. And he will finally tell me his name. But he'll always be my demon.

Kai

The smell of mold invades my nostrils as I step inside the gloomy attic. A startled flock of birds rises into the air, taking off for the hole in the roof. That roof is a disaster, with multiple missing shingles and cave-in on its outer layer, so as the birds frantically make their way out, I'm not surprised to see more debris and pieces of broken tiles rain through the openings. The wood floorboards creak under my soles as I walk toward the busted window, leaving footprints in several years' worth of dust and grime. The entire house is basically a ruin, and the lawn is covered with so many overgrown weeds that it took me ten minutes to find the back door. I crouch beside the window and set my big rectangular case on the rotten floor, causing another cloud of dust to rise into the air around me.

To enhance the precision of the shot when firing a sniper rifle, getting into a stable position on the ground and using the bipod mount for leverage is best. Unfortunately, that's not an option here, so I need to improvise. I flip the left bipod leg down and then brace the rifle's stock against the side of the window frame. Gripping both the leg and the frame with my left hand to support the weapon, I push past the piercing pain in my injured arm and lean into my shooting position.

The shit ton of strung-up bare bulbs over the garden's lawn doesn't provide much illumination, but the tree behind the stage is covered with enough of them to create a perfect backlight that gives me a great view of my target. I focus my aim on the middle of his chest, right beside the champagne glass he's holding. Then, I slowly start raising the scope, letting the crosshairs slide up and halt on the bridge of his nose. I don't hold my breath, keeping my breathing to its normal rhythm. Breathe in. Breathe out. Pause.

In.

My target raises his glass.

Out.

I pull the trigger.

From this distance, it takes the bullet a little over one second to reach its mark.

One second. Less than it takes to draw a breath. A single beat of a heart.

But it's enough to shatter a fragile dream.

Enough to extinguish a tiny ember of hope.

I'm a second too late to notice a blonde woman with a red silk scarf tied to her ponytail standing in the crowd.

The man on the stage jolts, while a line of blood trails out of a red hole in the middle of his forehead. He slumps backward, sprawling on the wooden platform. Some of the people in the crowd drop to the ground the instant they realize what happened, while the rest are scrambling away in hysterics. Several men have pulled out weapons and are rushing for the cover of tables.

As typical with the human species, the urge to save themselves is stronger than the need to help others. I've seen it countless times before and I found it quite interesting to watch. But now, I'm not looking at the people running like a mindless horde. My scope is fixed on the blonde woman climbing onto the stage. What the fuck is my tiger cub doing there? She has lost her red scarf, and her hair falls loose down her back and around her shoulders as she drops to her knees next to my target.

My stomach plummets as I watch her grab the front of the dead man's jacket, frantically shaking him. I adjust the scope to zoom in on her face. Tears slide down her cheeks while she screams, pain and grief etched into her features. I zoom in again, focusing on her mouth, and the rifle nearly slips from my hold. I'm too far away to hear her cries of anguish, but I can still feel them echo through my ears and bounce within my chest, shredding me on the inside. My lungs contract; I'm gasping for air, but there is no air to draw in. I've been sucked into a vacuum, suddenly frozen in a fraction of a second, the moment I've deciphered what she's been saying.

Dad!

Chapter Twenty-Two

Nera

For some reason, I expected it to be raining on the day of my father's funeral. Like it did when we buried Elmo. And Mom. It's strange to be standing at the cemetery, watching the casket being lowered into the ground on such a beautiful sunny day.

Zara is next to me, clutching my hand in hers so hard, I fear she'll break my fingers. She and our father never had a good relationship, but his death shook her more than I could have anticipated. Thank God I sent her home before everything went down that night.

As I lift my eyes off the casket, my gaze falls on the man in a prison uniform standing across from me on the other side of the grave. Two guards flank him, even though his hands are cuffed in front. I haven't seen our stepbrother in over a decade, and if I passed him on the street, I'm not certain I would have recognized him.

The Massimo I remember had wavy dark hair that brushed his nape, with a few untamed stands that would always manage to fall over his cleanly shaven face. He was tall and athletic, but not overly muscular. Mom once told me that the girls who hung around him often joked that he should leave Cosa Nostra and become a model, gracing billboards and the covers of fashion magazines.

The man who returns my stare has nothing in common with the young man I remember. His outfit has short sleeves, revealing a multitude of dark tattoos covering his arms, hands, and even his fingers. The first two buttons on his shirt are undone, and I can see that, in addition to his neck, his chest is inked, as well. His hair is completely shaven off, but stubble covers the lower part of his jaw. And, since I last saw him, he nearly doubled his body weight—all pure muscle. If it wasn't for his eyes—black and calculating, just as I remember—I'd think they brought the wrong inmate.

I didn't expect him to be here today. When Mom died, he wasn't allowed to attend her funeral, so I assumed he wouldn't be coming to Dad's, either. Strange, how I always think of Laura as our "Mom," never a stepmother. But I don't have that many memories of Massimo, and he's always remained a "stepbrother" to me.

When the cemetery caretakers start pouring the soil over the casket, Massimo approaches, keeping his eyes firmly locked on me. His guards closely follow in his wake.

"Munchkin," he says as he stops in front of me. Even his voice is different—deeper, gruff.

I bite my lower lip, unsure if I want to hug him or take a step back. The last time I saw him, I was five, and even back then he seemed formidable and somehow distant. It's been so long, I'm not certain if I know who he is anymore. He cocks his head to the side, and a corner of his lips tilts upward, just like it did when he would catch me sneaking into the kitchen when I was a kid. It's one of the few clear memories I have of him.

I swallow hard, trying to keep my composure, then take a step and wrap my arms around him. "Hello, Massimo."

"Let's go, Spada," one of the security guards barks, tugging on Massimo's arm.

Our stepbrother takes a backward step, out of my arms. "We need to talk."

I nod. "We'll come tomorrow."

"Just you, Nera," Massimo says, then his gaze moves over to Zara.

My sister has been standing motionless this entire time, her eyes glued to the ground, avoiding looking at our stepbrother. She must be unsettled seeing Massimo for the first time. Zara was not even four when he was sent to prison, so she probably feels as if she's meeting a stranger.

Massimo lifts his handcuffed hands and lightly brushes Zara's cheek with the back of his fingers.

"Hello, Zahara." His voice is strange as he says it. Softer. Almost like it was before.

My sister just keeps staring at the ground, her body stiff. Her knuckles look nearly white as she grips the hem of her blouse. Massimo's hands fall from Zara's face, and then he walks away with the security guards trailing after him.

"Zahara?" I lift an eyebrow.

No one calls my sister by her full name. When she was little, she couldn't pronounce it, so she kept referring to herself as Zara, and it kind of stuck. I doubt anyone in the Family even remembers her actual name.

She takes a deep breath and lifts her head, her gaze slicing directly to the large figure in an inmate's uniform getting into the prison transport van.

"What's going on?" As far as I know, she didn't have any contact with Massimo for nearly fifteen years, but both of their actions say otherwise.

"Nothing," she chokes out and quickly strides in the opposite direction.

As I follow behind my sister, faint tingles run down my spine. I stop, my eyes search the crowd of mourners heading toward the parking lot, but I don't see my demon among them. He did mention that he'll be back in about a week, but it's been only four days since he left. Taking a look around one more time, I hurry after Zara. I've probably just imagined that I felt him. God knows I wish he was here with me.

I grip the balcony railing and stare at the glow of the city before me. Zara has been staying with me ever since our father was killed. She's taken over my bedroom while I've been sleeping on the couch in the living room. As soon as we returned from attending the burial, she shut herself inside. I can't figure out if it was the funeral that shook her or if it was seeing Massimo.

Coming face-to-face with my stepbrother after so many years certainly shook me. I also can't help but wonder what he'd like to talk to me about, especially after he refused to have us visit him all this time, and now has made it clear that he wants to have this discussion with me alone. However, when I called the correctional facility to arrange the visit for tomorrow, I was informed that Massimo started a fight when he got back today and has been placed in solitary confinement for a week, which will be followed by a two-month ban on visitors.

The gusting wind blows a curtain into me, and as the smooth material touches my arm, that subtle tingling sensation spreads across my skin, entrenching itself into each of my pores. Just as it does when my demon is watching me. I sigh and rub my palms over my arms. Even though I know he's far away at this moment, doing God knows what in Mexico, I still glance down to the street below, hoping I'll see him lurking in the shadows.

But there's no one there.

Kai

I stare at the balcony across the street, eyes glued on my tiger cub as the wind blows into her beautiful but grief-stricken face. The black hole that has formed within my chest is sucking me in, as if trying to swallow me whole into its oblivion, drowning me in despair and helplessness. Nothing I can do now to turn back time, to undo what I have already done. No way to atone for my darkest sin. There is no forgiveness for my deed.

The stabbing ache at my temples has gotten worse, most likely from the lack of sleep. Other than a few hours I caught last night, right here on this roof, I haven't slept in days. I reach for the bottle of water at my feet to take a big drag, then put it back next to the empty fast-food container. Sustenance was the last thing on my mind, but I could feel my body shutting down, so I bought the first takeout I found. I don't even know what the hell I ate.

Ignoring everything I'm feeling, I keep my vigil. My cub leans away from the railing and heads inside, shutting the balcony door behind her. Through the still-open curtains, I watch as she prepares for sleep. She disappears for ten minutes, but returns wearing her pajamas and lies down on the couch in her made-up bed.

For a few minutes, she remains bathed in the light of a floor lamp before she turns it off. Darkness descends and veils my view of Nera's place. And I keep watching, even though I can't see her anymore.

Chapter Twenty-Three

Nera

Two months later

"I still haven't decided who it's going to be, but you'll be informed well in advance," Batista Leone says from his big office chair.

"I will be informed?" I stare at him, flabbergasted. It's been only two months since we buried my father. And barely a month since Leone took over the position of don.

"Yes. You'll have sufficient time to pick out a dress and have your wishes regarding the decorations adhered to."

"You're not marrying me off to anyone, Batista."

"It's Don Leone for you." He slams his palm on the desk, his eyes bulging under his thick white eyebrows. "Forget your old privileges, girl. You're nothing more than an asset now. An asset I plan to use well."

My whole body tenses. No one would have dared to talk to me like this before, not even him while he was an underboss. But he's the don now, and the truth is, he can do whatever the hell he wants. If I say no, he'll just proclaim me a traitor to the Family and order someone to make me disappear. Bile collects in my throat. I feel sick.

"I'm considering someone from the Albanian organization," he adds. "Or maybe Salvo."

I raise an eyebrow. Salvo was never a fan of Leone, and he never tried to hide it. I was rather surprised when I heard Leone appointed Salvo to be his second-in-command, but now things are starting to make more sense. Keep your friends close, and your enemies closer. Leone is going to try to win Salvo over by giving the new underboss my hand in marriage.

"Is that all?" I ask through my teeth.

"Yes." He reaches for the newspaper on his desk. "You're dismissed."

The chair makes a screeching sound on the floor as I spring up. Both fury and despair are raging within me as I walk toward the door. I've almost reached it when Leone's voice stops me.

"I think you've forgotten something, Nera."

I shut my eyes for a moment to pull myself together, then turn to face him. Approaching his desk on rubber legs, I lean over and peck the ring on his outstretched hand. "Have a nice day"—I swallow—"Don Leone."

His lips widen into an egotistical smile, and then he's back to reading his newspaper.

Only once I get inside my car do I allow myself to fall apart. I lean my forehead onto the steering wheel and let out a sob—a mix of grief, helplessness, and worry. Grief over my father not being here anymore. Helplessness because I have no idea what I'm going to do. But worry is all about *him*, my demon. It's born of fear that something has happened to him, because it's been two months, and I haven't heard from him at all.

Anguished, I'm spiraling into a dark abyss at the possibility that he won't be back as promised. But he has never broken his word before, so I have to believe that if he said he'll return, that day will come, and he'll be there—no matter what. Every night for the past ten weeks, I've been waiting for him on my roof, standing in the cool darkness till the sun rose on the horizon, but he's never shown. Chilled to the bone, I've even thought I felt the familiar prickles on my skin. They've always told me when he's near.

I've been so worried, I've made myself sick, and that goosebumps-raising sensation is always there. Like yesterday, when I ran out to the grocery store to get myself more crackers. Saltines seem to be the only thing I can keep down lately as I stress about my demon night and day. Two days ago, I felt it too, as I went to the fabric store with Zara. And on Saturday, taking my car to get washed, I waited in the line up and felt the tingles all over my flesh. I think I'm going mad.

I look up and squeeze the steering wheel with all my might. Maybe he'll return today. He'll come to me this evening. If I believe with all my heart, it may just happen. He'll show up and he'll, somehow, make everything okay.

Yes.

I brush away my tears and start the engine.

"Where are you going?" Zara asks as she leaves the bathroom and sees me putting on my jacket.

"To the roof. I need some fresh air."

"It's almost midnight."

"I know." I grab the knob. "I'll be back soon."

Up top, I take a seat on the makeshift bench and just stare into the night. That prickling feeling at the back of my neck is driving me crazy. It never abates. Never ceases.

The moon is full, just like on the night my demon and I met, but tonight, its silver brightness is shrouded by clouds. It's probably going to rain. And hard. I can already feel that shift in the air. The storm is about to unleash.

My eyes wander over the buildings beyond the narrow road before me, noticing the few random windows that are still lit. I glance to the rooftop across the way as the wind picks up, making me hold my jacket around me a little tighter. The bleak darkness is all I see. Minutes pass. The wind continues to blow. I rise off the bench, ready to head back inside, when the moonlight briefly parts the clouds, illuminating that dark horizon on the other side of the street and a figure leaning over the railing.

I narrow my eyes. It's . . . him.

My stomach drops.

What is he doing there? Why hasn't he come to me? Maybe it's not him but someone else? No. Even in this low light, I would recognize him anywhere.

Confused, I take a step closer. The figure quickly retreats, disappearing from my view. I wait. It can't be my demon. He promised he would come to me as soon as he returned. He knew I would be waiting.

Hurt pierces my chest, and it almost feels like a tangible pain. It was him.

All those instances when I *thought* I felt him, but disregarded the sensation as my desperate hopes . . . Was he actually there all those times? It's been weeks! I've been falling apart, terrified something had happened. I've been so fucking scared for him that it made me physically ill. And all the while, he's been following me around in secret. Not even letting me know he's okay. After everything we've been for each other.

I was ready to leave my family just so I could be with him. My hand flies to my mouth, stifling a sob. He was at my father's funeral! And still, he stayed away, not bothering to ask me how I was doing. I thought... I thought he loved me. But, you don't let your loved ones hurt alone, without offering comfort. Was it all a game for him? Was I? A silly girl persuaded to fall in love, only to be dumped in her most desperate hour? He left me when I needed him the most.

Lies.

It has all been lies and nothing more.

"Why?" I scream into the night.

The answer to my question is sudden, relentless rain. The heavens open, raindrops pelting my face and mixing with the tears streaming down my cheeks.

"Fuck you!" I cry. "Crawl back into your darkness, and stay there!" I yell so loud that my throat hurts and the last word ends up being a gut-wrenching whimper.

Turning around, I head toward the door back into the building, feeling as if I'm crumbling on the inside.

I'm not coming here ever again.

---- Kai ----

Idiot!

I bang the back of my head on the wall behind me. The concrete rooftop is awash from the heavy downpour, leaving me slumped and soaked as my butt stays put and I sit alone in my misery. Propping my elbows on my upraised knees, I grip my head and shut my eyes, trying to erase the image of my cub staring at me with shock written across her face. Shock, disappointment, and so much damn hurt.

I bang my head against the wall again. And again.

Reckless idiot. Two months ago, I made a deal with myself. I'll keep watch over her from afar, but I'll never, fucking ever, allow her to see me. I knew she'd feel hurt when I didn't come back. Knew she would probably never forgive me for breaking the promise I made her. She'd likely forget about me after some time. She might even think I had died.

I could live with all that.

But I can't live with the look of betrayal and utter pain on her face when she noticed me on this stupid-ass roof. Or her anguished shout into the darkness that I keep hearing in my head on constant repeat.

Why?

The need to rush to her, to drop to my knees and beg her forgiveness, is eating me alive. But how can I ask her to forgive me? Forgive the most horrible thing I've ever done? Just confessing my actions would bring her more heartache. All because of a man she let into her home. A man she allowed to touch her, kiss her, and make love to her. A man who assassinated her father without a thought. If she knew, she would hurt so, so much more than she's hurting now. Because now, now I'm just the man who left her.

And that man now needs to leave, for good.

My chest feels like it's being crushed, squeezed as if a great weight is bearing on it. I tilt my head up, staring at the nearly obscured full moon while massive drops of rain bounce off my face. That treacherous glowing orb, its power over the dark deceived me into believing the starlight could be mine after all. And for a fleeting moment, I held that radiance in the palm of my hand. Held *her*, and knew peace.

The pressure in my chest intensifies, and it feels like everything inside of me starts breaking. I take a deep breath and let out a beastly roar, hoping the night will swallow the torment tearing me apart.

It doesn't go away.

I bang my head on the wall one more time, then take out my phone, blindly punching the number. Kruger answers after a single ring.

"Send me the details for the Mexican job," I manage to croak out.

Twenty-two hours later

The small private jet lands on the narrow runway with barely a bump as the wheels touch the paved ground. I, however, feel that thump as if it's a fucking earthquake, rattling my entire being. More than three thousand miles separate me and my tiger cub now.

Good.

I rise from my seat and grab the bag with my equipment from the custom-modified luggage compartment. The long case with my sniper rifle is lying across the seat in front of mine.

"When do you want me to come get you?" the pilot asks over his shoulder.

"Ten days. Same time." I open the cabin door and unlatch the airstairs, letting them expand. "Where's the vehicle?"

"Up ahead and to the left of the runway, hidden in the bushes." He points through the cockpit windshield. "The key is in the ignition."

I nod and descend the steps.

The air is thick and heavy, humidity clinging to my skin as I head in the direction indicated to me. Aside from the light marking the runway, there's no other illumination. Not surprising, considering we're in the middle of bumfuck nowhere, at a seaside airstrip barely larger than a football field. I don't even bother checking the surroundings, don't bother with the recon before approaching a vehicle in a hostile territory. My gun stays secured inside the holster. It makes me a sitting duck to any potential threat, but I don't really give a shit.

I don't fucking care about anything anymore. I've lost my tiger cub. Everything else is meaningless—my life included.

The beat-up truck is right where the pilot said it would be. As I open the back door on the driver's side, the cab light remains off. I'm about to place my gear inside when I feel a sharp sting on my nape. The years of training finally kick in. Swinging around, I rip out the dart lodged in my neck.

My hand reaches for the gun, but my fingers seem to have lost the ability to grasp the weapon. It slips from my hand and falls to the ground with a thud. I try to blink out the haziness that overcomes my vision. It doesn't help. I stumble, my back hitting the side of the truck. Blurry shapes of a dozen or so men approach, their flashlights blinding me when they draw near.

"Well, what do we have here?" a heavily accented voice says. "That motherfucker wasn't lying after all."

The face of a man materializes in front of me. Even with befogged vision, I still recognize him from the mission documents Kruger sent me yesterday. Alfonso Mendoza. The leader of a Mexican cartel. My target.

"You must have really pissed Kruger off," he laughs. "He requested we teach you a lesson, then send you back once you remember how to bark on command." He leans in close. "But, I think we're gonna keep you instead."

The Mexican swipes the shotgun off his shoulder, and the cold metal of the barrel connects with my temple.

Chapter Twenty-four

Nera

THE DOOR ON THE OPPOSITE WALL OPENS WITH A SCREECH, breaking the silence in this bleak room, and Massimo steps inside. I still find it hard to process that this scary-looking man in a prison uniform is actually my stepbrother. When I thought about him over the years, wondering how he's doing here, I've always imagined him in a suit, for some reason.

The chains around his ankles rattle as he walks toward the chair on the other side of the table. The guard who brought him in lifts Massimo's wrists and connects the handcuffs to the iron loop affixed to the tabletop. Massimo glances up, his eyes zeroing in on the camera mounted in the corner. The guard nods and leaves the room. The red light indicating that the camera is live turns off a minute later.

"Nera." Massimo leans forward and places his elbows on the metal surface, the action making the muscles of his inked arms bulge.

"You said we needed to talk." I meet his gaze.

"I hoped it would have happened sooner, but something came up, messing up my plan, unfortunately."

Yeah. From what I gathered as the guards escorted me here,

Massimo almost strangled some guy when he got back from my father's funeral.

"But you're here now, and I need you to bring me up to speed," he adds.

"Leone took over."

"I know. Who voted for him?"

"I don't know. It's not like I'm invited to the Family meetings."

"Ask Salvo."

I arch my brow. "As if he's going to tell me something like that."

"He will."

"Why don't you ask him yourself? He can come see you and tell you whatever you want to know."

"I want Salvo exactly where he is now—as an underboss, with no obvious ties to me."

"How do you know that Leone promoted him?" I ask.

"I have my sources. Has Leone made any moves regarding the Camorra situation?"

"As far as I know, no. My guess is, he'll try to pay them off."

"Pay them off?" he tenses, and something dangerous flashes in his eyes. "For what?"

"The investment they've made into our casinos earlier this year."

Massimo's jaw clenches. "Who the fuck allowed them an in into our business without consulting me?"

So, it is as I suspected. My stepbrother has been involved in Family's dealings all along.

"My father," I say. "But Leone was the one who came up with the idea. Their plan was to pay Camorra off before the annual meeting, so the Family wouldn't find out. That all kind of went off the rails at the start of summer, but Dad made a new deal with Efisio after Alvino's death. He was going to announce the partnership they struck at the party, but then he was killed before he had the chance."

"Mm-hmm. And who knew that Nuncio was going to make that announcement?"

"He told me. And I assume Leone knew, as well."

"And you're absolutely sure that Leone was behind the idea to involve Camorra in the first place?"

"Dad told me so."

Massimo leans back in his chair and starts tapping his handcuffs on the metal table, the slow beat reverberating through the room. "I need you to describe the party to me. Who was there, and everything that happened during it, from the moment you arrived to the moment that shot was fired."

I take a deep breath and start talking, telling him everything I remember of that night. It's not much. I was still euphoric from what happened the night before and wasn't paying much attention to anything. But I tell him everything I can recall. Massimo listens without interrupting, his face getting darker with each word.

"And Leone wasn't on the stage with Nuncio?" he asks after I'm done.

"No. He was standing to the side, by the drinks table."

Silence falls between us, the metal on metal tapping the only sound in the room.

"Leone wants to marry me off. He still hasn't decided whether it'll be someone from the Albanian organization or Salvo."

"Good. I'll make sure he picks Salvo."

"I'm not marrying him, Massimo. Or anyone else." I lift my eyes from his hands and meet his gaze. "I'm pregnant."

His eyes widen. "Who's the father?"

"It doesn't matter."

Massimo lunges forward so suddenly that I flinch back in my chair. "Some bastard got my sister pregnant, and it doesn't matter?" he roars, pulling on the chains.

"No. He's not from the Family."

"Is he going to marry you?"

"No. He's . . ." *What the fuck is he?* I wonder. "He's gone."

Massimo stares at me, his nostrils flaring, then slowly lowers himself back onto the chair. "Get rid of it."

"I'm not 'getting rid' of my child!"

"No man from the Family will marry a woman who's pregnant with someone else's kid, Nera. Especially if that woman is the daughter of a don. If it's a boy, should he ever covet the leadership position, as your son, he'll have the backing to take the reins. He'll forever be considered a threat by those desperate to hang on to their power."

"Don's position is not hereditary."

"Nope, but you know very well that just being a familial relation to the previous don is enough to get the necessary support."

"I will leave."

"There is no leaving Cosa Nostra, Nera. You know that, too."

"I can try."

"And you'll end up dead before your child ever has the chance to be born. Leone will have you killed. Just like he killed your father."

"What?"

"Seriously? You haven't connected the dots already?" Massimo leans over the table, his eyes piercing mine. "Leone never would have allowed things to come to a point of 'paying off' Camorra. He orchestrated the whole deal just so he could later 'reveal' it to the Family, present your father as a traitor, and take his place. He probably convinced Nuncio not to tell me anything about it for that sole reason. And he won't hesitate to dispose of you if it meets his needs."

"Oh God." I stare at him.

"Are you serious about keeping the baby?"

"Yes."

"And how far are you willing to go to keep your child safe?"

"To the depths of hell, if need be."

"Good. Because that's exactly where you're headed," he says. "Now, listen up, and do exactly as I tell you."

My stomach volleys between somersaults and steep drops as I listen to my stepbrother's plan, and by the time he's finished, I feel like throwing up. He wasn't kidding when he said I'd be headed to the depths of hell.

"For how long?" I choke out.

"Until I'm out."

"That's almost four years, Massimo! I can't do it."

"That's the price of your freedom and the safety for your child." A smirk pulls at his mouth.

As I watch the calculating glint in his eyes, a realization settles. "You weren't just pulling some strings from here, were you? You've been the one dealing with the Family affairs all these years."

"Nuncio was a good man, but he didn't have the bloodthirsty edge to make the necessary decisions." The smirk on his face widens into a smile so terrifying that I involuntarily lean back. "I've been running Boston Cosa Nostra since I was nineteen, sis."

I shudder. "There must be some other way."

"There isn't." He cocks his head to the side, his piercing gaze holding mine. "It's a fair trade. Four years of your life in exchange for freedom. For you and your kid."

A *trade*. Just hearing the term makes me want to cry. Looks like my demon was right on that account—nothing is ever free.

"Swear it," I insist in a raspy whisper.

"I swear on my honor."

I nod. "I'll do it."

Slowly, I rise from the chair, trying to process everything. I'm at the door when Massimo's voice reaches me, pulling me up short.

"What happened to Zahara?"

"Nothing 'happened' to her. She has vitiligo. It's just a skin condition. If you would have let us visit, you would have known."

"I was counting on my sentence being reduced, but each of my applications for parole got rejected. And I'll bet Leone was somehow behind that, too." He lifts his hands in front of him, straining the chains. "I didn't want either of you to see me . . . like this. Believe it or not, I care for you, Nera. You're my family. I would have never forbidden Nuncio to marry you off when you turned eighteen if I didn't give a shit."

My eyes drift down his huge body sprawled on the chair, then up, over his tattooed hands and arms, halting on his face. "Or maybe you just wanted the chance to arrange a marriage that would further your plans."

His lips widen into a devious smirk. "That, too."

"Well, prison might have changed you on the outside, but inside, you're still the same cunning guy I remember."

"Never presume you know a person unless you've lived their life, Nera."

"Yeah"—I grab the doorknob—"I've realized that exact thing recently."

Chapter Twenty-five

Nera

"Enter."

I close my eyes just for a moment as I reach for the handle. While driving, my body shook so much, I was afraid I'd lose control and crash into something, but once I parked in front of the Italianate-style sandstone building, an unusual calmness came over me. It was similar to the tranquility right after a storm on the ocean, when the air still feels charged with electricity but the water turns to liquid glass. That's how I feel now. On the outside, I'm a serene iceberg floating on a calm surface, while underneath, a damned current is pulling me apart. But, I'm ready to do whatever it takes to ensure my child's safety.

I push open the door and step inside Don Leone's office.

"I was rather surprised when I got the call from the gate," Batista Leone says without lifting his eyes from the leather ledger in front of him. "I've decided to marry you off to Salvo."

My black heels click against the ornate wooden floor as I approach his desk and take a seat on a visitor chair set before it. I place my purse on my lap, take out the first of several folded papers, and leaning forward, drop it over the ledger he's been perusing.

"You should be asking, what can *I* do for *you.*" I smile, then add, "Batista."

Leone's head snaps up upon hearing me utter his first name. "How dare you!" he barks.

"Look at the document before you say something you'll regret."

He grabs the printout of the investment contract that he and my father signed with Camorra and starts reading, his face turning redder by the second.

"I wonder, what would the Family say if they saw that." I reach into my purse again, taking out the next set of papers. "Or perhaps they'd be more interested in the shell company that you set up, that also—so conveniently—was hired to complete all of the renovations in our casinos. And charged triple the rates for the actual, finished job. Stealing from the Family, Batista?"

Leone rips the investigator's report that exposes him as the owner of said company out of my hands, and the color on his face fades rapidly.

"And how about this?" I pull out a stack of photos. One has him kissing a woman half his age. Another is black and white and somewhat grainy, but it clearly shows him banging the same woman from behind, inside a hotel room.

"Fucking the wife of our biggest investor? Tsk tsk tsk... I don't think Adriano would take the news well."

Leone's face is now a sickly shade of yellow.

I have no idea how Massimo managed to obtain all this stuff, and I don't really care. The moment Salvo brought the documents to me, I came straight here.

"But those are all small things, yes? I'm sure the Family will let them slide." I offer him a condescending smile. He knows very well that the moment these come to light, he'll be a dead man. "So, how about this? Arranging a hit on the Cosa Nostra Don so you can take over."

What little color was left on his face, disappears, leaving him as pale as a corpse. There is no greater offense in Cosa Nostra than killing the don for the sole purpose of taking his position. The hierarchy structure has been established to ensure stability, security, and prosperity for the members. If it was common practice for subordinates to kill their higher-ups, it would cause chaos. And chaos would never be allowed to take root in Cosa Nostra.

He keeps his eyes on mine as he reaches inside the desk drawer. My guess, he's going for a gun.

"Do you really think that I would have come here alone and shown you all of this without some kind of insurance?" I cross my legs and lean back in the chair. "If something happens to me, copies of these documents will be sent not only to the capos, but to every single member of the Family, too—from our biggest investors to the lowest soldiers. They'll tear you apart and make an example of you within hours."

"What do you want?" he barks. "You don't want to marry Salvo? Fine. I don't give a fuck."

"Oh, I do want to get married, Batista. But not to your underboss." I smile. "I'll be marrying you."

"What?" he snaps, half rising from his chair.

"Believe me, I find the idea of being tied to a disgusting old pig like you sickening. But that's what's going to happen." I pause for a moment, then continue. "On Sunday, you're going to announce our engagement. The wedding will be set for the end of this month."

"Why?"

"Because, being your wife will mean I can ensure the Family's best interests are protected." I cross my arms over my chest and pin him with my gaze. "You'll still be Don, as far as most people are concerned, and they can continue to bow to you and kiss your hand. You'll be allowed to go around peacocking as if you have all the power and respect. But that's all you're going to do.

"Starting today, I'll be making all decisions regarding the Family dealings, businesses, and private matters. To everyone, it will appear as if you're still in charge. And, in four years, when my stepbrother gets released from prison, you're going to resign due to medical reasons, and give your full support to Massimo as the next don."

"You're crazy."

"No, Batista. I'm not crazy. I'm determined, and if you have an ounce of wit in that traitorous mind of yours, you'd understand that a determined woman is much more dangerous than a crazy one." I pull out the last piece of paper from my purse and throw it in front of him. "The list of my preferences for the wedding reception. Make sure they're followed. And please, do make sure you wear a tie that doesn't have the stains from your last three meals on it for our special day."

I can feel his eyes drilling into my back as I walk away. When I reach the door, I stop and look over my shoulder. "Oh, and one more thing. When my child is born, you're going to claim the baby as yours. And God help you should you ever slip up and tell a soul that it's not true."

The door shuts behind me with a soft click.

When I'm back in my car, heading to my place, I scan the shadows of every alley I drive past. Looking. Searching. Hoping.

I'm still hopeful that, any second, my demon will materialize out of the dark. But I know he won't. There are no more little pricklings at the back of my neck. No more awareness of eyes that follow my movements. Nothing.

I never wanted him gone. I didn't mean those hateful words I yelled at him from my roof that night. He should have known. After everything that happened between us, he should have known that I couldn't live without him.

And still, he left me.

Kai

"We should try starving him first."

I pull on the chain attached to the shackles that bind my wrists and stare down Mendoza's man as he wipes away the blood from his broken nose. He's just a few steps in front of me, but I can't reach to finish him off. The other end of the chain is bolted to the floor, allowing me a range of only about twenty feet.

The guy pulls out a knife and takes a step forward. The dozen or so men standing in a wide semicircle around us start cheering. I'm not sure what Mendoza has in store for me in the long run, but for the moment, it seems I'm here to provide entertainment for his soldiers. Before he dumped me at this compound, he told his men they were free to do whatever they wanted with me, as long as they keep me alive.

In the first two weeks after I was captured, I killed three of his goons who tried a sneak attack on me and wounded several others. Now, there are bets being placed on who'll be the first to overpower me.

My opponent takes another step closer and swipes his knife at me. I dodge and manage to deliver a kick to his knee, sending him sprawling on his ass to the dirt. A few of the spectators rush toward us, trying to help their comrade, no doubt. But they are too late. Before the fastest of the bunch got to me and kicked me in the stomach, I'd already buried the knife between my opponent's shoulder blades.

A boot connects with my forehead, snapping my head to the side. The next kick catches my ribs. I focus my gaze on the sky as more hits land all over my body, welcoming the pain. Hoping it'll be strong enough to overcome the ache in my heart.

It's not.

Chapter Twenty-six

Nera

Two months later

PRINTOUTS, FOLDERS, AND NOTEPADS ARE SPREAD IN front of me all over the oak wood surface of Batista's oversized office desk. Well, I guess it's mine now. Along with the problems my dear husband caused while he was in charge for a handful of weeks. Venue leases that he didn't get renewed. Contracts that needed to be reviewed and signed, and are now way past overdue. And a horde of angry investors breathing down my neck, demanding revenue projections for the next year. A whole mess that Batista was ever so eager to dump on me so he could spend most of his time in one of the Family's strip clubs.

The smell of old furniture and the stink of cigarettes infused into the upholstery and drapes is absolutely nauseating. It's been a little over a month since we got married and I moved into his house. With all the outstanding work that's been thrown at me, I didn't have the time to remodel this room, but that's something I'll need to rectify soon.

A hard knock sounds on the library door.

"Come in," I mumble as my eyes keep gliding over the credit statements our bank has sent.

Salvo steps inside and takes a seat in the chair on the other side of the desk. "We have a problem."

"More investors have called to say they're not happy with how the Family finances are being handled?" I sigh. "I don't think I can deal with them today."

"We found a mole, Nera."

My head snaps up. "Someone has been talking to the authorities?"

"Worse. It looks like one of our security guys is on Salvatore Ajello's payroll."

I lower the documents. The issues with our credit lines suddenly seem like a minor inconvenience. "Are you sure?"

"Yes. One of my men has been working him since this morning. He started singing an hour ago."

"Okay. I'll visit Massimo and see how he wants us to handle it."

"There's only one way to handle this situation, and Massimo will tell you the same thing. We can't wait till tomorrow anyway. Someone told Brio we caught a traitor, and he just arrived at the facility where we're holding the guy. I assume some of the capos, if not all, are on their way there already, too. They'll want to personally see this issue be resolved."

My breath hitches. The punishment to those who betray the Family is death.

"I'll go wake Batista," I say. "And tell him he needs to go take care of it."

Salvo holds my gaze and, even though he's trying not to show it, I can see the concern in his eyes. As well as the pity. "It has to be you, Nera."

I rear back so suddenly that my office chair rolls a full foot across the floor. "Batista is the don. Since he loves parading around so much and having people kiss his hand, not to mention his ass because of his boasting about how he fixed the clusterfuck my dad created with Camorra, he should be the one offing people."

"The rest of the Family may not know that you're the one actually holding the reins, but the capos do. You were successful in paying off part of Camorra's investment in our casinos, but that fact will only keep them at bay for a short while. The capos need to be convinced that you are capable of doing what is needed for the sake of the Family."

"I'm not killing anybody, Salvo."

He places his elbows on the desk, leaning forward.

"There have been hushed comments among the capos. Brio has brought up the possibility of opening a discussion regarding the change in leadership at the next meeting. If they deem Batista unsuitable for the role and decide to vote him out, you'll end up as collateral damage." His eyes trace over my chest and stop on my stomach. "Everyone believes he's the father of your baby."

My hands immediately fly to cover the already rather telling bump, as if merely cradling it can protect my child from the things Salvo is insinuating. I thought Batista claiming parentage would protect my child, but that can only work if he's the don. If Batista gets thrown off his throne, Massimo won't be able to take over. I will never get my freedom, and, no matter the gender, my child will face the fate I'm trying to prevent. If it's a boy, sooner or later, someone may try to kill him. If it's a girl, she'll end up being married off to who knows who. And I wouldn't be able to do anything to prevent either one.

Horror roils in my stomach, its toxicity overtaking my whole body. How can I bring myself to end a man's life? Kill someone who didn't do anything to me specifically? I grab the armrest and squeeze it so tightly that my knuckles go white. That man might not have done anything to me directly, but he is a threat to my baby. Taking a deep breath, I pick up my purse and head across the room. "Let's go."

"Where?"

"To wherever you are keeping Ajello's spy," I whisper.

I will do *anything* to ensure that my child is safe. If it means selling my soul to the devil by killing a man, so be it.

Chapter Twenty-Seven

Nera

Three years later

High-security prison outside of Boston

EVEN AFTER THREE YEARS OF WEEKLY VISITS, THE RATTLE of chains inside this silent room as Massimo takes a seat across from me at the metal table still wraps around my spine like cold dread. As always, the guard secures the shackles to the metal loop and leaves. A few moments later, the camera in the corner of the room turns off.

"I told you, Nera," my stepbrother says through his teeth, "one visit per week only, or someone may suspect there is more to this than just a warm family reunion."

"I know."

"So what the fuck are you doing here today?" he roars.

Before, Massimo's outbursts made me shake like a leaf. I would sit in this chair and endure his rage, too afraid to talk back to him. Not anymore. After everything he made me do, not to mention all the things I've done without his orders since we started this charade, his yelling has absolutely no effect on me.

Following my first kill, there were two more of Ajello's infiltrators that required my personal "attention." Each time, I pressed a gun to a man's head and pulled the trigger without even the slightest shaking of my fingers. I've also condemned several of our men to death by sending them to New York to spy on that bastard. He discovered each one. I got them back—in pieces—by special courier delivery.

There were more. An employee in one of the casinos who was caught stealing. A bookkeeper who forged the accounts and skimmed off the top. They may not have died by my hand, but I was the one who gave the orders. It was their lives or the safety of my little girl. Not a choice at all, in my eyes. Keeping my child safe trumps everything else in this godforsaken world.

"I'm certainly not here because I had an urge to see your face, Massimo." I cross my arms under my chest. "Batista's health is getting worse."

My stepbrother's expression transforms from rage to concern. "What is it?"

"He had a brain aneurysm. It was a minor one. He's being sent home in a couple of days and is being placed on special meds to hopefully prevent another, but the doctor can't assure us that it won't happen again, or tell us how serious it may be if it does." I grit my teeth. "You need to get out and take over before he dies."

"Do you think I fucking like it here? Do you think I would let myself rot in this dump if there was any way to get out sooner? I have eight more months till release. Let's hope he lives long enough."

"And if he doesn't?"

"If he doesn't, we're both fucked, sis."

Kai

Alfonso Mendoza's compound, Mexico

The sound of an explosion penetrates my hazy consciousness. I crack my lids open, but I can't see anything other than darkness. The ground under me shudders as several more detonations go off somewhere close by, then, a cacophony of yells and screams add to the overall mayhem. Everything in me wants my eyes to stay open, but they keep shutting as if my lashes are weighed down with lead.

Automatic gunfire. Coming closer. More screams, shouts. I'm guessing one of Mendoza's rivals is attacking the compound. Whoever it is, or whatever else may be going on, I don't particularly care. My mind wants to return to the dream I was having before the noise chased it away.

A stand, laden with vegetables, and a beautiful woman lifting various greens for me to smell.

It seemed so real that I could almost inhale the pungent scent of dirt, but for some reason, I couldn't recall her name.

I know her.

I know her very well.

My heart beats faster each time I see her. She's always in my dreams. But lately—the past few days, or maybe it has been weeks—her name escapes me. Every time, it's at the tip of my tongue, but I can't remember it.

The echo of running footfalls. More gunfire, closer now. I push it all away, slipping back into my dream.

I'm sitting on a roof, the woman is snuggled into my side. Her hair is tied up at the top of her head with a red scarf.

What is her name?

"Holy Mother Mary, Jesus, and Joseph," a male voice says somewhere near me. "East corner. Get your ass over here. Now, Az."

Another voice joins shortly after, but I block both of them out, trying to hold on to the vision in my mind.

A soft female voice, saying something next to my ear. It's her again. Reading to me. Something about . . . cows?

Her name, what is her name . . . ?

"Hold him down. I don't want him going berserk thinking I'm an enemy."

Hands grab my legs, the sensation dissolving my dream, just as I almost grasped it. I flip over, hitting the distraction with my foot. I want my dream back!

"Jesus fuck! I told you to hold him down, damn it!"

Something heavy lands on top of me. I roar and headbutt the son of a bitch who planted his ass on my chest. A sting of a needle in my thigh. I thrash around, trying to get the man off me.

What is her name?

Fog invades my mind, making the voices of the men more distant.

Delicate hands. Gentle fingers with manicured nails, cleaning the cut on my arm.

Cub. My tiger cub.

Yes, that's her name.

Chapter Twenty-Eight

Kai

Two weeks later

A MUTED CRUNCH SOUNDS AS I TWIST A MAN'S HEAD TO the side, breaking his neck. I lower the body to the ground, then use my lockpick to open the basement door. It took me four days of careful observation to learn the guards' movements so I could swiftly dispose of all six of them. If I also had to crack the alarm system, I might have had to pick another location, but Felix was kind enough to blackmail Az into handling the tech for me.

Wooden steps lead up to the ground-floor hallway. I turn right and head to the living room where the TV is on, broadcasting the news. A man is slouched on the couch, facing away from me. I silently approach him and press the barrel of my gun to the back of his head.

"Hello, Captain."

His body goes rigid for a moment, but then he relaxes. "I see you finally got yourself free. Took you long enough, Mazur."

I keep my gun butted up against his skull as I take out my second weapon with my other hand. "Yes, it seems that way." Aiming at his left knee, I fire. Kruger cries out just as I shoot his other kneecap.

Circling the couch, I take a seat on the recliner set across from it. Kruger is pressing his hands over the mess that was once his knees, glaring at me with a mix of misery and anger etched into his face.

"Sorry about that," I say. "I'm not exactly in peak physical condition to chase you around should you try to slip away."

A low, slightly hysteric chuckle escapes him. "Understatement of the century. Based on how awful you look, you must have gotten the VIP treatment at Medoza's. Did they just starve you, or was it something more lavish?"

"I'd say I received an all-inclusive package."

Kruger snickers again, the sound coming out unhinged but quickly dissolving into a pained whimper. I don't enjoy watching anyone suffer. Unless specifically ordered otherwise, my kills have always been fast and efficient. But this . . . seeing Lennox Kruger wriggle in agony, brings me immense joy. And it has nothing to do with the fact he served me to Mendoza on a silver platter.

I cross my arms and meet his slightly frantic gaze. "Was it a setup?"

"Of course it was a setup, you motherfucker!" he yells, spit flying out of his mouth. "You fucking quit on me?" He draws a hurried breath, eyes flaring as rage paints his face red. "For a woman?" The words are becoming harder for him to spew out as he seems to lose all control of his emotions. "I made you, you bastard!" he screams. "You needed a lesson. But that cocksucker Mendoza didn't follow through on our deal to send you back."

"I'm not talking about Mexico." I growl in an even tone while raw rage tears me up inside.

Kruger's lips widen into a sinister smile, and he leans back as if infused with new energy, forgetting his wounds.

"It was, wasn't it? That last hit you sent me to complete. The Italian big leaguer."

"You're mine, Mazur." He sneers. "You would have been nothing without me. I took an insignificant wad of shit and shaped it into a magnificent art piece. No one can take away my creation!" he chokes out with a snarl. "Did you even know the woman you were seeing was a Cosa Nostra princess?"

No, I didn't. I only found out a week ago when Felix dug up info on her for me. I lift my gun and shoot Kruger in his left shoulder. "Continue."

He glares at me, his face contorted into a pained mask. Beads of sweat collect at his hairline, and his breathing is fast and shallow, but he keeps his back ramrod-straight. He's always been a tough son of a bitch.

"You know, at first, I considered just killing your little cunt. But then, I saw a hit contract on her father up for grabs. Having her lover kill her only parent? Fate was smiling on me, I couldn't pass up this perfect gift of circumstances." He falls into maniacal laughter. "Do you know that she's happily married now?"

Pain explodes in my chest, just as it did when Felix told me that detail. My cub got married. I knew it would happen one day, but a part of me still died when I heard it.

"I guess I did her a favor after all," Kruger continues. "A wife of a powerful, respected man. She ended up way better off than she would have if she stayed with you."

"I know."

"Did you already go to see her? To watch her like a creep, as you did before?"

Rising from the recliner, I approach the man who orchestrated everything that led to me losing the only thing I've ever wanted for myself—my cub. Her husband might be a better man than me, but no one will ever love her the way I do.

I wrap my hands around Kruger's neck, squeezing his trachea

until his face turns blue. "Have a nice fucking time in hell, Captain. When I join you there, I'm going to kill you all over again."

Kruger gasps, struggling for breath. I squeeze harder. His eyes are bulging, staring at me from his aghast face, as sounds of choking leave his lips. I savor his audibles as if they are the most beautiful melody, and keep squeezing, even after his body goes still.

When I leave Kruger's home, I get into my car and head to the airport. Going back to my tiger cub at last. I couldn't risk doing so before taking care of Kruger, but now, nothing will keep me away. She might not be mine anymore, but I'm still hers. And I will watch over her and make sure she's safe until my last breath.

Chapter Twenty-nine

Kai

Two months later

THE SHINY BLACK SEDAN CRUISING DOWN THE STREET ahead of me starts to slow down, stopping at the red light. I ease up on the gas pedal, maintaining a safe distance, and let another vehicle slide in ahead of mine as I pull up to the intersection.

She stayed out late tonight.

I planted a GPS tracker on Nera's car, just in case, but I'm not reliant on a fucking device as far as her safety is concerned. For the past two months, I've been watching over my cub, following her every move whenever she left her home.

Am I back to being a fucking stalker? Yup, but it means I get to continue keeping her safe.

She doesn't leave the mansion that often, usually only once or twice a week. And she always returns home before the dinner hour. It's nearly midnight now, so something unexpected must have happened. Does it have anything to do with the death of her husband?

I watched her at the funeral yesterday, hidden behind the shrubs on the elevated part of the cemetery's terrain. The position presented me with an undisturbed view of everyone who attended.

That damn gathering nearly caused me to lose my shit. More than a hundred people huddled together, and every one of them was a potential threat to my cub.

For over an hour the scope of my MK 13 kept moving from one person to the other while I assessed their body language and searched for any abrupt movement in Nera's direction. A shitload of mourners, most armed as evident by the bulges beneath the men's suit jackets. Only after my cub finally slipped inside the car with her sister and left the cemetery grounds was I able to breathe normally again.

I hadn't even caught a glimpse of her face while she was there. She hid it behind a gauzy black veil. Was she crying over losing her husband? She probably was. Nera has always cared deeply for the people around her. She must be hurting now. That realization makes me want to dig up the asshole's corpse and kill him myself. Not to cause her more pain, but because he had what I wanted.

I never saw them together, which is a blessing, in a way. If I had, I'm not sure I would have been able to resist sending a bullet through the man's head. I'm glad the asswipe is dead, and that fact makes me feel sick. Nera married him, so she must have loved him. Regardless, I can't pretend I'm not glad the fucker is six feet under.

The light changes to green, and Nera's vehicle makes the left turn, heading north. I follow for half an hour, keeping three cars' lengths between us until her sedan pulls up in front of the tall iron fence. Her new home. I park down the street and wait for the security guard to open the gate. A moment later, my cub's car disappears from view.

Leaning back in my seat, I watch the iron barrier roll back into position. It's well-oiled and it doesn't make a sound as it closes, but I still hear the clank of metal in my head. As it does every time she disappears behind that thick iron gate, it feels like a slash of a knife across my chest.

Each night since my arrival, I've imagined ramming that damn gate with my car to force my way inside and to claim back what's mine. A foolish delusion of a desperate man. Tonight, I don't even have the energy to dream. Yet I can't make myself turn the car around and leave. This is as close as I can get to her now, and I want to stay a bit longer.

"A bit longer" ends up being over an hour. When I step inside the apartment I've rented that's only a few blocks away, it's one thirty in the morning. I throw my jacket on the back of the kitchen chair and head to the fridge, grabbing some leftovers to heat up. While the bowl of mac and cheese spins in the microwave, I pull out my phone and navigate to a familiar site hidden on the dark web, entering my login credentials. Normal people browse social media and news apps when they need a distraction; I check out listings for hit jobs. Not that I have the time to take on a job at the moment, considering my sole purpose since getting back stateside is watching over Nera, but old habits die hard, so I still do it from time to time. Maybe I'm just sentimental.

I peruse the listing, checking out the locations and details, when one particular entry attracts my attention. The target is in Boston, and the contract has been claimed earlier today by the Sicilians—a team of ruthless hitmen who strike hard and fast, eliminating their mark in less than twenty-four hours. I click on the entry, and the black-and-white image of a woman starts to load.

My fucking heart stops.

It's Nera.

The earth falls out from beneath my feet.

Some unknown cocksucker put the hit out on my cub.

I don't spare even a second to go to my bedroom for extra

weapons, just storm out of the apartment. Panic floods the pit of my stomach as I race like a maniac down the few streets that separate my building from the neighborhood where Nera's home is located. If it was anyone else but the Sicilians, I would have more time to deal with this threat. But fucking Rafael De Santi prides himself on the turnaround time for any contract his organization takes on. They are going for the kill. Tonight.

Well, not on my fucking watch!

My hands are shaking as I hit the brakes in front of the formidable iron gate that bars the entry to the property and fly out of the car. The entryway is still shut, thank fuck, and I take my first full breath since I saw that kill order. That is until I notice the cut wires peaking out of the power box attached to the side of the gatehouse. Security guards are nowhere in sight.

Terror grips me anew as I grab at the metal rod on the rolling gate and push it open. The obstacle moves easily to the right. No doubt the locks and the alarm that are part of the gate's circuits have been neutralized. Fucking bastards are already inside. I slip through the opening and run along the south side of the fence, straight toward the mansion.

The windows along the east wing of the ground floor are lit. The drapes are drawn open, and I can see the female shape sitting behind the large desk in a spacious room. This must be Nera's home office. Air leaves my lungs in a great puff while the relief washes over me. She's alive. I allow myself only a second to soak in the sight of my cub, then resume my mission.

The Sicilians always work in teams of four: two men at exit routes oversee surveillance and direct the movement inside the perimeter, one provides cover fire or backup as needed, and the lead man goes after the mark. Their typical MO for executions is strangulation while the target is asleep, so the appointed assassin could already be hiding in Nera's bedroom, lying in wait until she turns in.

Knowing their moves gives me an advantage, but only if the appointed cutthroat doesn't get wind of my being here. If he or his buddies spot me, they'll change their tactics. There's no way I'm gambling with Nera's life. If the motherfucker is already in position, Nera's safe as long as she remains in the study. That means I can leave the lead assassin to be dealt with last, after I dispose of the other three.

I spy one of the surveillance guys near a thick oak tree, standing guard close to the main entrance. Using the shadows as cover, I creep along the mansion wall until I'm right behind him, getting the drop on the man quickly and wrapping my arm around his neck. A moment later, a tiny crunch echoes over the silent struggle, confirming I've fractured his cervical vertebrae. I lower the body to the ground and head toward the rear of the house, once again hidden among the darkness like the demon cub claimed me to be.

Another Sicilian is crouching by the garden feature of some sort, close to the back door of the house, his head is tilted up. I follow his line of sight and spot the third team member scaling the drainpipe toward the roofline. The moment the climber disappears over the edge, I charge the man on the ground. We both end up in a drained fountain from the force of my onslaught. I slam my palm over his mouth and bury my knife in his guts, all the way to the hilt. The man keeps struggling, his hand reaching for my throat. I shove the blade deeper into his flesh and twist the handle of my Ka-Bar when pain explodes in my left side.

"Die, you fucking rodent," I growl as I withdraw the knife and thrust it up through the underside of the guy's chin into his skull. I don't bother checking the wound on the side of my torso where the bastard cut me, just hustle after the man who made it onto the roof.

The skin on my palms burns as I grip the ice-cold metal downspout tucked into the L corner of the mansion. It takes me less than a minute to reach the summit, but it seems like hours of precious time. Time I don't have to waste. Painful pulsing just above my hipbone tells me that the damn Sicilian got me good, but the injury is meaningless to me. I will fucking crawl if I have to. No one is harming my cub today. Or ever. For as long as I live. Grabbing the edge, I haul myself over the lip and onto the roof.

The moon is hidden behind the clouds, but a few stray beams penetrate, illuminating the black-clad figure crouching on the far end, attention focused on the lawn below. Whereas I was just thanking my lucky stars for the flat roof, now I'm cursing the fucking thing. There aren't any obstacles in the way for me to sneak up on the son of a bitch. With little choice, I take out my gun and screw on the suppressor. As the man raises his hand to his earpiece, likely to contact the rest of his team, I aim at the back of his head and send the bullet fly. The guy jerks forward and sprawls facedown on the surface of the roof, hanging partway over to the edge.

I feel the blood seeping through my shirt as I approach the body to check for pulse. The stabbing pain in my side gets worse when I jump to the balcony below. The not-too-wide deck happens to be right above the study where I saw Nera earlier. The light spilling from the ground-floor room turns off just as I throw a look over the railing. My time is up, yet I still haven't disposed of the last of Rafael's men. Fuck. With a gun in hand, I open the balcony door and slip inside the room.

It takes me a moment to get my bearings since I've never been inside Nera's home. However, I've scouted the grounds and looked at the building blueprints the night I returned to Boston, so I have a general idea of the layout. Her rooms are on this upper floor, but face the other side of the property. With no time to waste, I sprint across the living room cluttered with pieces of fabric and some other shit, and step out into the hallway. There's only one other door, right in front of me.

"Yes, I'm done for tonight, Timoteo." The ring of Nera's words reaches me from the downstairs hallway, echoing through the stillness. "The capos will be here at ten tomorrow. Please make sure the conference room is ready."

A jolt of pain rips through me, but this time, it has nothing to do with the wound in my side. It's been more than three years since I've heard her voice. Or got this close to her. No more than a few dozen feet separate us, but it still seems like every inch of that distance is a mile long. I squeeze my eyes shut for the briefest moment, just a heartbeat of time to commit the melodic sound to my memory, then ready my gun and open the door to her private rooms.

The suite is dark, but after all the time I spent confined in the pits of Mendoza's dingy hangar, my eyes are well used to seeing in low light, so it takes me less than ten seconds to confirm my prey isn't in the room. I don't even need to do a thorough check of the vicinity. In my line of business, the hunter tends to develop an instinct for feeling out the surroundings. From the moment I stepped inside the room, I knew I was alone in there. But not for long.

The glass door leading to the balcony is slightly ajar. That's the point of entry I would use. Since I eliminated the man on the roof, my guess is the would-be killer will try to climb up from the lower level. I walk across the carpeted floor and take a seat on the recliner positioned near the bookshelf. It has a direct view of the exterior deck through the open drapes.

Just for a minute, the eerie silence envelops me. Then, the muffled sounds of heels on the hardwood floor echo through the hallway I crossed moments before, getting closer. Leather squeaks as I squeeze the armrest with my free hand while a storm rages within me. Facing my cub once again was never the plan. Witnessing the hate and condemnation in Nera's eyes once she finds me here will be torture worse than anything I've ever experienced. I don't care. There's nothing I wouldn't endure for her. I survived letting her go. I'll survive this, too. At least long enough to make sure she's unharmed and safe.

The suite door opens, and Nera steps inside. For a moment, I forget how to breathe, too shaken by the sight of her. Her proximity. My twinkling star, one that shines even in the darkest gloom. I watch her as she walks to the center of the room and looks around as if trying to peer into the shadowy corners. As if she had done so many times . . . before.

"Long time no see, tiger cub," I rasp.

Nera becomes so utterly still.

I take a deep breath and turn on the lamp beside me. My God, she's even more beautiful than I remembered.

"I thought you were dead," she chokes out, a mixture of shock and hurt written all over her face.

I was. Still am. Dead. I've been dead most of my life. The only time I've actually felt alive is for that short period I spent with her. All the days before and after, are a fucking wasteland.

"Did you miss me?" I ask and regret it the instant the words leave my mouth. Even in low light, I can see her muscles tense up. I'm just making this harder on both of us, but I can't control myself, it seems.

"It's hard to miss a man whose name I don't even know." Nera's voice is barely audible but I detect the slight trembling in it. The hurt in her expression is plain to see now. But I notice something else. A glistening in the corners of her eyes. I must be the most selfish son of a bitch on earth, because seeing her tears ignites the fire in my chest, and I feel a tiny spark of life returning into my dead existence. Maybe she did miss me. A little bit.

Fighting the gravitational pull of a star, my eyes shift away from Nera's face and zero in on the movement behind her. A hand, clad in a black leather glove, grips the balcony railing next to a grappling hook fastened over the edge. The last of Rafael's men has finally decided to show up.

"I missed you, too, cub," I whisper. Raising the gun, I aim at the man now standing on the balcony. "Do not move."

Part 2

present

Chapter Thirty

Nera

Present day
The Leone Villa, Boston

THE SOUND OF BREAKING GLASS AND SOMETHING LARGE crashing to the floor explodes behind me. My heart is beating so fast it feels like it will burst out of my chest, but I remain perfectly still. He told me not to move, and when it comes to my safety . . . I trust him completely.

"That's the last one," my demon says and slowly lowers his weapon. "Call your security and tell them to sweep the property and pick up the bodies. There's one at the fountain in the back garden. One by the oak tree close to the front door. And another on the roof."

"Alarms?" I ask.

"Compromised. You'll need to install new ones."

I throw a glance over my shoulder. The body of a man dressed in black clothes and wearing a balaclava over his face is lying on the balcony. "Mercenaries?"

"Yes. Sicilians. One of their hit teams." He lays the gun next to the reading lamp on the side table, groaning in the process. "Congratulations. Your head is worth two million nowadays."

Dread ignites somewhere deep inside me. Something is wrong. I dash across the room and grab the lamp, turning it toward him. The front and side of his shirt are saturated with blood, and some of it is seeping onto the chair's upholstery.

"Shit." I kneel between his legs and start unbuttoning his shirt. "Bullet?"

"A knife." He cups my cheek, tilting my head up. "It's good to see you again, my tiger cub."

I press my lips together to hide their quiver, peer into his eyes, and suddenly, it doesn't feel like it's been almost four years since we last saw each other. Same eyes. Still so haunted. But there are new secrets in their depths.

He's alive.

Is this real? I'm terrified this could all be a cruel, cruel dream.

Breaking his magnetic stare, I glance away to take in the changes. Little differences he can no longer conceal now that I can see him in the light. Like one of the strands that has escaped his braid and had fallen over his somewhat gaunt face. He's lost a lot of weight, and his hair seems to be shorter, the ends reaching about halfway down his breastbone.

"Where were you all this time?" I ask and resume unbuttoning his shirt.

"Not important."

I shake my head and pull apart the sides of the button-down, revealing his chest and stomach. A shocked gasp leaves my lips. There's an almost four-inch cut above his hip, running vertically over his ribs. The same general spot as that bullet wound nearly five years ago.

"We need to get you on the bed." I take off my blazer and press it over the cut. "Can you walk?"

"Yes."

"Okay." Straightening up, I take the gun off the table, flick on the safety, and slip it into my waistband behind my back.

He raises an eyebrow. "Confiscating my weapon, cub?"

"I can't have guns lying around my living room," I say and extend my hand toward him, "Come on."

His eyes hold mine as he wraps his calloused fingers around my wrist, his thumb pressing right over my pulse point. Since I've met him, the look in his eyes has been somewhat surreal, as if a fiend was lurking behind those icy grays. Are his eyes the last sight his targets see before leaving this world? They might feel fear, but in their place, I'd welcome the view.

"You're losing too much blood," I whisper.

His eyes crease at the corners. He pulls my hand to his mouth and touches his lips to the tips of my fingers. It's the faintest of kisses, but it feels as if hot iron is branding my skin.

And I almost fall apart.

"Blood lost for you is blood well spent," he says against my trembling palm.

A viselike grip squeezes my chest. This man. How dare he? After what we had. After losing him. And now . . . Now he says *this* to me? Words that make my heart race, reigniting that desperate yearning for all those things I dreamed of for so long. To be his. Have him as mine. To breach this chasm between us, break through the invisible barricade keeping us apart. He'd taken a bullet for me, but he never let me behind his guarded walls.

I pull my hand out of his hold. "Let's go."

He slowly rises off the recliner, towering over me. I forgot how tall he is.

"This way." I wrap my arm around his waist and nod toward

the door that separates my bedroom from the open floor living and kitchen area of my apartment within the villa.

With my palm putting pressure on his hand as he presses my jacket to his side, I help him across the central space. We're at the threshold of my bedroom when his body sways forward, and I barely manage to get him steady.

"Your luck with the knife-welding riffraff in my neck of the woods hasn't changed, I guess."

"They still think I'm too pretty," he slurs.

We reach the bed in a few slow strides, just in time because, in the next moment, he drops to the mattress, unconscious. I lift his legs atop the covers one by one, then run to my sister's suite, which is just across the hall from mine, occupying the other side of the upper level.

"Zara!" I whisper-yell as I shake her shoulder. "Wake up. I need your help."

"What?" She blinks slowly, then squints her eyes at me.

"Come on." I shake her again before rounding the bed to check on my daughter, sleeping on the other side.

When I'm not around at bedtime, Lucia won't go to sleep unless my sister tucks in beside her. Since the two of them can't fit on the little toddler bed, my daughter ends up sleeping across the hall at Zara's. I adjust the duvet around her tiny body, then grab my sister's hand and drag her to the kitchen in my suite.

"I need the first aid kit and clean towels," I say as I pull out a pot from the cupboard and put it into the sink to fill with warm water. "And get me the soap from the bathroom. Now, Zara."

She blinks at me, then turns on her heel and rushes out the door. As soon as the pot is half-full, I take a clean kitchen linen from the drawer and carry both to my bedroom.

Removing my demon's shirt will be impossible, so I just leave it and focus on washing away the blood from his abdomen and side. The water quickly turns red as I rinse the cloth.

A sharp intake of breath sounds behind me. I turn around to find Zara staring from the doorway, a bunch of towels in her hands.

"It's him," I say. Two words, but they are enough.

Her eyes widen, sweeping over the huge blood-covered body lying on my bed, then she approaches. Kneeling on the floor beside me, she takes one of the towels and presses it over the knife wound.

It takes us ten minutes and three pots of water to clean the blood enough for me to focus on the cut itself. Based on the length of it, it'll require about fifteen stitches.

"I'll take it from here," I say and use a cotton ball saturated with antiseptic solution to clean the skin around the wound. "You can head back. Can, um . . . can she stay with you for the rest of the night?"

Zara nods and rises, walking out of the room. The door shuts behind her with a muffled click a moment later.

Once I'm done disinfecting the angry flesh, I take out a syringe and a vial of anesthetic from my kit, ready to pump him full of pain meds, but strong fingers grab my wrist.

"No."

I press my lips into a thin line and look up at my demon. "I'm done sewing you up without an anesthetic."

He narrows his eyes at me, his gaze searching mine. The look is cautious, as if he's trying to find evidence of deception. I lean forward, directly into his face.

"And you're getting a shot of antibiotics right after," I bark.

"Want to know what I did to the last person who came at me with a syringe?" His voice is low, with a dangerous timbre to it. "I squeezed the life out of that dickhead."

"Good thing I have a horse tranquilizer in my kit." I pull my hand free and jam the hypodermic into his side next to the cut.

As I pull the syringe away and reach for the needle and thread, he just watches me in silence. I'm struggling to focus on what I have to do, overwhelmed by being able to touch him again after all these years. So many questions roll through my mind—questions I want to yell into his face and demand answers to.

Where were you? Why didn't you come, at least once, if only to let me know you're alive? Why did you leave me?

I don't ask any of them. What's the point?

I begin the first suture. Even with the anesthetic, it must hurt, but he doesn't make a sound. This is probably the fifth time I'm sewing him up, and not once has he complained. I work my way through all the necessary stitches, and if it wasn't for a slight change in his breath, I might have thought he felt nothing at all.

"I'll go get you some water. Do you want something to eat?" I ask as I secure a thick dressing over the wound.

"No."

"Okay. I'll be right back."

When I leave my bedroom, I head over to the kitchen counter to get my phone out of my purse.

"Mrs. Leone?" Ernesto, my chief of security replies on the second ring. "Is something wrong?"

"There are bodies you need to dispose of. On the roof. At the entrance. And at the back door." I open the fridge and reach for the bottle of water. "And there's another one on my balc—"

The crunch of glass under heavy feet echoes from the living room behind me. I turn around just in time to see my demon toss the body of the dead hitman over the railing, down to the frost-covered lawn.

"It's under my balcony, Ernesto," I correct myself.

"Bodies?"

"Yes. Get rid of them. And call the alarm company, have them here first thing in the morning." I throw the phone onto the counter and reach for a glass from the cupboard. "I'll see if I can find you some clothes."

I pour water into the glass, avoiding looking at him. The hardwood floor creaks beneath his shoes as he rounds the island separating the living room from the kitchen and comes to stand behind me.

I grip the edge of the counter and close my eyes. Still reeling that he's here. His absence left a gaping hole in my chest, nothing in the world could fill it.

"I thought you forgot me," I whisper.

Warm breath fans the back of my neck, sending a shiver down my spine.

"Even when I was on the brink of madness, barely alive and unable to grasp where or who I was, I remembered you." His voice is raspy next to my ear. "Where's my gun? There are things I need to take care of."

The familiar hurt pierces my chest. He's leaving . . . Again.

"On the top shelf by the front door."

His touch disappears. I keep my eyes focused on the glass of water as I listen to his retreating steps. A few moments later, I hear the front door open and then close with a heartbreaking click.

He's gone.

Chapter Thirty-one

Nera

THE EYES OF SIX MEN FOLLOW ME AS I STEP INSIDE THE formal dining room, which had long ago been turned into a meeting space at the Leone Villa, and take a seat at the head of the long black table. This was Batista's spot up until a year ago when his health no longer allowed him to be here. My inner circle always knew that I was making the decisions for the Family, even with my husband presiding over meetings like this, but once he was too sick to attend, we dropped the charade completely.

I lean back in the plush black leather chair and sweep my eyes over the faces of the men present. Salvo is sitting to my right, his face set in hard lines. He's probably blaming himself for last night's situation, and I'm sure Massimo will hold him accountable as well once news of the assassination attempt reaches my stepbrother. I'll have to make sure that doesn't happen, or Massimo might kill Salvo the moment his sentence is done. As the underboss, Salvo is already burdened with so much work, and I can't expect him to personally oversee my safety, too.

The men remain silent while my gaze moves from one to the next, pausing on each face for a couple of moments. Who's the bastard who ordered the hit? I knew something like this could happen as soon as Batista died and I announced that I wouldn't be stepping down. No one expected that. A woman, officially leading a Cosa Nostra Family? Such a thing was unheard of. But I didn't expect anyone to be so bold as to try to kill me in my own home.

"So, do you think it was Ajello?" I ask, even though I'm sure it wasn't New York Don. The culprit is sitting right here in this very room. I just don't know who it is, yet.

Six pairs of eyes stare at me, but no one says a word. I'm sure Ernesto has already filled them in on the events of last night, including the number of bodies he had to collect from around the house. The man, or men, who ordered my assassination are now most likely banging their heads on the wall, wondering if someone spilled the beans and warned me. They must be dumbfounded by the fact that the entire team of hitmen was neutralized, and baffled about who might have done it.

Maybe they think I did it myself. If I wasn't furious, I would laugh. The image of my demon sitting on that recliner covered in blood after he took out the killers rises in my mind, and right on cue, an ache hits me square in the chest.

I can't believe he's back.

I can't believe he left.

Again.

I push the thought away and, leaning forward, cross my hands on top of the table.

"Or maybe it was the Albanians," I add in a calm tone. For now, I'll let them all believe that I think it was an outside job.

"Dushku," Brio agrees. "We've been partners with the Albanians for decades, and you've cut ties with them without a proper explanation. I can understand how they would see such a move as a betrayal. A move, which I might add, you've made on your own, without consulting with the rest of us."

"Popov gave us better rates." I meet his gaze. "Or are you suggesting I should have rejected his offer and kept working with Dushku, even though that would have meant unnecessary financial losses for the Family?"

Brio clenches his jaw. "Of course not."

"Then I don't see a problem. I appreciate your concern, but I need your full focus on the casinos. Leave any objections about our arms supplier to me and Salvo to figure out." I turn to the underboss. "Do we have anyone on the inside with the Albanian group?"

"Two soldiers," he confirms. "But they are not high enough on the food chain to be privy to that kind of information. If it was Dushku, he would have kept it on a need-to-know basis." Salvo says. "But, I'll send someone to New York again. On the off chance it was Ajello, we must be completely sure."

I shake my head. "No. Ajello has been keeping his word and staying out of our business. Let's keep it that way and focus on the Albanians for now. Unless someone here has another idea?"

There are some muted mutterings, but no one offers up other suggestions. As expected.

For over three years, I've been following Massimo's guidance and minimizing any potential conflicts between our Family and our partners, as well as with our competitors. I can handle the business aspect of the Family, but I won't be able to manage a Mafia war with another criminal organization. Cosa Nostra is strictly patriarchal. Getting capos to follow a woman's directives is difficult, but as long as those orders bring in a lot of money, it's doable. But if the war does break out, the capos will never allow me to make the necessary decisions. I know Massimo will handle any potential conflict once he gets out, and based on what he has hinted, it's going to be a shitstorm. I just need to weather the next six months until then.

"Well, now that that's settled, let's go over today's business agenda." I turn toward Brio. "I need the casino revenue details from last week."

He starts spilling the numbers, beginning with our largest casino, and I school my features to show nothing but calmness, while panic swarms deep within my guts. I've spent the whole night sitting next to Lucia, watching my sister and daughter as they slept and wondering how I'm going to keep my family safe.

Ernesto had the window in my living room upstairs replaced first thing this morning and has already contacted the alarm company. The system will be upgraded later today. Three of the six men who were on guard duty last night were killed, so I instructed him to assign at least eight to each security shift from now on. Will that be enough?

The idea of running away once again forms in my head. Dare I risk it? With me out of the picture, whoever wants me dead could simply take over, leaving me alone. Or will they send hitmen after me again? Dear God, what am I going to do?

Brio has finished rumbling about the revenues at the casinos, and Tiziano has taken over, giving updates on business at our strip clubs. The anxiety plaguing me doesn't subside. I take a deep breath and squeeze my hands into fists, trying to relax. My throat feels like it's being throttled, as if someone is trying to suffocate me. Years of pretending to be someone I'm not, of doing countless horrible things just so these men would treat me as an equal, are crushing me to the core. I'm tired of inflicting fear on others only to keep them from realizing how utterly terrified—all the damn time—I actually am. They are predators—the moment they smell fear, I'm dead. How much longer can I keep this up before I crack? As I watch the grim faces of the men seated around the table, a silent scream builds in my chest, clawing at my insides, fighting to be let out. I can't do this anymore!

The mahogany double doors on the other side of the conference room open, and a man steps inside.

My heart stops its incessant thunderous beating in my chest.

For a fleeting moment, a stillness settles as all present gape at the newcomer, but then, everyone leaps out of their seats, reaching for their weapons.

"Sit down," I order. "And put away the guns."

It amazes me how strong and controlled my voice sounds, considering the upheaval that exploded inside my mind the moment my eyes landed on my demon standing at the threshold. He's dressed in a perfectly tailored black suit, and even though the rest of the men here are in similar attire, he, in a way, seems more refined. Silver eyes meet mine and then shift over the men returning to their chairs, assessing them somehow.

"Who the fuck is this?" Ernesto barks from his spot at the end of the table, which happens to be closest to the door. "And how did he get through the gate without me being informed?"

My demon's gaze travels back to mine while he takes a step forward, coming to a stop just next to Ernesto.

"Your head of security?"

"Yes," I reply.

"My condolences, cub."

The swipe of his hand is nothing but a blur. A great red arc of blood sprays the table and the faces of the men seated around it, and some of the droplets end up on my hands. Nobody moves, everyone too shocked by the sight of Ernesto's body slumped in his chair, his throat gaping open, while a river of crimson flows down his chest.

The thing about Cosa Nostra's higher-ups is that they don't often witness people being slaughtered before their eyes. Unless there's a situation that demands personal retaliation, typically, it's the soldiers who handle all the dirty work.

Salvo is the first to come to his senses and reaches inside his jacket, going for his gun again. I grab the underboss's wrist and shake my head.

"I guess I should introduce myself," my demon says as he grabs Ernesto's corpse by the scruff of the jacket. He tosses the body to the right where it hits the wall with a loud thump and crashes to the floor. His eyes don't deviate from mine even for a second while he casually takes a seat on the now-empty chair and crosses his arms over his chest. "I'm Kai Mazur. Mrs. Leone's new chief of security."

Angry murmurs quickly turn into yells, deafening in the room, as the men all speak at the same time, demanding to know why they were not informed about the change or how someone from outside the Family was allowed to take over Ernesto's position. I tune them out, their voices nothing but white noise, and focus on the man seated directly across from me at the other end of the long table. He stares back, his jaw clenched tightly and eyes slightly narrowed. It reminds me of how he looked at me all those years ago, the night we first met.

The tumultuous state I've been in since the start of this meeting feels like a minor discomfort compared to the storm brewing inside me now. Too many things are hitting me at once. I've finally learned his name. And apparently, he's planning to stay.

I want to kiss him. And hit him. And send him to hell—all at the same time.

I take a deep breath and shout, "Everyone, shut the fuck up!"

The silence lasts for only a few seconds, then the yelling match resumes.

"This is outrageous!" Brio roars.

"How dare you hire someone without consulting with the capos first?" Armando.

"I won't tolerate an outsider!" That one is Tiziano.

"No one can get away with killing a member of the Family without suffering the consequences!" Brio again.

My attention is only on him—Kai. I watch as he reaches inside his jacket. The air stirs, and my eyes catch a blur of movement. In the next instant, a sizable black knife is embedded in the middle of the table, right in front of Brio, who has been the loudest. Silence descends once again, and, this time, it envelops the room.

"I can hire anyone I want," I say. "And I don't need your approval to choose my own security."

I have no idea what I'm doing. I'm not completely sure if my demon is serious about sticking around or for how long, but I can't let anyone in the room come to that conclusion. A few mumbled words ring out, but no one contradicts me.

"And as far as Ernesto is concerned—" I continue, but Kai's deep voice from across the conference table interrupts.

"Ernesto," he says in that husky voice I love so much, "is an example of what will happen to anyone who is entrusted with Mrs. Leone's safety, but fails to do his job properly."

The capos' eyes bounce between the knife lodged in the center of the conference table and Kai.

"Nera"—Salvo leans toward me—"I don't think this is—"

"We're done for today," I cut him off. "You're all free to leave."

Chairs scrape on the polished wooden floor as the men rise and file out one by one. I know they won't let this go so easily, but that problem will have to wait for another day. Salvo is the last to walk away from the table, and as he reaches the door, he stops and gives me a pointed look.

Massimo won't like this, his look says.

He closes the door after he exits, leaving me alone with the man who broke my heart. Shattered it so completely, that I'm fairly certain I'll never be able to piece it back together.

Kai

"I thought you left."

Each word from Nera's lips pierces my chest like a dagger. I know she's referring to last night, but it still takes me back to that time on the rooftop when she screamed into the brewing storm.

"I didn't," I say.

"So, you just decided to barge in, interrupt my meeting, and slaughter my head of security?"

"Correct. And I'll do the same to anyone who's a danger to you. Whether directly, or because of their incompetence."

"I don't want you here . . . Kai."

Another strike to my chest, this one cutting deeper than the previous one. I hate my name, but I love how she says it. "It doesn't make a difference, tiger cub. I'm staying until I'm convinced you're safe."

"It's not your job to keep me safe."

"Maybe not. I'm still going to do it."

"And then, you'll leave for good?"

"Yes," I lie. As long as I live, I'm never leaving her again. "You've changed. What happened?"

"Life." She buries her hands into her hair and looks down at the black wood surface in front of her. "Life happened."

"Any guesses on who might have ordered your assassination?"

"Likely one of the capos."

"I'll dispose of them tonight."

Nera's head snaps up, her eyes finding mine. "You're not disposing of anyone else without my permission."

"I won't allow a potential threat to you to draw a single breath more than necessary!" I bellow. "Can you imagine my shock when I came across a contract for a hit with your picture on it? Or when I saw that the Sicilians already took the job? I couldn't fucking breathe—too worried about your safety—while I was running around your home, trying to pick them off before one of the bastards could get to you!"

"Do not raise your voice at me. You saved my life, and I'm grateful for it. But that doesn't mean you can yell at me."

"You could have died," I growl. "The kill order on you is closed now, and there won't be one again. But that doesn't mean that whoever submitted it won't try using other means."

This morning, I called Rafael, the head of the Sicilian group, and made sure they dropped the job. Then, I made another call—to a guy who acts as a mediator for all high-level hit jobs. I explained, in excruciating detail, what would happen to his insides after I'm done with him unless he takes down the listing of Nera's hit. And, I extended the threat to anyone who considers taking on the job of killing my cub. I might not be sociable, but I know most people in my line of work. And, more importantly, they know of me.

Nera closes her eyes and swallows, gripping the handrests of her chair. Her hold is so hard that her knuckles are white, but she doesn't seem to realize I can see right through her present bravado. It's the first sign of unease she's shown since I walked into the room. Even when I slashed the throat of her security chief, she barely batted an eye. When I got back to Boston two months ago, I noticed right away that she seemed different, but it was only today that I became aware of how significant that change is.

"All right," she whispers and meets my stare. "You can oversee my security, and you'll be compensated for your services. We'll sign a contract with a six-month duration."

My body tenses, each of her words scorching my soul. She wants to give me money in exchange for keeping her safe?

"I'm not signing a fucking contract with you, cub," I growl. "And why six months?"

"That's when my stepbrother gets released from prison. He'll be taking over this shitshow from that point on." She rises and walks across the room until she's standing right next to me. "I'll inform the household members and staff about the change in the security department. Someone will come to escort you to your accommodations. They are in the other building."

With those words, she steps over the dead body lying in a pool of blood and leaves the room.

I grit my teeth and fix my gaze on the knife buried in the tabletop, trying to smother the urge to go after my cub. To take her in my arms and hold her to my chest like I wanted to last night. Like I've dreamed of doing every day for the three years I was rotting away at that damn compound, and during these past months, while I've secretly been watching over her again.

But I won't do it. I won't let the hands that killed her father touch her ever again. If I do, I won't ever be able to let her go. The cold shoulder I can handle. I broke the promise I made to her, and I will accept the consequences of that. I will even sign that damn contract if it makes things easier for her.

Leaning forward, I wrap my fingers around the handle of the knife and pull out the blade.

But I will not be sleeping in the other building.

Chapter Thirty-Two

Nera

"Yes, you're to follow Mr. Mazur's orders with regard to all security-related matters," I say into the phone.

"But, Donna Leone . . . we had that surveillance equipment installed three months ago," the butler says on the other side of the connection. "It's top-of-the-line."

"Did he elaborate on why he wants the equipment changed?"

"I tried asking, but that brute put a knife to my throat and warned me to either replace the equipment with what he ordered, or he'll replace my head. I didn't find it funny."

"He wasn't kidding, Timoteo. Just do what he says." I cut the call and approach Zara, who's standing by the window, looking out at the yard beyond, and ask, "Is he still doing 'interviews'?"

"Yup."

Kai had the entire security staff, all three shifts, called in. He had them line up in one long row next to the staff quarters building, like prisoners facing a firing squad. At first, I thought he might be asking each man about their credentials, special skills, or something like that, but he just told them to stand still. Twenty-six men, and all they've been doing is standing there with their backs to the wall for more than twenty minutes.

"What the hell is he doing?" I say under my breath, watching my demon as he waits in the middle of the lawn—hands in his pockets, observing the security guys.

"I'm not sure this was a wise decision," Zara whispers.

"Yeah." I press my forehead to the window frame. "But it's the only way to keep us safe. Other than you, he's the only person I trust completely."

"He left you, Nera. You were pregnant with his child, and he just disappeared."

"He didn't know."

"If he called you, even once, he would have."

"Let me rephrase." I let out a sigh. "He's the only person I trust with our lives."

"Are you going to tell him about Lucia?"

"No."

"He has the right to know."

"As you said, if he bothered to call, he would have known."

I'll let him believe what everyone else believes—that Lucia is Batista's daughter. With her light-brown hair and pouty lips, she looks like a tiny version of me. Except for her eyes.

Zara wraps her arm around my shoulders. "Did he tell you why he left without a word?"

"He didn't."

"And you have no idea what the reason could be?"

I close my eyes and bite my cheek, instantly tasting the metallic tang of blood in my mouth.

"No," I lie.

Several rapid gunshots ring out outside. I flinch, my eyes snapping open. Below, on the lawn, Kai is putting away his gun. My gaze flicks to the line of security staff, spotting three of the men slumped on the ground, their heads aren't as intact as they used to be. I grab the handle on the window pane, pushing it open, just as Kai steps toward the men.

"These three were on guard duty last night when the premises were compromised." Kai's deep voice reaches me. "From now on, if a fucking squirrel breaches the perimeter without being neutralized, I'll kill each man working that shift. Is that clear?"

The security team gapes at him dumbfounded, then nods in unison.

"You're dismissed." Kai turns around and heads toward the driveway. Several cars are spaced around the area, and a man walks among them, inspecting the underside of each vehicle with a strange-looking tool. Is he searching for an explosive device?

I watch as Kai takes the tool from the man and continues to inspect the cars himself, taking his time with every vehicle. It feels strange to think of him as anything other than "my demon," but I like his name.

When he's done inspecting the last of the cars, he throws the mirror-on-a-stick thing back to the guy and heads off toward the gate, where the new surveillance equipment is being installed.

"I'm gonna check on Lucia." I leave my sister to her snooping at the window and trudge across the large living room.

Being the don's wife, I was expected to live with my husband, but when I arrived at Batista's home, I made it very clear I had no intention of sharing my living space with him. At the time, he was already having difficulties climbing the stairs, thus, he mostly used the ground floor where his office and other business rooms were located. I, therefore, claimed the second level, which consisted of two sets of suites—one for myself and one for Zara. She took the smaller one, which faces the backyard, and I ended up with the spacious three-bedroom apartment that I had remodeled to my tastes.

I head into my bedroom, where Lucia is having her afternoon rest. She usually naps in her own room, but when she dozed off in my bed after lunch, I didn't want to chance waking her.

As I pass by the open-concept kitchen on my left, my eyes catch on a bunch of colorful magnets hanging on the fridge. Lucia likes to play with them—a lot—so some are chipped or had to be glued together. I make a detour and stop in front of the mosaic of souvenirs. They seem completely out of place in the contemporary, white kitchen. My fingers brush over the magnet with a picture of a bridge, a long diagonal crack mars the middle of it, and a sad smile pulls at my lips. It's the one *he* brought me. The night of the ill-fated party, I wanted to move it to the central spot, but the magnet fell out of my hand. Looking back on that moment, now it seems like it was some kind of omen.

Kai

"I want the surveillance feeds to stream to the guardhouse, the main computer in the office on the ground floor, and my laptop," I tell the security specialist who's fumbling with the main alarm box on the wall. "Make sure there's no lag."

"Um . . . I don't think that is necessary, sir. All footage will be transmitted to our headquarters, and we have a team who will monitor it twenty-four seven."

I take a menacing step toward him and pin him with my gaze.

"Of course." The man backs away two paces. "No problem at all."

I nod and head to my car, parked on the driveway at some

distance from the other vehicles. The case with my sniper rifle is on the back seat, so I take that out first, then open the trunk. Two big sports bags holding my extra weapons are on the right side of the cargo space, but I decide to leave them for now and only grab the duffle bag with my clothes.

A short man in a penguin-looking outfit approached me earlier, letting me know that my room was ready, and I could find it on the first floor of the staff building. I look over my shoulder toward the structure in question. It's located nearly two hundred feet from the main house. Not happening. Knowing I have another type of "battle" on my hands, I leave my sniper case inside the trunk and head to the front door of Leone Villa.

In the entry hall, a maid is busy cleaning the glass doors leading to the office. When she notices me, she throws her rag on the floor, then hightails it out of there. Must have been the lucky one who had to clean the blood in the meeting room.

As I climb the stairs to the second level, I take in my surroundings, registering the details I missed when I scouted the house this morning. The walls are covered in wainscoting. Oil paintings in oversized ornate frames. An enormous vintage grandfather clock. A crystal chandelier and matching sconces on the walls. It looks like a museum. It even smells like one. Nothing about this joint is remotely similar to my cub's rooms upstairs. Her space is all modern, like her apartment long ago. She even still has her garden weeds, all lined up in pots along the walls and windows.

There are two doors off the landing. The one on the right leads to a separate unit. I used the balcony of that one to get inside last night, after I took care of the hitman on the roof. The double door in front of me leads to Nera's suite. I grab the knob and step inside.

Nera is standing by the breakfast bar separating the kitchen from the dining area, a mixture of confusion and alarm written all over her face. A yellow heart-shaped bowl, partially filled with cut-up pieces of oranges and apples, sits on the marble counter before her. Half of an apple is lying on a cutting board.

"What are you doing here?"

"I stay where you stay." I nod toward the big brown couch in the middle of the living space. "That'll work."

"That's not what we agreed on." Her voice seems calm, but there is a subtle undertone of panic in it.

I approach the breakfast bar, stopping on the opposite side. In the middle of the counter, a parsley plant is growing in a clay pot. The herb's faint aroma tingles my nostrils. "We agreed I'm going to keep you safe. I can't do that by staying in a separate building."

As Nera's mouth opens to deliver an undoubtedly scathing retort, her gaze sharply swivels to the left. I reach for my gun and snap my head around to follow her line of sight. My eyes land on an open white door across the room, and everything inside me freezes. A tiny little girl, wearing pink pajamas with white flowers all over them, stands in the doorway, clutching a teddy bear to her chest. A shock of tangled dark-blonde hair—so similar to my cub's—partially obscures her face.

"I'm thirsty, Mommy," the girl mumbles and sleepily rubs her eyes with the back of her hand.

I jerk as if someone's stabbed me straight in the heart. All air leaves my lungs as an avalanche of feelings crushes my chest.

Shock.

Hurt.

Betrayal.

I release the hold on my gun and take a step back, not taking my eyes off the little girl.

Since making my way back to Boston, I vowed that this time, I wouldn't get closer than is necessary to keep my cub safe. Felix informed me she got married, but that crackpot didn't mention anything else. And it never occurred to me that she and her late husband had a child.

Nera dashes to her daughter and scoops her up. The girl drops her little chin on Nera's shoulder and tilts her head, her innocent eyes twinkle as she watches me with interest.

"This is Lucia." Cub's voice penetrates the stupor that has overtaken me. "My daughter."

I grab onto the edge of the breakfast counter, squeezing it with all my strength, and close my eyes. I have no right to feel this heartbreaking ache and simultaneous anger, but both emotions are shredding me on the inside.

"I'm sorry, I didn't know." I make myself say and release the marble rim I've been gripping like a lifeline. Of course, she doesn't want someone like me anywhere near her child. "I'll take my things to the staff quarters."

Picking up my duffel, I head toward the suite's door. My mind is spinning, but I know I can make this work. During the day, I'll do rounds around the property and stay out of Nera's view, but there is no way I'll leave her and the girl alone and unguarded in the house at night. I'll just grab the sleeping bag I keep in my trunk, and take up a position outside of their door once everyone goes to sleep.

As my hand lands on the knob, I can't help myself, so I steal another look at them. Nera didn't bother to turn around. She's still standing with her back to me, clutching the little girl to her body. I meet the child's gaze, and she giggles and buries her face in her mother's hair.

Watching the girl clench Nera's locks with her small fists, a strange feeling blooms inside my chest. It's a combination of pain, longing, and jealousy, but there's also happiness. My cub has someone of her own now. Maybe, in another life, that little girl could have been mine, too.

"She looks just like you, tiger cub," I say softly and turn to leave.

"Yes. Except for her eyes," Nera answers, her voice hoarse and trembling. "She has her father's eyes. Pale-gray, like the break of first light to end a starless night."

I swivel around so fast that my duffel bag hits the door frame. Faint ringing settles in my ears, getting louder with every heartbeat until my head feels like it's going to explode.

Nera is still in the same spot as before, but she's facing me now, while tears streak down her cheeks. "Your eyes, demon," she says, barely above a whisper.

Her muted words are another blow to my chest, powerful enough to make me stagger back, hitting the door behind me. The duffel's strap slips off my shoulder, the bag landing on the floor with a thud. I don't even register that I'm walking across the room until I'm standing right in front of my cub and the little girl. My hands rise of their own volition—left one to touch the soft little cheek and the right to cup the tear-soaked smoothness that has haunted my dreams—when reality crashes down upon me.

The spray of blood.

Screams.

Death.

A discarded red scarf on the ground by my cub's feet as she cradled her father's body in her arms. The vibrant red hue of the silk, a mockery of the ribbon of blood trickling from the red hole in the center of his forehead.

My fingers cease just an inch from heaven. I take a deep breath and lower my hands, retreating a step. Then another. I back away from the only thing I ever wanted, all the way across the room. My back plasters to the wall, and all I can do is watch them.

Chapter Thirty-Three

Lucia reaches toward the toy dinnerware set scattered on the carpet by my bed and lifts a miniature cup toward me. "Tea for Mommy."

I take the offering and pretend to drink while observing Kai. He's crouching beyond the threshold and hasn't said a word to me in the last four hours. When he backed away from us in the kitchen, I was so damn heartbroken. He hasn't asked to hold Lucia in his arms. He hasn't even touched her. He just . . . retreated.

He simply stood there with his back against the furthest wall while I gave Lucia her fruity snack, and later while she drew with the crayons Zara bought for her. When it was time for Lucia's dinner, I sat her in her high chair while I prepared the meal. Kai moved a few steps to the side and continued to watch her from afar. His gaze hasn't moved off her for even a second in all that time. It felt like he was trying to absorb our daughter with his eyes.

Just as he's doing now.

"Blue for boys," Lucia suddenly exclaims, takes a blue plastic cup with a coaster, and, scrambling up to her feet, heads toward Kai.

He blinks, pales, and his eyes widen in alarm. Lucia stops in front of him and lifts the toy cup. Based on the expression on his face as he looks down at her outstretched arms, you'd think she offered him an explosive device. Slowly, he takes the cup from her—it looks ridiculous in his huge hand—then mimics my action of pretending to drink.

Lucia smiles, then places her hand on top of his head and giggles. "You have girl's hair."

Kai goes so utterly still, even his breathing has stopped altogether, but the emotional turmoil in his eyes is completely at odds with his unmoving body. Our daughter proceeds to pet his head in the same way she usually does to her plushies, then dashes around him into the living room where Zara is straightening out the cushions on the sofa.

Since coming over an hour ago, my sister has been trying to appear busy with chores around my apartment while keeping her cautious eyes on us. She's always been protective of Lucia, but I'm surprised at the lack of any other reaction from her. No questions, no accusations, no demands. She hasn't uttered a word about finding Kai here. And it's not because of her old reluctance to speak around people she doesn't know. This is different. Nothing that I recognize in her at all.

"We're going to take a bath," Zara says as she scoops Lucia into her arms. "And I'll put her to bed."

I nod. "Okay."

My demon follows them with his eyes until they disappear through the bathroom door, then slowly rises and comes over to take a seat beside me on the bed.

"Does . . ." He swallows while staring at the white wall before him. "Does anyone know?"

"No. Other than my sister and Massimo, our stepbrother, everyone believes she's Batista's."

"Why?"

"Because it was safer that way."

He bends his head, focusing on his clasped hands between his wide-spread knees.

"I need to check your wound," I say.

"It's fine."

"I still need to check it." My shoulder brushes his arm as I stand up, and a shiver runs through me from that incidental touch. "I'll go get my first aid kit."

The medical supplies box is in the kitchen, and as I round the breakfast bar to retrieve it, laughter rings out in the bathroom. It tugs on my heart, making me smile. I can picture Zara getting fully drenched while giving Lucia a bath.

When I go back into my bedroom, Kai is by the nightstand, looking at the picture frames lined up on the top.

"Take off your shirt," I whisper.

His jaw hardens. "I don't think that's wise, cub."

"It's nothing I haven't seen before." I take a step toward him and start working on the first button.

I had this idea of how I was going to appear indifferent. I'd check the cut on his side and be done with it as if it's an ordinary task. After all, he's the one who created this distance between us. I told myself I could do it. I can pretend that there is nothing left between us anymore.

Wrong. His closeness, his scent, the heat of his body as it seems to seep into mine even when we're not touching—and with all of that, my feelings are threatening to burst free. The need to lean into him and bury my nose against his skin, to feel safe and loved again, is overwhelming.

I barely manage to unfasten the first button. My fingers shake and my vision blurs with unshed tears. I take a deep breath and move to the next, and then the next, working solely by touch rather than relying on my sight. Once the last button comes loose, I let go of his shirt and keep my eyes fixed squarely on his chest, not daring to meet his gaze.

The gauze over the cut is covered in dried blood. Carefully, I peel it off, then apply a thick layer of antibiotic cream. The wound doesn't look like it's infected.

"Are you taking meds?"

"Yes."

I start applying a new dressing. "Keep taking them for at least five more days. Just in case."

It's so damn hard being this close, with my whole being aching to snuggle up to him. To feel his warmth enveloping me. I've always felt as if nothing could touch me when I was in his arms. How could he leave me?

"I thought you loved me," I whisper. "I guess I was wrong."

Kai's arm shoots out, wrapping around my waist and crushing me to his body. I can feel the rise and fall of his chest. His breathing—fast and shallow. His other hand comes to the back of my head, fingers tangling in my hair. Warm breath tingles my skin as he lowers his head until his mouth hovers next to my ear.

"You were." The husky timbre of his voice reverberates through me, all the way to my bones. "But only about your use of past tense. Not only do I *still* love you. I fucking live for you, tiger cub."

My breath hitches. I wrap my arms around him, holding him tight.

"Every breath," he continues. "Every heartbeat. Every drop of my blood is yours. It has all been yours from the moment we met all those years ago. If you want it, I'll carve my fucking heart out and lay it at your feet. It's yours, and always will be."

It's not just my hands shaking anymore; my whole body is racked by tremors. I dig my nails into his back with all my strength, while tears unabashedly flow down my cheeks.

"So why did you leave me?" It was meant to be a scream but it ended up as a pained whimper. "Why?"

His embrace gets stronger, squeezing me as if he's trying to merge my body with his. In the next moment, he lifts me and sets me on top of the dresser. His palms move up my arms, slowly, as if savoring the touch, then over my shoulders to cup my face.

"Ask me anything, but that." The look in his eyes as they meet mine is so full of torment and sorrow. "If I tell you, you'll hate me forever, cub. Say the word, and I'll confess every dark sin of mine to you. Just not that one."

I take his face into my hands and press my forehead to his.

When my father was murdered, I was too shaken up to think about anything at all. But after some time, as I lay awake in my bed, waiting in vain for my demon to return, thinking was the only thing I could do. That call he received the last time we were together. The way my father was killed—one shot to the head. And then, my demon disappeared into thin air. It took me a while, but eventually, I connected the dots.

"I already know," I whisper. "I know it was you."

Kai jerks and starts pulling away, but I wrap my legs around his middle, holding him in place.

"I was so angry and hurt when I realized it was you," I continue. "For a while, I even hated you. The only man whom I trusted absolutely. The man who said he'll never do me harm. The love of my life..."

"Please," he chokes out, "don't say it."

"The man who killed my father." I finish with a shaking breath.

Shudders pass through his body, faint at first, but then his entire frame begins to shake.

"I didn't know, cub." A tear slides down his cheek. "I swear, I didn't know. When I saw you there, rushing toward him, and realized what I had done . . . I wanted to die, Nera. I'd rather kill myself a thousand times than cause you the slightest anguish. But I didn't know. The fucking barely literate bastard that I am, I didn't even bother to read the bio of the target. Please, believe me. I didn't know. I didn't fucking know."

I close my eyes and drop my head, burying my nose in the crook of his neck.

"Take my gun, cub. I'll kneel before you, so you can shoot me in the head." His voice sounds so broken, making me hurt from the weight of pain I can hear in it.

"Sometimes, fate likes to play a harsh game with our lives," I say into his neck while I run my palm over his braid. "I know you'd never intentionally do anything to hurt me."

"I am so sorry, cub." His hand is on my back now, pressing me to his still-shaking body.

I loved my father. Realizing that my demon was the one who killed him, almost crushed me. Almost. But I forgave him. Nearly as soon as I grasped the truth. I loved him too much not to. Yet, he still left. And that *did* crush me.

Destroyed me.

Condemned me to hell.

But, my heart knows . . . I'm going to forgive that, too.

I straighten and cradle his face with my palms. His eyes are red-rimmed and glassy. Lost. Wiping away the moisture from his cheeks with my thumbs, I take a deep breath. "I forgave you. For my father. Years ago."

"Some things can never be forgiven, tiger cub."

"They can. When you love someone, you can forgive anything."

"Not this."

I lean toward him until my lips brush over his. "How about a trade, then?"

"I have nothing to offer you, cub. Only my blood, my life, and the army of ghosts at my back everywhere I go."

"Then, I'll have you just the way that you are, my demon," I say into his mouth. "And I don't care about the ghosts."

Kai

Something breaks inside my chest, causing physical pain. It's so massive that, for a moment, I can't draw breath. My eyes bore into Nera's, looking for lies or deceit. There is none. Just tenderness. Love. I don't deserve it. Don't deserve her. But I'm going to take it anyway.

"Done." I bite her lower lip, sealing the bargain. "I was already yours anyway, tiger cub."

Years of waiting to see her again, dreaming of touching her one more time while knowing I'd never get another chance. Longing. Pain. Rage. Love. Everything that was brewing inside me for so long finally explodes. I grab the sides of her silk shirt and tug at the soft fabric, tearing it off her body and causing a small yelp to leave Nera's lips. She pushes my shirt off my shoulders and sinks her teeth into my neck while my hands find the delicate black lace that holds her full breasts. I tear it off, too, then slide my hands up her thighs, raising her skirt.

"Ass. Up," I growl.

Her arms wrap around my neck as she nips my lips. "It's so hot when you bark orders at me, demon."

I hook my fingers on the string of her panties and slide them down her legs. My cock is stretching the fly of my pants so taut that I barely manage to lower the zipper.

"I've dreamed of being inside you again for years," I say next to her ear as I trail my palms down the small of her back to grab her ass, positioning myself at her entrance. "I've imagined how you'll smell. The tiny sounds you'll make." Slowly, I slide inside her warmth, one agonizing half inch at a time, savoring every single moment. "I've wondered if it would feel the same. Like before."

A strained noise leaves her throat as she takes me into her wet core. Her eyes are closed and her hands are in my hair, pulling some of the strands free of their restraint. "And does it? Feel the same?"

"Even better." I thrust to the hilt, then grab her chin, tilting her face to look at me. "I've missed you so fucking much."

I'm about to blow, but I make myself stop and hold still, capturing her gaze with mine. The sensation of being inside her, our bodies joined in the most intimate of ways—is this how it feels to be alive?

"Can you grasp the vastness of nothingness within my soul if you're not near?" I pull out, then slide into her again. Small tremors quake her body, and her eyelids flutter like the wings of a butterfly, but her amber orbs stay pinned to mine. "Everything is gray and empty. You are my lifeline, tiger cub, because there is no life for me if you're not in it."

"I wanted to die," she manages through ragged breath, then gasps as I plunge back into her heat. "When I thought I'd never see you again, I just wanted to die."

One of her hands slips down, grabbing my chin and mimicking my hold. Our breaths mix as we gaze at each other with unwavering stares. Pain shoots across my scalp when she squeezes my hair in her fist. The jolt travels straight to my pulsating cock inside her spasming walls, revving up that need for release.

"Don't you fucking dare leave me again," she says through her teeth.

"Over ninety-nine million," I growl as I keep slamming into her.

"That's how many seconds I've spent without you. And every single one felt like death, Nera." I crush my mouth to hers. "Never again."

My eyes are locked on hers as I pull out and push into her again. And again. And again. The dresser rattles from our unrelenting rhythm, banging against the wall with each hammer of my hips. Nera's soft whimpers transform into moans, ardent and getting louder. So I slide my palm over her lips.

"Bite down on it, cub."

Two rows of white teeth sink into my flesh. I use my free hand to grab her leg, opening her wider. My cock wedges deeper with every thrust, the pressure in me building. We can't be any closer than we are now, but it still doesn't feel like enough. I increase my tempo, slamming into her at a devilish pace. Her teeth clamp harder on my hand.

With the lights flooding the room, I can soak up every delicate detail of her pretty face. Her brilliant eyes, twinkling like two distant stars. The perfect bow of her rosy mouth. Tiny, button nose. Every one of her features is engraved on my mind, and still, I can't stop watching her.

Thrust. Mine! Another. Another. The dresser wobbles. My tiger cub! My shining star. I should pull back, go easy—I'm being too rough with her—but I can't. What if *this* is just a dream? What if I wake up and she's not here? I pound into her faster. Harder. More.

Her dark-blonde hair has come fully undone, and it's plastered to her sweat-dampened cheeks. Rugged breaths, fanning my skin. The smell of our vigorous lovemaking. And the muffled mewling sounds that manage to escape her throat.

Mine. All mine.

Nera's body starts to shake, her pussy pulses around my cock. As she releases her bite on my hand, I crush her to me and slam my mouth to hers, swallowing her scream as she unravels. Wave after wave of tremors racks her body. I hold her gaze through every ebb and flow. My beautiful tiger cub. My lifeline. Coming undone for me.

But once isn't enough. I need to see it again. Right fucking now. I pull my aching cock out and press my thumb to her quivering core, massaging her clit with slow but firm strokes. A moan leaves Nera's lips as she arches her back, her eyes closed.

With my free hand, I seize her chin, squeezing lightly. "Look at me."

Her eyes flutter open, shining like the starlight I tried catching so long ago.

"I need to make you come again, cub. I'll keep taking you over and over until I'm convinced you're real—here in my arms—and not some figment of my imagination. I need to watch you shatter under my touch. Again. And again." I slide two fingers inside her and lean to whisper in her ear. "I'm going to fuck you until my damn cock bursts and my brain finally accepts that you're with me and I'm not dreaming. You're mine." I curl my fingers upward. "You got me, cub?"

"Yes," she mewls.

"Good." I pull out my fingers and lift my hand to lick her juices off. Then, I impale her on my throbbing cock.

Rugged breaths. Moans. Panting. Our sweat mixes as I pound into her relentlessly, driving my dick deeper into her with every thrust. More. More. Again. Again. I almost lose it when Nera buries her nails in my shoulders. Breaking the skin. The dresser drawers rattle, and a loud crack splits the volatile thumps and the slapping of our naked flesh. The fucking thing is going to break. Grabbing Nera under her ass, I shift us to the left and press her against the wall next to the battered piece of furniture.

Every time I plunge into her, she sucks in a breath, letting out tiny little gasps. My God, she's so fucking beautiful, and the sounds she makes are driving me insane. I quicken my pace, keeping our gazes connected. I know I'm out of control, but I can't rein myself in.

"I love you so fucking much," I rasp as I marvel at the sensation of having her body shiver in my arms while her pussy spasms around my length. A low moan leaves her lips, and then she shatters in my embrace.

"I love you too, demon." Her voice is hoarse.

"Good," I growl and crash my mouth to hers. "Because we're moving to the bed now."

Nera

"How many people do you need me to knock off?"

I lift my cheek from Kai's chest and narrow my eyes at him. "No one else for now. Please."

"Someone has put up two million to have you killed. I'm going to take out anyone who's ever seen that hit order just to make sure the motherfucker cannot follow through."

I would have smiled at his statement if I wasn't certain he was being deadly serious. "We made a deal, demon. When I find out who's after my head, you're free to do whatever you want with him. But you won't mess with how I'm handling this business."

"Oh, I'll find the man who dared to hurt you," he growls. "And when I do, I'm going to enjoy the sounds of his screams while I rip off his arms. And his legs. Then, I'll twist his fucking head off and put it on a spike to rot."

"I don't think a warning of such magnitude will be required."

"It won't be a warning. It'll be a guarantee to everybody else." He tilts his head and drops a kiss on my chin. "Will you tell me about her? About... our daughter."

I smile and lay my face on his chest again. And then, I tell him. I tell him how my water broke while I was in the middle of a meeting with the capos. How I thought she was the most beautiful baby when they handed her to me for the very first time, even though she was screaming like a banshee. About Lucia's first word (No!). Her favorite toys and songs. How she bit Adele, one of our maids, when the woman tried to take away her teddy bear to get washed. I tell Kai everything I can think of until my lips feel numb from all the talking. He listens in silence, his arms holding me pressed to his side while his chest rises and falls in quick succession. Even after I run out of stories, he doesn't utter a word, just keeps stroking my back with his trembling fingers.

"I've been taking photos of her, almost every day. I wanted to have all the big and small moments recorded so I wouldn't forget them. And... and so I could show them to you, if you did come back one day," I whisper into the darkness. "Will you tell me where you were all this time?"

"In hell, cub. Instead of seeing my baby girl being born, I was in hell. Where I belong."

I lift my head, trying to see his face but it's too dark. Throwing one leg over his hips, I climb on top, and press my palms over his cheeks. They are wet.

"You belong here," I say. "With me. And our daughter. But I need to know, Kai. I need to know. No lies. And no more secrets."

I can hear the pounding of his heart, feel the movement of his chest under me. Slow, deep breaths. His palms rest on the small of my back, stroking my skin.

"I can endure a lot of things, Nera, but to see you with the hatred in your eyes? That, I couldn't bear. So, I spent days and nights following you or lurking on the rooftop across from your apartment. Watching you. Having you so close, yet so out of fucking reach at the same time, was the worst form of torture. I never meant for you to see me that night." His hand glides up my back and into my hair. "I heard you, you know? When you shouted off the roof into the darkness."

"I didn't mean it. I was hurt and—"

"I know." He kisses my forehead. "You had every right. I couldn't make myself come before you and tell you the truth. But my silent presence, no explanation, was hurting you. I needed to take myself as far from you as possible because, I was afraid that if I didn't put enough distance between us, I'd crawl back to you. Just to have you near. To be able to see you once in a while. But my toxic proximity would only have poisoned the rest of your life. So I took a job in Mexico.

"It was meant to be a simple recon mission. Gather the intel on the latest trouble brewing between the cartels, and get out without being spotted. But I was ambushed before I even left the airfield."

I squeeze my eyes shut. I've never had any dealings with cartels, but I've heard the stories. "What did they do?"

"It doesn't matter."

"It matters to me!" I press my lips to his. "It matters to me, demon."

"Anything and everything they could think of. Don't ask me to put those images in your head, cub. Please. Just . . . don't."

"How long?"

"Three years."

A pained howl leaves my lips. I wrap my arms around his neck and bury my face against his chest. All those new scars I saw on his body make sense now. "But you escaped?"

"I didn't. My . . . friends came to rescue me. I didn't know I *had* friends. I never expected that anyone would ever come for me. Especially those two idiots. They nearly blew me up along with the rest of the compound where I was held captive. Fucking Belov and his obsession with explosives. I'm going to kill him next time I see him. And then, that motherfucker Az pumped me with enough sedative to put down a goddamn elephant. I'm killing him too, the first opportunity I get."

"They saved your life." I nuzzle his neck with my nose. "You should be thanking them."

"I don't thank people."

"I know. But maybe you could make an exception this time?"

"I'll think about it." A kiss lands in my hair. Silence reigns for several long minutes before he speaks again.

"I was half dead when Az and Belov got me out and brought me back to the US. It took me a couple of weeks until I was functional enough to track down the bastard who set me up and kill him. My old boss. He knew about us, and I didn't want to risk him coming after you once he realized I was back." His fingers are in my hair, gently tugging. "After, I came back to Boston and watched over you from afar. Even though I knew you weren't mine anymore. Not after what I did. I thought I lost you, cub."

"You never lost me." I kiss his chin. Then his collarbone. "I was always only yours. Even when I believed that I'd never see you again." I sweep the strands of hair from his face, then kiss his cheek. "Even when I believed that you forgot me or no longer cared."

"Forgot you?" He grabs me around the waist and flips us around, pinning me under his weight. "How could one forget the sole light in the miserable darkness of his life?" His rough palm glides down my rib cage and hip, then lower. A long slow caress of his finger through my folds before he slides his cock inside. Sucking in a breath, I grab his shoulders. I'm still sore after the frenzy of our earlier lovemaking, but it doesn't matter. I lift my hips, taking more of him. Needing to feel more of him in me.

"While I was confined, most of the time I didn't know where I was. Or if it was day or night. And sometimes, I didn't even know *who* I was." He pulls out and lowers his head until his face is a hair's breadth above mine. "But even though I was delirious, disconnected from reality, scattered flashes from my memories kept invading my mind." He slides back inside, sinking deeper. "A red scarf. Warm hands, sewing up my skin. The taste of chocolate cake." His hand grips my chin, tilting my head for a kiss. "Soft voice, reading some nonsense about cows to me, while a delicate finger moved under the words so I could follow."

"Kai . . ." His name comes out as a strangled moan.

The moonlight streaming through the window is falling onto him, bathing his rugged face in a pale glow. I can see his eyes now, gleaming like two silver flames, burning into mine. Two stellar beacons with immeasurable gravitational pull. And I—I am their willing captive, ready to fall in. I never imagined that I'd have someone who'd look at me like that.

"You, my tiger cub, were the only thing I remembered." He lowers his head and buries himself inside me. "My everything."

CHAPTER Thirty-four

Kai

"I'M HUNGRY."

I turn around, my eyes zeroing in on the owner of the tiny voice. Lucia is standing at the threshold, her head tilted to the side as she watches me with interest clear in her wide, pale eyes. My eyes. My heartrate skyrockets, thundering so hard and fast that I nearly feel each punch on the inner structure of my ribs. Our child. My daughter. The urge to hold her in my arms is clawing at me. But I'm too trepid to make a move.

Last night, Nera told me all about Lucia. And later, she let me know how she came to be the head of Cosa Nostra in Boston. For the past three years, she's been stuck in a fucking nightmare, and even though she didn't say so with her words, I know she willingly dropped herself into this shitpit to protect our little girl. She had to be strong, and she was. My fearless tiger cub.

After Nera fell asleep, I snuck out of the bedroom and tiptoed to the room next door. I stood in the doorway and watched Lucia's little sleeping form. I didn't dare to come any closer, simply listened to her breathe as she lay curled under her fluffy yellow blanket. Then, around three in the morning, I crouched by my baby's bed and watched her cherubic face. She looks just like Nera when she's sleeping. I've never seen a more beautiful sight.

My daughter.

It felt like I was observing a miracle. How could something so perfect and innocent ever come from me? Would I taint her if I touched her? Would I stain her with my sins?

Her tiny hand was resting on a pillow, and I wanted to reach out and take it in my own. That yearning was so powerful that I had to grab onto the frame of the bed so my hands wouldn't wander to her uncoerced. When I finally made myself leave, I couldn't even stay away for fifteen minutes. I returned and spent the rest of the night watching Lucia sleep. Once dawn broke, I headed back to Nera's bedroom, fearful that my daughter would be frightened if she woke up and saw me at her side.

"I'm hungry, Rapunzel-boy." Another tiny whisper, but more determined now than before.

I blink. Rapunzel-boy? Must be the hair. I just had a shower and didn't braid it as I normally do. Lucia scrunches her tiny nose at me and spins around, running away. I dash after her.

The plush carpet muffles the sound of her small feet as she hurries into the kitchen area and stops next to the high chair positioned at the breakfast bar. She looks up at me and raises her hand, a teddy bear clutched in her grasp. Is she offering me her toy?

"Up," she says, bouncing on her tiptoes.

I don't understand what she's asking and feel like a complete idiot.

"I'm hungry. Up."

My eyes ping-pong between the high chair and my daughter. My hands shake as I bend to grip her around her waist, lifting her. I've never held a child, and I'm terrified of dropping her or unintentionally hurting her somehow. As carefully as I can, I place Lucia into the chair and throw a frantic glance toward Nera's door. Now what? Should I go wake her up? Or should I—*Ouch.*

"I want to eat, Rapunzel-boy." Lucia grins at me while tugging on my hair.

"Okay. What do you want to eat?"

"Cookies!" Her smile widens. "And ketchup."

"Um... Those two don't go together. And I don't think there's enough nutritional value in cookies. I mean... they aren't good for babies."

Lucia furrows her eyebrows at me, her eyes narrowing into crinkled slits.

"I'm not a baby." Another tug on my hair. "I'm a girl."

"Yes, well... Um... Do you want scrambled eggs?" I ask. It's one of the few things I know how to cook.

"No."

"Sausages?"

She shakes her head, disgust written all over her cute face. "Yucky."

"A sandwich?"

"I want cookies, Rapunzel-boy. And ketchup. And pickles."

I look at Nera's closed door again, but there's no help coming.

"Okay. I'll have a gander."

I find a box filled with honey cookies in one of the cupboards and get the ketchup and a jar of pickles from the fridge. A couple of small plates with cartoon characters are drying on the rack next to the sink. I take one and place a few cookies on it, setting it and the ketchup in front of Lucia on the breakfast bar. The pickle jar I leave sitting on the side of the counter.

Lucia opens the ketchup bottle and squeezes at least half of the contents over the cookies. Then, she fishes one of the wafers from the mess and starts nibbling on it. I take a seat on the other side of the breakfast bar and stare at my baby girl. Her chair is covered in red stains and so is the top of her pajamas. Ketchup is smeared all over her face. Cub is going to kill me.

I grab a paper towel off the holder on my left and start cleaning the disaster around Lucia while she follows my every move with her inquisitive eyes. Once I'm done with the chair, I rip off another few sheets of paper towel to clean her face. My hand is halfway to her before I stop myself. The texture of the towel seems too harsh for her soft skin. Without a better alternative, I drop the sheets and very slowly extend my hand, intending to wipe away the smear of ketchup from her little cheek with just my thumb.

Lucia stills. I freeze, as well. Panic explodes in my system.

I've scared her.

"I'm sorry, I . . ." I start to pull away, while an ache, sharper than anything I've ever felt, pierces my chest.

"You forgot my pickles," Lucia grumbles, snatching my hand with both of hers. She holds my index finger and my pinkie, pulling them toward her face. My heart stops beating as she presses my hand over her mouth, rubbing her face on my palm as if it's a towel to wipe away the ketchup stains. When she's finished, she looks worse than she did before, with red splotches all over her nose and some even on her forehead.

"Mommy doesn't like me do that," she declares and flashes me a toothy grin. "I like it very much."

I swallow and look down to where she's still holding on to me. So tiny. How can her fingers be so tiny? I move my thumb and stroke her teeny fist.

My daughter.

Gingerly, I turn my hand to capture one of hers in mine, caressing the now sticky little fingers.

"Wanna play hairdresser?"

Not moving my eyes off the precious treasure in my palm, I lean over and kiss the ketchup-covered tips. And nod.

Nera

I'm floating in that incorporeal void between wakefulness and slumber until a faint draft invades the room from where the balcony door was left slightly ajar. A chill skims over my exposed flesh. As I blink away the sleep, for a moment, my mind is blissfully blank, but then yesterday's events crash down on me all at once.

I roll over and glance at the other side of the bed. The sheets are wrinkled, but Kai isn't there. Panic grips me in its icy fist and, for a few seconds, the only thing I can do is stare at the indent on the pillow. A moment later, I'm scrambling out from under the covers and running across my bedroom. I pull the door open, nearly letting it crush against the adjacent wall, and rush through only to stop short at the threshold.

Kai is sitting on the floor in front of the sofa, his back leaning against the cushioned edge. One of his arms is raised at an awkward angle, holding up a round wicker basket overflowing with Lucia's elastics, clips, and other hair accessories. My daughter is perched behind him, on the same sofa's edge, worrying her bottom lip with her cute baby teeth as she tries to secure an oversized pink silk flower at the top of her father's head. Meanwhile, the bulk of Kai's hair—with the exception of a skinny, clumsily tied together ponytail hanging in a skewed mess at the back—has fallen free over his face. My poor heart flutters at seeing my demon, holding absolutely still while his wide-open eyes, peering through the strands, are wildly flitting around the room.

"I found them in the kitchen an hour ago," Zara says next to me. I hadn't even noticed her presence, too entranced by the sight in the living room. "Apparently, Lucia woke up and went into your bedroom. Since you were still asleep, she asked him to give her breakfast."

I press my hand over my heart and swallow. "What did he do?"

"I found a box of cookies, ketchup, and a jar of pickles. Hopefully, he didn't give her all of that at the same time." She tilts her head toward the man in question. "I don't think he's been around kids much. Look at his face. He seems utterly terrified."

"Yes." I blink away the tears threatening to spill. "I told him the truth last night."

"Why?"

"No lies. Only secrets." I smile, then elaborate after Zara gives me a confused look. "That's been our thing from the beginning. But not anymore. No more secrets left."

Zara nods. "Are you going to see Massimo today?"

"Tomorrow. I'm meeting with the investors at the Bay View casino after lunch." I glance at her. "You still won't tell me what's going on between the two of you?"

"Since I was three, the only time I've seen Massimo is at our father's funeral. Outside of old photos, I didn't even know what our stepbrother looked like before that. What could possibly be between us, Nera?" Her voice is dry and slightly shaky. "I have to finish that pantsuit for Dania tonight. Will you be back for dinner?"

"Yes." I wrap my arm around her waist, giving her a hug. "Thank you for helping me take care of my daughter."

"Always." She hugs me in return and heads to the dining table, her attention immediately drawn to the page in her sketchbook.

I lean my shoulder on the doorframe, watching my demon hand Lucia a Disney Princess hairbrush. His eyes find mine and lock as our daughter lifts a strand of his long hair and starts to back-comb it.

Chapter Thirty-five

Nera

"What's going on?" I ask as six enormous SUVs make a U-turn on the driveway and park in a perfect line, side by side.

"Sicilians are late," Kai says and wraps his arm around my waist, pulling me close.

The doors of all the SUVs except for one open simultaneously. Men in black tactical clothes exit the vehicles and line up next to each other along the edge of the road. There are twenty of them, and every man carries several weapons strapped to his body.

"Sicilians?" I'm gaping at the small army on my driveway. "The same Sicilians who tried to kill me?"

"Yes. A mistake I'll never forget."

The driver's door of the lead SUV opens and a tall, heavily muscled man steps out. He's wearing a three-piece gunmetal gray suit with a black shirt underneath, and a black tie. The Sicilian looks around and heads toward us, his hands in the pockets of his pants. Dark aviator sunglasses are obscuring his eyes, but the accessory can't hide that something isn't quite right with his face. The skin on his chin and cheeks seems mangled somehow, which makes it hard to pinpoint his age, but everything else about him tells me he's young. Probably midtwenties. He doesn't seem to be carrying any weapons, but Kai's gaze is fixed on him as if this man is the one who presents the biggest threat and not a platoon of armed mercenaries.

"You're late, Rafael," Kai barks.

"My apologies," the newcomer says. "You asked for twenty men. I had to pull a team off a job scheduled for this afternoon. That required adjusting some logistics."

"Dropping a job?"

"Of course not. I'll be taking care of that contract myself." The guy removes his sunglasses and turns to me. I barely refrain from recoiling. His face is a mess of scars and battered skin, as if a wild animal had mauled him. He probes me with his penetrating gaze, with eyes that appear to be his only undamaged feature. "I'm terribly sorry for the misunderstanding that occurred two nights ago. We had no idea that the contract we accepted involved Mazur's girl."

Before I can respond, light reflects off a silver blade. I suck in a breath, staring at the wicked-looking knife Kai is holding against the guy's neck. Blood wells at the spot where the tip nicked the man, and a thin trickle slowly slides down the cold steel. The Sicilian doesn't even blink. He just looks at Kai and raises an eyebrow.

"You do not stare at my woman, Rafael." My demon's voice is low but charged with menace. "You got that?"

"Noted."

Kai slowly lowers his knife. "I've sent you the blueprints for the house and the property. You better do your job right, or I'll slaughter every one of your men, and then I'll be coming after you."

"Your family is safe in our hands." The Sicilian puts his sunglasses back on, and my eyes catch on the multitude of raised scars crisscrossing his skin from his wrists to the tips of his fingers. Nodding at the armed guys standing at attention, Rafael heads back to his car.

The men disperse. Five run up to the house, taking guard positions on the corners and by the front door. Two go to the staff quarters, a two-story building to the left. And the rest of them rush off in different directions across the lawn, heading toward the perimeter walls.

The leader, Rafael, takes another look around, then gets behind the wheel and drives off.

"What happened to his face?" I whisper.

"No idea. Our paths crossed a few times over the years. I first met Rafael while doing a job for the Camorra syndicate about a decade ago, maybe a little less than that. He was still a kid, eighteen perhaps, and his face was normal. When I ran into him again a couple of years later, he was like that," Kai says and ushers me toward his car.

"So, care to fill me in on why you have his men stationed all around the house?"

"I'm not taking chances with my girls' lives. The pricks you have as security couldn't guard a damn library."

"So you hired the team of hitmen instead?"

He opens the car door for me. "Exactly."

"And how much did it cost?" I ask as I slide onto the passenger seat. "Sicilians are expensive."

"A bit more than the original contract for the hit."

I follow him with my eyes as he rounds the hood and drops into the driver's seat. The amount of money needed to hire a small private army of this caliber must be insane. He mentioned the bounty on my head was two million, so he must have shelled out at least two and a half for this. Maybe a full three. It's an absurd fee, even by Mafia standards. "Did you pay three million, or did you manage to persuade them to accept only a point-five increase?"

With a quick movement, his fingers seize my chin. He leans over, bringing his face in line with mine.

"The safety of you and my daughter has no price tag," he grits out, then clashes his mouth to mine. "Let it go, Nera."

"No lies." I take his lower lip between my teeth and bite it. Hard. "And no more secrets."

His eyes flare dangerously. He lands one more quick kiss on my mouth and starts the car. "Zero, cub. Rafael accepted a new contract, tacked on protection with a zero."

I watch his profile as he steers the car down the driveway. He's never lied to me before, but I know Sicilians wouldn't work for free. We're nearly at the gate when it finally dawns on me. A zero tacked on to the original price. Twenty million.

"Tell me about your subordinates," Kai says as he makes a turn. "Start with the blond. The one who was high at the meeting."

"Armando?" My eyes widen in surprise. "He's in charge of the soldiers who collect the debts. His father is one of our investors and had insisted Batista make his son a capo. I had no idea Armando was on drugs."

"Watery eyes. Runny nose. His suit was two sizes too large. He must have lost a lot of weight recently. And he was fidgeting with his sleeves, pulling them down, most likely to hide the scratches. He's a heroin addict. There are needle marks between his fingers, which means he's been using for years."

"I haven't noticed any of those things."

"I might not be able to read written words very well, but I'm adept at reading people," Kai says. "Drug addiction requires money. An addict would resort to any means to get cash if he doesn't have deep pockets. If daddy dearest insisted on a job, maybe he got tired of sonny-boy blowing through the greenbacks he wasn't earning himself. So, I'm sure blondie is already taking a cut of the debts he collects. But would he have anything to gain by your death, even if he did somehow have enough to pay the bounty?"

"Killing me won't magically open the Mafia bank, so I don't think money is the motive. Whoever ordered my hit, did so because of a principle. No woman held a leadership position in Cosa Nostra until me." I lean my head back and sigh. "It's probably one of the older members. They stick to their traditions. Brio—he's the one with black glasses—was the loudest voice opposing me taking this role. He manages our casino operations, which brings in a lot of income. Or maybe the finance guy, Primo. He handles money laundering and investments. He was sitting to the left of Ernesto. Both of them could easily afford the Sicilians' fee."

"What about the guy who was sitting on your right?"

"Salvo, my stepbrother's best friend. He's been helping me since Massimo thrust me into this shitstorm. It's not him."

"I didn't like the way he was looking at you." Kai stops at the street light and takes my chin between his fingers. "I don't share, Nera. Not even in the platonic sense. You better make sure he's out of my sight if you want him to keep sucking air."

"There's never been anything between Salvo and me. I can't be certain, because he's never mentioned it, but I think he's in love with my sister."

"Don't care. Next time I see him looking at you, he's dead." Kai captures my lips with his.

I step inside the lobby of our largest luxury casino and take a deep breath. The ceiling is high, and there are at least a thousand square feet of mostly empty space, but it still feels as if the walls are closing in on me. Meeting with our investors might not be as nerve-racking as meeting with the capos, but even after nearly four years, it still gives me anxiety. Too many numbers. Too many details to remember. I'm always afraid that I'll forget or miss something.

Image is everything in our world. If I lose the appearance of being the calculating, capable bitch I've tried so hard to be, they'll stop supporting me. Without the backing of our investors, the capos will team up and knock me off the top seat. If that happens, I'll be prey for the wolves, and I'm afraid that not even my demon and an army of mercenaries will be able to keep me and Lucia safe then. I've been tiptoeing on a razor's edge between composure and losing my shit for months, but now, feeling Kai's presence as he walks just a step behind, it doesn't seem so terrible.

A man in a flashy suit rounds the corner, heading toward me. Bile rises up my throat as I watch Lotario's approach, a big sleazy smile plastered over his face. I forgot that it's the end of the month and all casino managers will be present at the meeting today. Including my slimy ex.

"Nera." Lotario hurries across the hall toward me, his hand extended. "We've been waiting for you."

He's nearly upon me, his limb a just few inches away, when Kai's arm shoots over my shoulder. The barrel of his gun presses to the bridge of Lotario's nose.

"Back. Off."

"Nera?" Loratio goes still, his eyes cross, staring at the gun. "What's go—"

Kai pulls the gun away and backhands Lotario so hard, that the man ends up sprawled on the polished tile floor several feet away.

"It's Donna Leone to you," Kai says, then fires his gun. Shards of slate explode from the spot next to Lotario's hand. "Come any closer to her than ten feet, and that's going to be your brain matter."

Lotario crawls back a bit, then stands up and starts dusting off his pants. His fingers are shaking.

"I don't think you met my new chief of security, Lotario. Do take him seriously." I smile and continue across the lobby in the direction of the meeting room. Kai comes up by my side and wraps his arm around my waist.

Lotario rushes after us, keeping close to a wall on our left.

"Um . . . What happened to Ernesto?" he asks while his eyes bounce from Kai's face to his hand resting on my hip.

"Kai decided Ernesto wasn't fit for his position. So he relieved him. Permanently." I wait until Lotario is out of earshot, then pull on Kai's sleeve and whisper, "*It's Donna Leone to you*'?"

"I like the sound of it." He looks down at me, his lips pulled into a small grin. "You were keeping secrets, too. Back then. Cosa Nostra princess, no less."

"You never asked, demon."

Kai's face falls. "I know."

The conference hall where the meetings are held is at the far end of the gaming floor, and I can feel a myriad of eyes on me the entire time I cross the distance. Big golden pendant lights shine down on the tables covered in green felt. The bold yellow pattern on the carpet matches the gilded relief decorations on the ceiling, making me feel as if I'm trapped in some weird maze and might not be able to escape. It's still early, and the casino is not yet open, but there are dozens of employees buzzing around, cleaning and preparing everything for the customers about to arrive while secretly staring at me. I come here at least once a week, but it's the first time I'm here not as Batista's representative, but as the official leader of the Boston Family. There are no windows in the building, and, despite the space being huge, I feel as if there isn't enough air.

I stop before the oak double doors with frosted glass panels in the middle and try to suppress a shudder. The urge to turn around and run away is overwhelming. My pause must be a heartbeat too long, and Kai's hold on my waist tightens.

"Just give the word," he says. "And I'll kill everyone inside."

I look up and meet my demon's gaze. He seems relaxed, as if we're out enjoying the night, but the look in his eyes is pure menace, and I can tell that his offer is absolutely serious.

Once, while we were still in high school, Dania and I had a sleepover, and we spent hours lying on my bed and talking about boys. I remember her saying that her dream guy would be considerate and nice, someone who would spoil her with presents and solve all her problems for her. It sounded ideal to my teenage ears. And as I stare at Kai's hard eyes, I realize that I've found my dream man after all. Only, he is as considerate as a hurricane blasting over the shore, destroying everything in its path. A wild, unstoppable force, one that could easily solve all my problems, but who chooses to let me handle my own shit because I've asked him to.

"I don't think that will be necessary." I smile and step inside the room.

Two and a half hours.

I look up from the printout of the revenues and lock my gaze with Kai's. He's leaning on the wall by the door, on the opposite side of the meeting room. The casino managers, sitting on the left side of the long conference table, are arguing across the dark-stained wood surface with the investors on the right, who are demanding various budget cuts. One of the moneymen starts shouting that he won't be putting more capital into a business that's showing a revenue decrease. I might be seated at the head of the table, but it feels as if I'm stuck right in the middle, being bombarded from both flanks.

The anxiety I've been feeling since before I even stepped a foot inside has multiplied several times over, but I've managed to keep it suppressed. Controlled. Detached. Composed. That's all I've allowed these vultures to see because that's the person I need to be in here. But at this moment, I feel like I'm going to burst at the seams, afraid I'll break down in front of them. I don't want to be in charge of this circus. I've never wanted to be in charge of anything. I just want all of this gone, so I can let go and have my meltdown alone.

"That's enough," I bark. My voice may sound steady, but the way I'm feeling is completely contrary to that state. "We're done here."

"What?" Lotario snaps from his seat at the end of the table. "I have workers coming tomorrow to update the flooring and light fixtures. These peanuts you've allocated won't cover even 10 percent of the costs."

"Then I guess you need to scale down your expenses," I say.

Lotario keeps arguing, demanding additional funds. More men have joined the yelling, their voices drilling holes into my brain. I swallow, my eyes finding Kai again, still leaning on the same spot. Our gazes lock, and, just for a fleeting second, I let him see the panic I'm feeling. He pushes away from the wall and reaches inside his jacket, pulling out his gun. He raises his hand toward the ceiling, and the sound of a gunshot explodes in the confined space. The ornate golden chandelier, a smaller version of those hanging in the lobby, comes crashing down on the tabletop.

Absolute silence descends over the room. Investors and casino managers stare at Kai open-mouthed.

"The meeting is over," he says nonchalantly and crosses his arms over his chest, leaving his gun in hand as a subtle exclamation mark on his statement.

"What...? H-how does he...?" Lotario stutters, his eyes glued to the shattered crystals spewed in front of him. "Nera, this is really not—"

Bang!

Lotario's chair tilts backward, then topples, his body hitting the floor.

"Does anyone else wish to add something?" My demon drags his eyes over the men. "No? Then, please wish Donna Leone a good day and be gone."

Nothing happens for a few seconds, and then everyone grabs their phones and organizers off the table. Several voices saying, "Have a nice day, Donna Leone," echo over the hurried rattle.

"Take the corpse." Kai gestures to the man in a light-gray suit stuffing his papers into a folder.

Removing Lotario's body ends up being a two-person job, one to hold the arms and the other the legs. When the last man leaves the room, and the oak double doors shut with a soft click, Kai turns around and locks them.

"That was interesting," he says as he crosses the room toward me. "I think I might come to like the bureaucratic bullshit."

I slouch back in the leather chair and close my eyes. "I think we agreed you'll stop offing my people without prior discussion with me."

"He was disrespectful. No discussion was needed." I feel the chair swinging around and then his breath on my face. "Why were you worried? Did you think one of these idiots was responsible for the hit?"

"No. These guys are only interested in money. As long as it's flowing, they won't risk creating unrest." I keep my eyes closed and inhale his scent. "I just... I don't want to be in control of every damn thing all the time. I don't want to make all the decisions. Sometimes, I just want to let go and, for once, let someone else be in charge."

A light touch settles on the side of my face, rough calloused fingers trace the contours of my chin. I open my eyes and find my demon leaning over, his head cocked and a dangerous glint in his eyes.

"Are you sure that's what you want, tiger cub?" His voice sounds deeper than usual. More husky. Just like a demon would when luring a mortal to sin.

"Yes," I whisper. I'm pretty sure he's not offering to review the revenue statements for me. "But only if I trust that person implicitly."

"Mm-hmm..." His fingers glide down my neck and collarbone to stop just above the button on my shirt. "Is there video or audio surveillance here?"

My breathing picks up. "Video only. The camera mounted above the door."

A corner of his mouth lifts. "Perfect."

Kai looks up, over his shoulder, and reaches inside his jacket with his free hand. He keeps stroking my cleavage with a light touch as he aims his gun at the camera.

Bang!

"Now, we can start." He slips the gun into his holster, and, grabbing me around the waist, lifts me onto the table. "Lie down."

Air leaves me in shallow puffs as I stretch out on the surface. His coarse palms glide along my thighs. Languid. Teasing.

"Do you always wear skirts to meetings?"

His touch is like fire on my skin. "No."

"You will from now on. Less obstacles in my way." He takes the string of my panties and starts to pull them down. "And no underwear."

"Okay."

I watch as he brings my black thong up to his nose and inhales. "I love your smell, cub."

Another deep breath in before he puts the black lace in his pocket.

His hands return to my thighs, pushing my skirt up. When he has it around my waist, he cups my ass cheeks and leans forward.

"Legs on my shoulders, Nera," he whispers as he lifts my butt. "And not a sound."

I grab the edge of the table and squeeze, setting my legs over his shoulders. Kai's eyes never leave mine as he bends his head and licks my pussy. With the first heated contact of his wet tongue, a shiver runs down my spine.

"I absolutely adore how you taste." Another stroke through my folds, more firm and deliberate, teases my clit. Painfully slow.

"Faster," I beg.

"I told you to be silent." He takes my clit between his lips and sucks.

My eyes roll back into my head. A moan threatens to escape, so I press my lips together and squeeze the rim of the table with all my might. Wetness pools between my legs as Kai's mouth releases my clit.

"Open your legs wider. Now, cub."

There isn't a moment of hesitation in my following that order. A shudder runs down my spine when I do as he commands. It feels so good. I've been accustomed to being in control for so long, and letting go of it makes me feel free again. A heartbeat later, Kai's tongue strokes up my slit, licking up my juices, then he seizes my clit once again. I can feel the sharpness of his teeth grazing over my sensitive flesh, and that sensation alone almost pushes me over the edge. His lips seal over my bundle of nerves, the suction turning hard and needy, while the tip of his tongue massages my clit. I gasp and arch my back, feeling the orgasm taking hold of me, but his mouth suddenly disappears.

"Not so fast, cub." A kiss lands on the inside of my right thigh. Then, on the left. "You only get to come when I give you permission."

"Why?" I mewl.

"You're holding the reins of this silly criminal empire of yours." A long lick to my folds. "And even though I'd enjoy offing every one of your subordinates and will extinguish all potential threats, I respect your need to see it through. But in bed"—a light bite on my clit—"I'm the one in command."

I almost come from his words alone. My thighs tremble like I'm running a fever as he carefully lowers my legs and starts unzipping his pants. I bite the inside of my cheek, wondering if he'll take me fast or slow. Where my demon is concerned, I never know what to expect. He releases his massive cock, and just the sight of it makes my core spasm. He grabs behind my knees, pulling me toward the edge of the table.

"What did we agree on, Nera?" The tip of his cock nudges my entrance, teasing my pussy with its girth.

"I won't come until you've given me permission."

A wicked smile pulls at his lips. "Good girl."

Slow. He's going to take me slow this time. I inhale, gradually filling my lungs with air while he slides himself into me. The pressure in my core builds with every minuscule movement, bringing me back to the precipice.

Kai pulls out, then starts pushing inside me again. Even more unhurriedly than before. It's pure madness.

"Faster, demon," I choke out.

"Hush." He glides his palm up my thigh, then over my belly, all the way up to my neck, wrapping his fingers around my throat. "The only sounds allowed to leave your lips now are your moans." He retreats, then plunges in hard, making me scream in rapture.

He moves his hand behind my neck, lifting my boneless self. His thick cock still fully lodged in me.

"Moans." He crushes his lips to mine. "And screams."

Our gazes remain locked while he pounds into me, every hard

drive making me choke on my breath. Between our labored breathing and the clapping of our flesh, I'm vaguely aware of the grinding of the table legs dragging over the wooden floor, providing the melody to the rhythm of his thrusts. The only thing I can do is wind my arms around his neck and hold on for dear life.

"Please," I whimper.

"Silence, cub." He moves his hands down my back, under my ass—squeezing.

My whole body starts to shake, humming with the need for release. All of my cells are a smoldering wire, strung super taut and ready to combust. I can feel the flicker of the spark that will set off the inferno, when he suddenly pulls out.

I grab the tied-up tendrils of his braid. This ache in my core is making me delirious. But Kai just tilts his head to the side, watching me. A wicked glint in his eyes matches a satisfied smirk on his face as he trails his hand across my abdomen to between my legs.

"I imagined doing this to you in that club. While you were dancing with that schmuck, I wanted it to be me." He slides two fingers inside me. "I couldn't handle it, cub. I knew I had no right to think of you as mine at the time, much less put my bloodied hands anywhere on you, but you were. Mine. And I wanted to snap his narrow little neck for daring to touch you." His thumb massages my clit in slow, tight circles, and each time he presses onto it, I come closer to falling off the cliff. "I fantasized about fucking you with my hand, and then with my cock right there in the middle of the crowd, letting every motherfucker in the vicinity know that you were mine."

The pressure inside me keeps building, more and more with every passing breath. Kai pinches my clit and removes his hand, only to replace it with his cock instead.

"You were mine back then just as you are now when I'm finally free to touch you, but I still need everyone to know that, tiger cub.

I want them to see you melt in my hands and picture your fervent face as you scream in ecstasy when I fill you with my cock." His mouth feathers over my ear, the tip of his tongue licking my neck. "That camera I shot? I'm afraid I missed, baby."

My eyes snap open. The feed from that camera is streamed directly to the surveillance company that handles the security at all of our casinos. And one of the capos is the owner of the firm. In a few hours, the whole of Cosa Nostra will see the footage.

"How does it feel to know that all of your underlings are watching as I fuck you in front of their eyes, Nera?"

I hold his gaze as I fight to draw in enough air, trying to contain the climax but losing the war. My nails dig into the skin of his neck as he slides in and out of my dripping pussy, every thrust pushing me further into oblivion.

"It feels like I'm only yours."

"Only mine," Kai roars and impales me so forcefully that my mind goes blank. "Now, you are allowed to come."

White stars burst before my eyes as I scream and shutter in his embrace. My vision blurs, obscuring everything except the silver eyes peering into mine, keeping me enslaved in their superheated fire as the most amazing orgasm rocks my body.

Kai bottoms out inside me as he takes my chin into a fingerhold, tilting my head up.

"So brave and beautiful. And only mine," he growls and explodes into me.

Chapter Thirty-six

Kai

"Kai." A light caress at the back of my head as Nera strokes the length of my braid. "We need to go."

"Okay," I say, not looking away from Lucia's sleeping form.

After receiving a message from her stepbrother, Nera went into her room to get ready. Apparently, he needs her to meet with someone today. Lucia stayed with me, playing on the carpet by my feet. Ten minutes ago, she suddenly got up, climbed onto my lap, and fell asleep in my arms. I don't like the idea of leaving her here, without me around to watch over her, but my cub said this meeting is important.

I stand up and carry my baby girl to her bedroom while Nera hurries ahead of me to open the door. The tight black dress she's wearing hugs her curves and makes her look even more serious than usual. She looks ready to slay armies.

Lucia's bed is under the window, covered with a colorful blanket that has pictures of cookies shaped like houses on it. I ordered it last week, along with a bunch of other stuff—a teddy bear that's several times Lucia's size, a dollhouse, a large set of farm animals, and an idiotic plastic ostrich that sits on a small toilet and shits tiny pink balls into the john.

I pull the blanket away and carefully lay Lucia on the bed, then cover her, tucking the edge under my daughter's chin.

"She will be fine," Nera says when I don't move from the spot. "Zara will be with her the entire time. And your army of hitmen has the house surrounded."

"It's been three weeks. I had someone check the GPS logs on all your capos as well as monitor their bank accounts, but we didn't find anything suspicious. The men I hired to tail your lot didn't report anything compromising, either." I wrap my arm around her waist and pull her against my chest. "I still think you should just let me kill them all."

"No. We have a deal."

"You drive a hard bargain, cub." I lift her and carry her out of the room. "Do you think Lucia likes the shitting ostrich?"

Nera laughs and kisses me. "She loves it. But you didn't have to buy her all that stuff. There are already too many toys lying around."

"I don't care."

"You'll spoil her."

"Children are meant to be spoiled." I stop in the middle of the living room and let Nera slide down my front to the floor. "I've missed three years of her life. I understand that presents can never compensate for that, but I need you to let me do this. I . . . I want her to love me. Please."

Nera raises her hand and cups my cheek. "Lucia already loves you, baby. But not because you buy her toys."

"Then why?"

A small smile pulls at her lips. "You should ask her that yourself, and she'll explain."

"But, she's a child."

"Exactly. Children have a way of looking into a person's soul. Ask her, and you'll see."

I swallow and quickly look away, hoping to God that my daughter will never get even the teeniest glimpse inside my soul. "I need to get my guns. Who are you meeting and where?"

"New York." She shudders. "Massimo arranged for me to meet with Salvatore Ajello. The don of the New York Family. A private plane is waiting for us."

"Your stepbrother is rather resourceful, considering he's locked up in a maximum-security prison," I say. "Why does he need you to meet with that sociopathic Italian?"

"You know Ajello?"

"You'd be amazed how much gossiping happens among the underground. A hit was arranged on him several years ago. I heard that the guy who took the contract was returned in two body bags."

"Yeah, Ajello loves mailing body parts as replies. I got a severed head the last time."

I halt at the threshold and spin around. "What?"

"He caught the man I sent to spy on him. Ajello sent back the guy's head, wrapped in fancy red paper. We agreed to stop spying on each other after that."

"The sick asshole sent you a damned head?"

"It was payback. I had Salvo dump the body of another spy in front of Ajello's building a few months earlier." She clasps her hands in front of her, looking at the floor. "There were two more before that. Spies. I killed them myself. I had to. If I didn't, I would have been labeled as weak and torn to pieces."

I stare at my tiger cub, lost for words. There's no actual bravery in doing something you're not afraid of. She's been thrown into a lion's den, alone and probably scared shitless, and still, she managed to climb out, leaving all the motherfuckers in the dust behind her.

Crossing the distance between us in two long strides, I stop in front of her and take her face in my palms.

"You will not feel bad for keeping yourself and your family safe," I bark. "You got that, cub?"

"Okay." Her lower lip trembles.

"Good." I bend so our faces are barely inches apart. "I'll never forgive myself for not being there for you. But, I'm here now, and no one will so much as look at you wrong going forward. Whoever dares, will instantly meet his maker. And if you decide you'd rather keep this weird criminal empire of yours, I'll off your scheming stepbrother the moment he's out from behind bars so he can't take it from you."

"I don't want it," she whispers. "I've never wanted it. I just want me and Lucia and Zara away from all of this. And I want you. With me. Always."

"You have me, cub. Always." I grab her around the waist and carry her into the bedroom. The fucking Italian will have to wait.

"What about the meeting with the capos you have this afternoon?" I hold the car door open and ogle my cub's pretty legs. Those sky-high red heels she has on are a real turn-on.

"It was just with Armando and Brio. I called them and canceled," Nera says and throws a look over her shoulder at the car that stops behind my vehicle. Two of her "security" guys get out. I place my hand on her hip, keeping her close, and head toward the small plane waiting on the tarmac of the private airfield we're flying out of. Nera's guys follow a few paces behind.

"I feel offended," I grumble.

"Why?"

"You think I can't keep you safe on my own?"

"They are just for show. Ajello will expect me to bring security. Appearances matter."

"Mm-hmm. Is your outfit for the sake of appearance, as well?" I nod toward her tight gray miniskirt and a low-cut red silk blouse visible under her coat.

"Nope. It was the only combination in my closet that was ironed." A corner of her lips curves upward. "Since you tore the dress I planned to wear to this meeting off me."

My cock hardens at the sight of her shapely legs as she climbs the stairs to the aircraft ahead of me. I would greatly prefer to tear off her clothes again and take her right here and now, in front of her dumbass security. But I can keep myself in check for a few hours more. Maybe.

There are four individual seats at the rear of the plane and two couches along the sides of the cabin's forward section. Nera heads toward one of the couches and starts to unbutton her coat. The two security guys take the seats in the back. The ding sounds and the seat belt sign lights up. The captain does his spiel and the flight attendant secures the door before takeoff. The engines rumble to life as the plane starts to taxi to the runway.

I'm placing Nera's coat in the overhead compartment when her barely audible gasp reaches me. My eyes immediately snap down to her. Hers are closed, and she's gripping the purse in her hands so tightly that her nails are leaving indents in the black leather. She's obviously still afraid of flying. But she'd rather keep it all bottled up than show weakness in front of her men.

I turn around and fix my gaze on the security guys.

"Into the bathroom." I nod toward the small door at the back. "Both of you. Now."

They look at me, clearly confused.

"Do I need to repeat myself?"

They scramble out of their seats and rush toward the lavatory. The first one grabs the handle and then looks at me. "Um. How long do we have to stay in here?"

"Until I come get you! Get inside!"

"Passengers are not allowed to use the restroom during take-off, sir," the flight attendant says from his seat near the plane's door.

"You don't say?" I raise an eyebrow and reach into my jacket for one of the throwing knives sheathed on the left side of my shoulder holster. "How about now?"

I throw the blade. There's a hollow sound as its tip buries itself into the leather cushion of the flight attendant's seat, right between the guy's legs. The man jerks, his eyes flaring while he gapes at me.

"Into the bathroom. Now."

He nods hysterically, unstraps his seat belt, and scrambles into the can. When the latch clicks shut behind him, I look down at Nera who's sitting stone-still, her hands in a death grip around the handle of her purse. I take a seat next to her, grab her around her middle, and pull her astride my lap. Her eyes are closed, and her breaths are fast and shallow—it's plain as day how terrified she is.

"It's okay, cub." I brush the back of my hand down her cheek. "They're all gone."

Nera lets out a long exhale and wraps her arms around my neck. The scent of her shampoo fills my nostrils when she buries her face against my shoulder. Her body is shaking badly, so I pull her even closer and stroke her back.

"We could have driven to New York," I say into her hair. "Like you did for your meeting with that Serbian guy."

"You were there?" Her muffled words mix with the roar of the plane's engines.

"Yes. Like I said, I followed you everywhere you went from the minute I set foot back in Boston. I just wanted to keep you safe."

"I felt you. Every now and then, I'd get that pleasant tingling on the back of my neck. I've always felt it when you were near." She slowly straightens, her eyes finding mine. "I thought I was losing my mind."

"It was the hardest fucking thing I've ever had to do. Not being able to hold you in my arms, have you next to me." I kiss her. "But I have you now. You're safe. I promise."

Nera

I stare into Kai's eyes and wonder how it's possible for them to be so warm and so sinister at the same time. Just like him. A guardian angel, and a demon. A man who continues to save me time and time again, but also sows death wherever he goes. A cold-blooded killer. A savior. The love of my life. And the only man in this world who has my implicit trust.

I let go of the hair I've been clutching but keep my eyes locked on his while I move my palms down his chest. The bulge in his pants has been pressing into my pussy this whole time. It hardens even more when I undo the button at his waist and start pulling down the zipper.

"My mind believes your promise, but my body and nerves are still in the grips of irrational fear," I say. "I need to feel you inside me, demon."

His hands slide down my back, over my skirt that got bunched around my middle, to my naked ass. I'm not wearing underwear, just as we agreed. Warm breath fans my face, his gaze rapt on mine as I wrap my fingers around his cock and pull it out. The plane dips suddenly, and I grab Kai's shoulders, leaning forward until I'm positioned just above his dick. Our ride gets bumpy and an overhead sign lights up with a ding.

"*Please remain seated and fasten your seat belts.*" The pilot's voice comes from the speaker. "*We're experiencing severe turbulence but should be through it in a few minutes.*"

I take a deep breath and lower myself onto Kai's cock. The plane starts shaking. Panic explodes within my chest, but I keep sinking onto his hard length, and with every inch that slides inside me, some of the fear recedes. He squeezes my ass with a force that makes me gasp, his chest heaves as his fingers dig into my skin. With one swift movement, he slams me down onto him, filling me to the hilt.

My entire body trembles with each powerful thrust, leaving me breathless and dizzy. He lifts me and slams me back down again. And again. And again. Every thrust sends waves of pleasure coursing through my body, making me shudder and moan uncontrollably. Desperately, I cling to him, my nails digging into his back as waves of pleasure crash over me.

Kai doesn't even blink while his eyes stare fixedly into mine. The low rumble of the plane and our labored breathing are the only sounds in our world. There are no words. And we don't need any. We've never actually needed to voice our thoughts, my demon and I. I can read the look in his eyes, just as he can do with mine.

You're safe. His eyes say.

I know. My own reply.

My body convulses as his unyielding cock rams into me from below, faster and deeper with each thrust. The turbulence around us is increasing, but I'm not afraid anymore. He said I'm safe. The overhead compartment across from us flies open, and something clatters to the floor. I slide my fingers into Kai's hair and slam my mouth over his.

"I love you," I whisper into his lips while everything around us shakes and rattles.

"I live for you, my tiger cub." His voice—raw and guttural—is gritty as it rolls through me.

Gripping his hair in my fists, I come, panting as I break apart. Meanwhile, more baggage compartments open, and things rain down all around us.

There are scary men in this world. But compared to Salvatore Ajello, they all seem like fluffy baby ducklings.

It's not his looks. The New York Don seems like any other wealthy businessman—an obviously tailored expensive suit, no jewelry other than a watch and a thick wedding band on his right hand, and dark hair peppered with gray slicked back in an unassuming style. No weapons in sight, but I'm sure he has a gun on him. And no bodyguards anywhere nearby. Still, just sitting at the table with him gives me the creeps. I don't understand why Massimo wants to do business with this man.

"So? What do you think?" I ask casually.

Even though we're in an upscale restaurant with more than fifty people dining all around, I keep expecting him to slam a severed arm or maybe a head on top of our table.

"Can't say that I'm interested, Nera."

I lift my glass and take a sip of my lemonade. "Why? We are ready to invest ten million over the course of the first year. Double that amount in the second one."

"You're dealing with Dushku," he says as if it's reason enough. Why would Ajello have objections to an assuredly prosperous collaboration only because of our ties with the Albanian syndicate is beyond me, but Massimo is obviously aware.

"I cut all ties with Dushku months ago. We're not doing any business with them anymore."

Ajello raises an eyebrow. "Any specific reason for that?"

"We have a new supplier now." I shrug, intending to leave it at that. Ajello doesn't need to know that Massimo is the one pulling the strings or that he ordered me to break from Dushku.

"Interesting. So, where will you be getting the guns and ammunition in the future?"

"From Drago Popov."

A dangerous spark ignites in Ajello's eyes. "A moment, please."

He reaches inside his suit jacket. My eyes snap to Kai where he stands on the other side of the restaurant, thrusting his hand behind his back.

No. I mouth and shake my head.

"Do tell your watchdog to relax," Ajello says offhandedly as he takes out his phone and presses it to his ear. "If I wanted to kill you, you'd already be dead."

I gape at him. Does the man have eyes on the back of his head?

"Sienna," Ajello says into the phone. "Looks like you forgot to mention that your husband is doing business with the Boston faction now."

A high-pitched female voice explodes on the other side of the line. I don't catch what she says, but she sounds rather cheerful—until she suddenly stops talking.

"I told you what I think about your spying schemes, Ajello!" A growly male voice booms from the phone's speaker. The man is yelling so loud I can hear every single word. "If you have a question for me, you know where to find me. Call my wife again, and I'll rip off your fingers and shove them up your ass. Maybe then you'll figure out what buttons to press!"

The line goes dead. I blink in confusion, staring at Ajello while he puts away his phone. He has a barely detectable smirk on his face.

"It's confirmed, it seems," he says. "I wish you luck in doing business with Popov's group, Nera. You're going to need it."

"Why?"

"A bunch of crazy savages, every one of them. But they are the best at what they do. Unfortunately." He rises from his chair. "Since Massimo has the Albanians out of the picture, I'm happy to discuss business. Tell your stepbrother I expect a call from him when he gets out and takes the reins."

I stare at his retreating back. How the fuck does he know that? Ajello's phone rings while he's still in earshot and I catch his response.

"No, Milene. We're not getting another cat. Two is more than enough . . . No, we're not getting a hamster, either . . . I know they are small. It's still a *no*, cara mia . . . Yes, I'm a very bad person. Love you, too."

Chapter Thirty-seven

Nera

"Stop," Kai barks, standing at the plane's door, looking out on the runway.

I halt immediately, bumping into his back. "What's wrong?"

"I'm not sure, but I have a bad feeling." He takes out his gun. "Clown A. Go get my car."

"Please don't call my security 'clowns,'" I grumble as he hands his car key to the man in question.

"Take off your coat and give it to Clown B. Put on his jacket."

I follow his order and quickly exchange my coat with the security guy. He's a bit on the short side but still looks rather funny in my three-sizes-too-small red coat.

Kai turns toward the pilot standing at the threshold to the cockpit and presses his gun to the man's forehead. "Call the tower. Tell them to turn off the runway lights and everything else that's close to here. Now. And cut the plane's power, too."

The pilot nods and gets back into his seat to radio air traffic control. If this was a regular airport, there's no way any of this could happen. I guess private airports are used to getting strange requests though, because, the runway lights turn off a minute later, followed by all other lights in the area.

Kai's car stops beside the boarding stairs built into the jet's door. The security guard exits the driver's side, circles the vehicle to open the back passenger door, and waits. In the absolute darkness that has fallen like a shroud, the lit-up interior and the headlights of the car glow as bright as a lighthouse on the coast.

"Clown B, pull up the hood and descend the stairs." Kai taps the tip of his gun on the man's back. "Slowly."

My heart rate triples as I keep my eyes fixed on my decoy while he descends the stairs. He's halfway to the tarmac when a gunshot explodes into the night. The man jerks back, then topples to the ground.

Kai takes a step out and starts shooting somewhere to the left. Incoming fire ricochets off every nearby surface. The other guard tries to get behind the car for cover but falls to the pavement, too.

"Cub, you need to get into the car. Stay low."

I hunch and rush down the stairs. Kai keeps raining bullets while he descends the steps—one at a time—behind me.

"Get in the back!" he shouts over the gunfire. "On the floor!"

I dive inside the car and slam the door closed. Kai walks around the hood, still blasting his gun. The instant he's behind the wheel, he hits the gas.

"Under the back seat," he says over the screeching tires as he cranks the wheel for a U-turn.

I grab the edge of the rear seat and lift, folding it up to open the hidden storage. Three handguns. A shotgun. Some kind of short rifle. Two other machine guns I don't recognize. Knives. Grenades. An Uzi.

"AK-47," he says. "Toss it onto the passenger seat."

I gape at the array of weapons, having no idea what an AK-47 is. "Which one is it?"

"Small, brown handle. Big curved magazine."

The short rifle. I grab the weapon and turn around to drop it on the passenger seat. When I look through the windshield, I notice a dark sedan driving a few dozen feet in front of us. And we're gaining on it. Fast.

"Why are we chasing the people who've just been shooting at us?"

"So we can kill them, baby. Get down."

I yelp and curl myself on the car floor, hands covering my head. The next moment, there's a violent wrench and a thundering sound as the two vehicles collide and come to a sudden stop. Getting myself as low as I can behind the driver's seat, I take deep breaths as automatic gunfire explodes overhead.

Should I help?

I am a lousy shot.

Doesn't matter.

Lifting the back seat again, I grab the first gun I can get my hands on. It's a lot heavier than I expected. I check the magazine—full—and pull the door handle. Using the open door as cover, I straighten and lift the weapon with both hands.

The dark sedan has stopped sideways, its left side heavily dented. A man is sprawled facedown on the ground by the driver's door, unmoving. Kai is in the process of dragging the second shooter out through the front passenger door. There's no one else in the back of the car; appears like my support isn't needed.

I lower the gun and approach the driver. He seems pretty dead, considering the missing chunk at the back of his skull. Reddish goo is splattered all over his neck and back. It looks like blood and brain matter. Swallowing bile and trying hard not to puke, I flip him over to get a look at his face.

It's one of the security guys from the Bay View casino. I'm fairly certain I've seen this bastard every week for the last six months, at least.

An anguished wail shatters the stillness. I jump to my feet and rush around the car. Kai has his quarry pinned to the ground and is in the process of breaking the man's arm. The shooter's other arm is listless and lying at an odd angle.

Crack.

I flinch as the man screams. With his face turned away from me, I can't see what he looks like.

"Cub. Can you open my trunk and see if there's enough space?" Kai asks conversationally as he turns to grab the man's leg.

"Enough space for what?"

Crack.

"To pack our friend," he says over the man's wailing cries and grabs the other leg.

"Umm . . . Is that necessary?"

"Yes." *Crack.* A greater intensity of screaming. "I don't have a rope to tie him up. Can't risk having him flee after he tried to kill you. I intend to question him when we get back."

"I'm not sure he'll be alive that long."

"He will." Kai lets go of the broken limb and it hits the ground, then grabs the man by the back of his jacket, turning him over. "I made sure to only fix his joints. No open fractures. I'm saving those for our chat."

I look down at the shooter. There isn't enough light to clearly see his features, so I take a closer step and gasp. "Armando?"

A pained whimper is the only answer I get before Armando's eyes roll back and he loses consciousness.

"The trunk, cub."

I nod and run toward Kai's car.

Two back duffle bags—the size of regular gym gear—are occupying the space of the trunk, but when I grab the first to move it, I barely manage to shift it. I open the zipper to have a look inside and gape. It's full of ammunition boxes. The second bag has more ammunition, along with several various caliber guns.

"Oh. I forgot about those," Kai says next to me. "I'll just put them on the back seat."

He adjusts his hold on unconscious Armando, propping the limp body under his left arm, and moves the bags. Clearing off space in the cargo area, Kai dumps my capo into the void as if the man is nothing but a rag doll, adjusts the broken limbs, and slams the trunk closed.

"I can't believe it was Armando," I say, staring at the closed trunk. "If it was Brio or Primo, I would have understood. They kept saying that having a woman leading the Family is a disgrace to Cosa Nostra."

"Well, it looks like they are happy with your leadership, no matter what they've been saying. I'll still off them for talking shit to you, though." He cups my cheek in his palm and smiles. "Are you absolutely sure you want to let your stepbrother take over?"

"Yes. And you won't touch Brio or Primo."

Kai's smile widens. "Okay. I won't touch them."

His hair came loose at some point during the skirmish and is falling haphazardly around his face. The bluish glow is bathing his rugged features, and glints reflect off raindrops sliding down his chin. I haven't even noticed it started raining. Or that the control tower must have turned on the airfield lights.

He saved my life.

Again.

"So . . ." I choke out. "Does this mean it's over?"

"We'll know for sure once I question him. But, probably, yeah. If there was anyone else involved, they wouldn't have sent a junkie to do the job." He pulls my lips between his teeth. "Still, I'll make sure the security on the property is even tighter tonight, just in case. You and Lucia will be safe."

I grip the front of Kai's shirt and jump into his arms. Our mouths collide in a storm of bites and kisses. His hands grab my ass, depositing me onto the lid of the trunk, and I cry out when my bare skin contacts the cold slippery surface.

"I'm afraid this will have to wait. Wouldn't want that beautiful pussy of yours to catch a cold now." He takes my bottom lip between his, sucking on it as he lifts me back into his arms. A few steps, and he lowers me onto the passenger seat, then takes off his suit jacket and drapes it over me. "Better?"

"Yes," I whisper.

Kai rounds the car to take a seat behind the wheel. The tires squeal as he reverses and floors the gas pedal, driving toward the highway.

Just two people heading home after work.

With a guest in the trunk whimpering over his broken limbs.

"Please show Mr. Mazur to the basement," I tell Timoteo when he opens the door.

The butler's gaze glides behind me and his eyes bulge out as they stop on Kai, who stands with Armando's body thrown over his shoulder as if it's a potato sack.

"Most certainly," the butler croaks. "Please follow me, sir."

Kai nods, then bends his head to whisper in my ear.

"I'll dump Armando downstairs to cool his heels for a bit, then come up to finish what we started." He places his hand on my hip, then slides it down my stomach and lower to press it to my pussy. I barely hold in a whimper.

I follow Kai with my eyes as he walks across the hall toward the basement door the butler is holding open. Armando's head and deformed arms are swinging left and right at my demon's back. The instant the door to the sublevel shuts, I rush up the stairs.

When I step inside the living room, Zara jumps from the couch, her eyes roving wildly over my tangled hair, half-untucked blouse, and Kai's drenched jacket to stop on my muddy shoes. "Nera? What happened to you?"

"We were ambushed when we landed and tried exiting the plane." I sweep away some of the strands falling over my face.

"What?! How?" She dashes across the room. "Are you okay?"

"Yeah, I'm fine. I'll go check on Lucia before Kai comes up. What did you give her for dinner?"

"Vegetable stew. Nera! Who attacked you?"

"It was Armando. Kai has him in one of the underground rooms, but he'll handle him later. I'll tell you everything in the morning. Um... Thank you for watching over Lucia, but I really need you to go now." I grab her waist and lightly push her toward the door. "Good night."

Zara stops at the doorway, looking at me over her shoulder. "Are you all right?"

"Yup. Just waiting for Kai. He should be here any moment. We have to finish an earlier discussion."

My sister blinks. "Discussion?" she asks, but then her eyes go wide as color creeps into her cheeks. "Oh. Um... I'll just go now."

As soon as she's out the door, I drop my phone and my purse on the dining table and head into Lucia's room. She's sleeping with a stuffed tiger Kai bought her under her arm. I sit down on the edge of the bed and reach out to lightly stroke my daughter's chin.

"Everything is going to be okay now," I whisper. "Your daddy promised he'll make sure we're safe. And he kept that promise."

A sharp intake of breath comes from behind me. I turn around and find Kai at the threshold, clutching the doorframe with an iron grip. His face is pale as a sheet of paper.

"She could have heard you. You should be more careful."

"We'll tell her soon anyway. She deserves to know." I stand up and close the distance between us. "*You* deserve her knowing the truth."

"Never." He watches our daughter, his jaw set in a hard line.

I take his chin between my palms, tilting his head down, making him look at me. "Why?"

"What will you tell her her father is?" he asks through gritted teeth. His tone is bitter, but every word is filled with pain and sorrow. "A hired hitman? A villain who killed her grandfather? Someone who can't even remember his own name?"

"No, baby." I rise onto my toes and kiss his jawline. "I'm going to tell her that her dad is Kai Mazur. The man who's been watching over me for years, keeping me safe. Who took a bullet for me. The man who has barely slept in weeks because he's been protecting us. Who spent hours simply watching her sleep, instead of getting rest himself. Our guardian angel. The love of my life." I tilt his head lower until our lips touch. "The man who loves her and her mamma more than anything else. Just as we love him. That's what I'll tell our daughter."

"Nera . . ." he whispers into my mouth.

"Kai. Let me . . . let *us* love you. Please."

A heavy, pained breath leaves his lungs. He closes his eyes and touches his forehead to mine. "It's the dream I've been dreaming but never dared to hope would come true. People like me are not allowed such ambitions, tiger cub."

"Well, we're going to live our dreams from now on." I kiss him. "And everything else can go to hell."

My phone starts ringing somewhere. I take Kai's hand and pull him along with me as I hurry toward the sound. I just want to turn the damn thing off, but as my eyes fall on the flashing screen, my body goes rigid.

"It's Ajello," I shudder. "He almost never calls. I need to take this."

"Want me to kill that psycho for you?"

"No. I just . . ." I mumble staring at the name on the screen. "I'm not in the right mental state to talk with him now, but I have to."

"Then, I guess I should help you with that." He takes the phone from my hand. "You haven't put on your underwear, have you, cub?"

"No. Why?"

A small smile pulls at my demon's lips. He sets the phone on the dining table and hits the speaker.

Kai

"I hope it's not an inconvenient moment, Nera." Ajello's voice comes through the line.

I keep my eyes fixed on my cub as I undo the button on her skirt and then rip the garment off her.

"Not at all," she says in a calm voice as she watches me unzip my pants. "What can I do for you, Mr. Ajello?"

Wrapping my arm around Nera's waist, I lift her onto the table. She opens her mouth to say something else, but I place my finger to her lips and shake my head. Then, I bury my cock in her in one powerful thrust.

"I heard you've had some trouble during your return. Is everything okay?"

I wait for her to draw a breath, then slam into her again. The phone slides toward the middle of the table.

"Quite fine." Nera wraps her arm around my neck and wets her lips. She looks like sin personified, with her cheeks flushed and her pussy swallowing my cock. "And how did you get that information, Mr. Ajello?"

"I have my sources."

Taking ahold of her wrists, I move her hands to the edge of the table.

"Hold tight," I whisper.

Nera grabs the wooden surface. My right hand is at the back of her neck, while the other grips her delectable ass.

"I thought we had an agreement regarding spying on each other." She arches her back as I plunge into her again.

"I have people monitoring certain locations. Private airports included."

"Why am I not surprised?" A hushed moan leaves Nera's mouth as I quicken my pace. Her lips tremble and her breathing hitches. "Is that the reason for your call?"

"No. I need you to pass a message to your stepbrother."

"I'm listening."

I grab Nera's chin between my fingers and seize her lips with mine. She tastes like rain, and wind, and the sun. Like life itself. I can feel her starting to come as her core quivers around my cock. With one last nibble on her lips, I pull out and carefully lower her to the table. The look she gives me is a mix of frustration and confusion. Holding her gaze, I widen her legs and dip toward her center.

"Not a sound," I say and bury my face in her sweet pussy, sucking hard on her clit.

"Tell Massimo, he owes me . . ." I miss the rest of the Italian's words.

Shivers run through Nera's whole body. I release her clit and slide my tongue into her opening as deep as I can.

". . . He'll know what for. One day, I'll collect," Ajello adds.

Nera is already shaking in ecstasy when I straighten and slip my cock to where my tongue has just been. I cover her lips with my palm and slam all the way in.

The phone line disconnects.

And Nera screams into my hand.

Chapter Thirty-eight

Kai

THE DRAPES ON THE FRENCH WINDOW ARE PULLED TO the sides, allowing me to see Rafael's men roaming across the front yard as the first rays of the sun break above the horizon. I stroke Nera's slender arm, starting at her shoulder and then continuing down to her palm. Careful not to wake her, I lift her hand to my lips and place a kiss on her fingertips. As I'm lowering her hand back to my chest, my eyes catch on her ring finger.

Since the minute she allowed me back into her life, the urge to have her marked as mine has been clawing at me day and night. I don't believe in ceremony. I don't need to sign some stupid piece of paper handed to me by a nameless clerk to claim her as my own. Or a geezer in funny clothes to proclaim her as so. If any man dares to approach my cub to steal her from me, I'll just snap his neck. But still . . . I stroke her ring finger one more time, then slip out of bed, grabbing my phone from the nightstand. As I head to the bathroom, shutting the door quietly behind me, I find Felix's number in my speech-to-text app.

06:34 Kai: I need you to do something for me.

A minute later, an audio file arrives. So he didn't forget my little problem with reading.

06:35 Felix: I'M SLEEPING!!

06:36 Kai: It's urgent.

06:36 Felix: Are you starved, dehydrated, and dying in some dump again? Because if you're not, it can FUCKING WAIT.

06:38 Kai: No. I need a priest. I want to get married.

A few minutes pass without a reply, and then:

06:40 Felix: Send me your location and stay put. Is it the Mexicans again? I'll have Sergei come get you out. When was the last time they drugged you?

06:41 Kai: I'm not high. Find me a priest and have him delivered by the end of the day, or I'm going to gut you real slow the next time I see you.

I send him the address as I return to bed and throw the phone back onto the nightstand.

Nera stirs and lifts her head off her pillow beside me. "What time is it?"

"Almost seven." I gather her back into my arms, move a strand of dark-blonde hair that's fallen over her face, and kiss her nose.

"Do you think it was wise to leave Armando in the basement overnight?"

"If you're worried about the wine that's down there, don't be. He can't drink it with his arms broken."

"I'm not worried about wine. What if he went into shock and died?"

"He wouldn't die of a few broken bones. Well, not right away at least. I'll go question him after breakfast. We need to know if anyone else was involved."

Nera tightens her hold on me and buries her nose in the crook of my neck. "I can't wait for the day when Massimo gets out, and we can leave this madhouse behind."

"But you make a magnificent Donna, cub. I could—"

"I don't want you to slay my stepbrother, Kai. But, thank you for offering." She sighs. "I just want all of us—you, me, Lucia, and Zara—away from all of this. A big house. Huge yard. With a bunch of animals for Lucia to play with."

"And no neighbors anywhere nearby."

Nera laughs into my neck. "And no neighbors."

"How long until your stepbrother gets released?"

"Five more months."

The bedroom door creaks open.

My head snaps up, and I stare in dread at Lucia standing at the threshold, holding her tiger plushie in one hand and a hairbrush in the other. She takes in the sight of me and Nera lying together in bed, her eyes bouncing from me to her mother. And then, she meets my gaze with a bold one of her own.

"Cub?" I whisper. "What should we do?"

"Why do you call Mommy 'cub'?" Lucia's tiny voice breaks the silence in the room.

"Um . . . well . . ." I steal a glance at Nera, hoping for help, but she just giggles into her hand. "It's a nickname."

"Why do you call her nicky name?"

"Because . . . I love her."

Lucia wrinkles her nose as if thinking about it.

"I wanna nicky name, too," she demands, then dashes across the carpet to climb on the bed. My heart races like a runaway train as I watch her crawl over and snuggle between us.

"Okay." I barely manage a reply. "How about *tygrysek*? It means baby tiger."

"I like." She grabs a handful of my hair and starts to brush it.

"I have a nicky name, Mommy. Rapunzel-boy loves me, too."

My lungs contract so hard that I can't draw a breath. Nera's hand grabs mine, squeezing it.

"Yes." I barely manage to speak. "I love you very much, Lucia."

"I know." She looks up at me, right into my eyes. "It hurts, but you let me make your hair pretty. 'Course, you love me."

Warmth erupts inside me, burning as hot as an exploding star. I almost melt from the onslaught of feelings overtaking me. I reach out and carefully stroke Lucia's soft cheek with the back of my hand. I'm not sure she'll ever understand the depth of my unconditional love for my two tiger cubs.

"I'll love you till the last drop of blood courses through my veins, *tygrysek*," I whisper.

"Yucky." She makes a disgusted face. "I don't want blood. I want breakfast. Can I have cookies and ketchup again?"

"No," Nera says next to me and rubs her eyes with her hand. She's been silent during the whole exchange. "But we can show Kai how to make oatmeal with fruit for you."

"Okay. Oatmeal is yummy." Lucia shrugs, takes the elastic from her ponytail, and tries to put it in my hair. "Last time Mommy made me oatmeal we had lotsa boomers and big rain, which made Mommy sad. But she told me a secret then. She said my daddy gotted lost a long time ago in the storm. But that he gonna find us one day. Are you my daddy, Rapunzel-boy?"

I feel like someone dropped a fucking mountain on top of me; its weight bears down on my chest. I can't move. I can't even breathe. I open my mouth to say something, but no sound leaves my lips.

"Yes," Nera says, her voice breaking. "He finally found us."

"Oh. Good." Lucia nods in a serious manner, then pulls on my hair with a quick tug. "Don't get lost again."

I close my eyes and kiss the top of her head. "Never again. I promise."

CHAPTER Thirty-nine

Nera

"We need to reschedule today's meeting," Brio's voice comes across the line. He sounds really strange. "I'm not feeling well."

"All right," I say. "I'll just have Primo come by so we can go over this month's numbers."

"I'm afraid Primo is indisposed, as well. He's still at the hospital. The doctors are trying to remove the remnants of rubber glue from his esophagus."

"What?"

A coughing fit overcomes Brio before he's able to respond. "We're both very sorry for disrespecting you. Please assure Mr. Mazur it won't happen again." He finally wheezes out the words.

I throw a look toward the kitchen where Lucia is sitting on the counter. Kai is standing behind her, braiding her hair. She wanted her hair done like his and wouldn't let me do it.

"I'll let him know, Brio." I cut the call and approach my demon. "Where did you go after breakfast?"

"To get you flowers."

My eyes wander to the bouquet of red tulips on the dining table. "And that's all?"

"I might have had a small errand to run on my way back." Kai shrugs.

"Did it involve my capos?"

"I haven't put a finger on them, cub. Only asked them to open their dirty mouths real wide."

"Kai—" I start but my phone rings again. A call from the gatehouse.

"Two men are at the gate, requesting to be let inside, Mrs. Leone," the guard tells me. "They say they are Mr. Mazur's friends and have a delivery for him. I tried calling Mr. Mazur, but he's not answering."

"It's the guard from the gate." I look at Kai. "Are you expecting a delivery?"

"Yes." He takes the phone from my hand, lodges it between his ear and his shoulder, and resumes braiding Lucia's hair. "Big blond guy? Whistling an extremely annoying tune?"

"Yes," the guard replies. "And another man. Dark-haired. Looking really displeased."

"Let them pass."

"Your friends?" I ask.

"Yes." He wraps his arm around Lucia's waist and sets her onto his hip. "Let's see if they brought the package I've asked for."

"A package?" I ask as I follow Kai down the stairs. Lucia is clutching his shirt and trying to attach one of her blue hair extension clips with a cute bow to the top of his head. Kai's long braid swings side to side across his back as he descends to the main level, the end of it is tied by Lucia's pink scrunchie. "And what's in the package?"

"A priest."

I furrow my brows. A priest? There's no time to ask for an

explanation, though, because Kai is already opening the front door. I trail him outside, getting a look at the two men on our driveway.

One is leaning on the hood of a beat-up SUV with his arms crossed over his chest. He's dressed in dark-gray cargo pants and a black T-shirt. Every visible inch of his skin, except his face and neck, is covered in ink. His hair is the palest shade of blond.

The other man is wearing a bespoke black suit that fits his large frame like a glove. His face is set in a dark scowl as he drums his fingers on the roof of his black sedan.

"I didn't expect you," Kai says, looking at the scowling guy.

"Albert blackmailed Az into helping me," the blond one blurts out. "He owes the old bat a lot of favors."

"Who's Albert?" Kai asks.

"It's Felix. Don't ask," the dark one, Az, replies as he clicks the small remote in his hand. "Can we get this over with? I have other things to do in Boston."

He heads around his car and leans over the trunk. Odd sounds emerge from inside the vehicle.

"Silence," he snaps, then pulls a man from the cargo space.

The guy's hands are tied in front of him and there's a gag in his mouth. He wriggles in Az's hold while he's dragged and then deposited a few feet before Kai. "That's my contribution."

"I have two!" The blond man grins and opens the back door of his SUV. "And mine are even dressed for the occasion."

He pulls out a man in a long black robe, tied and gagged as well, and then another fellow in similar circumstances, but this one is garbed in a white vestment adorned with intricate gold details.

"You weren't specific in your request." The happy blond beams like a kid at Christmas as he pulls both men toward us. "So I got you one Orthodox and one Catholic. Az's is Protestant. Now you have one of each. Take your pick."

"Jesus fuck." Kai sighs next to me and squeezes the bridge of his nose. "That's not a priest, Belov."

"What?"

"This one"—Kai gestures at the first guy pulled out of the SUV—"in the black gown . . . He's a fucking JUDGE!"

"Oh? So he can't perform a wedding? Shit. I'll off him and get you a new one."

"A wedding?" I ask, confused. "What wedding?"

"Is this the bride?" Belov points his finger at me. "She looks like a nice person. What the hell made her want to marry a motherfucker like you?"

"Kai? What's going on?" I ask.

He looks at me, his eyes boring into mine. "We're getting married."

My lungs stop drawing air. I stare at my demon and my heart swells to double, then triple its size. "We are?"

"You didn't even ask the poor thing if she wants to marry you?" his blond buddy challenges.

"Shut up, Belov," Kai growls, his gaze never leaving mine. "You are my reason for living, cub. And, in this life, I don't need a signature or a ceremony to confirm that you're mine. You are. And I'm yours, every cell of my body. Till my dying breath. And even when I perish, in whatever afterlife awaits." He cups my cheek in his palm and bends his head so our noses are almost touching. "But I want to do this thing right."

"So you had three priests kidnapped?" I choke out, trying to hold back tears.

"Just two, apparently. And a judge. Will you marry me, tiger cub?"

I bury my fingers into his hair and kiss him back. "Every day of my life."

"Mommy. Daddy," Lucia chimes in from Kai's embrace. "Can I have cookies and ketchup for lunch?"

"Yes," Kai and I whisper into each other's lips.

"You have a kid? And you let her eat cookies for lunch?" The happy pal's voice interrupts us. "That's, like, super unhealthy."

"I'm going to count to three, Belov," Kai says as he keeps attacking my mouth. "If you're still there when I finish, I'm going to strangle you."

"Ungrateful motherfucker," Belov mutters. "Next time you need a nice selection of priests, call someone else. And what the fuck is that shit in your hair?"

Kai

The lanky guy in a long black gown looks around the spacious office, his eyes frantically flitting about the place as if searching for a way out. He finally realizes there's no escape and no one around to help him, so he turns his gaze to me.

"I-I have never performed a marriage ceremony before," he stutters, tugging on the collar of his dress shirt underneath.

"Then, you better be amazing at improvising," I say and pull my girl closer to my side. "Which one would you prefer to go first, baby? Orthodox, Protestant, or the judge."

"Um . . . I don't have a preference." Nera rises to her toes and whispers in my ear. "Maybe you should untie them first. They seem a little freaked out."

I look at the three men standing across the boardroom table. The judge is still pulling on his collar, his hands shaking. The Orthodox priest—an older guy in a white gown—has his back straight and is trying to feign composure, but sweat is dipping from his forehead by the bucketful. And then, with a shock of messy hair and glasses sitting askew on his nose, the twentysomething-year-old Protestant priest appears to be ready to puke. His face is so pale it seems green.

"They'll manage as is for a few more minutes," I say and nod at the three men. "Let's have all three do it together, at the same time."

"At the same time?" the green-faced guy chokes out. "But . . . we have different rituals. The vows are different. And what about—"

"I'm a fucking judge!" the black-gowned man screeches, throwing his tied-up hands in the air. "I'm going to put all of you lunatics in jail!"

"I love weddings," Sergei chirps on my right. "I should have brought snacks."

"Belov," I warn, but the idiot just keeps rambling while the judge continues to yell about handcuffs and life sentences. I shouldn't have let the crazy Russian stay, but he insisted that I needed a best man.

"You know, I only had one priest at my wedding," he says. "Three makes it so much merrier. When you guys are done here, I'm taking them to Chicago to have them marry me and my wife all over again. Angelina is going to love it . . ."

On the other side of the table, the judge is still bellowing out threats, pointing his finger at me. The Orthodox priest is fidgeting next to him, his eyes turned toward the ceiling, mumbling a prayer while trying to untie his hands. Between them, the green-faced guy is hyperventilating; a minute more and he's going to faint. A couple of Rafael's men are aiming their semiautomatic weapons at the clergies and judge, yelling for them to calm down.

" . . . Maybe I can find a real Catholic priest on my way home? If I can't, the judge will have to do," Sergei continues. "Do you think my wife would notice the difference?"

I reach behind my back and take the gun out of the waistband of my pants. I stuck it there after I took Lucia up to Zara's, getting my little girl away from Belov's fucking loud mouth and nonstop shit. *Would his wife notice the difference if I shoot this asshole?* I take a deep breath.

The overhead lamp here is much smaller than the chandelier at the casino, but it'll serve its purpose. I aim at the point where the chain connects to the ceiling and fire. A loud bang explodes inside the room. Almost instantly, the fixture hits the floor, right between Rafael's men and our unwilling guests.

"The three of you are going to start the ceremony now. You"—I point the gun at the Orthodox priest—"will go first."

He quickly nods.

I shift my aim to the Protestant one. "You're going to repeat after him."

The green-faced guy swallows and nods, too.

"And you"—I double-point my gun at the judge—"will make sure to follow swiftly after them. Am I being clear?"

All three of them nod like fucking bobbleheads.

"Good." I lay the gun on the table and turn, taking Nera's hand in mine.

"Blessed is everyone that fears the Lord..."

I stare into my cub's eyes as the first priest speaks, followed by his Protestant counterpart and then the judge, but I ignore the actual words being said. The words are nothing but those early distant stars—their glow overshadowed by much brighter things. I don't care about the words or the ceremony. The only thing that matters is this enormous, indescribable love I feel for the woman in front of me, and the look in her eyes that says she feels the same.

"...Blessed is the Kingdom of the Father, and of the Son, and of the Holy Spirit... Um..." The priest clears his throat. "I need the Bible for this part."

Without breaking our locked stare, I push the gun I've left lying on the table toward the priest. "That's my Bible. Proceed."

"Um . . . yes. So . . . *And of the Son, and of the Holy Spirit, both now and ever, and to the ages of ages . . .*"

"You can't have us married with a gun," Nera whispers while the priest turns toward the east, lifting the weapon in the same way he would the Holy Scripture.

"I don't know much about marriage vows, cub, but I know they mention loving, cherishing, and keeping their partner safe. In good times, and bad. I won't swear to you over a bunch of old papers. I'll give you my oath on the weapon which will take the life of anyone who would ever think of doing you, or our daughter harm." I lift her hand to my lips and kiss the tips of her fingers. "I'm yours. And you're mine."

"I'm yours," she whispers back, her eyes glistening. "And you're mine, Kai."

"*. . . join them together, for by You is a wife joined to her husband. Join them together . . .*"

Reaching into the pocket of my pants, I take out a pair of white gold rings. I bought them this morning while my florist buddy was depollinating the tulips.

"Would you please be my wife, tiger cub?"

"Always, demon."

I slip the smaller of the two bands on her finger, and watch—breathless—as she slides the other one on mine. Then, I grab my wife around her waist and crash my mouth to hers.

"*Amen,*" the three voices say in unison.

Boisterous clapping fills the room, but it's suddenly cut off by the sound of something big hitting the floor.

"Fuck, Mazur," Sergei exclaims. "Your priest number three just fainted!"

Nera

"Is he really taking them with him?" I ask, watching Kai's blond-haired friend trying to stuff the poor judge into the trunk of his SUV. The two priests are sitting tied and gagged in his back seat.

"Looks like it," Kai responds.

Belov slams the trunk closed and, whistling to himself, gets behind the wheel. Two quick honks of his horn and he drives off, heading toward the gate. Kai tightens his hold on my waist.

"Should we go consummate the marriage right away, or check on our prisoner first?"

Shit. I completely forgot about Armando. "Maybe we should—"

I don't finish the sentence because Kai pushes me behind him and takes out his gun. Peeking around him, I notice a sleek black car advancing up our driveway.

"Who the fuck let that vehicle through the gate?" Kai yells.

The car stops a dozen feet from the stone steps. The driver's door opens and a man steps out. It takes me a moment to recognize him without his prison uniform. He's wearing a stylish gray suit and a perfectly pressed white shirt underneath, just as he was the night the police led him out of our home. But it's the only similarity to that twenty-year-old man from so long ago.

"Hello, sis." Massimo fixes me with his gaze.

"It's okay." I take Kai's wrist and lower his hand. Only when he's put away the gun do I face my stepbrother again. "Massimo, I didn't expect to see you out for a few more months."

"Me neither. But it looks like someone important pulled some strings and got me released sooner." Massimo climbs the stairs and stops in front of us. "I hope you don't mind?"

"I think I'm going to celebrate this day as my second birthday," I say. "I fulfilled my part of the deal. Are you going to fulfill yours?"

A menacing glint flashes in Massimo's eyes as he probes me with his unrelenting stare. Then, he switches his focus to Kai. He looks my demon over as if assessing the level of potential threat, and his attention falls on our joined hands. Ever so slightly, Massimo's eyebrows rise.

"Yes," he says when his eyes meet mine again. "You're absolved of any further obligations to Cosa Nostra. I'll make sure everyone in the Family is informed."

"Not good enough, Massimo. I want a written statement that I'm not considered a part of the Family anymore. And I want every capo's signature at the bottom."

"You want Cosa Nostra to officially disown you? That's never been done, Nera. Not in Boston, at least."

"I don't care. You promised me full freedom. I won't settle for anything less."

Massimo crosses his arms at his chest—the action threatens to burst the seams of his suit jacket because of his bulging biceps—and narrows his eyes at me. He doesn't like my terms, but he won't dare break his word.

"Fine," he says.

The burden that has been crushing me for the past four years dissolves and vanishes with my next breath. I'm finally free.

"Are you going to stay here, or return to Nuncio's house?" he asks.

"I'm not staying here a second longer than necessary. And you can have my father's house if you want." I squeeze Kai's hand. "My family has different plans."

"All right. I'll transfer the amount for the value of the home to your account. Will you tell me where you'll go?"

"Maybe," I say. It won't be easy to forgive him for what he has made me do.

"Very well. Let's go see Armando now and wrap everything up. From what I heard, you were too busy to question him."

I don't bother asking how he knows about Armando. Even locked up, Massimo has always had a way of being well aware. I turn around to head inside, but Kai's hand slips from mine. I look over my shoulder and find Kai standing in front of Massimo, his hand wrapped around my stepbrother's throat.

"The only reason you're not bleeding out on this threshold is because, for a reason I can't fathom, my wife still cares about you. Even after everything she had to endure while your ass was locked up." His voice is low and threatening. "Be careful, because if that ever changes, I'm going to find you and rip out your fucking throat."

The corners of Massimo's lips curl upward.

"I see you've chosen the right man, sis. I guess I won't have to worry about you anymore." He takes Kai's wrist and moves his hand away. "Let's go see Armando."

When we get down to the basement, the stink of urine and other bodily fluids hits me like a hammer. I press my palm over my mouth and nose and take a peek from behind Kai's back. The capo is lying on his side, his limbs at unnatural angles to his body. His eyes are open but empty, staring into nothing at all. What looks like white foam is smeared around his mouth and has slid to the ground around his head.

"Dead?" I ask.

"Yes." Kai crouches next to the body and presses his palm to Armando's ghostly white face. "Cold. Considering the temperature in this room and the fact that rigor mortis is still present, he was killed during the night." He tilts Armando's head up, observing the foam around his mouth. "Poisoning. Cyanide most likely."

"It wasn't you?" Massimo asks as he comes to stand next to Kai.

"Death by cyanide ingestion is not overly pleasant, but much faster than what I had planned for the motherfucker. Someone sneaked in last night and killed him so he wouldn't talk." Kai rises and faces my stepbrother. "We're leaving within an hour. This is your shit now, and you're going to sort it out real fast. If I catch even a tiny grumble that anyone from Cosa Nostra has mentioned my wife's name, in any way, you're dead."

"This is a Family matter," Massimo growls, his eyes swiveling back to the body. "As soon as it's announced that Nera is no longer a member and I have taken over, whoever wanted her out of the picture will switch their attention to me."

"Perfect." Kai takes my hand. "Let's go pack Lucia's and your things, baby."

"Can we have ducks at our new house?" Lucia chirps from my arms.

"Yes," Kai says as he puts the last of my suitcases in the trunk. I want to leave this dreadful place as soon as possible, so I've only packed my and Lucia's clothes and some toys. Someone can send us the rest of our things later.

"And pigs? I love pigs!"

My demon throws me a concerned glance. I just smile and shrug.

DARKEST SINS

"If we have to," he says and reaches to take Lucia from me.

"Where's your sister?"

"She's probably still packing," I say, turning to look at the front door just as Zara steps out. Massimo is right behind her, carrying her suitcases. "Are you ready to go, Zara?"

"Yes," she says but doesn't make a move to approach us. Her eyes are cast down, toward the ground at her feet.

Massimo walks around her and descends the stone steps, but instead of bringing my sister's things to Kai's car, he approaches his own vehicle and opens the trunk.

"What's going on?" I ask, volleying my gaze between my sister and stepbrother, who's now holding the passenger door open.

"Zahara," Massimo says in a soft voice, so uncharacteristic for him.

Zara looks up, meeting his enigmatic expression. For almost a full minute they just stare at each other, having a private conversation with their eyes, before my sister finally turns to me. Her expression is guarded, and a sense of unease creeps over me as I try to decipher the reason for the guilt that's written all over her face.

"I'm sorry, Nera," she says. "But I decided to leave with Massimo."

What?

Shock. Confusion. Disbelief.

"I don't understand." I'm still trying to process her words as they hang heavy in the air.

Zara slowly descends the steps and comes to stand before me. She tilts her head to the side, a small smile tugging at her lips.

"I'm so happy for you, Nera. You finally found your peace and joy." She wraps her arms around me, burying her nose in my hair, and whispers. "Now, I'll try to find mine, too."

"But . . . Zara . . ."

She takes a step back, releasing me from her embrace. "I have to go now, but I'll call you tomorrow. Okay?"

"Okay," I say, staring at my sister's back as she walks toward Massimo's car and gets inside.

Our stepbrother slides into the driver's seat. Gravel crunches under the tires of his vehicle as he reverses and speeds off in the direction of the gate. Ten seconds later, the car disappears from view.

They're gone.

My sister just left with our stepbrother, whom she doesn't even know. She was barely four when he was locked up.

What the fuck is going on?

epilogue

Nera

One month later

MY WRISTS STRAIN AGAINST THE SMOOTH SCARLET fabric, affixed tightly to the bedpost while Kai's rough hands glide over my bare chest. I feel every ridge and callus on his palms as they explore my body, caressing every inch of my skin.

"Did I tie it too tight?" he asks as he bends to lick my nipple.

I shake my head. When I brought the scarf and asked him to tie my hands, he said no. It took ten minutes of persuasion that involved my tongue and his cock until he relented.

"I have to admit," he says as he continues his exploration, his fingers tracing delicate patterns along my abdomen. "I love the sight of you bound to our bed. At my mercy."

His hands move lower, caressing the curve of my hip, leaving a trail of heat in their wake. I gasp as his fingers dip between my thighs, teasing me. My breath catches in my throat as the anticipation builds. Each touch, each gentle stroke, ignites a fire within me that only he can sate.

"You're so beautiful, cub," he says as he slides two fingers into me. "Especially when you get aroused just by my finger."

He watches me intently, his eyes filled with hunger. With each strum of his thumb over my clit, he pushes me further to the edge. He delves deeper, setting my body ablaze with a scorching heat that threatens to consume me wholly. He knows me so well, able to unravel me with the lightest brush of his fingertips. I arch my back, offering myself completely to him, craving more of his touch, as the satin sheets beneath us rustle with each movement.

"Please," I pant.

He smiles and withdraws his hand, leaving me empty and yearning. A muffled groan escapes my lips at the loss, but before I can utter a single word, he swiftly flips me onto my stomach. The silk binds around my wrists tighten, holding me firmly in place.

From behind, he positions himself between my legs so that his hardness presses against the wetness coating my thighs. I feel his hot breath on my nape.

"Mine." With a forceful thrust, he plunges deep inside me, filling me to the brim. A cry escapes my lips, muffled by the soft pillow under my face.

His grip on my hips tightens, fingers digging into my flesh as he pounds into me relentlessly. With each powerful thrust, he hits a spot deep inside me that sends waves of pleasure crashing through my entire being. I clench around him, desperate for release, my body trembling with anticipation. Kai's thrusts become more urgent. He claims me as his own, marking me with every hard drive of his cock. His hand reaches around and finds its way to my throbbing clit, his fingers expertly teasing and stroking in time with his feverish rams. The dual sensation overwhelms me, pushing me to the edge of sanity.

My nails dig into the fabric beneath me as I come with a moan, at the same time as he explodes into me.

Kai's chest rises and falls against my back, our bodies pressed together in a tangled mess of limbs. He unties my wrists, and we collapse onto the satin sheets. The scent of sweat and sex hangs in the air.

"Do you think Lucia heard us?" I pant.

"After an entire morning of chasing the ducklings, she'll be sleeping for at least another hour. Don't worry. We have time for another round." He spoons my body with his and kisses me. "But I have to ask you something first."

"What?" I mumble into his lips.

"Will you marry me?"

I lean back and arch an eyebrow. "We're already married."

"I'm pretty sure that our ceremony wasn't technically official."

"I thought you didn't care about papers and words."

"I thought so, too." He takes my chin between his fingers. There's so much tenderness in his gaze as it connects with mine. "But I can't handle the idea of you not being mine in every possible way. Legal mumbo jumbo included. So, will you? Marry me? Again?"

I laugh. "Yes."

"Good." He pulls me in for another kiss, then rolls us over until I'm atop him. "Time for round fou—Did you hear that?"

"No. What?"

"A car just pulled up." Kai leaps from the bed and heads for his gun lying on the shelf where Lucia can't see or reach it, then steps out onto the balcony.

"Jesus Christ, Mazur! Put something over yourself, you exhibitionist fuck." The male voice comes from the outside.

"I told you—tomorrow!" Kai whisper-yells over the railing.

"Can't you do what you're told for once, Belov?"

"Sorry, I'm busy tomorrow. We'll have to get you remarried today!"

I wrap the bedsheet around me and rush toward the balcony. Kai's friend, the chirpy blond fellow, is standing on our driveway, holding a tied-up man over his shoulder.

"See?" he says and taps the guy on the backside. "I've got your marriage officiant ready."

"Why is he tied-up?" Kai asks through his teeth. "I told you I want a real wedding, you idiot."

"Oh, don't you worry. I've made sure your socially awkward ass will actually get married by the book this time. Justice of the peace, the witnesses, the guests—I've got you covered."

"What guests?" Kai snaps. "I didn't invite anyone."

"I know. But as I said, I've got you covered on that account, as well." Belov grins and places two fingers between his lips, making a loud whistle.

In the distance, a rumble of a vehicle comes to life, and, a minute later, a big blue bus slowly rounds the curve and stops behind Sergei's truck. At least thirty visibly alarmed people in elegant clothes are sitting inside.

"Your guests." Kai's pal theatrically bows, motioning with his hand toward the bus.

"Baby?" I nudge Kai with my elbow. "Is that what I think it is?"

"Yes. That maniac hijacked someone's entire wedding for us." He turns around and scoops me into his arms. "I'm sorry. I really wanted to do it right this time. We can send that idiot away and have a normal wedding later this week."

I rake my fingers through the long black hair that's fallen over his face. The man of my dreams. My demon. The love of my life. "It would be a shame to pass on such a nice opportunity. Especially considering the great lengths your friend took to get us guests and all." I smile and press my lips to his.

"All right," he mumbles into my mouth. "But we're still doing an actual legal wedding next week."

"Third time's the charm?" I laugh.

"Yes. That asshole downstairs married his wife again, using our priests and the judge. There's no way I'm letting fucking Belov have more weddings than us, tiger cub."

The End

Thank you for reading

Thank you so much for reading Kai and Nera's story! I would be honored if you could take a few minutes of your time to leave a review, letting the other readers know what you thought of *Darkest Sins*. Your reviews are always appreciated. Even if it's just one short sentence, it makes a tremendous difference to the author. The more reviews a book gathers, the greater its exposure in the online store of your choice. And a few words of your honest feedback can help the next person decide whether to give Kai and Nera a try.

To leave a review for Darkest Sins on Amazon, scan the code:

What's Next?

As for what comes next... Please don't be mad at me. I know many readers have been eagerly awaiting Arturo and Tara's story, and it is coming. Soon. ☺ However, the next book will feature Massimo and Zara.

I never planned for this couple, but from the moment these two met "on page" at Nuncio's funeral, their story invaded my mind, begging to be written. It will feature a forbidden (i.e., stepsiblings), age-gap romance. The title of this upcoming book is *Sweet Prison*, and you can check out the blurb and preorder by scanning the QR code below.

Sweet Prison (Massimo and Zara, Book #10)

Also, since many of my readers have been asking for the spinoff featuring the kids of the Perfectly Imperfect characters, I'm happy to announce that the 2nd generation series—Mafia Legacy—is in the works! I'm so grateful for all the love and support you've shown for my stories, and this is my way of saying "Thank You." The first book of the Mafia Legacy series is titled *Beautiful Beast* and will be released this summer. *Beautiful Beast* is a loose retelling of the *Beauty and the Beast* fairytale. This bedtime story, however, will include a kidnapping and an age-gap romance between Vasilisa Petrova (Roman and Nina's daughter from *Painted Scars*) and Rafael De Santi (the Sicilian, who appears in *Darkest Sins*).

Before the release of *Beautiful Beast*, meet Vasilisa in *Daddy Roman*, a bonus scene available free on my website: www.neva-altaj.com
Read the blurb and preorder *Beautiful Beast* by scanning the QR code below.

Beautiful Beast (Vasilisa and Rafael, Mafia Legacy Book #1)

About the Author

Neva Altaj writes steamy contemporary mafia romance about damaged antiheroes and strong heroines who fall for them. She has a soft spot for crazy jealous, possessive alphas who are willing to burn the world to the ground for their woman. Her stories are full of heat and unexpected turns, and a happily ever after is guaranteed every time.

Neva loves to hear from her readers,
so feel free to reach out:

Website: www.neva-altaj.com
Facebook: www.facebook.com/neva.altaj
TikTok: www.tiktok.com/@author_neva_altaj
Instagram: www.instagram.com/neva_altaj
Amazon Author Page: www.amazon.com/Neva-Altaj
Goodreads: www.goodreads.com/Neva_Altaj